The Wild Orchid

CLUNY CLASSICS

RICCARDO BACCHELLI
The Mill on the Po (THREE BOOKS)

ROBERT HUGH BENSON
Come Rack, Come Rope
Dawn of All
Lord of the World
The Light Invisible
None Other Gods

GEORGES BERNANOS
A Bad Dream
A Crime
Joy
Under the Sun of Satan

ORESTES BROWNSON
Like a Roaring Lion

MALACHY G. CARROLL
The Stranger

G. K. CHESTERTON
Wanderings over the World

MYLES CONNOLLY
The Bump on Brannigan's Head
Dan England and the Noonday Devil
Mr. Blue
The Reason for Ann & Other Stories
Three Who Ventured

ALICE CURTAYNE
House of Cards

GERTRUD VON LE FORT
The Pope from the Ghetto
The Veil of Veronica

MARIELLA GABLE, O.S.B. (EDITOR)
Many-Colored Fleece: Short Stories

JOSÉ MARÍA GIRONELLA
The Cypresses Believe in God (TWO VOLUMES)
One Million Dead (TWO VOLUMES)

RUMER GODDEN
A Breath of Air
Five for Sorrow, Ten for Joy
In This House of Brede

CAROLINE GORDON
The Life and Passion of Aleck Maury
The Malefactors

NATHANIEL HAWTHORNE
The Shattered Fountain: Selected Tales

CARYLL HOUSELANDER
The Dry Wood

ELISABETH LANGGÄSSER
The Quest

BRUCE MARSHALL
Father Malachy's Miracle
The Month of the Falling Leaves
The Accounting

FRANÇOIS MAURIAC
The Dark Angels
The Desert of Love
Genetrix
A Kiss for the Leper
The Lamb
The River of Fire
Thérèse: A Portrait in Four Parts
The Unknown Sea
Vipers' Tangle
What Was Lost

DOROTHY L. SAYERS
Whose Body?

IGNAZIO SILONE
Fontamara
Bread and Wine
The Seed Beneath the Snow

SIGRID UNDSET
The Burning Bush & The Wild Orchid
Four Stories
Images in a Mirror
The Longest Years
Madame Dorthea

LEO L. WARD
Men in the Field: Eighteen Short Stories

The Wild Orchid

A Novel

Sigrid Undset

Translated from the Norwegian
GYMNADENIA
by Arthur G. Chater

CLUNY
Providence, Rhode Island

CLUNY MEDIA EDITION, 2022

This Cluny edition is a republication of the
1931 Alfred A. Knopf edition of *The Wild Orchid.*

For information regarding this title
or any other Cluny Media publication,
please write to info@clunymedia.com, or to
Cluny Media, P.O. Box 1664, Providence, RI 02901

VISIT US ONLINE AT WWW.CLUNYMEDIA.COM

ISBN: 978-1949899931

Cover design by Clarke & Clarke
Cover image: Nikolaus Joseph Jacquin, *Orchis militaris*,
in *Icones plantarum rariorum*, vol. 3 (1781)
Courtesy of Wikimedia Commons

Contents

Book I

Book II

Book I

Chapter One

Paul was one of the last wave of passengers—those who came at a trot through the gloomy station without stopping at the newsstand. They slackened speed on seeing the train standing peacefully in the sunshine at the outer platform, puffing clouds of steam into the bright spring sky.

With the corner of his eye Paul caught a glimpse of his mother's face behind the window of a carriage. She knocked on the glass, but he pretended not to notice and went on.

The train gave a jerk, and the boy jumped on to the platform of the nearest carriage, opened the door—the corridor was thick with people, so the compartments must be packed. A heavy smell of paint, tobacco, and human beings surged out upon him. So he stayed outside on the platform, pulled his college cap over his eyes to keep off the sun and stood leaning against the end of the car with his hands in his pockets and his books under his arm.

The train rattled on, and before his lowered eyes the bright rails flew over the dark, wet ground—slipping behind sheds and heaps of coal, disappearing beneath uncoupled railway cars.

It was when he was in this mood, bored with himself and somehow out of sorts in his inmost heart, that he paid most attention to all external things. For instance, how finely the golden-yellow ragwort showed up against the faded old grass on the slopes of the railway cutting. All colors were so sweet and friendly, as it were, now that they had just escaped from snow into sunlight. The faded greens, reds and yellows of the little houses on the slopes of Ekeberg had taken on such charming tints, and their old tile roofs were browned by the sun. The firs at the top of the hill shone with a vivid olive green, and the naked boughs of the other trees were tinged with violet in the strong spring light. And the fiord was almost white, the water gleamed so in the sun—the sky shone serenely and the radiant fine-weather clouds floated through space.

Mother, thought Paul—of course she guessed he had seen her and had deliberately passed their carriage. And of course she guessed why he had done it, today of all days. And he knew she must be sick about it.

But, damn it all, she might have known beforehand what he would think of this latest idea—letting Tua go up to her father's in the daytime to practice on Lillian's grand piano. Not likely that he would care to sit and listen to Tua cackling away about father and Lillian and Lillian's grand piano. Anyway Tua hadn't the pride of a louse; he had actually heard her speak of Lillian as "my stepmother." Charming stepmother—father's faux-pas was what he called her—to himself, of course. Barmaid type. That was the expression Rolf Hagen used of a blonde and buxom dame they met some days on their way from school. It fitted the old man's wife to a T. He was sure Lillian's hair never used to be that butter color—it was hand-painted, he would bet anything. And those fat red earlobes of hers with big white pearls screwed into the flesh, they were enough for him! She looks like a dressed-up steamer stewardess, thought Paul—awful! and then her officious landlady's hospitality! Just like going to a summer boarding house, he thought, the few times he couldn't get out of going there. Only that his father had set up a boarding house for his own private use. Good cook—huh, she'd jolly well need to be! The next thing would be that Tua was to go and take lessons in cookery from Lillian.

The train slowed down and clattered over the Ljan viaduct. He looked down into the little ravine below. The tops of the willows were golden-yellow and silver-grey with catkins—and the slope was turning green down in the depth—and he felt that little voluptuous thrill that always came when he stood outside on the platform as the train crossed the lofty iron bridge. The trees along the heights had that newly washed, faded yellow tint on their stems—it always filled him with a joyful sense of spring—and the sky behind them was so blue, so blue. And now they were across the bridge and entered the cutting with his beloved red granite exposed to view, and the moss in the puddles swelled with moisture and the tufts of heather stood out bare and pale and fresh—and in one place he saw a sheen of blue anemones under the spruces. With all these little things he had formed an oldstanding and affectionate intimacy as he passed by every day in the train. But today they were not able to distract his thoughts, which continued to revolve about this new and annoying notion of his parents.

Of course he understood that it was for the sake of their future that his mother wanted them to keep up the connection with his father. But his mother ought surely to understand that he intended to claw his way through the world exactly as he would have been forced to do if his father had been dead. All he asked was to be spared any more talk of his father and this new wife of his. Oh, if only his mother had had pride enough to refuse to have anything to do with that couple in Pilestredet!

This new arrangement that Tua should go there twice a week, have dinner there and practice and then go home by the seven o'clock train—this was meant of course to give her some kind of standing in town. She had picked up some awful girl friends—it wasn't altogether amusing for him either to meet her round the handstand with that crowd—you couldn't call Tua decorative in herself, and then she wriggled and giggled and swung her pigtail, trying to do the flapper, which didn't suit her a bit. She simply ought not to be allowed—

But why couldn't the lanky youngster go straight home from school by the two-twenty—and take Sigmund with her? To come to that, why should all four of them have to hang about in town, waiting over an hour for mother to come from her office—so as to go home with her, all in a bunch?

It looked so funny. And he was utterly fed up with this going about in a herd. There they sat in the train, morning and afternoon, all five in a row, like a delightful family group. Mother with a book for the journey to town, and the papers on the way home. The children with their school-books—little Sigmund, who was only in the second form, was inattentive, looked out of the window, disturbed them with questions, and his mother would answer without looking up from her book—"Go on with your lesson, Sigge dear!"

His mother had hauled Sigmund up to her office, let him sit there looking at foreign magazines—this was last year when he was in the first form and only had to be in school by ten. And the little chap had got into the oddest ways during the hours he had to spend in town between coming out of school and catching the train. He went by himself to Deichman's reading room and tramped through museums—the little fellow was getting so odd and unlike other boys that it was positively serious!

That was the feeling that worried Paul all the time—they were an odd family. It seemed as if there must be something odd about them all—about his mother and himself and the little boys. Something that made people notice them. They were not like other people and they did not live like other people—

There were two other boys in his class whose mothers were divorced. But Frederik's mother lived in Skoweien and had a telephone and gave parties and was just like any other lady in every way. He didn't know whether Frederik was at all fond of his mother; at any rate he seemed to be quite free of her. And Toralf's mother had married again in Denmark, and his father lived in Bordeaux; Toralf lived with a grandmother and two aunts who fussed over him and shepherded him—but he did exactly as he pleased behind their backs.

But he himself was surrounded by his mother's being as by an invisible net—that was Paul's feeling; his mother's will and his mother's vehement opinions and the impatience born of her capability, his mother's—he didn't know what it all was, but she held him by a hundred threads which all met in her hand, and by these she led him. Though she never made a row or ordered him about—because she was so fearfully liberal-minded—he couldn't tell how it was, but the thought of her always weighed upon him and made him feel worried and shy and ill at ease whenever he did or said or thought anything that he believed she wouldn't like if she knew of it. Though she never pried and asked questions, like these ordinary mammas the other boys had. Dash it, he was proud of her too—he saw she was very different from these coddling mammies and he wouldn't have changed her with anyone. But all the same it worried him so fearfully that she was different from everyone else.

At any rate he didn't know of anyone else's mother who had a business and came to town every morning with her flock and collected it again at the station and took it home—under her wing as it were. And he had never heard of any other woman going and buying a brand new, unpainted wooden house in the middle of a field, and then painting it herself and doing all the carpentry and everything single-handed, just like a man, and digging and manuring and planting and sowing, till she had made a garden of the field. Of course he was proud of her—he'd like to see the lady who could do all the things his mother had done—

And then her knowing such a lot and reading about all kinds of things that ladies as a rule haven't the smallest inkling of—

Besides, she had the sort of looks that made people notice her, Paul felt. Her eyes were so tremendously brown and bright and big, and her hair, that too seemed much browner than any other hair he had seen—lustrous and flaming in its waves; its color was exactly like a chestnut, the moment you take it out of its husk. And clothes looked different on her from what they did on other women, though she never dressed so oddly as Rolf Hagen's mother for instance.

As to his father, he looked as ordinary as you like, though to be sure there was quite a stylish cut about him—especially with the new type of wife he had gone in for, he did look downright ordinary. That was a damned odd thing too—Paul looked down on them for it—and at the same time he envied them, because he instinctively felt that they got off certain things by being like that. To tell the truth he loved his mother, with a kind of savage pride at the bottom of his heart—but at the same time there was something painful and disturbing in the thought that people could not help noticing her.

THE train stopped—Paul had been standing outside the second car, so he was carried a good way beyond the station building. He saw his mother, his two brothers, and his sister go out through the gate; they did not look out for him or wait. At once he felt nervous and uneasy; he followed them slowly. Hans took the turning to the post office, but his mother and Tua and Sigmund went straight along the main road and never looked round once. When they were out of the village Paul started to run after them.

His mother heard him, and then she stopped and turned.

"'day, mother."

"Good day," said his mother with a nod. "You very nearly missed the train today, Paul!"

"Not a bit of it. I just saw Hagen part of the way home, and then you see there was a breakdown on the tram line—"

"Ugh, that loathsome youth," Tua began; "I can't imagine how you can go about with him—"

"Mind your own business"—Paul eagerly seized the chance of a quarrel with his sister, to postpone the subject he dreaded to hear of—"I don't think you can say much; those girl friends you're so fond of showing off with—"

But she did not take it up, and it came after all:

"Father and Lillian sent you their love. Lillian asked why you never come to see them—"

Paul made no answer, and Tua went on in a cheerful tone:

"We're all to go there on Sunday."

Paul walked on in silence. In the ditch the young leaves of the meadowsweet were coming out among the withered grass, and the boy noticed how red they were. By the little pond in the field stood some big osiers, and their tops were now like gold filigree, as the catkins were fully out. A gust of wind came and broke the little blue mirror—for a moment the water was dark and furrowed.

"I shall have to go over my mathematics on Sunday," he said.

"Oh, you—" said his sister. "You've been slacking the whole spring—you can very well slack another Sunday—"

"That's just why I can't—the exams are coming on—"

"Pooh, exams—a lot you care about them—"

His mother was leading Sigmund by the hand. She said nothing.

THEY were sitting at the coffee table in the veranda. Tua had gone indoors, and Paul was getting up.

"Sit down again, won't you?" said his mother, and she began to ask him about the school. Paul was dreading what he knew would come next.

"I think, Paul—you ought to go with the others to your father's on Sunday. It's a very long time since you were there, isn't it?"

"I can't spare the time; you heard me say so."

"Yes, yes." His mother crossed her legs and clasped her hands on her knee. "Of course if you can't spare the time—"

"I'm bound to do some preparation—"

"Yes—no doubt you are." His mother smiled faintly.

She had lovely, deep red lips and strong, fine teeth. It suited Julie Selmer to smile, even if it showed up all the wrinkles in her brown-complexioned face. Her dark eyes gleamed and took part in the smile.

Her forehead was broad and low, but her face narrowed towards the chin, which was small and fine. Julie Selmer would still pass for a young woman—gave an impression of fullness too—though in fact she was now rather thin. She did nothing to make herself look younger than her age, and there was a radiant air of vigour about her, surrounded by her four children—two of them nearly grown up.

"Well, of course, if you haven't time there's no more to be said—"

"You know, mother, the stuff one learns in the train doesn't stick too well—"

"No, I dare say not," she said, becoming serious.

"Well naturally—if you want to go anywhere—" It sometimes happened that their mother went into town to see some friend she seldom had a chance of meeting, when all the children were at their father's.

Paul felt bound by his word, so he sat indoors the whole of Sunday morning and tried to mug up mathematics. Through the window he saw his mother digging in the kitchen garden—she was bareheaded, in an old underskirt and a rainproof coat.

He had a great mind to go down and help her. It was the kind of weather he loved, too—in spring. Big blue-grey masses of cloud drifted over the sky; now and then the sun broke through, and then everything was gilt by the sharp, piercing sunlight. The wind roared and howled in the little copse outside their garden wall, and the birches that stood on their side of the stone wall flogged the air with long, lithe branches that bore a pale green veil of young buds. On the other side of the garden the big field stretched right away to the road—now it was beginning to put on a tinge of green. The road itself could not be seen from the house, but whenever a gust came it raised clouds of white dust which showed where it ran.

Paul sat with his head in his hands and his book open before him. He was thinking that if only this invitation had not come, he could have walked to Gjer Lake by the secret path he knew of, through the woods. He had such a fancy for a walk—just now, while the snow still lay on the shaded slopes and the forest kept its good cold air and had not begun to breathe a scent of growth and warmed earth. The smell of snow and mouldy twigs and cold water—

He decided to take a look at his geometry—that was anyhow more interesting. His mother had gone in and there was a pleasant smell of broiling fat from the kitchen. The boy looked forward to dinner.

Paul was scribbling in an old book of geometrical problems when his mother came in.

"Well, how are you getting on?" She laid her hand lightly on the back of his neck. "Come in and have something to eat, my boy."

She had changed for dinner into her black Sunday gown, with a white handkerchief round her brown neck and crossed over her bosom.

There were pork cutlets for dinner, and stewed nettles with hard-boiled egg. And preserved pears and plums to follow.

Julie had painted the walls of the dining room a pale mauve above a high white wainscot, and had had the furniture lacquered in yellow. All along the shelf of the wainscot was ranged a service of yellow earthenware ornamented in white relief—this was Julie's pride; it came from the home of her childhood.

The sun shone into the room while they were at table, and the short white muslin curtains fluttered lightly in the draught. It was a charming room when the sun was on it. It gave Paul an intense feeling of well-being to eat his fill of this good Sunday food. And after all it was cosy to sit alone with his mother. But he had nothing to say, so he just gave the necessary answers while his mother talked on—chiefly about the school and the garden.

"It's so windy on the veranda. I think we'll have our coffee here, Paul."

While he cleared the table for her, his mother took down the coffee pot and cups from the shelf on the wall. As far back as the children could remember it had always meant a special occasion when the yellow service was used. And when his mother had lighted her cigarette she offered him one.

"I say, mother," said Paul, blowing rings, "I don't feel like working this afternoon. Are you going to do any more in the garden—if so I might help you?"

His mother smiled and fixed her great eyes on her son.

"Thanks—if you can spare the time—it wouldn't be a bad idea—"

THEY sowed the beds and Paul sharpened little sticks and stuck the seed bags on them, as they were emptied. He set them up at the end of each bed, although his mother knew perfectly what had been sown in every row.

Then he collected the stalks of potatoes, beans, and peas, and wheeled them in a barrow to the bottom corner of the garden.

The sky was darkening, the clouds grew denser and greyer, and the wind had almost dropped. "I believe we shall have rain tonight," said his mother. "I do hope so!"

She put a match to the heap of rubbish. Thick yellow smoke curled into the air and Paul's nostrils were stung by the grateful scent of burning weeds. His mother stood leaning on her rake, dark and gypsy-like in her mud-stained blue skirt and rainproof coat, lighted up by the flames which shot out of the rubbish, red and crackling. Now it was burning almost smokelessly with long waves of flame, little white sparks danced in the quivering air above the bonfire and the heat drove them away.

Paul ran for fresh fuel—eager as a little boy. With every load he heaped upon the fire the thick yellow smoke surged up for a moment—then the flames burst out, red and gleaming and volatile.

"There, Paul, that will do—we must leave some for another evening. The little ones must have their turn at burning rubbish—"

She had seated herself on the grass border, and Paul flung himself down by her side. He would have liked to do as Sigmund would have done—crawl up to her and lay his head in his mother's lap. But he did not.

"Come along," she said all at once. "Let's go over to the wall and see what's come up." As he rose to his feet she linked her arm in his.

Along the stone fence at the edge of the little copse there was a strip of ground that Julie had left undisturbed. Some tall birches stood there, and a few rocks, and wild roses and juniper bushes grew in the fine, long grass. His mother had planted kinds of wild flowers here—cowslips and anemones, violets and lilies of the valley.

She walked slowly, now and then letting go the boy's arm and stooping down. She parted the long, withered grass with her fingers, searching for signs of sprouting. The ferns thrust their coiled-up, snail-like shoots into the air, and in the warm corner she had cleared for them among the rocks she found a tuft of fragrant violets.

"I'm so excited to see if anything will come of the gymnadenias I put in here last year—"

"Gymnadenia?" asked Paul. "Isn't that some kind of orchid?"

"Yes—white, with a sweet scent—I got some roots from Ringebu last year, from Halvdan. But you can't always be sure they'll come to anything."

Dusk was falling fast. The red embers of the bonfire glowed in the grey spring evening.

"Well, my boy—don't you think it's time I went in to get tea ready? You'd better put out the fire before you come—in case the wind should get up again tonight."

Paul lay on his back in the grass, gazing up at the slowly drifting dark grey clouds above the naked boughs of the apple tree. A single drop of rain fell on his face.

It was not blowing much now; there was only a gently flowing movement in the air, a soft, moist drift. Deep within him he had a feeling that the spring was something which was flowing over him, swelling from one second to the next, that it would wash over him and pass on.

"Gymnadenia," he whispered softly.

It was such a pretty name. He imagined tall stalks with shining wax-white flowers among the dark juniper bushes. He saw them gleaming above the grass, where it was finest and the shadow was shot through with spots of light. No doubt they smelt like butterfly orchids—

"Gymnadenia," he whispered again. As he rolled over on his side he caught the fresh, acrid scent of crushed blades of grass where he had been lying. "Gymnadenia," he whispered, as though it were something that awaited him at some point of his life. "Gymnadenia—so lovely—"

SPRING went by, and the month of June. The children passed their examinations; Paul was moved up into the third form with a fairly good report, and Tua passed the lower school examination with optime. Their father and Lillian gave them an extra good dinner in the Fairy tale Room at Holmenkollen to celebrate the event.

Herr Selmer, who was Chief Clerk in a Government office, wanted to take his eldest son with him to The Skaw for the summer holidays, but Paul said no, thanks; he had planned to go on a walking tour with two of his schoolfellows. So they took Tua instead; she was delighted and wrote effusive letters home about the marvellous time she was having and all the nice things her father and Lillian gave her.

All that spring and early summer Paul searched the grass under the juniper bushes to see if the gymnadenias were coming up. And they did come up; his mother showed him the shoots. She was glad to find the boy interested and talked about how amusing it would be to raise a collection of Norwegian orchids in that little strip of wild ground along the stone fence.

Julie Selmer was to stay at home all the summer, she and the two small boys. But Paul started early in July on a three-weeks' tour.

The day he came home again—he was in his room having a rub down, and his mother came and knocked at the door; she had clean clothes for him—"Have you seen them?"

"Seen what?" asked Paul, as he took the clothes through the crack of the door.

"The gymnadenias," she answered with a smile. "On the chest of drawers. I put them there for you."

Wrapt in his wet towel, with bare feet, he padded across the room. There stood a little vase with some small green-looking flowers in it. Paul took it up. Frail stalks, with a few insignificant whitish little flowers growing up them. They had the faintest of scents.

"Aren't they sweet?" cried his mother from the other side of the door. "Fancy, eleven have bloomed out of the twenty I put in!"

"Yes—I should think they were sweet," said Paul.

He was frightfully disappointed. Was that what they called *gymnadenia*—?

Chapter Two

In summer the veranda was like another room. It was entirely enclosed by greenery—Virginia creeper, aristolochia, and honeysuckle. Only where the steps led down into the garden could you look out under an arch of leaves at the closely packed masses of red and yellow flowers; their colors and the afternoon sunshine had a dazzlingly warm effect contrasted with the cool green shade within.

That year Paul had been away on his walking tour for more than five weeks. He came home one afternoon in August, so sunburnt that his brown hair looked light and yellowish against the skin, and his old brown tweeds had faded to the color of hay. The whole boy smelt of sunshine and road dust and wood smoke and cattle and greased boots sodden with water. It reminded Julie of big dogs basking in the sun in a farmyard on a summer afternoon.

She had given him his dinner out in the veranda, and to finish it off she had treated this grown-up son to a whisky and soda. She sat with her eyes on her sewing and smiled now and again at something Paul had to tell her—but all the time she saw nothing but her big lad and fed on the sight of him, her eyes sparkling with enjoyment.

So that was how he looked—like a great hulking fellow, big and tall and broad-shouldered. The old basket chair creaked and squeaked when he moved—he was lying huddled up, in his shirtsleeves and with waistcoat unbuttoned—his big feet in ski-boots straddled far out on the floor. Julie could have laughed with happiness, so handsome she thought him, with his low, broad forehead and his nut brown hair, to the curls of which the summer sun had given a glint of gold—those curls which he could not keep in check, short as he might cut them. He had had his hair cut in Nesby too, he told her, because it was so hot with all that thatch.

Below the smooth young forehead the eyebrows showed like straight strokes; at the temples they bent sharply downwards. And he had such fine eyes, clear and grey, dashed with yellow in the iris. The nose somehow had not kept pace with the growth of the rest; it was straight and shapely, but too small and stumpy—his father too had just the same nose; Erik's looked as if it had never grown up. But the mouth, Paul's mouth, was downright handsome—big, clean-cut, with narrow, delicately curved lips that were still bright red and fine with youth.

It was already a good many years since Paul had outgrown her, but Julie had never got over her delight in having to look up when she wanted to look her eldest son in the face. Hans too was taller than she, and Sigmund looked like being as tall and broad-shouldered as Paul.

They took up a lot of room with their heavy tramping in her charming, bright little doll's house. When she established herself out here she had followed her own taste without restraint—and at that time her taste was simply a reaction, as it were, against everything she had broken away from. Big, dark town apartments, huge upholstered pieces of furniture which reminded her of corpulent, wheezing sisters-in-law, cascades of cream-colored lace curtains and dismal velvet portieres, heavy, useless ornaments of nickel and majolica and copper—vases and urns and pots which no human being had ever intended to be used to pour anything out of; treasures that Erik's relations had dumped on her as remembrances of the wedding and Christmases and birthdays.

In an indefinite way Julie felt it as a triumph. These boys of hers who were growing so big and so heavy—she had anyhow succeeded in plucking them out of the massive, pretentious frame in which they would otherwise have grown up—the grave solemnity which nothing could disturb. Even Erik's jealousy had been a double offense to her and had driven her rebelliousness to the utmost limit, because no passion had been able to get the better of the man's abysmal, self-conscious gravity. It had been present everywhere—in the endless yards of dark plush portieres which descended over all the lofty, sombre doors, it spread itself over the wide expanse of Brussels carpets, it bowed obsequiously in the form of vast, over-padded armchairs, opening to receive ponderous bodies in their embrace.

She had carried off her sons to fresh air and light and sunshine, she had taught them to dig the ground and to tend trees and flowers and animals, to do carpentry and painting. She had sent them out and let them tramp the country. People of their sturdy build must be made to feel that their place was not indoors. That need not prevent them from loving their home; she knew that her boys did love her home, where all the colors were light and bright, all the lines straight and clean and tapered, where the trim little muslin curtains did not shut out the daylight. They stumped about with a certain wariness; if a chair crashed under them it was not altogether for want of caution. Perhaps they had learnt a lesson for life, to have a kind of respect for frail and tender things—to deal as delicately and carefully as they could with all that is dainty and bright and easily broken in this world.

Paul reached for his glass. His mother suddenly put out her hand and took her son's—for the fun of feeling how small hers was in the grasp of Paul's brown paw. Though her hand was not so very small for a woman's, and it had grown strong and rather coarse with honest work.

"You know, it's very jolly to see little Polleman's dear little face again—"

Paul laughed good-naturedly. One day his mother had taken him and Hans, one under each arm, and told them laughingly:

"Now you must soon begin to call me little mammie—" So long as they were children their mother had never been in the habit of calling them pet names; if she now did so occasionally, it seemed like a sort of abdication—so her sons laughed and did not dislike it.

"Hans might just as well have gone with you," Julie remarked. "As you didn't take either the climbing or the geology too seriously."

"Of course he could—that was just what I said. But if he didn't want to—"

"I can't make out why you didn't care to go with Paul and Nikko, Hans."

"No," said Hans, without looking up from his book. He kept to the other end of the veranda, as usual, where stood a broken-down sofa, waiting for its final dissolution. Hans used to sit there with his feet on it, his knees drawn up to his chin and his book balanced on them—all the summer.

"Next year you can take me with you," said Sigmund. The twelve-year-old had drawn his chair close to his mother's and was engaged in some experiment with buttons and a piece of elastic he had found in her work box.

"Yes, I dare say. You might come and work for us—"

"But how in the world did you come to end up in Hurdal?" asked his mother.

"We were broke. And Nikko's father was there with his regiment, you see—"

"Have you been borrowing money, Paul?" She frowned slightly.

"Ten crowns. But I'll settle that myself all right—I wrote some stuff in the hotel at Fagernes—something about the mountains in Hallingdal. And if I don't get it into the paper I can sell some books."

Julie gave a little laugh and shook her head.

"Anyhow, Hurdal's *fine*. Along the lake. Nothing grand or wild, you know, but big old birches and pine forest, that sort of thing—fairy tale scenery. And we didn't come across a single herd of schoolmistresses—"

"Now, now!" Julie put her work together. "Oh, look here, Sigmund, what have you been doing with the buttons for Tua's winter coat—pick it all up again. It's time I went to the kitchen—" She took the opportunity of giving her youngest's hair a little tug, then stopped behind Paul's chair and stroked the back of his head with two fingers:

"By the autumn, when it's grown a bit—I wonder how you'd look with a side parting?"

"Not a chance." He snatched his mother's hand and took it away, but kept hold of it for a moment. "No, I tell you what, mother, if one has to have curls although one's a man, there's nothing for it but clippers. Unless one's going to be a singer, or stand behind a grocer's counter—"

"Or be a parson," Sigmund put in.

"Hush, boys, now you've got to behave yourselves—" Julie disappeared into the house, as Tua and Herr Garnaas came up the garden path.

"Where's mother?" asked Tua.

"In the kitchen. She couldn't wait for you any longer."

"But I say—is it so late—?" Tua dashed into the house. The young bachelor of divinity sank into Julie Selmer's armchair and fanned himself with his straw hat.

"It's a fine walk up to Melstad Water. Your sister and I went all the way to Lunde—"

"I dare say you'll have a whisky and soda?" asked Paul politely.

Herr Garnaas mixed himself one—very pale and weak—and drank to his future brother-in-law. Paul had a feeling that Garnaas drank not for the sake of drinking, but simply to show that he was not at all narrow-minded. He did all he could to make it clear that he was by no means narrow in his views—and nothing he did made any difference; Paul still suspected him of doing it simply to parade his liberal-mindedness.

Halstein Garnaas was decidedly a handsome man—with something markedly frank and boyishly alert in his face and air and manner; he had soft, curly fair hair which was brushed up into a sort of halo about the pure white forehead, and blue eyes which seemed to be asking a question, they were so round and open under strongly arched brows. The mouth was small, with red and curling lips and a forcible, prominent muscle on each side; the chin was round and shapely with a sharp cleft. But he was already rather corpulent and mealy of complexion—though he was fond of games and open-air life and had put in a year at a workshop to study the social problem, and he had done his military service all right.

That was what he had come to talk about today—on account of Hans, who meant to try for the Military School next year, when he had passed his matriculation.

"I confess that to my mind it doesn't seem quite the thing that young men of a certain class of society should be allowed to do their military service in a different way from other folks—"

"That's all bosh—why, it's the only way we can get enough officers—and that about 'a certain class of society'—The boys in my class who got into the Military School—one was the son of a schoolmaster in some god-forsaken place in Solor, another was the son of a missionary in the South, and another came from a shop in Dröbak—"

Garnaas flushed slightly:

"I mean the real working class—I *know* from my own military training how much bad blood it may set up—"

"The real working class—" Paul snorted. "All I can see is that those who are a bit smart either push themselves forward and become political leaders, or else they make their way in some other branch, and then they give up the *Socialdemokrat* and take the *Aftenpost* instead and they're much more bourgeois than we are. Well, naturally I agree that everybody ought to have a right or a chance to get what he wants out of life—so I dare say I'm a socialist too as far as that goes. Only the things they want—it seems to me they're not so very different from what middle-class people want—something like plaster figures made in the same mould. Some are still unpainted—but of course they may be just as much entitled to be painted and gilt, instead of being left naked and white till they're grey with dust—"

"You know very little about the movements going on in the depths of the people, Paul, I can see that. There is a real thirst for justice and truth in all the relations of life!—for greater freedom and beauty in one's existence—"

"You evidently don't know—" Paul was annoyed, particularly because it would be no revenge if he retaliated by calling the other Halstein; on the contrary, he would probably like it. "You evidently don't know what a thirst there is among the bourgeoisie for justice and truth and greater freedom in all directions. The only thing is that besides this thirst there is a hunger—to have a good time oneself. And when once they've more or less satisfied their appetite, it's such an effort to have to get up and make way for others—"

Garnaas looked as if he would come out with a protest. But he checked himself and nodded seriously instead: "That's interesting. So you're a socialist—not so much from sympathy with the ideals of the social-democracy as from lack of sympathy with the ideals of the upper class?"

Paul grunted.

"But you yourself, Paul—what is your ideal? In what direction does it lie? Won't you tell me?"

Paul made his voice infinitely meek and mild:

"Will you excuse me, Herr Garnaas, if I beg you to be kind enough not to use that word—ideals? It's so embarrassing—"

"I beg your pardon." Garnaas nodded again. Then he said, in a voice as gentle and subdued as Paul's: "Yes—yes—I remember that feeling."

Paul was speechless with astonishment and anger. It was exactly as if the other had accepted his sure thrust. But the next moment he played into his hands again:

"Of course you're a freethinker—like your mother?" Garnaas said it with a little friendly smile.

"I? Not at all—" replied Paul sourly. "I don't believe in anything at all, as far as I know—"

"And you think that in order to be able to call oneself a freethinker—a man who thinks freely—one must have something to believe in?"

"At any rate it seems to me that those who say they're freethinkers have a much better notion of what they believe and don't believe than you theologians."

At that moment Tua appeared in the doorway. She had been in the dining room laying the table. There seemed to be so little of Tua, among her tall brothers, and she was neither ugly nor pretty; her head looked too big with the thick brown plaits which she wound up in a wreath, and strands of hair always straggled over her forehead. But this summer even Tua had acquired something of a cheerful and self-confident womanly air:

"Oh no, Halstein"—she cooed laughingly to her fiancé; "please leave off teasing Paul"—and she bestowed on the boy a smile that was brim-full of sisterly banter.

But the theologian was not quick-witted enough, this time:

"Really, my dear Sif—it's your brother who's trying to tease me—"

Paul picked up his rucksack from the floor, and Sigmund jumped up—Paul had said he had bought him a knife for a birthday present up in Valders.

"Oh, look here, Hans," Tua scolded in a tone of annoyance, "why must you always put your feet up on the sofa?—mother and I have just patched it up and then you boys go and dig fresh holes in it with the heels of your boots. It's simply not fit to be seen—"

"It's *got* to look like that—it's a tradition in the family. We call it Fagin's den—Oliver Twist, you remember," Paul explained to Garnaas, as he went in with his rucksack. Sigmund trotted behind him. Their tramping rang through the house.

THE boys' room had no sun on it at this time of day; a cool green light came through the big birches outside the windows. Paul had begun to change—he was holding up his trousers and staring dreamily out of the window, while Sigmund rummaged high and low for a spare strap for his braces—there ought to be spare straps in one of the drawers—telling his brother meanwhile about the telephone extension he was rigging up to the wood shed and the hen house.

The ink-stained writing table in the window was a mass of litter, the contents of Paul's rucksack topping all the rest. He swept clear a place to sit on, picked up the saloon rifle which lay there among shreds of cotton waste and empty cartridge cases, cocked it and looked down the barrel:

"I've told you you can't have my saloon rifle if you leave it lying about in this state—"

His own iron bed over in the corner under the sloping roof showed signs that the boys had been lying on it outside the bedclothes. On the top shelves of the bookcase at the foot of the bed stood his brothers' school-books—in holiday disorder, with dirty paper covers that were torn and creased. On the bottom shelves lay balls of fetid limestone, with a black lustre, a block of conglomerate, specimens of gneiss and granite, fossil-bearing limestone and a particularly fine piece of porphyry. By the door to the stairs stood a nest of sloping shelves; he had made it himself for the small specimens in cardboard boxes: the copper ores gleamed faintly under their coating of dust. It was when he was about twelve that he used to half kill himself dragging home bits of rock for his geological collections. They began with a piece of granite with garnets in it and some copper ores, given him by his father. This was while they were still living with him.

For that matter he still had the idea of being a geologist. He intended to take a science degree and had been working pretty hard the last few terms. But sometimes, as on this very evening, he had a feeling that all these childish collections were nothing but a memory of the past—an ardent and secret hobby.

By the door of his mother's bedroom—against the only wall that was not dwarfed by the roof—stood an old bookcase of dark rosewood. The doors of the lower half were scratched and knocked about, but the upper part with its pilasters and ornamental cornice and the green silk curtains behind its glass doors gave it a very grave and distinguished air in the battered surroundings of the boys' room. His mother had formally presented it to Paul some time ago, and he used it for all the books he cared about; besides them he kept in it ammunition and tools and things like canes and straps and wax for his skis.

It gave Paul a strange feeling of contentment simply to sit here and find himself at home again—he recognized all the familiar objects that belonged to his and his brothers' den with a kind of placid goodwill—

Somebody struck the piano in the drawing room below.

> "Clad in robe of heavenly blue
> In my dream I saw you—"

That was Garnaas. He had a fine voice. And when Sigmund instantly snatched the damaged accordion that Hans once upon a time had imported into the room and drew from it a discordant noise, Paul intervened at once:

"Shut up, boy! Mustn't be a cad—" And it dawned on him that possibly the youngster might misunderstand the lack of enthusiasm for Tua's beloved which prevailed in the family; at any rate Sigmund must be admonished to abstain from such demonstrations.

For the first time it crossed his mind as a surmise that Tua was the one who had actually put in practice the results of their mother's liberal principles of education. It was his sister who had chosen for herself when she announced at home that she wanted to be confirmed. And after she had matriculated she joined some sort of Christian students' movement—what it really was, nobody in her family took the trouble to find out. But in her vacations she had taken part in summer meetings in Norway and Denmark, and at one of those she must have come across this man Garnaas—Paul had met him once or twice last winter at their father's. But this summer she had asked her mother if she might invite her friend out to Linlökka. Julie Selmer's reply was an uninterested and friendly yes, by all means. Since then the young man had found his way here five Sundays in succession.

Julie received him with a friendly tolerance, and the boys took their cue from her. And if in Sigmund's case nature got the better of discipline and he displayed a certain inquisitive interest in his sister's affairs—when Tua and Garnaas strolled with their arms round one another's waists in the little copse behind the house or sat holding hands in the veranda—his mother and Hans gave him to understand that one doesn't notice such things.

Paul had not heard a word about Garnaas having become an institution, until today when he came home. He concurred in his mother's tacit view of the affair. Herr Garnaas did not fit into their scheme of things—but if Tua thought he suited her, then of course she must do as she pleased.

But he sang nicely anyhow.

And simultaneously with the sudden recognition that it was Tua who long ago had emancipated herself from their mother's control and had now taken her destiny into her own hands, he recalled his and Nikko's visit to that boarding house in Hurdal, and the memory acquired a savor of adventure; its images seemed strangely drenched in sunshine and summer and sweetness. Once more he caught the scent of her, Aina's girl friend—first on the path through the woods: a branch had taken hold of her big white hat, and he had to help her. His unpracticed fingers fumbled with the stiff frills of tulle, and a long curled feather gently stroked his skin. She raised her arms to take out the hat-pins and the warm scent of her body reached him—she bent to free herself of the hat, and he caught the perfume of her hair; it was cinder-blond and fluffy, piled up over the whole back of her head in smooth, sinuous tresses which had a sheen now of gold, now of silver. Her hat had the same scent, when at last he had freed it from the spruce twigs and handed it back to her.

In the afternoon they had lain in a haycock down in the fields, all four of them, drinking lukewarm port, and bits of dirt kept getting into the wine, and midges and flies clung to the sticky glass. Nikko and Aina had withdrawn to the other side of the haycock and were petting in the unembarrassed way of an engaged couple—and he lay with half-closed eyes letting the sun bake him; the hay tickled the back of his neck, it was blazing hot, and his heart was hammering—his body was in a tumult with this big, white-clad girl lying beside him, so close that he could feel the warmth of her, and her slightest stir rustled the hay under them both.

It needed only a trifling movement of his hand, which lay so indolently beside him, as though it were asleep on its own account. He might easily have touched her as if by accident. He wanted to, but even more strongly he would not. Deep within him a dream began to stir, a dream that he hardly dared acknowledge to himself, such was his fear of being laughed at if he should chance to give himself away to anyone—a longing for adventure, and a terror lest at the very moment when he tried to make a reality of it, it might prove cheap and shabby.

For of course, though personally he was what people call inexperienced, he knew a good deal. He was constantly made the victim of confidences—perhaps because his friends and their girl friends understood that they ran no risk of his claiming the customary return and making them listen to his own story. Especially when they grew sentimental, late at night for instance, after a number of drinks, when they used high-flown words and phrases that were familiar from novels and poems, then it was that a vague misgiving clutched at his heart: there was such a glaring disparity between all these high-falutin words and the reality, as experienced by these young people who hung out in diggings or in fly-blown boarding houses in Christiania. Although he could guess that these borrowed, gassy words were often spoken in bitter earnest. He would never forget the time when Nikko broke off his former engagement—she was manageress of a millinery establishment and almost old, couldn't be far off thirty. One evening last winter he had walked and walked with her through the streets down by the fortress, and as she talked he had felt a catch in his throat time after time—what made it so terrible was that she who confided in him in this way was an elderly lady, and was losing her looks too. But now Nikko must have found out that there is a Nemesis in life, as he was fond of saying; since he had got mixed up with Aina he had been as skittish as a flea in a hot pan. For although Aina had long ago given Nikko the final pledge of her unreserved affection—in spite of his lack of personal experience Paul was not too innocent to guess that Aina had played this game of forfeits before.

She was not exactly pretty and unmistakably a provincial who was a trifle out of her element in Christiania. All the same, Paul too felt that she was attractive—above all in a purely physical way, besides which she had that solicitous and sympathetic manner with men which they generally call motherly—there had been enough motherliness in Paul's life to make him feel instinctively that those women who are motherly with grown-up men, cannot, as a rule, stand children. In addition to this, Aina had read quite a lot, including a fair amount of serious literature, and she could talk quite sensibly about what she had read. Altogether Paul imagined he had a pretty clear notion of Aina and was mildly interested in her, so far as was consistent with his fastidiousness and with his loyalty to Nikko.

But this friend of Aina's was so utterly different. He was certain she was—"innocent" was an expression he was ashamed to use even to himself; there was something indelicate about it. But he was certain she was by nature refined—damn it, yes, deep she was, and proud and reserved—

"Clad in robe of heavenly blue
In my dream I saw you—"

—her robe had been white, by the way, light and full with a mass of flounces, with a touch of green at the throat and a wrinkled green silk belt. And he thought she reminded him by turns of a water-lily and of a lily of the valley and of a swan—especially a swan, with her huge white hat frothing with tulle and feathers. She was big, a rather valkyrie-like figure, but her face was placid—well, she didn't look terribly intelligent exactly; but you can't call that a fault in a woman, so long as she herself doesn't suffer from any illusions on that score—and she had big, gentle, pale blue eyes.

She gave the impression of a great, calm white swan in that bare and brand new summer boarding house. There was such an awful smell of paint in the dining room, and the only other male boarder—a hollow-chested business man who was related to the proprietress—diffused a powerful scent of creosote around him, and the meat and beer and pudding and coffee and bread and butter were all of the same lukewarm temperature. They had been obliged to take coffee in company with the other boarders—the creosote man and a married woman with three daughters; the youngest of them had a harelip. They sat in the drawing room at a table which rocked whenever anyone moved, splashing the coffee into the saucers. The hare-lipped child played on an old piano, terribly out of tune, which stood in one corner, and on a sofa placed across the other corner she sat—above her, also across the corner, hung a large picture of the house with flagstaff and flag flying and the avenue of birches looking like a row of sticks topped with spinach.

She looked so strangely and touchingly out of place.

After that they were to go for a walk, all four. But Aina dropped a hint that the other couple need not hang about them all the time. After which she and Nikko vanished through the gate that led to the wood. And Paul was left with his new acquaintance—in a paddock among big old birches; at the bottom of the slope the lake gleamed white in the heat-haze.

He said something about these birches that had grown into the shape of candelabras being so fine—and she answered in surprise, yes, fancy, they did look just like candelabras; that must be a special kind of birch? Paul explained: no, it came from lopping, from people having lopped the trees for fodder—and she replied, oh. Then they stood for a few moments stealing glances at each other, and he couldn't help laughing, and she looked at him, surprised and a trifle suspicious—and he jerked his head in the direction of the gate through which the other two had gone: "Well, well, if they're so taken up with each other as all that—there's nothing to be done. We shall have to get on as well as we can without them, Fröken Arnesen."

"Yes—it's so nice here," she said in a weak and uncertain voice, turning her fair face towards the lake, which lay calm and pale in the afternoon light, with great dead, oily patches of sunshine on its surface.

They went down to the shore and sat on the turf wall looking out. And certain it was that she said nothing specially remarkable. But it seemed to him, as she sat there, that she dwells in a closed world of young girlhood. And he had a feeling that perhaps she was rather lonely and forlorn—maybe so lonely that she would not have repulsed him if he had tried to make advances; but somehow he had not the heart to do it, he would leave her in peace in her unapproachable kingdom—he grew rather melancholy about it, and made the most of his own sweet sadness. For they would have to leave the following morning, he and Nikko.

They did not make a very early start. And the two girls accompanied them as far as the local store. When they parted he said to Fröken Arnesen:

"It would be pleasant if we could meet in town in the autumn—"

She served in a glove shop, he knew. And her name was Lucy. He almost wished Nikko would tell him something about her—but still more he wished Nikko would not. He was fond of Nikko, he was a good chum—only Nikko and women were a sphere he was unwilling to enter more than he could help. Nor had it anything to do with their friendship, as far as that went.

His mother came to the door.

"But—bless my soul, Paul, aren't you ready? We must have supper at once—Herr Garnaas has to catch the ten o'clock, you know."

Paul took up the ancient pair of braces that Sigmund had found and drew out one of the straps, which was new. While he finished dressing his mother turned over his soiled linen which Paul had thrown on to the writing table.

"It's no use mending these—you'll have to get some new shirts. How do you like Herr Garnaas?" she asked with studied indifference.

"Like?"

> "The sun was shining the livelong day—"

came the voice from the drawing room—

> "And by night the moon shone down—"

"You can hardly expect me to make up my mind about a person I've only set eyes on two or three times—"

"No, of course not. Well, if you're ready, come down to supper."

Some atavistic instinct or other impelled Julie Selmer to accompany her daughter and the young clergyman part of the way to the station. Paul stood at the gate and watched them go. His mother had wrapped herself in the kind of long, dramatic shawl that she loved.

The evening light was pale and cool, and the mist was rising from the little pond in the field. It was a potato field this year; the dark green luxuriance of the leaves seemed to be sucking in the spots of white blossom—now that they had closed for the night. And there was such a good, cold smell—of dew and of the dust of the white road—and from the big bed above came the strong, sweet scent of white tobacco flowers.

From the south came the noise of the approaching train. Paul waded along the fence through the currant bushes which reached to his waist.

In the twilight he tore off a handful of currants and filled his mouth with them—some were not properly ripe yet. He stopped where he could have a view of the train as it passed on the level below. The long row of lighted windows—that familiar sight struck him as so beautiful. At times it seemed as if just these things which one knew so well had a kind of new attraction.

The latch of the garden gate clicked—Paul turned and crossed the lawn to meet his mother as she came up the path. Julie put her arm through her son's, as they stood looking at the shining constellations of the tobacco plants.

"Paul—" said Julie; "I want to tell you what I've been thinking. How would it be if you took a room in Christiania this autumn? Then you wouldn't be tied by the trains every day. And now that you boys are getting so big, there isn't much room for you all upstairs—"

"No-o—"

"If you find you don't like it, then you know you can come home again when you choose—next year at any rate, because then Hans will have to live in town—"

It's much better to send this big boy away from home before he takes it into his head that he wants to go, thought his mother.

Chapter Three

Paul had tried three separate sets of diggings in the course of five months before he came to lodge at the Gotaases in Schwensens gate.

The first and the last places he had lived at had been, not downright dirty, but what Paul thought almost worse, half dirty. He could not break himself of an uncomfortable feeling every time he came across traces of the unknown persons who had lived here before him—on the bedclothes and the tablecloth and the worn-down chairs. In the first room he had had the stove was full of litter and refuse and combed-out hair—it had given him an odd, unpleasant feeling in the stomach when he hastily put a match to it. Of course it was not for trifles like this that he gave notice. But when he had lived there a fortnight or so he began to miss one thing and another—a tie-pin and a silver pencil case and money. The bare thought of having to speak about it or ask questions filled Paul with shame. His landlady was a little, flabby, middle-aged widow; her sons were both in some kind of business, and there was something about them which in an explicable way made Paul think of pocket fuzz—perhaps it was because they had black borders to their nails and rings on their fingers. The girl was tall and pale, with fluffy hair and breasts that waggled—she looked as if she had nothing on under her dress. Paul did not care to conjecture which of them it might be—it was all the same; he could not possibly make a row here. After a time he discovered that someone rummaged his drawers while he was out; but at this his own sense of guilt became so intolerable that he went out to look for another room. Then he paid the widow a fortnight's rent in advance and left the next evening.

The next place was clean and tidy, and the landlady was a nice elderly lady, refined and motherly and altogether just what a clergyman's widow ought to be according to the best traditions. She proposed at once that he should breakfast in the dining room—it was so uncomfortable to eat in a bedroom that hadn't been "done." Paul's den looked out on a little garden—it was a ground floor in Underhougsvei—and that year it was so mild even in November that when he opened the window, before getting into bed, he could smell the cold, pure scent of the violets that bordered the flowerbeds. He happened one day to mention his fondness for that scent, and that evening there was a little vase on his writing table with a bunch of the last dark violets.

The very first morning, as Fru Jensen poured out his coffee, she asked if he was not a son of Julie Randall? Dear me, then she had known his mother—her late husband had been curate in the parish when Julie Randall was engaged to the deputy magistrate and Fröken Benedikte, Paul's Aunt Benedikte, to Doctor Wangen, but of course he wasn't a doctor then—and Paul's grandfather, Doctor Randall, they had known well—his grandmother she could just remember, she died the same year they, the Jensens, came there. Altogether Fru Jensen's reminiscences brought out a whole panorama of Paul Selmer's relations, near and more distant; she had photographs of them; she even had a portrait of his mother as a girl.

And when Julie came in one afternoon to see how the boy was getting on in his new lodging, the widow produced coffee and cakes on an extensive scale, and Fru Selmer had to promise to come to supper one day before long, and she begged Paul to invite his brothers and sister; he really must.

Paul had an acute attack of study—did not miss a single lecture, dragged home books and read till far into the night. It was really homelike at Fru Jensen's—the walls of the sitting rooms were covered with photographs in oval frames and Thorvaldsen reliefs. And then there was that strange, rather confined atmosphere to which Paul had been accustomed ever since he was a little child to associate with the idea of aunts—a smell as of wardrobes full of old clothes, and a scent of old gloves in the hall.

But six weeks later, when Paul looked in at his mother's office to get his monthly allowance, he told her he was thinking of moving to the boarding house where Henrik Alster lived—they were to share a room; it would be so much cheaper—

"But my dear boy," said Julie Selmer; "you mustn't think of that. You surely know I would rather you paid a little more and lived comfortably. And at Fru Jensen's it's so homelike—"

"*Too* homelike."

His mother looked up at him; then she smiled, and Paul smiled back, rather worried. Neither of them said any more about it. And Paul went home and told his landlady that a friend of his—and so on.

It began by Fru Jensen dropping into reminiscences—ah yes, how charming Doctor Randall's daughters were—no indeed, one could never tell how it would turn out—and it was better so. And what a charming couple Julie Randall and Erik Selmer made, and so much in love with one another! His father was living in town, wasn't he? No, of course, one could understand that none of the children cared to live with him; Herr Selmer's new wife—hadn't she been housekeeper at Röllstulen Mountain Hotel?—In short, she thrust her nose into all the things that Paul wouldn't discuss with anyone to save his life. But to keep her off with civility was more than he could manage—just now they had got on to the same topic again—his parents.

So Paul moved. But he made no bones about stealing the photograph of his mother as a girl out of Fru Jensen's album.

It was a portrait of Julie in a comic old-fashioned dress, with a bodice fitting skin-tight over the splendid shoulders and high young bosom; she had a waist like a wasp, and her skirt was tucked up over a kind of bustle. She stood leaning over the back of a chair with a book in her slender fingers. Her hair was twisted up in a way that reminded you of the crest of a helmet, and below the fringe her great eyes looked out—serious and expectant—as though with a challenge to life.

Paul stood himself a frame for it and set it up on his writing table. There Julie saw it one day when she came to see him.

"Goodness!" she said with a loud laugh, "Just fancy, we really did dress like that! Can you imagine anything more awful? And we used to think ourselves charming!"

So Paul was to try living in a boarding house and sharing a room with Alster.

It was a dark ground floor somewhere in the neighborhood of Holbergs Plass; there were ten or twelve boarders, mostly young people. The landlady kept to her kitchen, and the one who in a way had taken upon herself to act the hostess to newcomers was a juvenile old maid whose greatest dread obviously was that she might not appear sufficiently liberal-minded. She was always extremely jocular, inclined to be intimate, especially with the young men, and she interested herself with profuse cordiality in the flirtations and engagements of the other ladies. It turned out, by the way, that she was engaged herself—secretly—to a third-class cadet who lived in the boarding house, a peasant lad from the west country, pale and small, with a hard, sharp face. When Paul came to hear of it he felt as bashful as if he had chanced upon some kind of unnatural vice.

There were endless little parties in the different rooms, lasting far into the night, and Paul found himself drinking *thé á la russe* by the dim light of pink and blue lamps in one lady's room after another; he allowed himself to drift into the life of the place, filled with a lukewarm curiosity: he was not too much bored by it either. He was well aware that he was a tall, good-looking fellow; the ladies said he was such a gentlemanly lad, and one or two of them confided to him that he was sweet—he had such refined ideas. Devil knows how they found that out, thought Paul, laughing to himself—he was certain he never said more than he could help to anyone.

There was a little girl, the daughter of a schoolmaster in the North, who was attending a commercial college—Paul was rather taken with her and felt inclined to cultivate the acquaintance. The first time he had taken Audhild to the Central Theatre and they had gone into the Grand for tea afterwards, she confided to him that she was secretly engaged to a man at Tromso. Well, that need not prevent their going about together and being good friends. Audhild told him a good deal about her Birger and began asking Paul what he thought about one thing and another—Gustav Wied and Rosmersholm and marriage and woman's right to be something more than just a creature of sex, and she compared what he said with Birger's opinions on the same subjects. Birger's ideas were really so refined, she explained; but Paul guessed that his own were still more effective, and that if he chose he might easily supplant Birger in Audhild's heart. It had somehow come about of itself, when they were alone in her room, that his arm at first had rested on the back of the sofa, and then had dropped to encircle her waist quite lightly. But after that it happened that they exchanged kisses. And she was good at kissing.

Paul began to have qualms. This was undeniably leading in the direction of an engagement—of the secret, boarding house kind. This lasts either till one of the parties moves to another address, when it fades out of its own accord, or till it is broken off in a longer or shorter series of scenes. Or else it drags on for years and finally is made public, and it has been known to end in marriage. Paul's heart misgave him, whichever issue he pictured to himself.

Nor was he getting any work done in this boarding house—he could not make both ends meet on his mother's allowance, and he would not ask her for more. So he took to writing little articles—about the geology and botany of different parts of the country that he had visited on his walking tours, and sometimes he got one of them into a paper. And then he gave some mathematical lessons in a little private school. Most of what he earned went in his outings with friends or with Audhild, but he did buy a pair of boots with his hard-earned money and was highly delighted to be able to tell his mother about it. Moreover, these lessons at the school and a little private tuition confirmed him in the decision he had arrived at even as a schoolboy—that a teacher was the last thing he would be in this world. Unfortunately it came to the ears of the schoolmistress that he had said something of the sort, and she informed him with her most amiable smile that he might be spared such a fate. He felt pretty small.

Then Henrik Alster was recalled by the uncle who was keeping him in Christiania. It had evidently dawned on his family in Nordmöre that Henrik was not made for climbing the tree of knowledge. And now he was to be put into his uncle's business.

Paul could not quite make up his mind what to do now. He could not afford to keep the big front room for himself alone and he certainly would not share it with a stranger. And when it came to the point he hated living among battered furniture of the worst lower-middleclass type and coming home to eat his dinner off a soiled tablecloth, while the maids took away other people's dirty plates and knives at the same time as they served him, and grimy table napkins in plated rings or worked bags lay all over the place. Secretly he began to be homesick—longed to get away from slovenliness and strangers, back to his mother's bright rooms with their slightly ingenuous stamp of artistic taste, and to live in a house which they had to themselves.

Besides which, he honestly desired to get out of this affair with Audhild that he had messed himself up in. Now they could never be alone without its coming to petting—it was not good for his peace of mind, but when he thought of her in her absence, he really didn't care much about her. His mother came to see him at the boarding house, and after each of her visits Audhild had a fit of rapture: "Oh, Paul, what a *bewitching* mother you have! There's something so distinguished about her. I feel I could have such confidence in her!" Paul was well aware that this feeling at any rate would never be reciprocated.—Besides, confound it, there was that fellow at Tromsö—provided always he was not an exaggeration.

What kept him from turning his nose homewards and moving back to his mother's was simply fright. Whatever happened, he did not want to be like his father and uncles—they had lived just like little boys under their mother's rule. It seemed as if they could not dream of doing anything but what she wanted them to do. Uncle Paul and Uncle Alarik had lived at home with her until the day of her death, and he remembered as a little boy how he had always regarded grandmother Selmer's home as the headquarters, where everything was arranged and finally decided. After his parents' divorce he had not seen so much of her, of course; she died the summer he was fourteen—it made a terrible impression on him to see how his father and the old uncles cried at the funeral. Soon after Uncle Alarik bought a share in a lawyer's business in the Uplands, and in the following year he was taken in marriage by his housekeeper—that was how Uncle Paul expressed it. Uncle Paul, the eldest, had always shown kindness to his nephews, had sent them ten crowns at Christmas and on their birthdays, but in return he insisted that they should come and thank him personally. He had gone on living in the top story of the villa on Hegdehaugen, even after the grandmother's death. Especially since Paul's father had married *his* housekeeper, Uncle Paul had tried to be nice to his divorced sister-in-law and her children—he always sent them picture postcards when he was away on a holiday, and a hamper of the yellow plums, if the old tree bore any fruit that autumn.

Of course—his mother was as unlike grandmother Selmer as she could possibly be. But he remembered his own feeling when he was still a growing lad—how his mother's being was like a net in which she had caught them all, and he floundered in vain, trying to get out of it. She had ruled over them by the very fact that she gave so few orders and never made a row—in a way she had left them far freer than other children. But she would smile, she would give that little laugh of hers—and then it seemed impossible to do anything but what she wanted. Just because she was so reasonable—never made a fuss about trifles, as seemed to be the practice of most other mothers. As the other day, for instance, he had gone home on the Saturday with Sigmund, and while they were at dinner Sigmund said: "I say, mother, I must break it to you that I'm going to have rather a bad report—I was sent up to the head—" "But my dear boy—what crimes have you been committing now?"—and her smile had been so bright and full of expectation. He remembered when he was a child, while they were still living at his father's, his parents had always quarrelled about this; his father had wished him and Tua to be patterns to their school—and Tua had been that—but his mother only laughed. She had never concealed the fact that she herself had been awful at school. And once he had heard his father say to Uncle Alarik: "It's evidently Julie's intention to stand up for the boys, whatever they may do—" and his mother had replied: "I hope I shall always be able to do so with a clear conscience—I can't imagine that *my* boys will ever do anything unmanly or dishonorable."

But precisely for that reason—because he so entirely agreed with his mother in everything—although he did not agree with her on very many points, it was not her opinions he agreed with, but in some far deeper and more intimate way he agreed with her—precisely for that reason he would not now live under her roof and be with her every day of his life.

QUITE by chance he saw one day an advertisement of a room to let in Schwensens gate; the name was Gotaas. And at haphazard he went to look at it.

The little woman who let him in had grey curly hair and was rather hunchbacked—her back was quite deformed, Paul saw, when they entered the sitting room from the dark hall. She dried her hands on a blue apron, had evidently been washing up.

The room took his attention away from her—its appearance was fairly amazing. There was the usual plush furniture and the round table with books and albums under the hanging lamp and pedestals with pots of flowers in the windows. But the walls were decorated in a way that roused Paul's liveliest curiosity: above the sofa between the windows hung a colossal oleograph of Jesus pointing to his heart, which he wore outside his clothes, and flames were coming out of it through a little chimney. Below the picture hung a crucifix. On the other walls there were oleographs of the Madonna della Sedia and of Joseph with the Child Jesus and a lily and a carpenter's rule in his arms, and then there were innumerable other pictures, representing Catholic saints, Paul guessed, and on shelves in the corners stood plaster figures of the Madonna and Joseph with the Child Jesus and the Child Jesus with a lamb in his arms.

They must be Catholics—that was rum. Somehow he had never imagined that there might be Catholics right in the thick of Christiania. Of course he knew the Catholic church quite well, they had lived close to it, in Keysers gate, when he was a child, but it had never occurred to him to wonder who went there. Some of the boys in the street went there to make a row—then a priest came and drove them off, he had been told. Paul had a sudden desire to lodge here—to try what it was like.

Fru Gotaas showed him the room; it was next to the sitting room and had a door leading straight on to the stairs. It looked inviting—like a monk's cell, thought Paul. There was an old-fashioned wooden bedstead which reminded one of a country parsonage, it was so piled up with pillows under the white crocheted coverlet, and above the bed hung a crucifix and a picture of a strange Byzantine-looking madonna, black on a gold ground. There was a corner-shelf with another figure of the madonna, without child this time, blue and white, and a rosary beside it. Then there were four or five more pictures of the same sort, and a crucifix standing on the top of the desk; and on the chest of drawers stood a figure of an old man in a black cassock; he carried an infant on his arm and two ragged children clung to him. Paul went over and took a look at it.

"Yes, this room belonged to our son who is dead," explained Fru Gotaas. "His name was Vincent—so that's Saint Vincent de Paul over there—but you know, we can take away all this, if you don't like it, and if you think of taking the room—"

"No, not at all, not on my account," said Paul. "I think it's cosy—"

He had already decided to try how it would be to live in this pious-looking cell. It certainly ought to inspire him to work, and the old green armchair was just made to read in. The place was clean and light too, and Fru Gotaas looked pleasant.

So Paul took the room. His last days at the boarding house were largely taken up with liquidating his friendship with Audhild—he maintained that it was unfair to Birger who was waiting so faithfully at Tromsö.—Audhild hinted that it couldn't exactly be said that they were properly engaged, but Paul refused to see this. He gave her to understand that the studies he had taken up were a slow business, and the position of a scientific man in Norway was so uncertain—and when Audhild shed tears and cuddled up to him, he didn't find it so very difficult to put on a melancholy face. And they agreed to meet now and then. *That* would not be too often, he knew very well—Audhild was the sort of girl who had to have the object of her affections about her every day, and there were at least two men in the boarding house who were ready to take over his part.

He moved to the Gotaases and installed himself and his belongings among the deceased Vincent's household gods. The pictures of Madame

Recamier and one that Audhild said was Beethoven—a group of people listening to music, framed in "Jugend" style—looked pretty dreadful in with all the rest. Paul couldn't quite make it out; for certainly the late Vincent's collection was at least as hideous in its own way. But Audhild's gifts would have to hang there for the present—as long as he had to be prepared for her coming to see him now and then.

"Schwensens gate?" asked Fru Selmer; "where on earth is *that*, Paul?"

He explained that it was up in the direction of Saint Hans' Hill.

"Oh yes," she said. "At any rate you'll be able to work in peace there—I don't suppose you know anybody in that part of the town." She asked what sort of people these Gotaases were.

The husband was something in a shipping business, said Paul—he came from Trondhjem. The woman was decent and seemed very kind. "They are Catholics, by the way—"

"*What* are they?" said his mother. "How funny!"

Chapter Four

Paul was comfortable in his new lodging. Though Heaven knows it was not exactly quiet. Almost every afternoon, when he came home and wanted to settle down to work, there was somebody in the next room.

Fru Gotaas had visits from a great many ladies of uncertain age. Some of them looked rather odd. They sat on the sofa under the picture of Jesus with the burning heart, drank coffee and chatted with Fru Gotaas in the kitchen through two open doors. So Paul could not very well avoid hearing what they said. In this way he found out that Fru Gotaas had been on the stage in her young days, a chorus girl no doubt, and some of the ladies were friends of hers from that time. A number of the rest were Catholics and shouted about meetings and societies, which seemed to be innumerable in that faith. Otherwise they discussed the affairs of their acquaintances. Paul had the impression that Catholics knew all about each other's concerns and were on the whole a pretty cheerful race—not particularly religious, according to his ideas of religious people, anyhow.

In the evening it was the children's friends who came; they played the piano and sang, and sometimes they had card parties, he could hear. There was a married son who visited them with his wife and two young children who made a terrific noise, and a daughter, Margrete-Marie, who was employed in an office—she was quieter and more serious, by the way, neither pretty nor ugly. The other daughter, Monika, was an overgrown flapper with a mass of curly black hair. Then came two boys, Wilfrid and Josef, but Josef was not the Gotaas's own child, as far as Paul could make out. They were a couple of smart, good-looking boys—Paul had occasionally walked home with them from town.

Of the husband, Gotaas, he did not see much. He was a heavy, corpulent fellow with a big, round head and thin yellow hair. He was very red in the face, had little eyes of an almost unnatural sky blue, and long yellow horse's teeth. He too was obviously an active member of certain Catholic societies—one whose members did good to others, and one, a Saint Joseph's society, in which they seemed to do good to themselves: they drank beer and smoked pipes under the chairmanship of a priest—so they evidently regarded Joseph the carpenter as a regular honest master craftsman and the Virgin Mary as a woman who was not so careful of her curtains as old Garnaas's wife. Tua's sweetheart had told them once that when his father wanted a pipe he had to sit in front of the stove and puff the smoke up the chimney.

One Sunday afternoon, when Paul wanted to go to the kitchen for some water, he had a fearfully embarrassing experience: he found Gotaas on his knees before the sofa in the sitting room with a rosary in his red hands. Paul stammered an excuse, but Gotaas merely smiled in a friendly way with his blue eyes and big yellow teeth and knelt on as if nothing had happened. Paul took plenty of time in the kitchen, but when he came back through the sitting room, the man was still on his knees counting his beads as impassively as could be.

Soon after there was a gentle knock at his door; Gotaas opened it with immense caution:

"I don't know—perhaps you might like a cup of coffee—the wife and children they've gone to my son's, it's Gjertrud's birthday, but I had to go down to the wharf for a bit, so I thought I'd look in at home—"

"Many thanks, but—" Before Paul could say any more Gotaas had vanished. After a while he came back with the coffee tray, which he carried so carefully that you could actually see him trying to keep his tongue straight in his mouth: "If you please—"

"Many thanks." Paul got up, feeling terribly awkward. "You must really excuse me, Gotaas, I had no idea there was anyone at home—I'm very sorry I happened to disturb you just now—"

"Oh, that doesn't matter," said Gotaas in a mild and drawling voice. And on seeing that Paul had turned red he smiled rather vaguely: "I'm so accustomed to that, I may tell you, for I always carry it in my pocket—" he fished out the rosary and looked with the same indefinite smile at the pale blue beads lying in his big red paw—"so that I can say them as I go to and from business, and at odd times, if I have to wait on the wharf and such like—"

"But I can't understand," said Paul, mildly interested in the phenomenon of the stout warehouseman and his little blue rosary, "how you can go on finding things to pray for, if you pray so often—"

"Pray for?" Gotaas's look was empty and stupid. "One doesn't exactly pray for anything in particular—well, of course—" he drawled, and said no more.

"I mean, for instance, you might pray for things you want—things you wish God to do for yourself or your family."

"Oh, I see. Supplications. Yes, I do that too—morning and evening—when I've finished with my morning prayer or evening prayer, then I do sometimes pray to God about my own affairs and such like—"

"Then do you Catholics say your prayers simply for the sake of praying, is that it?"

"Simply for the sake of praying—how do you mean?" Gotaas looked perfectly idiotic. "Well, what else should one pray for? Except of course sometimes, when one prays because of something one wants to obtain. But generally one prays for the sake of praying. It's the same thing when you're with ordinary people just—as a rule you're with them for the sake of having their company, because you like them and think it's cheerful to have them to talk to."

"Ah, in that way—" Paul looked rather doubtfully at the other. Gotaas's expression was empty—or far away, he did not know which. "But then it was doubly unfortunate that I happened to disturb you—"

"Oh no. It's different all the same, you see, when it's God. For nobody disturbs *Him*—"

"How do you mean?"

"Well—if you're talking to a man, then you will be disturbed if somebody comes—but with God—" he scratched his head. "It's like this—we are in Him, everything is, so if you, for instance, leave your room and go past me and speak to me and into the kitchen and back again, it's in God all the time. It's the same as at Mass—one isn't disturbed there either if folks walk in and out—I don't know if you see what I mean."

Paul shook his head: "That's a thing I know nothing about."

"Oh no, I dare say not. But what I was going to say—we were all going to my son's this evening, after service, and we may be a bit late. So I thought I'd ask if you would be so kind as to look after your own stove tonight—"

Paul said he was going out to supper—"but that's all right, it's always warm enough when I come home—"

"But seeing you sleep with your window open—isn't it too cold when you get up?—Monika can run home and see to it—"

"Thanks, there's no need at all. But what about you, Gotaas, aren't you going to have any coffee?"

"Thanks, I'll take a cup in the kitchen."

SPRING came with days of bitter wind. The fields in Vestre Aker were bare of snow, and the osiers hung their golden catkins over ponds of ice cold water which reflected the pale blue sky, till a gust of wind came and ruffled the surface to a dark steel blue.

Paul was suffering from the sensations of spring—he was depressed and full of nervous expectation. Along Ullevoldsvei the lilac bushes were bare and whitened by the sparrows, with great, yellow-mottled buds which could not burst, and the auriculas in the little beds had begun to stir but came no farther. There was a tinge of green over the birches in the churchyard, and here and there a spot of color from tufts of blue anemones and crocuses on the graves. But every time a gust of wind came it raised a swirl of filthy dust and filled his eyes with it.

So he took a day off for a good long run in the Nordmark—one could put on one's skis at Frogner saeter.

He came home again with his skis over his shoulder at the hour when the shops were shutting and the gas lamps were lighted. The yellow light of the street made the pale evening sky above the roofs seem a very deep blue. It was a discovery Paul had made when he was no more than a child, how strangely blue the twilight showed outside the range of lighted lamps, and ever since he had been fond of this light, as if it were a secret into which he had been specially initiated.

Down in Bogstadvei he caught sight of a girl who stood looking into a jeweller's window. There was something familiar about her—the next moment he remembered where he had seen her—

"Good evening, *fröken*."

She turned and shot a glance at him, angry or scared or suspicious.

"I don't know whether you remember me—Selmer's my name—we met at Tveter last summer, I was with Haagen Nicolaysen—"

"Oh," she said without a smile, but her blond face cleared as though with relief. "Yes, now I see—you were so fearfully tanned then, I didn't recognize you—"

"Perhaps we're going the same way?" They began to walk, and Paul rummaged his brains—what the deuce was her name now, Lucy, but what was the rest of it—? Meanwhile they chatted about Aina and Nikko. He soon discovered, however, that she did not know Aina very well, it was more or less an accident that they had been staying together at Tveter, and she had only seen Nikko that once. Paul had not had much practice in making conversation for ladies—it was usually they who did the talking; but evidently this one was not exactly a chatterbox. Paul did his best, but it was hard work to set her going.

He had a vague feeling that the dress she was wearing did not suit her—at any rate not so well as the white summer frock last year—though she had a nice figure. She was in a close-fitting brown walking dress, and on her head she wore a white sailor-like hat, but as big as a tambourine. Or was it her face that looked tired? She was dark under the eyes. And it made him nervous that he couldn't hit upon her name—it wouldn't do to call her nothing but Lucy.

It turned out that she lived in Dahlbergsti, so his way took him past her door. They crossed the Bislet field—it was grey as a desert under the wide, cloudy vault of the spring sky; the twilight seemed to grow much lighter and paler now that they had quitted the streets and the gas lamps; there were breaks in the clouds too, and faint traces of the afterglow. She carried herself well, thought Paul, very upright—and all at once he saw that it was her shoulders and high, firm bosom that were so shapely, but about the hips there was something in the long basques of her coat that was ugly—it reminded him of Tua's clothes which never fitted properly, as their mother said. And the big pancake hat was jammed down like a lid on her wavy hair and white face.

He told her about his ski run; there had been some snow-flurries inland, and as he came down Kobberhaug it had been exactly like February. On the northern slopes there was still about six feet of snow, he had measured with his sticks.

"Are you fond of skiing?"

"Oh—I'm not very good at it. But I'm fond of—of beautiful scenery"—she said it shyly, in a low voice—"but I don't know so many people here, so it isn't very often I get away from town. And then one likes to stay in bed late on Sundays, when one has to be at business all the week—"

"Why don't you come with us," Paul blurted out, "some time or other, some Sunday. There are a few of us young people who go out pretty often on Sundays—"

"Thank you, but I don't know—" the little suspicious look came back.

"My sister and her fiancé—" It slipped out of his mouth. Never in his life had he been on an excursion with Tua and her sweetheart, and he had never thought of trying it either.

"But anyhow I can ring up and ask you, can't I, some day when we're going—?"

The end of it was that she replied with a bashful yes, thanks, it would be fun—she would like very much to come out some time this spring, but she didn't quite know. Anyhow he got her address: Fröken Jensen's flower shop in Bogstadvei.

They had reached her door, and he said good evening—"Fröken Arnesen—" He said it tentatively, under his voice, and turned red, for he was not perfectly certain that that was her name. They were standing together in the light of the dairy window—she looked at him in some surprise when she noticed his confusion, and then she too became confused and slipped away from him with an almost inaudible good night and thanks for seeing me home.

THEN Paul discovered that this business of arranging an excursion in the Nordmark was easier said than done. It had always been the others who made the arrangements, when he did not go by himself—which had generally been the case; he had not thought of that before.

Nikko was busy getting engaged, properly this time, to a girl of their own set, the daughter of one of old Nicolaysen's colleagues; so he was not available. Then there was Aaser, a pleasant fellow, but it would be hard to make him understand that Lucy wasn't another Aina. What if he rang up the boarding house where he used to live—they ought to be two couples—but Audhild and Halvorsen who was her present fancy—no, that wouldn't do very well. In fact, going through his whole acquaintance, there was nobody he really cared to ask—he was afraid they would misunderstand Lucy, either in one way or the other.

He began to wonder whether he should not simply ask her out to Bygdö—to begin with. It was pretty there now, anemones and everything. Or find a pretext for calling at the flower shop; perhaps they might fix up something. If he only knew where she had dinner—poor girl, it would be some place that was not up to much—but if it was good enough for her, it would surely be good enough for him too, and he had every reason to save money.

Then one Friday afternoon he came home and saw a girl standing at the Gotaas's door and ringing the bell. He knew that slender figure in navy blue with the big knot of auburn hair:

"Hullo, is it you, Randi—what are you doing here? Good evening!"

"Hullo—are you living here?" she said in astonishment; she had seen him take out his key.

She had to leave some books for Margrete-Marie and let her know about a meeting of the League of Mary, but there didn't seem to be anyone at home.

"But can't you come into my room and wait?" asked Paul.

"Fancy your landing here," she said again, when they came into his room. "And all Vincent's things in their places, I see." She put a finger into the little holy water stoup that hung by the bedside. Paul sometimes used it as an ash tray, but took care to wash it out afterwards—he had a feeling that it would be tactless not to do so. "And there you have the Madonna del perpetuo soccorso—" she pointed up at the black and gold picture.

"Yes, I wonder if it's a bad reproduction? But I can imagine the original must be very beautiful. It's Byzantine, isn't it?"

"Yes. But I don't think it's up to much as a work of art. It's rather curious—but these miracle-working pictures never are. I wonder why—I must remember to ask a priest one day. If I come across one who looks as if he was interested in that kind of problem." She gave a little laugh—her mouth was charming when she laughed—red as a berry, with little sharp teeth.

She was really very pretty—Paul remembered he had thought so, even when they were at school together. She had a little triangular face, the kind of pink and white complexion that goes with red hair and freckles, and big grey eyes with long reddish blond lashes. And then she was neat—in a blue walking dress with a pink blouse; there was something tidy about her from the blue hat with a mass of violets underneath the brim against the splendid dark red hair, to the tips of her little brown buckled shoes that peeped out under the skirt.

"Then do you know any of the Catholic priests?" Paul asked with interest.

"Yes, indeed I do. I'm a Catholic myself, Paul—I was received into the Church last winter."

"*You* were? But what on earth put that into your head, Randi?"

"Because I believe the Catholic Church is the right one, I suppose." She laughed again.

"Well, all churches are that, aren't they, to those who think they have use for them—"

Randi laughed again and shook her head.

"You weren't a Catholic when we were at school—?"

"No. I was a rank heathen in those days."

"Was it through the Gotaases that you turned?" asked Paul.

"No, far from it. I got to know Margrete-Marie and Monika in the League of Mary. And after that I met the old people at church, and you can guess I was awfully glad when they asked me to come and see them, and now I've been here pretty often—"

"Are they what you might call shining lights among the congregation?"

"Yes—that's to say—" Randi laughed again—"because everyone who knows them is so fond of them. Because they're so devout and so good-humoured and are always willing to help everyone they can, and pray for other people's sorrows and difficulties and so on. Fru Gotaas, poor thing, with all those odd friends of hers—she can certainly say with Saint Peter: Silver and gold have I none; but such as I have I give you—"

"I see," said Paul rather reservedly, for it had never occurred to him that there was anything significant or out of the ordinary about the Gotaases. "Did you know Vincent Gotaas too—?"

"No. He was already in hospital when I became a Catholic. But I have heard a good deal about him, you may be sure—Amongst other things, the priest who is my confessor, was also Vincent's. So, you see, I have heard how he died—it was the deathbed of a saint, they all say—"

Paul frowned slightly. It sounded to him as if the girl was talking a kind of jargon—religious jargon which put his back up. Besides, he wanted a cigarette so badly just now, but wondered if it would do to light one. He remembered Randi had smoked like a chimney the year they were freshmen—but probably she had cut it out now.

"By the by, there are a whole lot of Vincent's books in one of the drawers of the wardrobe," said Paul for the sake of saying something.

"You're not likely to have read much of them," said Randi with a smile.

"No—to tell you the truth, they don't look tempting exactly." They both laughed. "What books are those you have with you, if I may ask?" he looked at one of them: *Conférences de Notre-Dame de Paris par le P. Henri-Dominique Lacordaire, Tome troisième*—"you're good at French, aren't you?"

"Yes, I'm taking French as my chief subject—thanks'"—she took a cigarette from the case he offered her.

"What do you suppose your father confessor will say when you have to tell him you've been smoking with one of your friends in his room—?"

"Are you potty—do you think we waste time in the confessional with rubbish like that—?"

"Then you don't think it a sin to smoke?"

"Sin—? All the same, I dare say I ought to smoke less. By way of fasting—"

"You don't mean to tell me that Catholics still make a practice of fasting? What in the world is that good for?"

"Well, that's a thing one discovers when one practices it." She laughed again. "It's easier to experience than to explain—to you at all events, I'm afraid." She looked so sweet and so straight sitting there in his basket chair—Paul had a sudden inspiration:

"I say, Randi—couldn't you come and join us in the Nordmark on Sunday?—I've arranged an outing with a girl friend, but the rest of the party have cried off—"

"No, I can't on Sundays. After High Mass—it would be too late for you, I'm afraid."

"Blow the Mass—it would do you much more good to come for a real long run than to sit in a stuffy church—"

Randi shook her head and looked as if he amused her.

"I say—do come! I really don't know anyone else I can get—I should hate to disappoint Fröken Arnesen, she's been looking forward so much to this outing. Be a brick, Randi, and come with us—she has to stand in a shop all the week, poor girl—"

Randi smiled faintly:

"I'm sorry, Paul—I have promised myself already as a chaperone on Sunday. Margrete-Marie and her young man want to make a trip to Maridal after church time, to pick anemones—"

"Can't we go all five of us? What do you want to go to church for in the middle of spring? You can leave that to the old folks—"

"You're good! But maybe—we might go directly after early Mass for once in a way—if you think it would be time enough to take the ten o'clock car. I can see what Margrete-Marie thinks about it."

AFTER a great deal of discussion Fröken Gotaas agreed to the proposal, and Paul dashed off to get hold of Fröken Arnesen as she left the shop.

It was a little flower shop, with only one show window, and Paul thought he would go in and buy some snowdrops—to see what it looked like inside.

It struck him that there were very few flowers, but the place had that peculiar scent—spicy and cool, with a suggestion of damp moss and freshly watered garden mould, and she stood behind the counter wrapping a flower pot in pink paper. She looked even paler here in the gloomy little shop, and her hair was a real silvery blond—it formed a sort of halo round the white face, and above her head some palms on high pedestals spread their stiff leaves. And her firm, high bosom in a thin, pale blue blouse. Paul could not help thinking of something romantic and Old Scandinavian, a captive shieldmaiden, for instance—and she just bent her head as he bowed, and looked down at the flower she was decorating with strips of crepe paper. This was stuff for which Paul had a very special contempt, because his mother had always loathed it; the first thing she did was to tear off the colored paper when she had a pot of flowers given her.

It was a little old maid who came forward and served him, and Paul bought a few snowdrops. Then he had to go, and he walked up and down outside the shop waiting for Lucy to come out. He went straight for her with his message—would she join him and some friends next Sunday?

Lucy Arnesen looked at him with that searching, rather suspicious expression which moved him so strangely: thanks—but she didn't think—"I don't know any of the others, so—"

Paul described the party in glowing terms, they were such friendly, straightforward people—the daughter of the people he lodged with and her fiancé, "and then Randi Alme, a school friend of mine, she's studying philology—a real good sort, I can tell you." It didn't occur to him that he had scarcely spoken to Randi since the summer they were freshmen, and that he hardly knew the other couple.

"Ugh, no," she said quickly; "I'm sure I shall be out of it with people like that—"

"Bosh!" He grew more and more pressing.

"But why in the world are you so keen on getting me?" she asked at last, and again she looked at him so oddly.

"Good Lord!" Paul burst out laughing; "do you think that's so strange? I thought we got on so well together that day at Tveter last year. Don't you remember we said it would be fun if we could meet again in town? And I was really so glad when I met you in the street here the other evening."

Now at last she too was laughing: "No, I'm blest if I remember anything of the kind—"

And then she gave in, and as he walked with her down through Homansby they arranged about the outing.

It turned out a huge success. The ten days since he had been inland had brought the fullness of spring, the sun shone, and great silver-grey clouds with shining white edges drifted across the blue sky, throwing blue shadows which swept over the green forests. The buds were just bursting on the trees of the southern slopes, and Margrete-Marie and Randi found blue anemones under the spruces, and in the undergrowth among the birches they found a few white ones, their buds still unopened and reddish brown, with the leaves bunched up. The ice on the tarns was so rotten that it was dry and grey, with stretches of clear water along the shore, and the bogs that he had crossed on skis last time, were now smooth sheets of water around flooded osiers.

It appeared that Randi also knew the people at the little farm Paul frequented, so they were able to borrow rugs and lay basking in the sun, looking at the white shimmer of light on the surface of the tarn, where the water lay above the ice and a long way over the shore. The great ridge behind towered up, dark with forest which drank in light from the air and breathed out coolness; on the far side the snow still lay deep. Paul knew all the little birds that chirped and splashed about in the field below, and had to tell Lucy their names; and on the little cornfield which had been ploughed last autumn the water lay in the furrows and the air quivered above the unpretending little heaps of manure.

Paul was in extraordinarily good spirits—they were certainly very pleasant company, all three, kind and with no nonsense about them. He felt safe on Lucy's account—no inquisitiveness and no criticism or impertinence; they took her exactly as she was and were pleasant to them both.

The fiancé, Karl Eberhard was his name, a Christiania boy who worked in an office—was a smart, outspoken lad, and played the concertina very nicely; they had borrowed one at the house. And when they had had their meal and the three girls went indoors to rest for a while, Paul and Eberhard went up the knoll at the back and made a bonfire. Eberhard was very keen on this, he collected dry juniper and heather till they had a roaring blaze—and then they sat down and got on very well together with pipes and silence.

Now and again they chatted about sport. Eberhard's mother came from a farm down in Aremark—his father was German. Before he was engaged he had often gone to spend Saturday and Sunday with his grandparents: "There's a church at Fredrikshald so it suited just right; I could go to Mass after I'd been up dancing the night before, and then home to sleep it off." He had been a Catholic all his life.

The birds were singing all through the forest as they went home in the evening.

"Don't you think we've had a very jolly day?" asked Paul, as he said goodbye to Lucy outside her door in Dahlbergsti.

"Yes—thanks for taking me out." But her eyes were strangely preoccupied, full of shadows as it were.

Fru Gotaas asked if he would not take supper with them. The hanging lamp was lit, and the world beyond the window was a deep purple in the dusk. Fru Gotaas's talk was of folks she had met at church.

"Was it Father Kindrich who preached today, Fru Gotaas?" asked Randi.

"Yes," she replied with a little sigh, and Gotaas laughed:

"Mother slept from the *Veni creator* to the *Credo*—she always does that when it's Father Kindrich."

Randi and Margrete-Marie had made up their flowers into nosegays.

"You'll take some of them to church tomorrow, won't you?" asked Fru Gotaas.

"Yes, of course. We shall take the best of them to Mary—we are in the middle of her month now."

There was a little bunch on Paul's table too, when he went into his own room. He raised the little vase, drank in the cool, acrid scent of growth and mould, as he smiled blissfully in the dim light.

Then he put the vase beside the blue and white Madonna on the shelf over his bed.

"*A vous, madame, et mille merci*," he said, as he made his best dancing school bow, laughing at his own fancy. But he felt so thankful that he couldn't help telling somebody about it.

Chapter Five

One day at the end of May he went down to see his mother; she was generally alone in the office about six. It had occurred to him that it was now three weeks since he was last at home, and in all that time they had only met once or twice to dine together in town. Now he would have a chance of talking till it was time for her to go, and then he would see her to the station.

It was as a practical bookbinder that Julie Selmer had first gone into old Mortensen's business, but after his death she had carried it on alone, with the jobbing printer's and the account book factory. Paul gave the three short rings, and she came herself and let him in.

"Is it you?—it's a rare thing to see you—" and Paul remembered that the last time he had called there had been lights in the offices. Now the three rooms were in dim daylight. The front room looked out on to the narrow street, the other two on to the yard. In his mother's office a crane darkened the window.

The offices had their own peculiar atmosphere of dust which gathered in the shelves full of printed matter, on the piles of writing pads in packages along the walls, together with the smell of machinery and printing ink which came in from the workshop beyond the double glass doors. To Paul this smell was full of romance—the romance of his mother who had taken her future into her own hands. Even the shiny black aprons she wore here had something of the glory of a ritual vestment—and there was a symbolic touch in the little blue and white china pot which stood on her writing table, with flowers in it in summer and winter. Paul suddenly made up his mind that one day next week he would buy some flowers and bring them to her.

"So you're quite comfortable at these Gotaases?" Julie asked, when Paul had told her about his outing on Sunday. "I can't really see, though, that they can be your sort—judging from the look of the place."

"Oh, that—at any rate they don't worry other people with it. They're extremely unaffected, decent people."

"Well, that's all right," said his mother rather absently. "But what I meant was, it looks so terribly vulgar, with those frightful oleographs on the walls. I suppose the Catholics as a rule take their religion pretty lightly, it's mainly ceremonies and that kind of thing—"

"I don't know about that. I have an impression that their religion means a good deal to themselves. But they don't make a fuss about it before strangers—you know, reminding them of it all the time—"

Julie smiled:

"By the way, that's exactly what I wanted to talk to you about, Paul. You know, Tua must go on living with your father and Lillian next year; she must be in town if she's to get any offers of work—"

"Besides which Halstein has opted for stepmother Lillian."

"But the thing is, Paul, we've agreed, your father and I—if Hans goes to the Military School this autumn, it will be best for him to live there too. Lillian has offered to get on with only a daily servant, so Tua can have the maid's room—"

Paul said nothing. His mother paused for a moment, then she went on hastily:

"So you see, it will be very quiet at home now; you can have the boys' room to yourself, or else Tua's room. Unless you think it's more convenient, on account of your lectures, not to be bothered with the train journey. You must do exactly as you please."

Paul hesitated a moment:

"I expect the end of it would be that I should cut the lectures—pretty often, I'm afraid."

"Maybe. As I say, you must do as you wish. *I* should be very glad to have you at home, but—but Paul, there is one thing I want to say to you. As both your brother and sister are to live there this autumn, I want to ask you to go there a little oftener. Your father feels it very much that you never come to see him."

Julie saw the shade of defiance that settled on the young face. They were sitting on opposite sides of her big writing table. The top of it was covered with red felt and the stuff had gone a little at the edges. Julie plucked at the frayed ends—then rested her elbows on the table, clasped her hands under her chin and looked across at her son.

"You haven't been there more than three times since you've been living in town?"

"No."

"That's not—nice—of you, Paul." She paused for a moment. "I've often thought I must talk to you about it one day. You're grown up now. And I've had a feeling that you have had a rather—erroneous impression—of how things were. That you have always imagined there was some connection between the facts that your father and I separated and that he afterwards married Lillian." As he made no reply, she continued, rapidly and with emphasis: "There is none, Paul."

The boy looked up—incredulous.

"No. It came about quite differently. I know for a positive certainty that there was never a shadow of anything but—purely business relations—between your father and her until a good while after he had moved to that boarding house of hers in Drammensvei. You see, we'd known her for many years—if you remember how it was at Röllstulen in the years when we used to go there in the summer. So you can guess it was just the right place for your father, when she came to town and opened a house here—an exclusive place, only for a few men of Erik's own set who wanted to have everything exactly as they had been accustomed—a home—"

"And then she went a step farther in the exclusive direction—decided to keep a home for father only—"

"Well, after all, Paul. I believe your father and she are very happy together. He and I simply worried each other—it got worse and worse as time went on. But naturally the amiable Selmer family were incapable of conceiving the *idea* that two people might agree to separate, unless one of the parties had a new partner in the background. So of course, when your poor father married Lillian, they came and wanted to apologize for having thought it was I who—And to show me their sympathy. All that I am saying to you now I have said both to your Uncle Paul and to Aunt Tinni and her parson husband; I have told them it was I who wanted a divorce because Erik and I were only making each other unhappy, and I said I was glad he had found a wife he could get on with. But of course, they don't quite believe that either."

The boy sat with his head bent, so that she only saw his short, light brown hair, which glistened with little rebellious curls, and below it a strip of his broad white forehead.

"Paul," she said entreatingly. "Paul—you may be sure it would have been far worse for us all if I had allowed myself to be bound by old outworn principles about morality and duty—if your father and I had gone on living together, wearing each other out for the sake of keeping up outward appearances, when everything behind them had fallen into ruin—"

"Ugh, no, mother—" Paul rose abruptly and went over to the window—"don't be so—melodramatic!"

Julie stared at the young back—tall, broad-shouldered, slim, a stripling's figure; she could not help thinking of the old word, stripling. Never before had he spoken to her in that tone.

"Paul," she said sharply. "You are much too young to judge of this. You know actually nothing—"

"No, that's just it," he replied from the window. "At any rate I can see that I know actually nothing about my father."

"At any rate you ought to have seen long ago that he is a thoroughly upright and generous character. Your brothers and sister have had no difficulty in seeing that. And you must really admit—I have never done anything to encourage you in your—unfriendly attitude—towards him. Even if what you have imagined had actually been the case—that he got a divorce for Lillian's sake—I've never made a secret of my opinion—that the fact of two people happening to be married doesn't give them any proprietary right over one another such as would prevent their regaining their freedom when their mutual relations are hopelessly undermined, and that the one must allow the other to seek happiness in a new connection."

Paul turned half round to his mother:

"I always thought you said all that because you were—well, chivalrous," he said in a low voice.

"Far from it." Her voice was sharp. "It's my most intense conviction."

"Yes, I see that now." He paused for a moment. "All the same it seems to me—that you could pick up four youngsters with outstretched arm and dump us down clean away from father and his family, so that we had no more to do with them—my word, you must be pretty cold, mother!"

Julie shrugged her shoulders, while thinking of an answer.

"You really can't say it was I who wished you to have nothing to do with him. And it's only yourself—Sigmund was so small at the time that it couldn't be helped if he was something of a stranger to Erik—but Tua and Hans have never been so; they've been there constantly, have spent whole summers with them in the country—"

"But what I can't make out is this," said Paul slowly; "that father agreed offhand—to let you keep all four of us—and bring us up according to your own ideas. For I can't imagine that the bringing-up we have had can have suited any code of *his*."

"Oh—your father has come round in course of time—he has had to admit I was right in a good many things."

"But he didn't admit that to begin with?"

Julie's face turned crimson:

"I may just as well tell you that too, as we've begun to discuss these things. I had a kind of formal right to make conditions. I loathed being forced to make use of it. For if I had been fond of him—in such a way that there had been any harmony or understanding between us—so that we were really a married couple, and not merely man and wife—then I should have been ready both to forgive and to forget that my husband had allowed himself to be lured on to thin ice by an enterprising female."

Her son said nothing, and Julie went on:

"This had nothing at all to do with his second marriage, you understand. It was a—lady—who came to our house and posed as my friend; a little sentimental, intriguing goose. In no circumstances could it be counted as more than a purely—casual—infidelity. And if there had been a remnant of anything vital in our relations—God knows how easy it would have been for me to forgive a thing of that sort—even if it might have hurt at the time. In any case—an affair like that, which a man blunders into from sheer simplicity—could never have hurt me a thousandth part as deeply as my husband's insulting me with suspicion and jealousy."

"I don't think you ought to have told me that, mother."

"Oh. You're grown up now, my boy. You'll soon find out that a thing of this sort—that doesn't make a man any the worse. Remember this—some women are like that, and men are a lot of softies who let themselves be fooled by a female, if only she's impudent enough. And we know it, those of us who have a grain of sense—we must put up with your taking an oleograph for a Raphael madonna, at any rate until you have learnt to look more closely. But we will not put up with petty suspicion. I hope anyhow that *you* may never commit your fate to a woman who has so little pride that she takes it as a compliment if you don't trust her."

The clock struck in the outer office.

"Now I've missed the train," said Julie Selmer. "So you can stay with me, and we'll have supper in town. I suppose the place on Saint Hans' Hill is open now. I'll just telephone home."

Paul made a show of protesting. His mother swept it aside:

"Then you can go home and get to bed early for once. You won't have far to go. Yes, Paul, your father agreed that I should keep you all, so long as I did not marry again. I made no proviso about his marrying again. And I have never done anything to keep you away from him—or make mischief for Lillian. On the contrary, I was glad when I saw he'd chosen her—I think highly of her—and the Krabys are a good old peasant stock—"

THERE were not many people on Saint Hans' Hill that evening, though it was mild enough to sit out of doors. Julie had chosen a little table away from the rest and seated herself facing the park, where the paths wound among bright larches and birches just in leaf. Usually it did not take more than this to make her indulge in a little exhilarating mood of adventure—the newborn mildness of the air and the breath of springtime from the lawns and tender leaves—the lights from the restaurant flooding the grey-blue twilight of the spring evening. And then all the sounds merging together—the roar of the town below, the jingling of trays as the waiters ran to and fro, the low hum of voices at the other tables, the twitter of birds from the trees of the park and the sound of footsteps dying away on the gravel paths.

She sat crumbling bread for the sparrows, and meanwhile she felt that little nervous fluttering at her heart. It took the form of annoyance, anger almost, with the boy. He sat there looking not so much unhappy as grumpy, he was just like a sulky child. Since it was one of her greatest delights to go about with her big boys, she felt her irritation growing with every unsuccessful attempt she made to start a conversation—to everything she said this unbearable youth gave the curtest possible answer and was downright surly.

"Come, come, boy!" she burst out. "This that I've told you can't possibly make things any worse for you! That there was no sort of guilt or disgrace on either side—that your father was not mixed up in any—vulgar, commonplace affair—but that we separated as free, honorable, conscientious people."

"Yes, I see that's how you look at it."

"Oh, Paul! Don't you think it's much better so—this gets rid of the misunderstanding between you and your father; you can now see him and respect him for what he is?"

"It'll be pretty late in the day—"

"Ugh!" Julie shook her head in despair. "You young people of the rising generation, you simply have no idea of anything. The world has changed to that extent, Paul, since your father and I were young—that it's utterly impossible for you to conceive the atmosphere we grew up in. There may have been a few things to object to—there may have been a good deal in the famous eighties that is easy to criticize after the event. But you should have seen how narrow and stuffy and small society was in those days, the people who made up the educated class in this country, in the towns and in official circles in the country. The men were often unutterably coarse, in the oddest, most naïve way; the women so terribly afraid of not appearing more stupid than they really were—and so well pleased with themselves and with the pure and wholesome life of this prim little corner of the world that it would have made you sick—"

"Well, mother—we learnt all that at school."

"All the same you can't understand how it felt to us who were young—when suddenly the windows were thrown open wide letting in a flood of new ideas, bold questionings, pitiless criticisms of all the old prejudices that we had been brought up to regard as sacrosanct—like a fresh breeze that swept away old barriers—"

"I remember when I was a child—as I lay in the nursery I could hear you all arguing in the drawing room till the fur flew, when you had company. Wasn't that the time when Aunt Tinni changed her name and wouldn't be called Albertine any more? I suppose it was on account of Krohg's book?"†

"You can't remember that," Julie laughed. "You were still a little mite that I used to cry over when you had a stomachache—"

Presently Paul said:

"Talking about what was swept away—I'm not so sure that that wasn't worth more consideration than all the rest—the conscientiousness that was in them, in the grandparents and a few who are still living, like Uncle

† Translator's Note: The novel *Albertine*, by the painter Christian Krohg, shocked many people in Norway and was very symptomatic of its time. It appeared in 1886 and has been reprinted recently. It was never translated into English.

Paul, and you may include Uncle Abraham and Aunt Tinni if you like, though of course they're pretty narrow-minded and there can hardly be anyone in the whole countryside who knows so little about human nature as those two. But they're terribly conscientious and quite certain of having done all that was in their power for the people about them. And they would never knowingly sacrifice a single ideal from motives of self-interest. Who do you think when it came to the point would stand up more steadfastly for what he believes to be true and right—even if he made himself unpopular—Uncle Abraham or, let us say, Halstein?

"I think they had a great deal—the old people that you speak of so sneeringly. They had faith in their duty to their country and nation—since they were more enlightened and their horizon was wider than that of a single parish or valley—and they paid no attention to criticism, however malicious, if it was ignorant or incompetent. And they were not to be bought, I fancy—I would almost say they would rather struggle in secret with desperate money difficulties than openly admit that they had an eye to their own profit or popularity."

"Some were like that—many of them were extremely loyal both to the ideals they had been brought up to believe in and to the people who were near to their hearts. But Lord save us, how narrow they were. It was just as if their hearts were the centre of a tiny little circle. And I can tell you that outside that circle there was often very little sign of their warm-heartedness."

"It's quite possible they ought to have extended their circle. Only it seems to me the circle has not been made larger, it has been wiped out. Leaving the point, the little ego, the heart which once was at any rate the centre of a little sphere, within which it shed its warmth. Now this famous warm-heartedness merely radiates into empty space—people love this and that and the world in general—and nobody in particular, in the sense that they would make any considerable sacrifice for any individual person. They preach about aims and missions in life and what a happy state of society it will be when everybody is so far advanced that everybody holds the same opinions as themselves and everybody loves everybody else and they all talk esperanto—and each heart burns for itself alone and keeps the crows warm—"

"Why should you not rather believe, Paul," said his mother seriously, "that these lonely burning hearts that you talk about are like—well, like beacons on the hilltops, while we are waiting for a new day?"

"Bah!" It was so heartfelt. Julie looked at him sharply.

She could not make up her mind about the expression of the boy's face—was it defiance or sorrow or just sulkiness in the clear grey eyes and about the narrow, clean-cut lips?

"Paul!" she said hastily. "You're not thinking of doing anything foolish, are you?—going and turning Catholic for instance. Because you're tired of dealing independently with—with the problems of life?—I'm not sure that it's good for your health to live with those Gotaases among all their household gods," she added, reflectively.

"Oh, not at all. You can surely understand I don't believe in anything of that sort." Instantly he felt that this was a card he had in his hand; he was looking at the side that was hidden from his opponent. He knew at once that he would ask someone, Randi Alme for instance—he would find out something of what Catholicism was.

"Oh, no, my boy." Julie shook her head. "You may be sure it would not have been better for you to grow up in a home like that. There wasn't a thing about which we did not disagree fiercely, there wasn't a point on which we were not at variance. We should have been simply forced to bring you up on—well, on purely conventional ideas which neither of us believed in or were prepared to defend—on lies, in fact. It is owing to my having freed myself, Paul, before it was too late, to my having a chance to avail myself of my abilities and create a new existence for myself, it is owing to this that I have been able to do something for you all. For I *know*, Paul, even if you won't admit it at the moment, because you're angry with me and upset—I have been able to do a great deal for my children."

"Good Lord, yes." There was something like resentment in his tone. "The danger is we may admire you too much—all of us."

His mother gave a quiet, happy laugh.

"All the same, Paul. Well, of course you'll only laugh, or jeer, if I speak of the subjection of women. But do you think I could have been what I have been to you, a person for whom you have respect, not just a mammie whose children look down on her as soon as their voices have cracked—do you think we could have talked together as we have done this evening, as two grown-up friends and equals, if it hadn't been for the 'eighties and liberal ideas and emancipation and all the things you treat so scornfully? I must tell you, Paul, the subjection of mothers was a reality which I have witnessed myself."

"So have I. Grandmother Selmer for instance."

"You impertinent young dog!—No, I tell you what—my respected mother-in-law, she was unique, thank God! Although perhaps the type was not so very rare. But actually it's one of the greatest benefits the woman's movement has conferred on the world—the very fact that women formerly had no legal rights and no definite external responsibility, favoured the development of that particular type—the dowager empress of China."

"Bah, the woman's movement—it wasn't a struggle for liberty at all—simply a necessary adjustment—to a new system of social economy." When he saw he had made an impression, the sentence was so current that his mother dared not contradict him offhand, he was emboldened to continue his candour: "No, mother, the bohème period and all that was really nothing but hunger riots. And the well fed refused to take any notice of the hungry, and those who had a wife for their own use would not listen to the distress of the young who couldn't afford to take a wife and had no prospect of marrying till they had got over the worst of their young days—and those who had ideals of their own that they stuck to even though it cost them something, wouldn't recognize that other people's ideals were also ideals and not merely immoral desires. Probably they can't have known themselves why they had just those ideals, for it seems to me it was not those they tried to carry over into the new age—loyalty and willingness to serve, even if those they served had no better sense than to be tyrannical at times—and that—that Spartan cleanliness, because it was a fine thing in itself to be Spartan and clean, no matter whether it was modern or old-fashioned morality according to date. Do you know, I think they behaved exactly like people who found a heap of rubbish had caught fire in the vacant lot next door and instead of helping to clear a space and let in the air and put out the fire and save their house, they took a pot in one hand and a pan in the other and ran away—they cleared out and only tried to save a few of their most cherished and least valuable prejudices—"

"It wasn't like that either, Paul," said his mother rather sadly. "You didn't live through that time yourself. There were so many contributing factors. By the way," she adopted a teasing tone—"letting in the air on a blazing heap of rubbish doesn't generally help to put out the fire, my boy."

Paul blushed in the dim light, recognizing that his simile had not been altogether happily chosen.

"And as regards the position of women—and of children too—in man-made society—a revolution is urgently needed there, whether you believe it or not."

"Yes, because there are so many of you who don't know who is the father of your children. It's the man—you can't get any nearer than that, when you're asked about their paternity. Why yes, as a rule you can tell who his grandfather's aunt on the mother's side was married to, and which of the daughters-in-law got the bracelet that King Karl Johan gave his grandmother, and things like that. But otherwise you're in just the same position as the hotel chambermaid who'd got a baby and was asked by the parson who was to be registered as its father: 'Please, sir, you'd better put down the Commercial Travellers' Association.' It's the man, you say; he has organized society."

"You're a damned impudent little donkey!" Julie laughed, but there was an undertone of temper in her voice. "The worst of it is—of course there *is* a little in what you say, but you're so one-sided and exaggerate most horribly—! Who'd have thought it, Paulinus, you have a few little ideas of your own, tiny child. You're *not* so stupid as your mother has been thinking all these years—"

She had arranged her veil and buttoned her gloves. She looked radiantly handsome in the blue spring twilight; as they passed the lights of the restaurant she made a festal figure in her deep mauve tailor-made, with a little hat that was almost all violets. Paul wondered—who on earth was it he had met quite lately who had a hat with violets on it—not Lucy, she wore a white sailor hat—no, Randi it was—

The elegance of his mother's figure and carriage struck him suddenly, with something like reluctance. Why the devil must they drag *us* into their affairs—? Can't the dead bury their dead? He felt an unutterable longing for a young girl—oh, tonight he wished he had had a girl to keep him company. Lucy with the proud high bosom and the pale face, as of a captive—he wished he could have pressed her to him and kissed her now. Or Randi—with Randi he could have walked and talked in the white streets, in and out under canopies of maples in the beams of the gas lamps. The violets would have looked so pretty against her warm auburn hair. She was really sweet. Or Audhild—oh no, he was so sick and tired of her, nobody at all was better than Audhild. But Lucy—at the thought of her a thrill went through every nerve in him—

"No, Paul, you're not to see me to the station—go home and go to bed, that's the best thing for you. Are you coming out on Saturday?"

"Oh yes, mother. I think I'll come with Sigmund."

He went straight home to his room, but he was not in a mood to light the lamp. He stood at the open window—looking out at the colorless sky over the roofs opposite.

This pain that oppressed his heart—it was that he had divined something intangible behind everything his mother said. Unconsciously he shrank from seeing it quite clearly—but behind all her fair words about his father he was aware of a self-satisfied, indifferent coolness which was much more heartless than hatred would have been. It was he himself who had whipped himself up into feeling hatred for his father, because he believed his mother to have been betrayed and the family abandoned—and if she always spoke well of him it was because she was chivalrous and high-minded and renounced her right to hate the man who had mortally injured her. And now they turned out to be nothing but baseless boyish fancies, all the ideas he had formed about his father. He did not know his father—but it dawned on him now that, whatever might have been the rights or wrongs of the breach between them—here was a man to whom a woman had quite coolly offered stones in place of bread.

He had never been able to dwell on any of the memories he preserved of his childhood, of the time before his parents separated, without touching tender spots within himself. Always that bitterness, for which there was no other reason than his own imaginations, and his passionate partisanship for his mother! And now he would have to try to remember his father, as he would have remembered him if, for instance, his father had died about the time they left him. But then of course he would have exaggerated in the other direction—made a hero of him and worshipped him.

That would not have been at all difficult. His father had the makings of it. For one thing he must have been a handsome man at that time—he couldn't remember very clearly what he had looked like; the image had gradually faded out as his father lost his hair and grew a little stomach. And then such memories as of that autumn when he was allowed to stay on with his father at Röllstulen, after his mother and the other children had left. He had never forgotten that autumn morning, the dazzling, fitful sunlight between heavy masses of cloud, the sharp glitter of water in the distance. They stood on the sweep outside the sanatorium, he and his father and Captain Tangen and Uncle Nicolaysen, with Shot and the other dogs—waved to the country cart as it bumped along the saeter road, and his mother and the children turned and waved back; Sigmund was still so small that he had on a light blue hood and sat in his mother's lap.

God, how happy and proud he had been, and what a pattern of good behaviour—and how awfully decent his father and his friends had been to him. Of course he was not allowed to shoot, but he had trotted by his father's side, once or twice at any rate, to look on and learn—had been given his first taste of the excitement and joy of sport, his first thrills as he watched the dogs at work and the birds fly up and his father shoot. It must have been the same year he was given his first saloon rifle as a Christmas present—from his father.

Lillian too he would have to change his mind about—at that time he had raved about her, he knew nothing more beautiful, except his mother; she was fair and round and always so kind to them. Often when his mother had said good night and gone downstairs Fröken Kraby would come with a plate for each of them—something good for them to eat in bed, cakes or dessert. And he had finished the caramel pudding, though he shuddered at every spoonful, so intensely did he loathe the taste of the burnt sugar. But he would not hurt Fröken Kraby by showing it.

Another of his Röllstulen memories was of his father's bearded kiss as he lay in bed—some time when he had come down from town no doubt. It gave him a sharp twinge at the heart when he thought of it—now they were two hopeless strangers. Did his father ever think of it—that once they had been little boys and he came in and kissed them as they lay in bed—?

Certainly he had been fond of his father—never wildly so, as he was of his mother; even his father's caresses were remembered as a sort of ceremony on solemn occasions. And occasionally his father had given him the cane, for particularly gross misdemeanours. He could not remember any other reaction to it than finding it was in order—that was what it cost to take a big liberty. His father represented justice, his father was good and safe, it was his father who lent him proper men's books, not story-books, But things like the Yearbook of the Tourist Association, and it was his father who looked at his sums and went through his school reports and saw to his skis.

Of course he had always taken his mother's part when he saw they were on bad terms, as he guessed they were pretty frequently, though they never made a scene when the children were present. But now and then he had chanced to wake at night and hear them quarreling terribly.

He remembered one night: his parents had separate bedrooms and he slept in his father's, but that night he had stolen in to Tua and crept up into her bed to comfort her; their parents were out, and she was quite beside herself and crying her eyes out—yes, now he remembered all about it. They had been to the confectioner's with one or other of the innumerable uncles of those days, and Tua had chosen a cake with a big lump of yellow custard on it, but when she had eaten it this uncle told her that now she would have a yellow beard when she grew up. And Tua was the sort of child who believed everything she was told, and afterwards it was a sheer impossibility to get ideas of this kind out of her head. So when she had gone to bed she began to howl over this yellow beard she was going to have. But at last they must have fallen asleep in each other's arms.

When he woke up he saw his mother standing in the light by the dressing table—his father standing by her in evening dress, with a strange and sinister look on his face. It was his father's voice that had waked him. And he had heard his mother say, in a loud, ringing tone: "Oh no, Erik—one doesn't fall in love a second time with a man like you!"

His father—he realized now that it must have been a cry of rage and pain; he did not understand the words, but the voice sent a cold shiver down his back, as when one amuses oneself by playing with edged tools.

His mother drew herself up—and her beauty seemed to the boy almost uncanny. Her rounded shoulders shone with black silk, but her bosom was exposed in a deep square, and at its point was a great swaying bunch of scarlet flowers and brown-bordered geranium leaves. She had similar fiery red flowers in her wavy brown hair—her cheeks were burning and her eyes aflame.

His father shouted something—and his mother's whole figure bridled up with a start, and the sheen on her black silk gown flashed with a strange white gleam:

"And you dare say that to me! You dare say that! It just shows how low you have fallen, Erik!"

He himself had tried to hide under the bedclothes—and then his parents must have heard a movement in the children's bed. When he ventured to peep out again, his father had gone; his mother was sitting at her dressing table, crying. After a while he called to her, in a hushed and frightened voice.

She came. And although he must have been a big boy then, about nine, she had taken him up in her arms and carried him back to his own bed. Her bare bosom was hot as fire against his cheek, and the spicy scent of her geraniums seemed hot too, her face was scaldingly wet. He remembered how cold and good his own bed felt when she laid him down in it. Meanwhile his parents did not exchange a word. And when a little later his father came over to him, he turned over on his other side and slept demonstratively. He was furious of course on his mother's account.

Paul heaved a sigh to the white sky. A pale gleam was beginning to show in the windows on the other side of the street, the air had a whiff of morning in it. He undressed, instinctively making as little noise as possible.

Well, there was no knowing—what his father had been up against. Jealous—and that had made his mother mad with him. But he could understand it, by gosh—

He could not even abandon himself to jeremiads about his parents' divorce having made one long disaster of his childhood, as he had heard other children doing. They put the blame on that, every time they got into any mess. He had not been unhappy in the years he had passed with his mother at Linlökka. Only he was never properly at peace, always uneasy, at half-cock as it were—there were thoughts which were never completely lost sight of, there was always something like an ache in the root fibres which had been torn across. And always the feeling that he was an exile and an outlaw from the first part of his childhood, that his father had wronged his mother. And now he would never be able to think of the years he had spent there, all his dear and joyous and amusing memories of Linlökka, without feeling the same rancour on his father's account—they had done him an injustice all the time.

He had consoled himself, hadn't he? Said his mother. Like hell he had—Lillian suited him much better, he got on with her—

All at once the tears forced themselves into Paul's eyes, scalding hot. He clenched his teeth with rage. Why should his mother want to say anything so—mean!

NEXT day towards evening he went up to his father's.

The Selmers lived on the first floor of a large brown wooden villa in Pilestraede. They had already planted their veranda boxes with pink climbing pelargoniums, which made a bright, fresh show against the dark woodwork—looked like a restaurant, it struck Paul; then he checked himself and stifled the thought.

He felt disheartened—downright ill at ease. For everything was different now—the situation was reversed, and he hadn't the least idea how he was to take it.

Fru Selmer was in the drawing room, said the maid who took his hat and coat. He could hear that for himself: a flood of notes fell upon his ear, some difficult piano piece or other. That too had been part of her business in former days, to entertain the guests at the sanatorium with music; she played brilliantly, but without much feeling.

He tried to get hold of the image he had once had of her—behind the bitter distortions of all these years—when he had been so fond of Fröken Kraby that he ate caramel pudding for her sake without turning a hair.

At that time she could not have been quite so stout, and her coloring was more credible. Now her whole face was an even pink, with a tinge of lilac from the powder, and the metallic golden yellow of her hair made no attempt to appear natural.

She was always as neat as a new pin from top to toe—the white pearls in her fleshy red ears put the finishing touch to her well-turned-out appearance. She had regular, quite well-cut features, but her face was very full now and so devoid of wrinkles that it had a look of being blown out; the eyes were pale blue with a permanent expression of interest and friendliness.

Fru Lillian Selmer was dressed in a white silk blouse with masses of tiny tucks, and a skirt of silver-grey cloth which fell about the hips and back in such a way that one could not help thinking of the hindquarters of a well-groomed galloway mare—for she carried herself exactly like the ladies in Reznicek's drawings in *Simplicissimus*: the chest thrust well forward, the head a little on one side, the stern stuck out—

"—Father not at home? Oh dear no, don't let me disturb you, I can go into father's room and look at the papers till he comes—" He knew that Lillian still took lessons from a well-known pianist and practiced several hours a day.

"Just let me tell the maid—you'll stay to supper, won't you?"

Obliging—that word seemed to cover the whole of Lillian. Shut up, you old devil, said Paul to himself. Isn't it a very good thing she *is* obliging, if she means anything by it—and kind—

Then it struck him that they had addressed each other in the familiar way—he had done so without thinking. Well, after all it had never come natural to him to address her formally—but he had done so, out of spite, ever since she had been his father's wife, till she had to do the same with him. He wondered what she thought now—! His late embarrassment was painfully accentuated.

The room was furnished in a way Paul had always heard described as tasteful—by people he would not venture to contradict. But he didn't like it. There was a thick carpet covering the whole floor, in soft, subdued colors. They had had deep, soft carpets like this at home in old days too, but his mother liked bare boards and smooth, hard mats. Over the carpet were scattered small rugs and skins, a polar bear's skin under the grand piano. Along the walls stood the heavy, polished mahogany furniture that came from his father's family, but the inlaid sofa had been covered in the same faded green silk as the new chairs. The woodwork of these was flowing and wavy, with plant designs; the chairbacks were carved in the form of some kind of umbelliferous plant. They had always given Paul a vague sense of loathing, those chairs. A salon—well, that was in fact what they called their drawing room in this house.

An old embroidered silk shawl covered the top of the piano, and on it stood a whole row of framed photographs. Including one or two of his mother: one with himself on her arm, and one where she had Sigmund in her lap and the three others grouped about her. There were photographs of him and Tua in students' caps. And how this exhibition of portraits had irritated him in old days—

The Krabys had a wing to themselves. And in the middle between the two families stood a big enlargement in silver frame, before which there was always a little silver vase of flowers: the portrait of a little girl of one year old, sitting in her shirt on a white fur rug. He had only once seen his little half-sister—one Christmas when he had been ordered up here.

Lillian appeared at the door. Paul felt as awkward as if he had been caught doing something he shouldn't. To save his face he took up a cabinet photograph of Tua and Halstein.

"Is this a new one? I haven't seen it before."

"No, they only took half a dozen. Your mother didn't think it particularly good."—They looked perfectly idiotic both of them.

"How sweet she was, little Margit. It was hard, her being taken from you—"

"Yes, it was a heavy blow. And your father loves little children—" Paul saw out of the corner of his eye that Lillian turned a deeper red than usual and her eyes grew moist. He went over to the brass Turkish table and picked up the evening paper.

"Pastor Johannes Dverberg—did you see that Uncle Abraham's brother is dead?"

"No, you don't say so! Is he dead? He wasn't so terribly old either—sixty-seven? Yes, he was the eldest of them all, next to him came Fru Horster—"

The news of this death came as a godsend; they discussed it under every possible aspect.

"Abraham and Tinni will come up for the funeral, no doubt. We must get the whole family together for a dinner here, one day while they're in town—"

Finally, however, the subject could be spun out no farther.

"What was it you were playing when I came in?"

She allowed herself to be persuaded to play it again, and Paul stood beside her and turned over. Then they talked a little of the opera at the National Theatre—she and his father had been to the first night. They were regular first-nighters. Tua and Halstein were going there this evening—no, they wouldn't be here; they were going to a club first and no doubt they would have something to eat there—

At last Paul heard his father's key in the door. Lillian got up and met her husband at the door of the room:

"Erik—Paul's here—"

Dash it, he could see that for himself—no, he must break himself of being annoyed at everything they said and did: that cheerful, twittering voice of Lillian's—now he knew that her mission in life was to make people comfortable and cheer them up—

"Well, how are you? Quite well again? Your mother said you were rather bad with influenza just after Easter—?"

"I? No. I stayed in bed one Monday—but that was nothing, just laziness. Hans was pretty seedy—away from school a whole week, I think—"

Then came Lillian with the news of old Pastor Dverberg's death, and they said over again all that could be said on that subject, and then came the maid and said supper was ready.

Herr Selmer was a tall, broad-shouldered man, rather corpulent now. His head was somewhat small, and his hair had withdrawn a long way from the high, smooth forehead; over the temples it was close-cut with a glint of silver. But the smart little pointed beard had kept its light brown color. The eyes behind the pince-nez looked worn and pale. Again Paul had the feeling that he must get his bearings afresh, after ten years' bewitchment—whether it was they or himself who had been bewitched he could not say.

The supper table was charmingly set out—with his table napkin folded fanwise, and each plate decorated with cut radishes and parsley, and cold mackerel with salad and horseradish sauce, and to begin with they had something hot and piquant served in shells. And he couldn't help thinking of the sanatorium.

Afterwards his father and he sat in the study; Selmer's room still went by that name, though it had been furnished with leather armchairs and a copper smoking table. But the walls were still covered with bookshelves and it was the big desk that dominated the room.

His father said: "You know where to find the cigars—or do you prefer a pipe?"—for himself he kept to a pipe, and they discussed tobaccos. And he asked if Paul would have a whisky and soda, and Paul said thanks. The door to the veranda stood open; Lillian was out there attending to her flower boxes; they could hear the splash of water from her syringe and the words she exchanged with the lady on the ground floor, who was also seeing to the flowers in her veranda, and from the street came the sound of people strolling in the spring evening.

And Paul sat tongue-tied and said nothing.

Then, thank God, his father began to ask about his plans for the summer. Paul didn't quite know. Well, for August he had arranged with Sigurd Aaser to go to Dovre—Aaser was going to be a botanist, distribution of plants—and he himself wanted to look at some old raised beaches. In fact they had thought of making a rather long tour, seeing some mines, working and disused, and ending up at Röros.

But what he would be doing the first part of the summer—well, he didn't know. Working—stay in town for the present, but of course he would go out to his mother's part of the time too.

—Lucy would have no holiday this summer; she had only been at the flower shop since February. So he would try to take her out a little in the evenings.

"They're quite well written, Paul, those little things you do for the papers now and again."

"Do you think so? I'm glad. Of course they're nothing more than popular, you know, but I think it's amusing to give people a taste for finding out something about their country—mountains and old moraines and so forth. I don't suppose you happened to see a thing I did last spring, I think it was in a Sunday number of *Pressen*—about a hermaphrodite chaffinch?" This was Paul's secret pride; quite a lot of the article had been quoted in a very scientific publication. "It was a bit out of my usual line. I had noticed the bird; it lived in the thicket outside our garden. Mother was angry with me for shooting it; she thinks little birds are little birds, whether they're normal or eccentric—"

"By the way, there's a thing I should like to ask you, father," he managed to say at last. "I remember an article in the Tourist Association's Yearbook about Vinsterdalen in Dovre, I don't know who it was by or what year, but if I may look through the set one day I shall be able to find it. I read it at home in Keysers gate; it used to stand in the shelf in the passage between the doors of mother's room. You remember, you had the latest years in your own room—"

"I've had to send those up to the attic, Paul—but I'll go up and get them out, and then I can send you the whole lot."

"Thanks. But I can come and fetch them myself."

Herr Selmer rose and went over to the bookcase.

"I have a book here—I don't know if it would interest you to have it?"

Paul went to look: "*Beiträge zur Kenntniss Norwegens*, von Carl Neumann—yes, thanks, I should think it would—"

"At any time, if there are books here that you have use for or would like to have for any reason, they're at your disposal. I remember as a child you always enjoyed being shown the English books of travel that I have."

"Thanks. Oh but, father, I don't think you ought to part with that—it's such a handsome copy." It was Capell Brooke in red morocco.†

"No, you'd better have it. I never look at it now—

"—You weren't at the station, were you, when the cabinet committee from Stockholm arrived?" asked his father.

"No. I say, father—have you any idea of how the situation will develop?"

"I presume the Storting will request the ministry to remain in office and carry on the administration as though the Crown were present. The country must have a government. This is no revolution, obviously—"

"No—?" said Paul. "I don't believe so either. You know, we've heard these Union politics discussed uphill and down dale as long as we've lived. But there's not likely to be any solution this time either—"

"I didn't think you were particularly interested in politics—?"

"Mm—not in jawing about them anyhow. I've had plenty of that—at

† TRANSLATOR'S NOTE: Sir Arthur de Capell Brooke: *Travels through Sweden, Norway and Finmark to the North Cape in the Summer of 1820* (London, 1823).

home and at school too—so that when they talk about these things it seems to me like hearing about Little Red Ridinghood and the Wolf all over again—"

"The present situation is to some extent different from anything that has gone before. It is a constitutional crisis—"

They stood there by the bookcase talking of the withholding of the royal assent, when they heard Tua and her fiancé outside in the garden. Soon after Paul said goodbye.

His father came down to open the street door and went with Paul through the little front garden, where the hedge of spiraea gleamed with white clusters of flowers in the light evening.

"Well, good night, Paul, and thanks for coming to see us."

"Thanks to you, father. Good night."

They gave each other their hands, Paul gave a hearty squeeze, and his father returned it—they waited a moment before letting go. Then the garden gate fell to behind Paul.

He was not in the mood to go home. Just as well look in at Aaser's—he had refused, saying he was engaged this evening. But the time was only a quarter to twelve—

But just as he arrived at the boarding house, Aaser's party were preparing to move on elsewhere—to a studio that Aaser's cousin and a girl friend of hers had taken. The two girls had just come back from a stay in Rome.

Paul was introduced, and it flattered him a little when Marie Aaser asked: "Aren't you the one who writes—you're going to be an author, aren't you?"

The crowd marched off and landed at the top of an office building at the far end of Kirke Gate. The others had had a good deal to drink at Aaser's and were already well shaken up. So Paul was the only one who religiously went through the exhibition of the two girls' pictures from end to end. Quite good, he thought, but rather weak and washed-out. However, Fröken Aaser herself was sweet, and there was a wonderful view over roofs and green treetops and the fiord and the islands in the twilight of the spring night. So he and she stood talking seriously awhile. After the agitation of the last twenty-four hours and the struggle to restore the balance of his heart, and last of all the impression of which he could not rid himself, of his father in that home of his—that he was a man who was concealing a defeat—it did him good to abandon himself to a melancholy he need not hide, because it was a natural pose and one that suited the situation. For he was the stranger who had dropped in from the night on the others' revels, the one who was alone and stone-cold sober in the midst of a merry party—standing with a sweet little girl painter at a studio window looking out on the Christiania fiord on a night in June. There was repose in it—just as one feels on flinging oneself down in a railway carriage at evening after tramping thirty miles or so during the day.

So when wine was produced—a Spanish country wine which tasted good—he felt much more at his ease. Somebody over on the sofa began to sing "*Ja vi elsker*—"[†]—Aaser no doubt, he belonged to the wildest democracy—and Paul joined in, standing by the window, with a feeling that he was making rather a show of himself. Now and again they danced, and then Fröken Aaser and her friend played the mandoline and guitar and sang Italian ditties, and then they danced again. The morning was well advanced when Paul left, with a girl who lived out in the Skillebask direction; he had offered to see her home.

The sky was full of little mother-of-pearl clouds, the Frogner creek was smooth and pale, and the fruit trees were in blossom in the gardens along Drammensvei. There was a scent of morning and brackish water and new leaves, and the birds twittered and sang. So when they reached the villa where the girl lived—Paul hadn't caught her name—he stayed sitting with her a good while yet on a dewy garden seat. Till a white form loomed up behind a window of the villa and the girl jumped up with a start:

"Goodness, mamma! Oh, now I shall catch it!"

Then he strolled slowly back into town, enjoying the stillness and the gentle warmth of the sun. The little lime trees down Karl Johan were a wonderfully tender green with their little silky leaves; the University looked so fine and venerable, standing deserted in the sunny morning—and he walked on, contented. The books his father had given him had been forgotten somewhere—probably he would find them at Aaser's. Still, he felt a little ashamed—as if he had been disloyal.

Just opposite Saint Olav's church he ran right into Fru Gotaas. Paul greeted her: "You don't mean to say you're out so early as this?"

"Oh, it's not so early," she replied in her mild, unruffled way; "it's half-past six."

---

† TRANSLATOR'S NOTE: The Norwegian national song, *Ja vi elsker dette landet…* ("Yes, we love this land…"). The words are by Björnson.

"Well, perhaps it isn't so very early to go home to bed. But it is early to be out for a walk—"

"Oh, I often go to the half-past six Mass," said Fru Gotaas.

Paul had a sudden idea. Fröken Aaser had told him that in Rome, after they had spent the night going round to festive little taverns, where there was music and you could see the life of the people, they used often to wander about watching the day break over squares and fountains, and end up in some dim ancient church with Mass and candles and clouds of fragrant incense. But he had never imagined the possibility of there being a Catholic Mass on weekday mornings here in Christiania—

"I say, Fru Gotaas—mayn't I go into the church with you?"

He felt rather foolish when she looked up at him—the little wrinkled face was so worn and innocent, her cape was green with age in the morning sunlight.

"Oh, I'm not drunk, Fru Gotaas. We've been enjoying ourselves all right, but not enough to hurt—"

"No, you're not *that*. Well, you know, the church is open to all."

Fru Gotaas led the way through a gate in a wooden paling and a door at the side of the tower.

He had never before seen inside the Catholic church. His first impression was that the vault was immensely high and there was something radiant and gorgeous about the interior; a flood of variegated sunlight through lofty painted windows. He followed Fru Gotaas up the middle of the nave, but when she suddenly dropped on her knees he slipped into a bench behind her and sat down. Fru Gotaas entered the row in front of him and crouched in a kneeling position with her hands before her face.

A priest appeared in the choir. Before him he carried something which was covered with a red silken cloth, and he wore a red chasuble, much finer than Uncle Abraham's red velvet with the thick gold cross. On his head he had a funny black thing. But the oddest of all was the little acolyte in red and white—fancy their having acolytes in Norway, looking exactly like the pictures from abroad—

When Paul had looked about him he discovered that his first impression of splendour had been rather misreading. It was all pretty cheap—a gingerbread Gothic of painted wood, and paper flowers everywhere. The altar up in the choir looked as if it might be a little finer, with two gilt figures of angels and a kind of cupola in the middle. And the body of the church was not so grand either as it seemed when one first entered it; the walls were a dirty grey and the painted windows nothing to boast of. It had impressed him with its size because it was so empty—only four or five people scattered among the benches and a few nuns at the very end.

But all the same there was something about it all which affected him sympathetically. There was something strange, exuberant or unreserved in the very abundance of rather vulgar adornments—as though the church made profession of something, without being ashamed, in overflowing joy. Even what was ugly in it was at any rate not ugly in the sedate, ostentatiously unpretending way that he knew from Fossbakke church.

He tried to grasp the meaning of some of the things the priest was doing before the altar. But the man turned his back to the people the whole time, and they could not possibly hear a word of what he was whispering while he moved about up there, doing things. And by degrees, as Paul discovered that the service must be in full swing, and the deep silence prevailed in the empty, sun-lit church, and the few people in the seats continued to kneel as though lost in self-contemplation, he felt a kind of thrill. Why yes, this was beautiful in its way; he suddenly thought he understood what people meant when they spoke of the invisible God—he could imagine that priest and congregation were gathered together here to worship something invisible. This form of service could not possibly have any other meaning, for there was nothing here of the priest turning to the congregation and concerning himself with them; it was rather as though this man took the lead in conducting some worship or other. And for the first time in his life he thought he could perceive some sense in divine service—in this silent adoration he could imagine that a Being was present to receive their souls. Of course, it must have been a similar form of Christianity that had possessed the force for so colossal an expansion—but then it was before it became a preaching religion that it had reached this country—

Paul woke up with a start—he must have been nodding—people were getting up and leaving the benches. Paul got up too—he thought it was over; then he saw that Fru Gotaas and the others were moving slowly up to the choir. It looked as if there was going to be communion, although it was a weekday. There were not so few of them either—about eight. Paul watched the administering of the bread with a certain curiosity—the priest had to drink for them all, he had been told, but he saw no sign of his doing so; he had replaced the chalice on the altar.

Fru Gotaas came back again, small and round-shouldered, walking with bowed head and her hands laid flat on her bosom, so that the tips of her fingers pointed upward. It looked seemly and solemn. Then she knelt down again in her seat. Paul tried to remember how people behaved when they had received the sacrament at Fossbakke—probably they just sat down on their posteriors. After all one would think it more natural to kneel.

If he had guessed there was to be communion and that it was for that reason Fru Gotaas was going to church, he would never have intruded in this way. And he felt still more sick about it when he was outside and Fru Gotaas came up to him—he could see she was trying to appear unconcerned—she began chatting—

"Incense—" said Paul for the sake of something to say. "Don't they use it here in Norway?"

"Oh yes, they do—at High Mass and benediction—"

"High Mass, is that a different kind of Mass from this—?"

"Yes, this was a low Mass—it's so seldom there's High Mass on a weekday, you know—only on the festivals."

"Then do you have a Mass like this every morning at half-past six?"

"No, unfortunately we can't have that. It depends on how many priests are in town. For one of them has to say Mass at the Institute and one at the hospital, and that leaves only the eight o'clock Mass in church, that's the one the school children go to and all those who have to go to offices and so on. So very often Gotaas and I don't get to Mass except on Sunday—"

They entered the flat. Paul heard that Monika and the boys were in the dining room.

"I'll bring you in a cup of coffee," said Fru Gotaas; "I think maybe you might be glad of a drop of coffee now—"

Paul met Randi Alme outside the University a few days later and went up and talked to her.

"And so you've been to Mass!" she said with a laugh.

Paul was nettled:

"Yes—and I didn't see any sign of you! And I should have thought you were the one who ought to be there. You don't strike me as specially keen, my girl!"

"I go to eight o'clock Mass every day," said Randi, turning red.

"All the same, if I was God, I expect I'd think there ought to be a limit to pestering people like this! He must get so sick of all your whining, if he has to have you running round every blessed day!"

Randi Alme laughed loudly:

"Ah, if you were God! Or if God were like us. 'What awful rubbish it is, all this twaddle about men having created God in their own image!"

She nodded and ran off to a girl who had beckoned to her.

Chapter Six

Paul accepted the invitation to the family party for Uncle Abraham and Aunt Tinni—as a kind of penance; he had not yet come upon any trace of Capell Brooke and Neumann. He had called at the studio, drunk *thé á la russe* and listened to what the two little girls had to say about artistic circles in Rome—but without result.

The evening before he had to go out to his mother's to fetch some clothes, and then he decided to stay there till the middle of the next day. It was such glorious weather, and there were various little jobs to be done in the outhouse; Hans was not much use at that sort of thing, and his time seemed taken up with being a freshman.

He was lying on the divan out in the veranda reading, in his shirt-sleeves, when the telephone rang. Reluctantly he padded indoors in his stocking feet and answered it.

"Paul—" came his mother's voice, loud and ringing. "The Union is dissolved. The Storting has declared the King deposed."

Paul was silent a moment—overwhelmed.

"Is it true, do you think—it isn't only a rumour?"

"No, far from it—the whole town's on its feet. You'll catch the train if you hurry—come in at once, boy!"

Paul told the maid as he passed her—he ran out with the flag and hoisted it. And Alvilde stood on the veranda steps and watched him. Then up to the boys' room to change. He just managed to fling himself into the train as it coughed up smoke into the summer sunshine at the empty platform; there must be a notice posted on the station wall, but he hadn't time to look.

He sat in the empty third-class carriage looking out at the familiar country that lay smiling in the summer day—for the first time it struck him that the hackneyed expression, "smiling landscape," meant something. Though everything was as he had seen it a thousand times before: the sunlight poured down upon the dense pine forest so that it seemed saturated with it, the houses were baking among the green fields, the bushes along all the brooks cast solid-looking shadows—

And so it was true—this country was now a free country.

My country, my country, my fatherland. Paul leaned his head right back lest the tears should flow.

Half-free—he had known very well they were a half-free country. Only he had not cared to join in the talk—it had been going on as long as he could remember, people wrangling over the Union, loud-voiced and voluble: one party shouting that we must fight our way to complete equality within the Union or else out of it; another striving to convince themselves and the rest that we were on an equal footing, our position was not humiliating or unworthy, a trifle uncomfortable perhaps, but when one weighed the inconveniences against the dangers that threatened the peninsula from the East—and the brother nations were indispensable to one another. And then we were the weaker of the two. He simply hadn't bothered always to listen to this or think about it, because he had never believed the talk would lead to anything but more talk—

And now—my God! He drew a long breath, quivering. Good Lord Almighty, what a lovely summer day—!

His friends and fellow students—were there any of his own age who interested themselves in Union politics?—a few peasant students from orthodox Liberal parts of the country, and a few sons of Storting members of the good-boy type who believed everything that papa and mamma believed—

The others skimmed over it and discussed social problems instead. Socialism, new morality, the materialist outlook, the abolition of religion. To tell the truth, he had regarded this as a continuation of the flight into talk and again talk. And to be sure he knew of nothing better to propose in its place, and he was certain that they firmly believed something would come of all this talk—as their parents' generation had believed something would result from the Union debates and newspaper articles and fiery speeches and echoing songs. But it never occurred to him that anyone expected him to believe—

Socialism would probably triumph, because the whole tendency of the age—mechanical, technical civilization—was to place power in the hands of the most numerous, not of the most intelligent. Until development called for fresh initiative—and then the most intelligent or enterprising among the masses would have a chance of climbing up, and then we should have an upper class and a lower class again, as normally. The new morality—all he could see was that it was sprouting and shooting up merrily; presumably it was as old as the human race, as you see when a forest has been cleared or trees blown down by the wind: the saplings that shoot up and spread have mostly been growing there before, in the shadow. In time the forest is there again—a new morality. That is to say, there *are* cases when the belt of forest shrinks—wastes and pasture take its place. Then there is nothing to be done—in that way a country is impoverished, unless people are willing to make sacrifices and wait a long time for a return.

The abolition of religion could not interest him, as he had never had any. But the more he saw of the iconoclasts, the more he was tempted to wish there had been something in the old religion that was real. People became so unbearably narrow-minded when they were emancipated. And the materialist outlook—he was never tempted to open his mouth and yawn so widely as when the talk was of some outlook on life, to say nothing of an outlook on the world.—He had confined himself to a couple of little maxims: never to believe a thing because there were many who believed it, and never to yield to the temptation of arguing thus: if others do it, I can do it too—

He had also noticed that those who were keenest in these discussions, in the Students' Union and in clubs and so on, were those whose line of study was chosen from the bread-and-butter point of view. Those who were to be schoolmasters and lawyers—parsons and doctors too. The lads who took up some scientific subject, they were far less inclined to talk wildly of social questions and a scientific outlook on life. Aaser with his flora of the calcareous slate, and Ingstad, the archaeologist, who had already taken a degree, they had no cut-and-dried scientific outlook on life; what they had was a good deal of exact knowledge and a capacity for accurate observation and for combining and drawing conclusions concerning the things they were working with. He himself had no scientific view of life, but he was beginning to know a few things, about the peat bogs of Norway, for instance, which later on might have some practical importance. And he had looked forward to helping Ingstad with his archaeological collection in the summer; Ingstad had proposed it—he was engaged in a work on the Stone Age and would be glad of the collaboration of one who had specialized a little in geology—

Now he supposed nothing would come of it—nor of that walking tour in Dovre he and Aaser were going to take. Paul laughed, nervous and joyfully excited.

To think that it was true. An end of talk, something had happened. And it was the old ones, for whom he, for one, had a sort of sympathy, because the young ones paid so little attention to them and he thought they had deserved this by their own incompetence—it was the old ones who had done it. It was they who had acted, when it came to the point.

And how we have misjudged them—but now—oh, now the whole nation will rally round them, ready to defend the liberty they have given us—

At Baekkelaget station a man gave him the first handbill—a crumpled sheet with just a few lines on it. Paul almost wanted to put it to his lips—

Outside the terminus he got his hands full of them. The next moment his mother came towards him—she came at such a pace, and the color of her mauve tailor-made was so intensely bright in the sunlight—

"Paul," she said with a laugh, almost embracing him.

She took his arm as they walked up Karl Johan:

"Oh, the flags, Paul, look at them! I've always thought the Norwegian flag the most beautiful in the world. Yes, its colors are hard—but they ought to be. Ah, now at last, at last—it's not merely a token of hopes and desires—which we consoled ourselves with to deaden our shame. God knows, we've had far too much bluster and big words—now we shan't need that any more. Look at the people, Paul, can't you see we've changed already—!"

They stood together on the outskirts of the crowd in front of the Storting. And when somebody began to sing "*Ja vi elsker—*" Julie joined in, while the tears poured down her cheeks. She pressed her son's arm against her side and sang with her head thrown back.

Strangely quiet in the side streets. His mother had to go back to business.

Paul was instinctively against the Bernadotte offer, "It seems like an attempt to sweeten the pill. Maybe it's wise. But if we have only claimed our rights—stood up for our constitution? And to the King's constitution it must be altogether indigestible—must taste like the most bitter of insults—which will only be made worse by our trying to coax him with a lump of sugar afterwards."

"He'll never accept it either. And Sweden—the Swedes have never begun to understand us really. Presumably they'll mobilize in twenty-four hours. It's tragic that it should be so—but it can't be otherwise. One nation never really understands an atom of what's stirring in another nation."

"But mother!" Paul laughed. "What's become of your pacifism?"

"Pacifism—that's another thing altogether. I've never denied that for us the question of national defense is the most important of all—"

Paul smiled with delight—wasn't mother's logic sweet?

"Do you remember what we were talking about last year? That I should try to be called up a year before my time? I wish I had done it. Of course, if we're in for it, you know I shall join up all the same—"

"I know you will." Julie looked up at her son, proudly. "All the same I too should have liked you to be wearing the King's uniform now"—she saw the boy's smile and corrected herself quickly—"with the colors, I mean."

Hans and Sigmund, Tua and her fiancé, had all drifted into the office.

"A gathering of the clan," said Halstein Garnaas. The sort of thing he would say.

Near by someone was playing "*Ja vi elsker*" on a piano.

THE afternoon sunshine was tinged with gold, and there was a cloud of dust from the fire engine going up the street. Tua and Garnaas walked in front, Paul and Hans behind.

Paul saw they were now exactly the same height, he and his brother. But Hans was much slighter and thinner in the face, his hair was darker too, and his complexion paler. He had passed his exam uncommonly well—must have pulled himself together a good deal the last half-year. He ought to have a good chance of getting into the military college. Anyhow they would both be in it.

And he couldn't yet grasp that it was true—that life had suddenly become so solemn. Every single thing—the familiar gardens and houses, Blaasen—that odd little knoll that had been left in peace while the town grew around it, with its briar thickets and its short grass—everything looked so fine in this new light of reality, beyond all words. Life is serious, life is serious, sang a voice within him—Lord, yes, he had heard that so often. Damned funny—that was what people said to check naughty youngsters! Oh, but to think that it was true after all—acutely true, making one's whole being tremble with solemn joy. Fatherland, Norway, life's seriousness—he dared say them out loud this evening, without feeling bashful—

"I say, Hans—if I was called upon, dashed if I couldn't shout it out loud this evening—Norway, my country, life is serious—"

"Don't be afraid," said Hans. "Halstein will say all that for us."

—But tomorrow he must find Lucy.

THE family party was rather a damper.

Paul scarcely had a chance of talking to his father. Once, when he did not happen to be taken up with any of his guests, his son managed to ask: "Have you any idea what turn it will take?"

Selmer shook his head:

"In any case the situation is serious enough to make us abstain from futile guesses. One thing I would say to you, Paul—make it a principle never to let yourself be drawn into discussing rumors." A spark of life came into the pale eyes behind the glasses: "but undeniably, one is tempted to envy you who are young. Whatever the cost may turn out to be—a state of things has been brought to an end which has meant a greater loss of energy to the country than I believe the nation has any idea of. Amongst other things it has taught the people to consume an immense quantity of speeches—and to believe that words are a species of deeds.—In itself of course war is always a disaster. But not always the greatest."

The others repeated what everyone else was saying, thought Paul. The Dverbergs were enthusiastic about the offer of the crown to one of the Bernadottes; the parson expressed the desire that it might be Prince Oscar.

"Ugh, no, Abraham," said Lillian. "How can you say so! I thought Prince Bernadotte and his consort had such very Low Church leanings, haven't they?"

Aunt Tinni wanted Prince Carl, because he was the perfect ideal of manly beauty, as she said, and a king ought above all to be the handsomest and most stylish gentleman in the country.—

Pastor Dverberg and Garnaas discussed the probability of this solemn national crisis bringing in its train an awakening of religious feeling.

"Undoubtedly, Pastor Dverberg, undoubtedly," said Garnaas. "We Norwegians are bashful in that way, we are shy of putting our deepest feelings into words. Many of us young men have had a kind of modesty of the soul which forbade us saying straight out how unspeakably we loved this beautiful country of ours. Now, now we dare say it—because we may be called upon to prove it in deeds! There is something similar in the Norwegian people's attitude to its God. But you may be sure there are thousands—millions"—he corrected himself—"of hearts which are raised on high today!"

"*Skaal*, Halstein," said Paul from his corner, but immediately withdrew into himself again.

But Halstein Garnaas raised his glass in acknowledgement, with dignified deprecation. He was used to nothing but everlasting frontier skirmishes with his future brothers-in-law, so he hadn't the remotest suspicion that Paul meant anything out of the ordinary by his *Skaal*, Halstein—

Paul thought: yes, God—today he ought to have existed. In the train coming along—he could have knelt down and clasped his hands. There ought to have been someone to whom one could give thanks and honor—with all one's heart, and even deeper, from the very depths of one's being. And prayed to for blessing. He saw this evening how men needed something of the sort—a God whom one could associate with. So that one was least alone when one felt most alone among men. If one could only reach out with one's soul and come in contact with an invisible one—who would help one to a deeper or higher vision of all that was irritating and disturbing, to look past the stupidity and platitudes and ridiculous expressions, into what was valuable in those one associated with, a common charity, a common vow which bound one to them. Just as he had thought a moment ago—why should I always be put off by Halstein's way of saying things? He means it; what he said about our country is the same as I feel about it, and what he said about God would have been the same too, if I had believed in God. And this evening of all evenings I must needs sit here taking exception to his comical jargon—

Meanwhile Uncle Abraham had reached the conclusion of a somewhat lengthy discourse: "—when life as now suddenly shows us its true countenance, and death stares a man in the face. To live without God, that is easy enough. But to die without God—"

"No," said Halstein Garnaas; "it reminds me of Grundtvig's beautiful words:

> To bid the world farewell aright
> In life's fair dawn or evening light
> Is hard for one and all;
> We ne'er could learn it here below,
> Did we not feel thee near and know,
> Jesus, thou'lt hear our call."

"Even you must admit that's beautiful, Paul," said Tua enthusiastically. "As you have such a feeling for poetry—"

But Paul loathed Grundtvig—he had had two Grundtvigian masters and they had used Seip's hymnbook at prayers all the time he was at school.

"In the first place it isn't true at all. To bid the world farewell aright—that's exactly what men have always been able to do; whatever they believed or didn't believe, they've always had the courage to die. It's no more than natural that men should insist on courage and pride being stronger than the fear of death—though it isn't everyone that succeeds in taking the last fence handsomely. The young—and the irreligious—often manage it best—any doctor or nurse you like to ask will tell you something about that. It is living without religion they don't manage so well, at any rate they don't succeed in living well and getting on in the world, without becoming odious and vulgar and narrow and egotistical—that may be an argument for the truth or anyhow the necessity of religion. But as to any real horror of death—that only comes in when one begins to mix up Jesus in it, and judgment day and all that. So I don't give much for all this talk about Christianity being essentially a means of comforting the sick and dying. As a narcotic at any rate it's a complete fiasco."

"No, Paul, you're wrong there," said Uncle Abraham weightily. "You do not know what effect the glad tidings of the forgiveness of sins through the blood of Christ has on a dying sinner who trembles for the wrath of judgment. I have witnessed that—oh, times without number! More specially in the case of the worst, the most hardened sinners. You must not be so sure, Paul—it may be your own lot, in the hour of extremity, to grasp at the gospel of salvation—"

"Yes, and it's you yourselves who have put this idea into their heads of a judgment after death. Though it hasn't been able to scare them sufficiently to make them behave themselves while they were alive and kicking. No, uncle, if I should ever be converted, as it's called, I hope it'll happen while I'm young and have my life before me and can live according to my faith and do something for God's sake."

"It's easy to hear that you live with Catholics," said Halstein Garnaas sarcastically; "and they haven't lost any time in influencing you."

"What do I hear?" Pastor Dverberg looked at his nephew in consternation. "May I ask if your parents know of this, Paul? Good God—has it come to this, a Catholic in our family! What do you think your grandparents would have said—No, my friend, you and I must have a serious talk about this—"

"No use, uncle, no use at all—" Paul waved his hand. "It's all settled; I'm to join the Catholic church in a week's time."

"Indeed you shan't! Erik—do you hear what Paul's telling us!"

"My dear Abraham," Lillian tried to calm him; "don't you see Paul's only chaffing, he's laughing all the time. You may be sure he has no idea of such a thing."

"Indeed I won't be sure. When once he's fallen into the clutches of people of that sort. Oh, they're more dangerous than anyone imagines in this country. Look what happened to Harald Tangen. He started going to the Catholic church, then one of those priests got hold of him, lent him books and worked on him in every possible way. And then the boy goes to Rome, that clever, cultured, bright young man. And now they say he's come home as a Catholic priest—!"

"What's that?" asked Paul with interest. "Harald—that was the second eldest of the Tangen boys, wasn't it, the one who was a cadet?"

"Precisely. And they say there's a danger that Emilie, the *charming* Emilie Tangen, will follow her brother. So now you can see what comes of associating with that kind of people. Oh, they're so sly—"

"Ah, I suspected as much," said Paul with a serious face. "The girl where I live brought home a birdcage the other day. But I guessed at once there was something mystical about it; of course it's a Jesuit that's disguised himself as a canary—"

"No, Paul, be quiet now," said Lillian with a laugh. "You must stop teasing your uncle," she whispered; "it's so awkward for us all."

PAUL walked to the station with Hans. On his way home he went along Karl Johan. There were still crowds of people about; he spoke to a few of his acquaintance, but refused to go in anywhere with them—didn't feel like it, without knowing why.

The sky stretched white above the dark trees of the palace gardens and the pale, empty building on the top of the hill. Its flagstaff was bare—well, of course, it generally had been bare, and besides it was night. All the same it seemed like a symbol tonight, the deserted white palace and the empty flagstaff.

And down below that strange monstrosity, the Storting building in grey brick, a kind of Old Man of the Mountain squatting on his haunches, with the huge paunch of the rotunda between his knees and the wings at the sides like two heads with a confusion of windows for little troll's eyes, squinting up at the house yonder—the foreigner's quarters. And so this odd grey troll behind the bushes of Eidsvoldsplass had had the true instinct; it had been the Storting after all that had fought for our national life all the time, and now the troll got on its feet. The Chosen of the People—oh hell, to think the day should come when there was nothing but bare truth in the phrase. At a word from the men in there we shall gladly march to the frontier—

There was a scent of lilac, and the dust seemed to hang in the air after all the feet that had been raising it all day long—a stuffy Independence Day evening air—tired air he had called it as a child, he remembered. But up in the tops of the tall poplars there lingered a gleam of light, and the sky was white.

Te Deum laudamus. Te Dominum Confitemur. Te aeternum Patrem omnis terra veneratur—

On the evening of the day when he had paid his early morning visit to the Catholics' God Almighty he had actually taken a peep at the lamented Vincent's library, though it did not look inviting—little books in black cloth with red edges. But in turning over one which made a special appeal to *"die gebildete Männerwelt,"* he discovered that it contained the Te Deum and the Miserere, and he wanted to look at those. From novels and plays and the like he had got the impression that the Te Deum was a sort of triumphal yell which Catholics are in the habit of uttering when they have had a real good time with a Saint Bartholomew or have put to death a few recreant noblemen, while the Miserere was more appropriate for the burning of heretics or the immuring of nuns who have kicked over the traces.

Of course he had had no notion of more than the opening words of them. But they turned out to be quite overpoweringly beautiful. Least of all had he expected that the Te Deum should end as a humble prayer: Vouchsafe, O Lord, to keep us this day without sin, or something like that, and—day by day we will praise thee—have mercy on us—in thee have we trusted, thou wilt not let us be confounded—it ended something like that. But the Miserere ended, if not exactly triumphantly, at any rate in a strangely high-spirited and cheerful strain—something about, then shall my mouth proclaim thy praise, and that the walls of Zion shall be built up again and the people shall offer sacrifices on the altars.

PAUL moved the lamp over to his bedside table and took out the little black book; he had put it away in the drawer. His talk with Uncle Abraham had encouraged him to look a little more closely at Vincent Gotaas's books. By the same token, this one was evidently by a Jesuit: Tilmann Pesch, S.J. that meant Societas Jesu, as far as he knew.

He read the Te Deum over again—luckily there was a German translation at the side. Good God, how magnificent it really was.

He went on to the next page:

> "Prayer of consecration to the Sacred Heart of Jesus: Most loving Jesus, Source of charity, Father of compassion and God of all consolation, who hast revealed to us poor and unworthy the unutterable treasures of thy most sacred Heart, in gratitude for the innumerable benefits conferred on me and the whole of mankind, especially for the institution of the most holy Sacrament, and in expiation of all the offenses which I and others have committed against thy sacred Heart in this mystery of the love that passes comprehension—I now offer up to this most sacred Heart my whole self and all that is mine—"

No. He found that if he was going to entertain himself for long with Herr Tilmann Pesch, S.J., he would certainly fall asleep and leave the lamp burning. So he put the book back in the drawer and turned out the light.

Chapter Seven

He was down in the fortress square with his mother on the ninth,[†] saw the Union flag struck and the clean flag run up.

The weather was rather overcast that day and there was a good deal of wind; the halyards swung in a wide curve, and the flag flapped loudly as it went up; on reaching the top it swept out in the tearing breeze. Paul felt himself turn white and cold in the face with emotion, and he dared not look at his mother—but she held his hand in hers and squeezed it.

Afterwards they went into the Grand and ploughed through the papers once more.

There were papers and papers and broadsheets and handbills and discussions of everything that had been in print. And the national song broke out spontaneously. And then all the rumours—it was not so easy to follow his father's advice and never descend to discussing rumours. Business as usual, let everyone go on with his work as if nothing were happening, that was the password. But one's work acquired a peculiar flavour of solemnity.

Paul borrowed books from his father and read up the history of the Union backwards and forwards. He even read the official gazette, but not from cover to cover. He had a good deal of talk with his father in these days. Erik Selmer was an old Conservative.

"You see, Paul, what Sverdrup meant by the will of the people was the will of the majority. I have no distrust of a majority on principle. But I have a distrust of all those who have confidence in majorities. Just as I have a distrust of all those who have confidence in a minority, because it

† Translator's Note: June 1905.

is a minority. It has nothing at all to do with the value of an idea, whether at a given historical moment it finds acceptance with a majority or with a minority which believes itself to be an elite.

"I remember, your mother in our young days, when—older people—protested against her radicalism, used to appeal to the fact that in every age the old had used the same language, bewailing the depravity of the young and praying to be preserved from the disasters which the ideas of the young must end in bringing upon the world. And the world had endured in spite of all, said she and her friends. Yes, but how—? What they forget is that in every age there have also been young people who laughed at the warnings of the old and were delighted with themselves and dashed off in the direction they believed to be that of evolution—imagined they were dancing before the ark, when they were just drifting with the stream. We may be sure the young did the same while decay was eating up all the old civilizations—the youth of the Renaissance laughed at their elders' prejudices against poisoning and extravagant courtesans. The world has been on the verge of destruction a good many times—and life has sometimes proved the old to be right in their jeremiads and sometimes the young in their trust in the future. But we forget the individuals who were the victims of every historical catastrophe, that is the point.

"Now there is no doubt in my mind that *today* the will of the people points in the right direction. At this juncture the majority desires the right thing. God grant it may continue to do so in five or in fifteen years. Today we are in league with the spirit of 1814, we are told. Your mother used to say, when she supported an idea, that it was in league with the future. I never thought *that* was in itself a recommendation—what does it mean to be in league with Friday fortnight, or with July nineteen-fifteen—? Maybe we are today in league with the spirit of 1915, but do we know what sort of a spirit that is?"

"You think that in one way or another ideas have a life and value of their own, irrespective of how many or how few people may believe in them on a particular day?"

"I think that moral values and truths are concrete and objective. To take comfort in the thought that one is in league with the future is equivalent to flattering oneself that one is on the side of the victors—a sufficiently contemptible line of thought. But one thing in any case is relative in this world—human intelligence.

"Won't you stay to supper?" asked his father. Paul looked at his watch.

"No, thanks, I'm afraid I can't. I have an appointment—"

And he went off to meet Lucy Arnesen as she left the shop.

ALL that everyone else was talking about and that formed as it were a background to all his thoughts and actions at this time—seemed scarcely to have touched Lucy's consciousness: "I don't understand such things—"

Paul thought there was a wonderful repose in this womanly nature which was content to remain within its own limitations. She did not understand much of what was going on, but there were so many others who understood just as little as Lucy, and that didn't keep them from cackling—they lacked the natural wisdom which made her confine herself within her own realities.

He could not resist picturing to himself what would happen if war broke out. Then she *must* be his, before he left for the front; when he thought of this the big, fair girl with the gentle, rather sleepy eyes and the pale pink, silent lips became the quintessence of life's patient capacity for enduring and renewing—woman, soil, home, race and all such conceptions—

At present however Paul conducted himself as the pattern of a respectful, considerate and unobtrusive friend. He came to meet her outside the flower shop several evenings a week. She continued to be very reserved, almost as though his attentions frightened her a little. Deuce take it, he was properly gone on her, so much so that he didn't know what he was going to do about her; if he yielded to his passion he could see it would not be easy to control himself. And as for seducing a poor young shop girl while the fate of one's country is in the balance—no, a man simply *can't* do that—

If it came to war—that would be another thing. Though he did not reflect why it should be.

Poor.—Her landlady had shown him into her room one Sunday morning when he came to take her out for a walk. A long, narrow room with one window on the ground floor, looking on to a yard. It was like a servant's room and reminded him of a place he had been to one day last winter, to take a parcel for Tua to a cheap dressmaker. The same untidiness and the same odour of poverty.

On the walls some picture postcards were stuck up fanwise: some of them were fairly offensive, though they could not be called downright improper, Lucy blushed when she saw him looking at them:

"Those are some things that were left behind by the one who was here before me. I let them stay, because I had nothing of my own to put up—it looks so bare with nothing on the walls—"

—Next day Paul went out and bought her two framed photographs. After long consideration he chose one of Charles I's children by van Dyke and Hobbema's avenue—they were good as works of art, without being beyond Lucy's comprehension. She accepted them after much protestation, almost shyly.—

This Sunday he wanted to take her out to Kongshavn bathing beach. She was not very enthusiastic, but gave in as usual, after he had spent some time in persuasion. She made a parcel of her bathing dress—a red one, he saw.

Afterwards, in the water, when he had swum a long way out, he caught sight of a red girl swimmer ahead of him; he thought it was Lucy and dashed after her. But it turned out to be a perfect stranger.

As they sat under the old horse-chestnuts, drinking coffee after their bath, he said to her:

"I tried to come up with you just now, out in the water, but when I got there it wasn't you at all, but somebody quite different."

"Oh no, I don't know how to swim. I was never allowed to bathe in the sea when I lived at home. My parents were religious—"

Paul had a soft place in his heart for this old hostelry—the little, low houses tucked in between the cliff and the railway line and the big old trees. He told her:

"My mother used to bring us here to bathe when we were children."

"I didn't think—" Lucy turned red, as she so often did when she spoke: "—I didn't think it was quite—proper, this place. So I thought when gentlemen came here it was too—well, they would never have brought any of their own ladies here—"

Oho, thought Paul. Was that why she didn't like it when he proposed coming here? Poor little Lucy. "Not a bit of it. In the morning at any rate anybody can come here."

But after that he generally took her up to Holmenkollen or to Bygdö baths. He himself preferred the small places which had not the character of a restaurant; the places he and his chums had frequented ever since he was a schoolboy. But he was afraid Lucy might misunderstand and think he was taking her to second-rate places because he did not care to meet people he knew. As far as that went she would have been right: he had no great desire to meet people he knew when he was out with her, though not for the reasons Lucy imagined. But he could scarcely have avoided it in the little huts in the forest, where you get thin coffee and primitive sandwiches at a cheap price.

The larger restaurants were more frequented by a public he did not know, business people and the like. Besides, he wanted the food to be good when they were out together—Lucy got her own meals, and perhaps it was no wonder she looked rather anemic. But it cost money. Paul wrote articles on fossils from Ringerike and ferrocyanides in the Gudbrandsdal, a summary of other men's work and old notebooks of his own which he worked up and filled in with brief descriptions of the scenery which he found so easy to make graphic. That brought him in a few crowns. Though the papers had such a glut of matter now that it was rather difficult to get things of this sort accepted.

HE had not been able to arrange any longer trips. Eberhard was in training at Oscarsborg, and to have three ladies on his hands wouldn't do. He had a thought of Hans—but his brother was—not snobbish either, but somehow so utterly out of place except in their own circle.

Anyhow, they were all leaving town now, one after another.

Randi knocked at his door one afternoon; Fru Gotaas had sent her to ask if he would come in and take coffee with them. Randi was going home in a day or two, taking with her Wilfrid and Josef, she told him; her father had given her permission.

"So your father has no objection to your being a Catholic?" asked Paul.

"Oh—to begin with he was not very pleased, I can tell you. Especially at my refusing to go to church—it's a regular custom at home that we drive to church a certain number of times in the year, you see." She gave a little laugh. "Father's idea is to be on sort of neighborly terms with Our Lord—he's willing to treat God with all reasonable consideration, but in return he insists that God is not to be unreasonable to him or interfere too much with his home life at Alme. There are many people all over the country who look at it in the same light, at all events among the older men. Ah well—I wonder how it was in the old days; there were once chapels of ease at Alme and three of the biggest farms in the parish—in Catholic times. The foundation and a bit of the wall of our chapel are still to be seen in the field north of the house—a particular kind of briar rose grows there; you know briar roses love old lime. Wilfrid and Josef are wildly excited about our going there in the evenings to say our rosaries together—"

"Don't you think it'll look odd if you start devotions of that sort?"

"Yes." She smiled. "Last Christmas Eve—you know, father insists on my going home for Christmas, so I've never been to midnight Mass. But Monika and Sister Blandina promised they would pray with me and give me their holy communion. So at twelve o'clock I lighted two candles in my room and tried to take part spiritually in the Mass, and meanwhile I said my beads. Then all of a sudden the door opened, and there was father. 'Mercy on us, Randi, what are you up to, girl?'—he probably thought I had gone in for some kind of idolatry; I had set up a little manger, you understand. Well, then I tried to explain to him what a rosary is. But when I had finished father shook his head: 'How can you believe it amuses God to listen to all that there, my lass?' he said.

"However, when I explained to him about the old chapel of ease, I could see the idea appealed to him tremendously. To have your own domestic chaplain—a young one, halfway between you and the farm servants, who might perhaps be put to doing a little office work. Father doesn't like the parson of the parish, I must tell you—and he's nothing but a parrot—

"But then we have a lay preacher—Brother Landfald he's called—and luckily he came one day to see father and explain to him what dreadful people the Catholics were—you know, all that folklore about confessionals and Jesuits and nunneries. Then said father, 'Well, if Brother Landfald says so, it must be three parts gossip and one part twaddle; there must be some good in the Catholics since he's so mad with them. I'm wondering if I shan't join you myself, Randi.' 'But then you'll have to receive instruction first, father,' said I. 'No, I'm too old for that,' said he. So that's as far as we've got."

Fru Gotaas appeared at the door: "Coffee's ready, if you please. Father Tangen is here," she said smilingly.

Paul looked with a certain curiosity at this man, the son of one of his father's old friends, who had gone and joined the Catholic priesthood. At first sight there was something odd in his appearance, with a white dog collar, a high-necked waistcoat and a kind of frock coat, lined like a uniform. Harald Tangen was a young man of middle height, powerfully built, with a thin, bony face of the type that is often called English—a hooked nose, big chin, narrow lips and prominent teeth; and he was very fair too, with sandy yellow hair, a reddish complexion and limpid, bluish green eyes.

He must have changed a great deal, thought Paul—he had not seen Harald Tangen since that autumn in the mountains, when the other was a boy of sixteen or seventeen; though the only impression he had of him was that he himself had envied the grown lad who had gun and dog and was praised for being a good shot—

Paul introduced himself: "But I don't expect you remember me—I was only a little boy then—"

Father Tangen said oh yes, he did, and asked after Paul's family—in rather vague terms. Well, of course he knew how things had gone with Paul's parents since that time—

Otherwise he did not say anything which struck Paul as out of the ordinary. There was nothing peculiar about him except the get up. On the contrary, it occurred to him afterwards, when the priest had gone, that there was nothing at all in his manner of that continual reminding the company that they had a priest in their midst—if only in letting people understand that they must not on any account allow it to damp their spirits—. He was like an ordinary man paying a call. In fact there seemed to be no humbug about him.

Paul stayed in Christiania—was out at Linlökka for a couple of days at a time and then back to town to work. He discovered that Christiania in summer is really a charming town. The evenings were wonderful, whether one went out to Bygdö, lay on the dry, sun-scorched ground a little way from the shore watching the white sails moving across the smooth, violet surface of the fiord which mirrored the great, pink-topped summer clouds over the wooded ridge of Nesodde. Behind them the devastated royal forest breathed resin and the scent of fir needles; children played noisily at the water's edge and people walked about the paths—the faint sounds only made one feel more deeply how vast and still was the luminous expanse. Little fiord steamers, crammed with people, came past with music on board; they set up little innocent waves which broke in ripples on the beach. Or else he and Lucy went up to Holmenkollen, saw fiord and town lying far below them in the soft twilight of the summer night, and walked home together through the woods.

So now he knew what it was to desire—not merely a pestering physical feeling towards something featurelessly corporeal—woman. But how it feels when another human being attracts everything that stirs in one's' body and mind, as a magnet attracts iron. And he could not help thinking of a conjunction with her as close as that of the iron with the magnet. His dreams either circled about a single night and the parting in the grey dawn, or else they soared into a distant future—when one day as a mature man he would look back on his path through life and thank his fortune for all the years he had lived together with his wife, that taciturn, prolific piece of human nature from which he had always been able to derive courage and joy, repose and faith in life. Even such things as her speech being—well, not quite correct—and the little she had to say being never particularly intelligent, made her dear to him: the fact that she did not possess much external culture had only served to preserve the natural fragrance of her being—oh, she was rich and deep and tender and unspoilt.

One thing which surprised him beyond words was that he could not help thinking of her having children by him. When he had read of such things in novels—that a man thought of a woman as the future mother of his children, or that a man desired to have children, he had always thought, nonsense, no man feels like that—unless of course he has a farm or an old business or something of the sort, which gives him special reasons for wishing to have an heir and successor whom he can bring up. But otherwise—it is another matter that a man is fond of his kids when once they are there and he has them about him every day—but heavens above! No normal young man goes round dreaming sentimentally about the children he may be going to put into the world. But with Lucy he really did feel like that—even now, before he had given her a single kiss, he knew that their relations would not be consummated until their child was brought to life.

Just because there was not a shadow of any so-called motherliness in her manner towards him. And not a scrap of coquetry—rather was she shy, yielded with some reluctance to his desire that they should be together. Was it that she divined as surely as he did, that nature had her design with the pair of them, and that she was alarmed, as at a fate from which there was no escape—?

As a sort of introduction to their relations he had proposed to Lucy to go out to Linlökka with him one day. But she refused absolutely—all that Paul said was in vain: his mother would be so glad; it was so quiet out there now that his brothers and sister were away on holiday, so his mother would be—well, in short, so glad. He was not so sure of that himself, by the way. Just because his mother was so liberal and all that, so full of love for the people on principle, he had a kind of instinctive doubt of her delight in being given a girl of the people for a daughter-in-law.

Lucy came from a little farm in the Tönsherg country, but did not keep up much connection with her people—she had mentioned a stepmother. Both her brothers had disappeared, one in the Arctic, the other in America. To tell the truth, Paul had never been able to appreciate very keenly this talk about classes: of course he saw the stamp of class in a person, in the same way as he saw his build or complexion, but to his mind everyone he met was far too much an individual to permit of his feeling democratic or undemocratic: he liked the lower middle-class stamp that he found in the old Gotaases, because he liked the Gotaases, and he disliked the middle-class air that was characteristic of Halstein Garnaas, because he disliked Garnaas. The same marks of tradition that he was fond of in his father and his paternal uncles seemed to him ridiculous enough when he recognized them in Aunt Tinni or Uncle Abraham. And ideas and expressions that he would not have forgone for anything in the world when they were his mother's because they belonged to her whole physiognomy, made him see red when any of the professors he didn't like took to airing them.

But his future was becoming somewhat of a problem to him now. He would take a science degree next year, and there was a post of assistant lecturer which he had a prospect of getting; probably he could get some lessons at a school too—and he could go on writing occasionally, only in his leisure time, of course, and because it amused him. He had a little money too; his father had made a division of his property when he married Lillian, and no doubt his mother had saved most of his father's contribution to the maintenance of the children. But the greater part of this money was invested in his mother's business—she had wanted to talk to him about it more than once, but then Uncle Alarik ought to be present, and so nothing had come of it as yet. But in any case he would be able to afford a fairly long stay abroad to complete his studies, when he was through the examination. Now he supposed he would get married instead—in six months' time or so. That is, if this crisis were settled peaceably—.

So long as Ingstad was in town Paul worked with him at the museum in the mornings. It was extremely attractive work—he became more and more interested in the points of contact between archaeology and geology; Ingstad took him into the ethnological collection and they looked at objects from other Stone Age cultures. And for a few hours Paul thought of other things than the settlement of accounts with Sweden and his passion for Lucy Arnesen.

Ingstad was married, and Paul went to supper with them a few times.

Fru Ingstad was pretty and charming, and they had a little girl who crawled about the floor and tried to stand up and walk. Sometimes she edged her way over to Paul and insisted on getting up into his lap; he was a good deal bothered and not a little flattered by her advances.

At the beginning of July Lucy happened to be alone at the shop for a week or so; Fröken Jensen had gone home to Sandefjord for a funeral. Paul was constantly in the shop during this time, and Lucy told him Fröken Jensen had promised her one or two afternoons off when she came back. And one day later in the month, when the weather was particularly brilliant, he went in, bought some roses for Fru Ingstad and persuaded Lucy to ask for the afternoon, so that they could go to the Ullevoldssaeter.

They went no farther than the Sognsvand. It was so broiling hot. And Lucy was not suitably dressed—in the white frock with the green neckband which she had had on the first time he met her, a year ago; she wore white canvas shoes. So they called at one of the cottages by the lake, got coffee there and ate the food Paul had brought in his rucksack.

Afterwards they lay down at the edge of the forest. Before them a field sloped down, so full of daisies that it gleamed in great silvery patches, and in the late golden sunlight the air above the overripe meadow seemed full of pollen.

Paul was giddy with the light and the sound of buzzing insects over the meadow and the close, hot scent of the forest. A streak of tall green bushes running through the meadow showed the course of a little brook which made its way down to the lake—it looked so cool. He was lying on a corner of Lucy's white skirt, so near to her that he felt how hot the thin, stiff material had been baked by the sun. And from beneath this dry, hot tulle breathed the warmth of her body, a moist and gentler heat, like the breath of the soil. Suddenly he raised himself on his arm—then threw himself upon her and buried his head in the scorching folds of the girl's dress under her bosom.

She gave a violent jump. Paul looked up, saw her face distorted as with extreme terror—then he let go. She struggled to her knees, then to her feet, stumbling over the flounces of her skirt, and stood with her fair hair in disorder about her pale, terrified face.

"But Lucy—" Paul got up too, snatched at her hand, as she was going to run away. "But Lucy, what is it—was that so terrible?"

"I didn't think you were like that—" she whispered.

"How do you mean, like that?"—he himself was trembling, with excitement and because her terror infected him with a sense of something fateful. He saw the flash of water behind the glistening osiers on the slope, the warm blue sky above the treetops—and this big white girl standing there in such fear of him that she shook.

"That I'm in love with you—haven't you guessed that before?"

"I don't know—" he caught her distressful pale blue eyes. "Sometimes—but then I thought, no, you didn't mean anything like that—" She burst into tears. "Oh, I know, it was foolish of me, but—I thought it was so—nice—to go about with you, so I tried to believe—you weren't thinking of anything of that sort—you were never anything but—kind to me—"

"But my dear Lucy—why should you take it in this way!—Do you think it such an awful thing that I should be fond of you?"

As she made no reply, Paul said in a low voice:

"Then you're not the least bit fond of me? I really thought so sometimes—that you cared for me. Then you don't?"

"Oh yes!" It came like a wail. She tore her hand from him and staggered a few steps to the big fir tree. And with her arms thrown about its trunk and her forehead against its old grey bark she stood there weeping as if she could not stop.

"Oh, but dear sweet good little Lucy—" now he had got his arms around her and drew her away from the tree, gathered her to him. She had bark in her hair, bark and resin on her dress "—but what in heaven's name has come over you, Lucy—Lucy, is it anything to cry about—that I love you and you love me—are you crazy, girl—?" and now he had got at her face, kissed her on the mouth, kissed her eyes and cheeks—oh, her soft, wet, warm skin—and with a deep, wild sob she surrendered herself and kissed him back, till Paul turned giddy; it was as though she sucked the breath and the very marrow out of him.

"But you are an odd one," he whispered, when they had to take breath. "Lucy—no, I can't make it out a bit"—instinctively he clasped her to him vehemently, for he was near guessing. "Do stop crying now, Lucy!"

She sobbed feebly with her face against his shoulder, trembled slowly and painfully and raised her unhappy eyes to his smiling glance—then she wept again:

"I didn't think you meant anything of that sort."

"Yes, but now you know I do mean it, can't you be just a little bit glad—look here, Lucy, now you must give in!"

“Oh yes. I am glad. Though I know it’s wrong—”

“Wrong? Why on earth should there be anything wrong in you and I being fond of each, other? You aren’t engaged to anyone else, are you?”

She shook her head vigorously.

“Well then, there can’t be anything wrong in your being engaged to me? Aren’t you allowed to be engaged even in that sect you belong to?”

“Oh yes—engaged—” she said in a hushed voice. Then she sobbed again.

“Well—and married, they allow that too, I hope?”

Lucy’s face quivered. She smiled a wretched little smile:

“Married—what are you saying—”

‘Yes, married—that’s a thing most people do sooner or later. So it can’t be so extraordinary if you and I do the same.”

“Oh no, Paul,” she whispered; “that can’t be.”

“Why not? If we love one another—that’s the chief thing, isn’t it?”

“There’s too much difference between us,” she said softly, looking down.

“There is this difference”—he crushed her to him, laughing over her drooping head: “that you’re my girl, but I’m only your boy. Hang it, do look a bit more cheerful, child!”

She nestled close to him and sighed.

“Lucy,” he said in a low and serious tone. “You know, don’t you—if anyone has given you a scare—running after you—in a nasty way—so as to make you afraid of men—you know you’re safe from all that now you’re with me.”

She looked up at him—he thought there were bottomless depths in her tearful eyes:

“That’s what I’ve thought all the time—that you were that sort—that you didn’t wish anyone ill. So you see, that’s just what made me think all the time, no, he can’t mean anything like that. Because there’s such a big difference between us, you know.” Seeing him smile, she said seriously: “Do you know, when I first came to town I was a servant girl—I had a place as nurse with a family in Cort Adelers gate—”

“Poor girl, was it horrid?” asked Paul lightly. Then he laughed: “That’s just like Cinderella. Now I know why I was so taken with you the very first time I saw you—you look exactly as I’ve always imagined Cinderella, and the youngest and prettiest of the three sisters in all the fairy tales—”

Lucy smiled shyly.

"Come, let's go down now"—he had his arm round her waist. "Or else Karen will think we've been breaking it off instead of getting engaged"—he plucked some dock leaves and held them to her swollen eyelids.

THEY were sitting down by the shore.

"Bless my soul, what a fit of chattering you've taken," he said at last, when they had been gazing in silence over the lake.

"Well, what do you want me to say?" she smiled awkwardly.

"Paul, for instance—that's not such a difficult name?" He seized her hand and pressed it. "Suppose I'd been called Maximilian or something like that—you'd never have managed that, my girl!"

WHEN he had said goodbye to her outside her door and given her a final good night kiss in the stuffy little hall, he continued to stroll about the streets in the summer night. He found himself in the upper end of Ullevoldsvei, where the houses were scattered over open fields.

Paul had glimpses of couples lying on the ground, he met lovers wandering about in the twilight with their arms round each other's waists. He blushed furiously as he walked alone.

So he would have to protect her. Just because she was so—well, so defenseless—he would have to do it. No behaviour of the kind that would have been excusable if he had been engaged to one of their own set.

He remembered her fright—and then her helpless surrender, every time he took her in his arms. Poor little Lucy—scared and burning with passion. Good Lord, it wouldn't be easy—young as they were—

But just because she was Lucy he must be on his guard for them both. With her the other thing would be so—well, downright unchivalrous.

Chapter Eight

"*We will not go back on the seventh of June.*" His mother handed him the little pamphlet as they took their seats in the train. It was printed in her office; Paul read it through and gave it back to her as the train stopped at Nordstrand. Julie Selmer leaned out of the window, talking to some people she knew—about the report of the Commission.

"We *can't* agree to it, that's as clear as day. There's only one thing to be done, refuse and take the consequences."

The train began to move. Julie put the pamphlet away in her handbag: "Well, what do you say?"

Paul replied quietly, quoting:

"The Great Powers demand a speedy and peaceful settlement between the kingdoms. The Norwegians desire a speedy and peaceful settlement. Why shouldn't the Powers give Sweden to understand that Sweden ought to lose no time in desiring the same? Then why the devil do we want to talk about refusing and taking the consequences? If we actually do not believe we are risking such a fearful lot, why must we pretend to believe we're venturing all?"

His mother looked at the young man attentively:

"I can't quite make you out, Paul. You're so—skeptical? And yet you won't go on that tour you'd arranged with Aaser, and talk about staying in town all the summer?"

"No, I don't feel inclined to go and stay up in Dovre and stand a chance of not hearing of it for days—if anything happens."

His mother looked up rather doubtfully.

"I was at Major Tangen's last evening," said Paul. "They sent messages to you, by the way. I wanted to find out if anything has been arranged about the training of next year's recruits and volunteers and so on, you understand—"

"I'm sure there won't be any difficulty about joining up—"

"The Major couldn't say anything definite, of course. But I met Harald there, the son who's a Catholic priest. We walked back to town together—"

"And I suppose he tried to convert you?"

"Ugh, no, mother, we didn't say a word about religion. Not directly anyhow," he corrected himself, as though recollecting something. "But you know, Harald Tangen has been a long time abroad. And he takes a much less optimistic view of the situation than you and your friends. Well, not of our military situation at the moment—both his brothers are officers, you know. The Tangens have always been Liberals, you remember. But he said, if we yield now, it will be difficult to get the Storting to keep up an effective force. And whatever form the settlement may take, peaceful or otherwise—and a war leaves bitterness behind—we shall hardly have much time to get over it before the storm bursts between England and Germany. And the Swedes and ourselves are bound by nature to gravitate in opposite directions in European affairs—"

"Oh, not at all," said his mother. "A European war has become an impossibility. So mutually involved as is the economic life of the different countries nowadays. Besides, the Socialists would be sure to put a stopper on any adventurous policy of that sort—a soldiers' strike would be declared immediately over the whole of Europe. That is precisely Socialism's real contribution to history so far—even now it is a fairly secure guarantee of the world's peace."

"Yes, that's what I heard in my cradle—perhaps that's why I have never been so cocksure it would turn out like that. And Harald Tangen took another view. He said something to the effect that the big capitalist interests which govern Europe, including the European press, were materialism reduced to a system, and the ideology of the Socialists was materialistic. But materialism is never anything but—what did he call it again?—an accident in a view of life which in its essence is the cult of humanity. But men's passions are always stronger than their reason. He told me many of his friends abroad are perfectly convinced that this generation is called upon to atone with its blood for the sins of the world, and that they are preparing to make good in their own flesh what was lacking in the passion of Christ, as he expressed himself."

"But that's sheer black medievalism. But of course he lives entirely in the middle ages, Harald Tangen."

"I don't know about that," said Paul reflectively. "At any rate he thought the nations were being imposed upon everywhere. Even here in Norway we don't know how little voice we ourselves have and what use we are to make of this new right of self-determination. That's what makes all these fine phrases seem to me so—sinister."

Julie shrugged her shoulders:

"My dear Paul, I'm afraid a policy the most important part of which is not carried on behind the scenes is inconceivable. One *cannot* tell the people *everything*!"

"Is it on those terms you are a republican?" asked her son caustically.

He had not been allowed to tell his mother of their engagement. Lucy was quite beside herself every time he spoke of doing so. Paul guessed that she imagined his family would do all in their power to separate them. He laughed at her in vain, telling her they were not lords or counts in a penny novelette.

"My sister went and got engaged to Halstein Garnaas—and there wasn't a soul in the family who had a word to object to it."

"Yes, but he's a man of college education," Lucy protested.

Paul was rather taken aback. It had never occurred to him to classify people according to their education—at any rate not according to that which they had received outside the nursery.

Lucy spent her evenings at home doing drawn thread work. She had a friend, an elderly lady who lived up in the Saw Mills district, and this Fröken Johnsen had a sister in America who was masseuse to "millionaire ladies," as Lucy said—and she sold their work over there; they sent it in parcels of Norwegian papers and were well paid for it; last winter Lucy had received ten dollars for a tea cloth. But it sometimes happened that the American Post Office discovered what was in the parcels, and so their work was lost, said Lucy sorrowfully.

She knew hardly anyone in town but this old maid—lived almost the life of a nun. Paul felt a smart in his eyes and a catch in his throat when he thought of the gentle, lonely girl, passing her days in the shadow.

He took her parcels for her to the embroidery shop in Markvei, to save her the long journey after she had been standing in the shop all day. And when he sat with her in her little room, he took her hand and drew the first finger, roughened with needlework, backwards and forwards over his lips.

If it came to a war, he wondered whether Harald Tangen might perhaps marry them secretly—

"Then there can't be war now, can there?" Lucy asked timidly; they had gone down to the newspaper offices to see the result of the plebiscite posted.

"Have you been thinking about it too?" He had never spoken to her about it. "What would you think if it came to war, Lucy?"

"I? I don't see how I could think anything, as I can't do anything. Thank God you won't have to go anyhow. Think how horrid it must be for Fröken Gotaas with her sweetheart in barracks."

Paul laughed and squeezed her arm against his side in the crowd. Thank God she was simple enough to be honest!

I wonder if it's always like this when history is being made before one's eyes, thought Paul. If an action is no sooner taken than it gets dusted over with talk? Or was there an initial defect in this action—the consequences of which would prove more and more fateful as time went on?

It seemed as though he had no real confidence in anything. The worst of it was he had no real confidence in those who said what he himself thought—we cannot raze our own fortifications, we cannot take a Fourth of November after the Seventh of June, as we had to take a Fourth of November after the Seventeenth of May.† But they had a bad habit of introducing little subsidiary clauses explaining that the danger they proposed to meet with their high-sounding declarations was not so dangerous after all. Or was it that they themselves did not believe that the crowds which flocked round them to listen could be persuaded to act?

So he was inclined rather to feel a kind of cold, bitter sympathy with

† Translator's Note: The reader may be reminded that on May 17, 1814, Norway was declared independent (of Denmark) and her new constitution came into being; but on November 4 of the same year, to the great disappointment of the Norwegians, the country was placed by the Powers under the sovereignty of the King of Sweden. It was this personal union with Sweden that was dissolved by the action of the Norwegian parliament (Storting) on June 7, 1905—at the time of our story.

the Government, who were willing to abandon the glories of the Seventh of June in order to retain as much of the reality as was necessary to put the country on its feet as an independent concern. He hated it—but at all events it was a definite position, and it looked as if the Government were working designedly to see it carried out. If only one could be spared the commentaries of the press, to the effect that this unavoidable retreat was in reality by no means so humiliating.

The same thing over again. It is not certain that the danger is so dangerous. The bitter medicine is by no means so bitter. Are we children?

And then the continual encouraging quotations from the foreign press—saying that foreigners admire us so much for this, that and the other.

The Government has the nation's confidence. Behind the Government of the Seventh of June stands the majority of the Norwegian people. Was that the cause of it? thought Paul—when the people rule, that is how it goes. If a nation is to be able to stand being told the whole truth, it must have someone at its head. And if a nation has rulers from whom it will stand hearing the truth, then it has no need to listen to them. It will follow its leaders blindly, if called upon—

So when it came to the plebiscite to decide the form of government, he thought, please God it won't be a republic anyhow. There must be at any rate one position in the country which never comes into the market.

It is true he could not work up much enthusiasm as he and Lucy stood and watched the procession on the King's arrival. Nor was the weather any help, to those who had not brought their enthusiasm with them, though the effect of the electric lights shining through the fog at midday and the thin coat of snow that covered the town had a strange beauty of its own. And as he chanced to be standing in a group from which no cheers were heard, he shouted loyally, as though at a word of command.

But there was a fairy-like beauty in the evening with all the thousands of lights shedding a rosy gleam on the misty air. He wandered up and down for several hours among the throng, with Lucy hanging on his arm so as not to be separated in the crush, and she was in raptures. And his conscience smote him a little on her account; they were to go to his father's later on, and no doubt she was dreading it horribly.

When Lillian told him they were going to give a party to celebrate the King's state entry, and if there was any girl he would like to bring they would be glad to see her, as the young people were to have a dance later in the evening—he answered, thanks, yes, he knew a Fröken Arnesen and he would like to ask her. Lucy began to protest, as usual, when he told her. He was nervous and out of humour—and suddenly he flared up: "I'm sick of this nonsense. This time I insist on your coming, do you understand?" She began to whine, naturally—she danced so badly, she said—"Well, then don't dance. What the devil does it matter? Yes, of course, if you're going to howl like this, you know I'll give in to you. Then I'll have to let father know. For I won't go alone. I suppose we can always squeeze in somewhere and sit and mope and growl at the bad service. But now I'm so fed up with this foolery of yours. There's nobody at home who'll bite you."

The solemn facade of the University, lighted up by two braziers and nothing else, looked splendid. Certainly the illumination was fine in the foggy winter evening.

They both had to go home and change before going to the Selmers'. Paul had to wait a long time outside her street door. The reflection as of a great fire lay over the town. And even up here in Dahlbergsti there were touching attempts at illumination with candles in the windows.

It was past ten o'clock before they reached his father's. The decorated staircase was crowded with guests and the doors were thrown open above and below—Lillian had got the family on the ground floor to join her, and the whole villa was made into one festal house.

Paul sat waiting, on a sofa which had been placed in the hall, with aspidistras grouped about it and a shocking version of the Venus of Milo on a pillar behind; in the ordinary way she lived in the bathroom. Hans spoke to him as he passed—the boy looked well in his cadet's uniform; he took the stairs two at a time, stopped near the top to talk to a girl who was leaning over the banisters—Molla Nicolaysen, but my word, how pretty she had grown, a real beauty; he hadn't seen her since she was a child.

Some girls came running downstairs—stopped as he rose and bowed: "Hullo, are you here—? What, are you here too—?"

Then he saw Lucy, at last she came out of the ladies' room that had been fitted up on the ground floor; he went to meet her. And felt a pang, of pity or bad conscience—he saw at a glance how she showed up against the other girls who were here.

She looked mortally embarrassed as she went upstairs with him.

Paul could not say what it was exactly, but her whole dress seemed to be wrong. She had on a pale green frock of some kind of thin silk, with a pattern of orange flowers in great bunches; her long pearl-grey gloves had folds of long standing at the elbows and wrists and smelt of benzine, and the artificial flowers she wore on her shoulder and in her hair reminded one of a second-rate theatre. The thought flashed through him that he had done wrong in forcing her to come. Then he shook it off—dash it, she was good enough as she was, she was lovely, lovely, lovely, no matter how dressed-up she might look.

But poor Lucy, he thought and could not help smiling, as Lillian surged to meet them in the drawing room—if only she doesn't scare the life out of my girl. And Lillian was the very climax—some kind of bluish silk lace all over the lady, and a diamond star in her bosom.

"Good evening, Paul—good evening, Fröken, was it Arnesen? Welcome, Fröken Arnesen, it was very sweet of you to come. How are you, Paul, quite got rid of your cold?—Fru Aarstad? You'll find her in the study or in the ballroom, I think—"

Paul knew pretty well everyone, and no one more than slightly. No—there was Nikko—

"You two have met before, haven't you?" Lucy looked guilty, Nikko a trifle annoyed; they exchanged a few words, then Nikko retired.

There were refreshments downstairs, and champagne. Herr Selmer proposed the toast of the new royal house, and did it uncommonly well, thought Paul.

The Selmers' dining room was cleared for dancing, and Lillian herself was at the piano. For dancing she could play simply spendidly.

But Lucy had spoken only but the truth when she said she danced badly.

Paul stuck close to her the whole evening, whether they sat watching the others dance, or he took her out for a turn. And when she was asked to dance by someone else, he kept an eye on her, ready to receive her as soon as she was free again. Herr Selmer came up to them: "May I have the pleasure, Fröken?" and Lucy followed him like a lamb led to the slaughter. Hans came up, stiff and smart; Lucy had the same despairing look as she danced off with him. Uncle Alarik, who was in town for the King's accession, without his widow, danced away with Lucy and handed her over to Hans; then turned to Paul:

"Charming young lady, Paul—perfectly charming! Who is she—one of your fellow students?"

"No. No, she's not a student. I met her last year at a sanatorium."

"Perfectly charming girl. I wonder if it'll suit your mother for me to come out and see her one evening before I go home—I thought of leaving the day after tomorrow—"

Tua settled herself to entertain Lucy, and Paul hurried off to get through one or two dances with old acquaintances meanwhile. And he could not deny it was refreshing to have someone else to dance with—

Tua was usually the acme of untidiness in Paul's eyes. But tonight she looked almost chic—white had always suited her best. "Don't you think we've made a good show?" she said radiantly. "But I can tell you, Lillian and I worked hard! Lillian is clever!"

Hans Selmer joined them: "Aren't you going to look at the fireworks? We're going to let off fireworks, Fröken Arnesen—I think you'll see them best from the veranda downstairs."

The guests poured down; they stood in the closed veranda and in the little front garden watching Hans and a couple of his friends letting off a dozen rockets into the night sky. They burst with a dull report and showered down their rain of colored stars through the thick, damp air.

Paul took Lucy's hand in the rosy twilight, as the others left the veranda: "Would you like to sit here—then I'll go and get you something to drink?"

There was a little semicircular sofa half-hidden in the portieres that divided the veranda from a kind of boudoir-like room inside. Paul brought some iced, orange-colored stuff in a long glass with straws:

"Are you beginning to feel tired?" He put his arm round her waist on the sofa. "Poor you, it must have been fatiguing to tramp about those crowded streets, wasn't it? Well—do you find my family so awe-inspiring? They're quite pleasant people, aren't they?"

"Your father looks awfully kind." She gave a little sigh. "Yes, and your brother and your sister—and your stepmother too. She is pretty and no mistake—"

The music began again on the floor above and the windows of the veranda shivered slightly, as the shaking of the dance spread through the house.

"Now we'll sit here and rest a little—" he laid his face against her bare shoulder and kissed it, as he clasped her waist more closely—"and then we'll go up and have just one more dance before we go home?"

"It's so silly that I can't dance," said Lucy softly.

"Yes, but you must learn. Poor girl, you weren't much used to dancing at home?"

"Oh, no! It was not to be thought of. Don't you understand, they looked upon it as a terrible sin!"

Paul kissed her shoulder again.

"Oh Lucy—I wish—I do wish I could get you to think it's fun being alive—"

Somebody came into the room behind. He heard the clink of glasses and then Lillian's distinct voice:

"Yes, *isn't* he a nice boy"—and in reply to a question—"yes, he's Julie's eldest. Why, can't you see how like Julie he is—?"

Paul had instinctively withdrawn his arm and sat up straight. Lillian's voice continued:

"Yes, you can't think how glad it makes me. Now he comes here quite a lot. And he's an awfully nice young man—he is really. Brings me flowers—and is so pleasant and attentive to his father. One must admit, Julie has known how to bring up those children wonderfully. And that Paul should have learnt to understand and appreciate his father—oh, I can't say how happy it makes me! You know, Erik has always idolized his children, poor man, and he simply loves Paul. When I think of all the nights Erik and I have lain awake talking about his children—I always tried to console him as well as I could—"

Paul did not know that he was crushing Lucy's fingers. He felt a pricking heat over his eyebrows—his heart was hammering terribly.

Julie, he said, Julie—

Oh, what a much cleanlier way they had in old days. Then a man might have a wife and a mistress, but what he might not do with propriety was to discuss one of his women with the other. Nor the family he had by the one, in sleepless nights—in the arms of the other consoler. It made him feel sick. So there was no hole to be found where those who belonged to each other by blood and heritage and all such obscure and powerful bonds could be free from interlopers. Oh, this was far more indecent than having two or three strictly detached families living parallel lives. And father, his father was not more of a man—foh!

"But who's that extraordinary creature he's brought with him tonight?" asked a man's voice in the boudoir.

"M-well. I haven't the least idea where he can have fished her up," said Lillian. "I suppose he's turned socialist—he's at the age for that—"

"Remarkable phenomenon—she looks like a painted deal wardrobe that has gone astray. Especially when she's dancing—"

There was a laugh, and a lady's voice said:

"Dear me, now I know where I've seen her—I was sure I knew her face. She serves in a flower shop in Bogstadvei—Fröken Jensen's."

"Little Jensen's not so bad, ha ha," quoted the man's voice—from a piece by Gustav Wied, Paul remembered.

"No—she's quite pretty in a way, you must allow."

"Yes—in national costume with a cow's tail she'd make an ideal pixie—or a Sunday saeter-girl without the cow's tail—"

"Presumably there's nothing at all against her," Lillian, clinched the matter; "it wouldn't be like Paul. He's quite exceptionally good in that way—"

Paul had put his arm round Lucy and held her head close against his chest: "You can't be allowed to cry over that," he whispered sternly. "It isn't worth it—"

TUA's voice cried "Lillian, Lillian—" and there was a sound of movement. After a moment, when Paul peeped in behind the portieres, he saw the boudoir was empty: "come along."

Herr Selmer and Doctor Aarstad were in the dining room opening bottles; Tua was with them. Paul led Lucy up to them:

"Fröken Arnesen is so tired, father. We won't go upstairs; I can hear they're in the middle of the quadrille, so if you'll be kind enough to say good night to Lillian and thank her. Very glad to have seen you, Doctor, please remember me to your wife. 'Night, Tua, and many thanks—remember me to Halstein, won't you—"

"Good night—are you coming out to mother's tomorrow evening? I've promised to go out with uncle—well, if you haven't time—. Good night, Fröken Arnesen, hope to see you again—"

HE took her arm as soon as they were out of the garden gate. And as they went up the little hill by the side of Blaasen, he slackened his pace.

"I'm sorry, Lucy. That you should be made so uncomfortable, the first time you met my family—"

"Oh, Paul," she shook her head. "It was only what I expected—I have no business in your family—"

"Don't say a thing like that—" he stopped and kissed her, "just because it didn't come off the first time—"

They were standing in the shadow of the odd little rocky knoll, which humped itself, white with a thin coat of snow and tangled with thorn bushes, against the fog which was still flushed with lights, though more faintly than before.

Paul kissed her cold face.

"Don't think too much about it. To tell the truth, everybody's like that—pulling each other to pieces behind each other's backs. You know the saying: eavesdroppers never hear any good of themselves. Though it was against our will we were eavesdropping—a piece of bad luck—"

She made no reply. And Paul said, as gaily as he could:

"But I think we ought to make it public at Christmas!"

Suddenly she spoke out, heatedly:

"Yes, to be sure folks are horrid at gossiping behind one another's backs—oh, they were cruel that way at home; it isn't that—. But they weren't like that all the same, witty and spiteful—I think *fine* people are far worse, I do—"

"Now, now, Lucy. Besides, she's only my stepmother—she's kind in many ways. But my mother is quite different. Wait till you've met her. Out at my mother's it isn't a bit like it is at Erik and Lillian's—" It struck him even as he said it, and his heart shrank up at the words: "Erik and Lillian"—but he knew it would be no use explaining that to her. So he only said:

"You feel that you're lonely, Lucy, and of course I know you are. But in a way I haven't anybody but you either. So we shall have to stick together—

"I love you," he whispered into the thick of the ruffled hair by her ear.

THEY stood outside her door in Dahlbergsti:

"Promise me you'll go to sleep at once," he begged; "not lie awake fretting over this. It isn't worth it, Lucy—"

She looked into his face with those strange, unfathomable, serious eyes of hers.

"Oh—I almost feel inclined to go in with you—so as to be sure you won't spend the night crying or anything of that sort—"

"Well, but—" she looked down and whispered, "you can if you like—"

He laughed rather irresolutely.

"Then the Lord above knows when I should leave again, my dear—I'm afraid it might be too late altogether—"

She looked up in his face and said in a strangely clear voice, but as if talking in her sleep:

"You can quite well come in with me—Paul."

He crushed her to him, kissed her with his teeth against hers.

"No," he said sternly. "I won't. I won't do that—Lucy."

Then he released her and ran a few paces—stopped under the gas lamp, and stood there watching her as she let herself in.

Chapter Nine

It was Lucy herself who proposed the skiing expedition, one of the last Sundays in December. She had not had much more practice with skis than she had in dancing and swimming—skiing trips had also been banned at home. But for a change she was fond of the sport; Paul discovered to his delight that she was at any rate fearless and keen at it.

It was dark, with a mist on the heights, and not much snow. Paul had a torch; he loved torches. But he was a little afraid of how she would manage coming down the slopes. Constantly he had to go back and pick her up, but she only laughed and shook the snow out of her clothes.

"Ugh—you'll soon be angry with me—" she stood with her hand on his back, while he fastened her ski. He had had to throw away the torch and light the lantern instead.

The mist rolled like smoke before the little gleam, as they crossed the lake. When they came near enough to see the hut, its lighted windows seemed like great red eyes in the fog.

"It's a long time since you were here, Selmer," said Berte, the woman; "oh yes, I know the young lady, you may be sure—it was she who was with you last time—"

Lucy had unpacked the food and was getting their supper ready.

"You'll have it in the bedroom, won't you?" asked Berte, as she got out plates and cups. "You'll have to sleep in the little room tonight; I've got some teachers from town in the big one—you know Fröken Pedersen, don't you, Selmer? And there's her sister with her, she's a teacher too, and her husband, I expect he's the same—"

"What about the attic—couldn't I sleep there?" asked Paul.

"No, it's in such a horrid mess up there. But aren't you two engaged?"

laughed Berte; "then what's it matter, if you have to share the little room tonight?"

Paul went into the kitchen, while Lucy was settling herself for the night. He sat in front of the stove talking to Berte, till the woman began to yawn and got up. "Well, now I think it's about time—"

In the bedroom a little kitchen lamp was burning on the table by Lucy's bed—she had chosen the one in the corner between the two windows. Paul could not help casting a glance at her: she had on some pale pink thing with lace on it and short sleeves; she had taken down her hair and plaited it, and this made her face strangely younger and more refined—he had never seen her except with her hair up, puffed out over a kind of pad.

"Good night," he said very softly, with his back half turned to her, as he put out the lamp.

He pulled off his outer clothes by the foot of the other bed, as noiselessly as he could. It was moonlight outside, he saw, when his eyes were accustomed to the darkness—a flood of faint milky light came in at the windows. Even the sounds of winding up his watch seemed to tear across his nerves like little cogwheels. Then he crept under Berte's heavy quilt, felt the coarse, homemade pillowcase against his cheek and tried to compose himself to keeping a knightly watch.

All at once Lucy's voice called, a strangely clear, flute-like note in the darkness:

"Paul—" And as he did not move, she called again: "Are you asleep, Paul?"

"No."

"Won't you come over to me—?"

He had one foot on the floor before he had time to think. And raising himself on his elbow, in the misty white moonlight that filled the room he could dimly see her sitting up in the other bed, with her arms stretched out. Then he got up and went over to her.

"You might guess"—her voice was full of tears and laughter at the same time—"You might guess—I should wish to give you everything you want in the world. You shan't have to want for what I can give you—" and her arms were around him the moment he bent over her.

He went for a short run on skis next morning, while Lucy was dressing. "Breakfast's in three-quarters of an hour—"

It was the same foggy weather today again; the wooded slopes had a slaty blue look from the thin rime on the firs. Paul went up the little cleft which divided the ridge behind the hut. A tiny brook ran through it; the little bushes on its course were bristly with rime. It was such a jolly little valley, a fissure clean through the syenite mass of the hill, and it had smooth walls covered with a wonderfully beautiful vegetation of lichens—Paul knew every inch of the valley.

He halted on reaching the top, where there was a view of the lakes on the other side. The mist lay on the ridges like a blanket, but down in the depths there were glimpses of a grey-white surface and grey-blue stretches of forest.

Ah yes, he felt his heart sinking under the weight of it. Her inconceivable sweetness, a love so wildly generous as he had tasted this night—And behind it.—As though a wall had fallen down, a wall on which he had painted his own naïve fancies—he was now confronted with the unknown that lay behind it—her past. Damned ungrateful, blackguardly of him to think of it on such a morning as this—but he could not avoid seeing it. She was not without experience—that hateful, vulgar word.

It did not make her any different; he had felt from the first time he saw her that she was the one he must love. It had been Nature's design with them the whole time to bring about what now had happened. Was it anything to dwell upon after all, that the fancy pictures he had painted as a background to her blonde beauty and warmth—that they were childish? As she was, so she had been all the time he had worshipped her. And this night could scarcely make him less certain that she was good and gentle as a summer meadow, incapable of being untruthful, she was so utterly powerless to make herself other than she was. They belonged to each other as Adam and Eve in Paradise—was it her fault that the world was no Paradise, and that she had not escaped unharmed through its jungle—the great fair girl who was so little able to defend herself and had no one to defend her?

It makes no difference, no difference—I *must* think it makes no difference, now that at last we have come together, we who *had* to come together—

The three-quarters had grown into an hour when he came to look at his watch. Then he turned and went down. From the top of the field he saw her standing at the door of the hut, he swished straight down to her, dashed across the bank of swept snow and caught her round the waist, sending his cap flying as he pulled up.

"Mine!" He pressed her to him. "Mine—mine—"

She looked up into his face—and he smiled down at her.

"You were away much longer than you said. I began to get afraid"—she looked down—"that perhaps you were angry with me for something—"

"Hush," he begged her instinctively.

"Perhaps you might have thought I was one of those who were ready for that sort of thing—"

"O God, Lucy. Do you believe I'm fond of you?" he asked in a low voice.

"Ye-es.—Only I was afraid you might not be so fond of me after that as before—"

Paul bent down and took off his skis.

"You're the biggest simpleton I've ever come across," he said teasingly. "I hope there's some coffee ready—?"

THEY came home by Slagteren. On the hill behind a crowd of little boys were practising ski jumping—evidently a class with their schoolmistress. Paul knew her as soon as she started off—why, it was Tua. The jacket of her skiing costume was fairly short, and below it hung something in bright pink—probably the edge of a Russian blouse. Paul had always regarded Tua with a certain brotherly vexation—she was so preposterously untidy and always gushing about something or other—he generally showed it too, without much pity. But now he was seized with a sudden tenderness; after all he was so fond of his sister, and that pink stripe across her back affected him by its touching innocence. So he hailed her.

She came uphill, red as fire, her face pouring with perspiration, her hair all over the place. He vaguely welcomed the sight of her as a kind of amends to Lucy for their last meeting—now it was Lucy who had the advantage, in a new green ski dress with Lapp embroidery and a square red Lappish cap on her head.

"You up here too—? How do you do, Fröken Arnesen! Oh, are you making for Frogner saeter?—Yes, aren't the boys doing well—Albin's a regular Holmenkoll champion already, and look at Oscar there!—Oh, isn't it marvellous that it's starting to snow now—we could do with a little more—"

IT was almost dark when Paul and Lucy reached Skjennungen. The snow which had been falling thicker and thicker now began to float down in big, light flakes. It was wonderful, thought Paul; he would have liked to go on and on forever through this giddy white mass sinking slowly over the forest.

All the same they had had more than enough of it when they came to Frogner saeter and shook the fresh snow from their clothes.

"Won't you come in?" asked Lucy, as they stood outside her door.

"No. I'm not going to compromise you worse than I have done"—he tried to speak lightly. "It's to be hoped they didn't hear anything last night, those teachers in the other room. But I shouldn't like your landlady to have anything against you on my account."

"Oh, as far as that goes," replied Lucy, "you may be sure she's made up her mind a long time ago that it's like that between us. She would never imagine a gentleman would spend so much time and money on a girl for anything else—"

Paul stopped her mouth with a passionate kiss: "Good night!" Then he ran off.

HE was standing in his room next evening—tying his necktie in front of the glass, when there was a knock at his door which led to the stairs. It was Lucy.

"Are you going out?" she asked, disappointed at seeing he had on his newest blue suit.

"Only to father's. It's his birthday today. Come with me, won't you? Then we'll tell him straight away of our engagement—"

"Are you crazy? I'm not dressed for it either. Besides—" she said, dropping her voice, "now, Paul—what do you suppose they'd think of your getting engaged to me, if they knew I'd already allowed you all sorts of things—?"

"They have nothing to do with that—it's our affair. Seriously, Lucy—I think this is just the moment when they ought to know you're engaged to me—my own people at any rate. So that you may get to know them—for all contingencies," he said, speaking firmly and rapidly.

She had turned red as fire; her hands trembled slightly, as she took the paper off a little parcel she had with her:

"Paul, there is something I must tell you—there, won't you have these"—she held up a couple of stalks of golden brown chrysanthemum. "I've so often thought I'd like to give you a few flowers—I noticed how fond you were of them. And now and then Fröken Jensen lets me take some—when they're not fresh enough to put in the window."

Paul put the flowers in a vase and placed it on the little shelf above the writing table, beside the crucifix.

Lucy was sitting in his armchair, her hands clasped on her little hag. "Paul," she said again.—"Perhaps you haven't time?" she asked, as he put on his jacket and opened the drawer for a handkerchief.

"Of course I have, what is it?" He sat on the edge of his writing table, moving the lamp away. "What is it, Lucy—? You look as if somebody had sold you a pup," he tried to be jocular.

"No, it isn't that—that I wish anything undone, if that's what you mean. But I think you're too good for me to deceive you. And so I want to tell you that I'm not so good as you think I am. I haven't been—straight"—she clutched at the tassels on the chair-arms, pulled them hard—"not always. But it's a good while ago now," she whispered rapidly, taking fright.

Paul felt a stiffening about his mouth, and his heart began to hammer abominably again.

"I must thank you for—for telling me that yourself, Lucy. I appreciate your wanting to tell me yourself"—oh, it sounded idiotic, but there was such a cursed pain at his heart. "For you understand, it doesn't come as a surprise—" bah, how stupid—

"Was it Nikko who told you?" she asked quickly.

"Nikko—does *he* know?" Hell—

"I don't know. But I expect Aina may have known about it. About the last—"

Paul said nothing.

"Because he was a gentleman, you might say. He was in the office at the shoe factory where I was packer—where Fröken Johnsen was manageress. And so then this bookkeeper began to take an interest in me; well, to start with he was just kind and nice, and it was he who got me the place in that glove shop in Karl Johan, you can guess I was delighted to get away from the factory, for there they didn't reckon you as a lady, but Carling treated me as a lady always—well, so then I thought the least I could do was to make friends with him in the way he wanted. Seeing that anyhow I wasn't innocent," she whispered.

Paul could not get a word out. He tried to find something—would have liked to say something kind. He raised his hand to stroke her face, but she was sitting so that he could not reach her without leaning far forward, and so he let it fall slackly on his knee.

"And yet really I've always been so afraid of that," Lucy wailed softly;

"I had such a horror of being a bad woman. And that was why I left that glove shop. Carling went to America a year and a half ago, you see, and then we stopped writing to each other; now he's engaged to another over there. And when the boss heard of it, he began trying to get hold of me. He wasn't nasty or brutal like, he was an elderly gentleman, you understand, a sort of uncle to Carling—but I was so terribly afraid all the same, I couldn't stand being there any longer. But then there was Fröken Johnsen, Jonsa as we call her, she's been so awfully kind to me always, she's a cousin of Fröken Jensen's, and so she got me the place with her—"

Paul remained mute—he hated and despised himself for his cruel curiosity or whatever it was. But *before*, Lucy, what had there been before—?

"Didn't you get any support from home then?" he asked, in a thick voice. "When you were in such a tight place—couldn't you have gone home for a while—?"

"Home! Oh no, that's the last place. That's just how it all began, I was thrown out, though I hadn't done anything wrong—

"There was a boy—I'd known him since I was a child; his parents belonged to the Friends too. Not that we'd kept company or anything like that, for that wouldn't do in our lot, but we got to know each other at meeting and walked there and back together and such like, you understand. You see, papa was an evangelist, I must tell you—well, we have a little farm too, but it's only two cows and some pigs and that, but as long as mamma was alive we had an old maid called Sister Sara, she looked after the farm, well, and I had to help too, for mamma was always in bed, as long as I can remember. But as long as mamma was alive it was all right at home, papa was kind, and I thought it was nice to go to meeting, for you know, that was the only pleasure I'd been brought up to. We weren't allowed to play either, they thought that was a sin—I expect that's why I'm no good at being bright or amusing. Well, I had a little playground all the same, with broken crockery and such like, up on a little hill behind the byre, and I thought it was fun when I could go up there, but I hadn't any other children to play with—but still I was always happy and contented in those days.

"But then mamma died, when I was thirteen, and Sister Sara had to leave, for papa married a widow the same summer; I won't say she was exactly bad to me either, but somehow it was so uncomfortable at home after she came. So when I was sixteen I went to Tönsberg to an old lady and took care of her for about a year, but then she died.

"But then the summer after that there was this boy, he was at home with his father and mother, and he was studying to be a minister. Not that the Friends thought anything of ministers, my word no, the State Church, that was pure heathenism and ungodliness—oh, what a lot of times I've had to pray that the minister might be converted and become a living Christian. Though he was a quite a kind man, as far as I know. But Otar's people had money, you see, and as they could afford to make a minister of him, they didn't see why they shouldn't. But the Friends didn't like it, I can tell you—they were looked upon as backsliders, they and Otar, after that. But you can guess, I thought he was awfully grand and smart, when he'd been in Christiania and a student and all.

"Now I must tell you, it's the custom where I come from that the young people sleep in the wash house in summertime. And our wash house has a window out to the garden, and then there's some big lilac bushes just outside—and so Otar came in to see me sometimes—pretty late—. Well, then one night when he was with me, my stepmother came and found us. And she simply wouldn't believe we hadn't done anything wrong.

"Never mind that—the end of it was that they gave me my journey money to Christiania and told me to get out—"

Paul slid down from the table, took her hand and raised it to his bosom. Lucy dropped her eyes as she went on:

"So that afternoon I took the train from Tönsberg. Otar went by it too. We were alone in the carriage. And then—they hadn't chosen to believe I was straight—and so I let him seduce me—"

She drew back her hand, blew her nose.

"Well, you know, that there with me and Otar—that didn't come to much. He paid for me a few days at a hotel down by the station, but you can guess it was too risky for him, seeing he was studying for the ministry. But then I knew two girls from Tönsberg who were in service with a lady in Observatorie gate and I was allowed to stay there till I could find something to do, but she couldn't afford to give me any wages. They were real kind, Janna and Olga, but all the same I was afraid to stay there; they were so shockingly flighty, and I had to share a bed with Janna. There were so many lodgers in the house and they carried on so with Janna and Olga—you understand. But they were kind. So I took that place in Cort Adelers gate, it was the first one I could find.

"No, that there with Otar, there wasn't any more of that. For it wouldn't do for me to come and see him in his room, and he couldn't be seen keeping company with an ordinary servant girl, you can guess. At first there'd been a sort of idea that we should get engaged. Well, now he's a curate in the North and engaged to a minister's daughter, I saw in the paper.

"But I was so afraid of getting into more of a mess—of being quite ruined and going to the dogs altogether, and this place was close to where Janna and Olga were in service, and they were always trying to get me to join in their goings-on—so I changed to a place out in Thorvald Meyers gate, and it was there I got to know Jonsa, and she looked after me and helped me.—But there, I haven't had anything to do with anybody else, only Otar and Carling—"

"And your people at home," asked Paul after a pause. "Haven't you heard anything from them since—?"

"Papa wrote to me—when he had found out that I had taken a place and meant to be straight—he wrote that if I would repent of my sin and confess and let myself be saved, I might come home again. I got wild, I did, and wrote back that they'd better send me my clothes first—for you've no idea how awful they'd been, driving me out in just what I stood up in—and my chest of drawers, for I'd been left a lovely antique chest of drawers by the old lady I was nursing at Tönsberg, mahogany, just fancy—. Because I hadn't done anything wrong when they threw me out. But I never got an answer to that letter."

"Oh, poor, poor, little Lucy—" He sat on the arm of the chair and held her head against his chest.

"Well, now you know all about me," she said with a deep groan. "So now you must do just what you think best."

"Think best." He laid his cheek against her hair. "If I could only—only get you to forget it all. So that you remembered nothing but me, and that you and I love one another."

"But how was it you knew," she whispered. "That I hadn't been quite good before?"

"Do you remember that day last summer, up at Sognsvand?" he asked in the same hushed tone. "When I took hold of you and you were so mortally afraid? That made me guess that somebody must have wronged you." At the moment all he remembered was that it was then he had guessed it.

Lucy nodded.

" 'I didn't think you were like that,' " he reminded her, quietly. "Do you remember?"

She nodded again: "Yes indeed!—What despair I was in. You see, I thought it was so terribly nice to go about with you, for I'd never met anyone who treated me like that. So I was utterly in despair when I found you were the same—passionate—"

"Well, but listen, Lucy—" Paul gave a little smile. "Did you really never wish that time that I would do anything like that—try to kiss you, for instance—?"

Lucy dropped her eyes, blushing:

"Ye-es—in a way I did. But all the same I didn't want you to. For I thought, then everything would be so terrible. And then it would soon be over—"

She quivered in his arm:

"Looking back on it now I think it's so shocking—I had no idea I could ever be like I am—so terribly sensual. So that I only wished I could die—when you held me in your arms—"

"Oh, you—little—" Paul's voice trembled with emotion. "That's because you love me, Lucy—"

She freed herself from his arms and stood up.

"It must be that. Though to be sure I thought the same with—before. But it wasn't anything like that—it was not the same somehow, I feel that now. Oh, I can't bear it, Paul—oh no, I can't bear it! I'm so afraid of myself—it's just as if I could wish I might die of it." She wept on his shoulder.

THAT evening he found there was something grateful in the soft and subdued atmosphere of his father's and Lillian's home—the thick carpets and drawn curtains and the silk shades on the electric lamps—and Lillian's playing, as he lay sunk in a deep armchair and smoked and smoked—

"Aren't you well, Paul?" Lillian brought him aspirin and a glass of water.

It was idiotic to dwell on it so much. Jealous—there would be just as much sense in that fellow in the engraving over there, Perseus, being jealous of the dragon. She did look like Lucy, by the way, the girl in the picture, standing up against the cliff with nothing on but her fetters. The youngest of the King's sons in the fairy tale might just as well take it into his head to be jealous of the Giant who had no heart in his body. Lord, if only a poor ordinary mortal could be as sensible and practical as a fairy tale prince—

But, but, but—

One of those beastly carriages on the Western Railway—"As they wouldn't choose to believe I was straight"—had anyone ever heard of such a reason—!

It was as though life had given him a blow in the face. Life, life, what do we mean by that—? He couldn't hit back.

He passed the house in Dahlbergsti where she lived. The front door was open. Paul went through into the yard. Her room was dark—he threw a couple of handfuls of snow at the window. Presently he made out her form within—she opened the window a little way.

"I only wanted to say good night to you." He jumped up on the dust-bin in the corner and made his way to her along the basement cornice.

"I wondered if you were awake. Lucy—you mustn't let anything worry you—you're not to lie awake thinking of gloomy things, darling!" He kissed her and jumped down; then went off home at full speed. At any rate he had calmed his own heart a trifle.

Chapter Ten

What Lucy had said of her landlady turned out true enough. She was indeed tactful—in an incredibly nauseous way. Poor thing, she was no doubt a decent person, worked hard in her cold milk shop and had to help her family—she probably thought she could not undertake to be a guardian of virtue. But her connivance was not pleasant. It was as though he himself were dragging Lucy down by exposing her—and himself to it.

And then he felt intensely uncomfortable with regard to the Gotaases. Of course he did not care a pin about what is called middle-class morality and propriety. He didn't give a damn for what they thought, all the he's and she's who lived in couples twenty-five years at a stretch and fought their way in the world, one flesh and one soul and one thought—for themselves and those belonging to them, even though they might cheat customers and creditors alike very handsomely and push aside other people's disgusting brats to get their own sweet and clever children on in the world. Who believed that a silver wedding and a notice about it in the papers was part of God's scheme for mankind, when he created them man and woman. And if neither of them had slept with anyone else, since the wedding at all events, they counted it a positive virtue that there should be a vice they had not indulged in. And talked about the immorality of youth so that one would think they had a gingerbread nut for a heart and a lump of dirt for a brain.

But of course he knew that the Gotaases took a different view of it. He had read enough of Vincent's books to know that to Catholics chastity meant something not merely negative—wait until you have the means to set up house according to your position in society—it was something positive. It had a value of its own, in such a way that it was worth renouncing even what is generally accounted harmonious human happiness—in order to consecrate one's whole life to keeping watch, as it were, on the city walls. It was simply a question of a call—whether one should marry and join the reserve so to speak, or try to be selected for the first line. There was at any rate something in this view which made a direct appeal to a man's manliness.

His former determination that there should not be anything of this sort between him and Lucy before they were married—that was not due to his holding that kind of thing to be wrong in itself. He had not considered it wrong when he knew of similar relations in the case of others. But it was different with Lucy—he had had a feeling that, if he made her his mistress as soon as they were engaged, she would never believe he would make her his wife. And now he was glad that at least he had taken nothing until she herself offered it as a gift.

His mother's morality *sounded* as if it ought to be easy and straightforward to follow: When two people are really fond of each other, it is no sin. For then it is beautiful. And what is beautiful is no sin.

God knew, he and Lucy were fond of each other. And it was beautiful—. But Paul could not get rid of a feeling that he was fighting a losing battle to defend what was beautiful in their love from the humiliations and ugliness that threatened to rise up against them on every side and deprive their youth of its splendour.

He himself had never had any principles either of religion or morality—at least he had never been able to bring himself to give that name to his private opinions and such things as a sense of personal cleanliness and justice. For he only reacted to impressions according to his nature—and according to his bringing-up, of course. He thought his friends—male and female—made themselves rather ridiculous when they talked about their subjective religious feeling and announced that my God is like this or that. He really had no craving to provide himself with a God who stood in the same relation to his worshippers as Mrs. Harris to Mrs. Gamp—he would prefer to choose an Indian god with sixteen arms and legs; then at least one would be secured against self-worship. But he would have to get along without any God Almighty—had no use for a God to approve his actions, and as he didn't know any God whom he could obey—

One evening, as he was leaving Lucy, he whispered, bending over her:

"You are the only one I have loved!"

She drew him down to her:

"But, Paul—you—you've been with women, haven't you—?"

He did not like her asking such a question. Or—did not like, that was putting it very mildly. But, poor girl, perhaps she was seeking a consolation for herself in the thought that he too had not been different from most people. If his life had been at stake he could not have said how much he had put into his relations with her.

So he said what he had heard others say:

"My dear Lucy—that's quite another thing. That has nothing to do with what there is between us."

He had made it a principle that they were to behave correctly the few times she came up to see him in his room. But unfortunately it sometimes occurs that principles are not strong enough. And Fru Gotaas knocked at the door, opened it without waiting for "come in," and shut it again in a hurry.

This took place at dusk.

"I'll come and see you in an hour's time," whispered Paul, when he had let her out on to the stairs. He thought he must die of shame—and die twice over, as he watched her back disappearing down the stairs.

Then he plucked up heart and went into the sitting room—it was empty; Fru Gotaas was in the kitchen filling the lamps. She turned towards him as he came in—and a fresh wave of misery swept over Paul, as he saw the look of distress on her old face, small and wrinkled, with pointed nose, under the untidy frizz of grey hair.

"Well, Fru Gotaas," he said as bravely as he could; "of course I shall leave at once. I know I have behaved disgracefully towards you—"

"Well, but, Selmer"—her plaintive voice cut into his raw nerves; "you're engaged to her, aren't you? I mean—you intend to marry her, don't you?"

"Yes, of course. As soon as I have something to marry on."

Fru Gotaas dried her hands on her blue apron; no doubt this everlasting gesture was purely automatic.

"It's such a pity," she said softly. "For Fröken Arnesen is such a nice, sweet girl—she looks so thoroughly good and kind, I think. And you're a good man too, Selmer?"

Paul shrugged his shoulders. In a way it would almost have been easier if she had given vent to severe reprobation. But the old woman was on the verge of tears—ugh, he felt an uncomfortable temptation to unburden himself of all his troubles and confide to her what a difficult position they were in.

"Yes, it's a pity," said Fru Gotaas. "It's so bad that you should both be going about in town here—and neither of you have a home. Couldn't you go back to your mother's?" she asked timidly.

Paul shook his head:

"There are practical difficulties in the way, Fru Gotaas. I shall have to see about taking my degree as soon as I can now, you understand."

"Yes, that's true, you must do that. But she—can't she go home to her parents—hasn't she any people she could stay with meanwhile?"

"No, she has nobody." He had seated himself at the kitchen table, under the little shelf with the alarm clock, and the Madonna. Against his will it slipped out of his mouth: "To tell the truth it's not at all easy for us, Fru Gotaas—"

"No, it is not." She sighed deeply. "But couldn't you get her to go away into the country meanwhile—to some nice family. She'll have her trousseau to make too, you know," said Fru Gotaas, brightening up. "Don't forget that, she must get her trousseau ready"—she beamed as if she had found a way out of all their difficulties.

Paul was on the point of answering bitterly: poor thing, where was she to get that from?—when it struck him: this was an idea. He had some money of his own—or he could arrange a loan, so as not to have to speak to his mother about it. "Upon my word, Fru Gotaas, I will propose that to Lucy—I'm sure it would be best for her to go into the country and make her trousseau—learn housekeeping and all that—"

"Oh yes," said Fru Gotaas cheerfully; "for even if you don't look upon these things as we do—you know, it makes it not nearly so solemn—when people are obliged to get married—the wedding and that, I mean—"

Paul felt a little chill go through him—

"And then about your parents," said Fru Gotaas. "For you mustn't forget that it would be so awkward for her—because she's not what you'd call the same class as you—and that would make it even worse for her, you must remember, if it were to look as if you only married her because you were obliged to—"

So she had an eye to that too, thought Paul with some surprise.

"Well—it was your lamp I was going to fetch—"

"I'll go and get it," said Paul hurriedly, and was gone.

The moment he entered Lucy's room he was met by that foul smell—the family who had the basement were vegetarians, and whenever the weather was mild the whole air of the place was poisoned. In fact poor Lucy could never get decently pure air in her room—the peculiar cold and mawkish odour of the milk shop came through, and the smell of cooking filled the flat, when her landlady was preparing her various delicacies—it did not help much if Lucy opened her window to the yard.

"What did she say?" asked Lucy in a panic-stricken tone, coming towards him. "Did she make an awful row?"

"Far from it. She didn't make a row at all."

"Oh no," said Lucy with a touch of scorn; "that kind don't think anything of it, do they?"

"Oh yes, Fru Gotaas said it was a great pity for you. Such a good, sweet girl as you are, she said to me. And by the Lord and all the saints of the Gotaas family, I think she's right. And then she said it was a great shame of me not to have made our engagement public and taken you out to my mother's. And there she's right again. For I must tell you, Lucy, I can't stand this any longer, treating you just as if you were a girl I was keeping." He gave a hasty toss of the head—it did him good to say it out brutally like that.

"Well, isn't that what I am?" said Lucy bitterly.

"Not if I can help it."

"Oh, Paul." She touched his arm timidly. "It won't depend on you. You'll see, that's how it will turn out. And then you'll be glad too that I wouldn't let you take me home and that. Because nobody will think it any disgrace for you to have had a love affair with a common girl while you were a student in town."

"Oh, be quiet!" He bit her shoulder through the blouse. "I hate to hear you talk like that," he whispered passionately—"that silly cynicism of yours—you're so stupid when you try to be cynical, it's not at all in your line. You imagine you've learnt wisdom from your misfortunes, but they've only made you stupid—" in spite of her resistance he kissed her pale face with its little huffy air.

"I only said it because I'm fond of you," she sighed at last.

"Yes. Yes. Yes. I know that. But it's so stupid. And really you're not at all stupid, Lucy—we won't talk, we won't even think of all the casual, outside things—we won't think of anything but that you and I were made to love each other, and therefore we must love. If you had had the chance of leading a safe and sheltered life before I found you—then you would never have been anything else than affectionate and happy and faithful and so on. Lucy, Lucy, you must stop talking like that—talk of the devil and he's sure to appear—don't you know that?"

She stood leaning against him, perfectly still, and accepted his caresses.

A little later, as he sat in the only basket chair watching Lucy laying their supper—he came out with his plan that she should go into the country and learn housekeeping.

"Do you feel already that you can do without me?" she asked in a low voice.

"Of course we should have to arrange so that I could come and see you." Some small farm, preferably a place where they knew him from his summer holidays.

"Well, where's the money to come from for that sort of thing?" said Lucy hopelessly. "For they'd want something for taking me—even if I could be of use to them. And I must have a few clothes too—"

"I'll see about that," said Paul, blushing violently. His whole young being shrank at the idea that this looked like paying his mistress.

"I can't stand your staying on here," he went on; "living and breathing in this smell of kohlrabi or whatever it is those hogs in the basement fill the air with."

"No," said Lucy longingly. "You may be sure I'd rather live somewhere else. But then—if you really want to help me—I'd rather have a better room somewhere in town—"

This was getting more and more complicated.

For if there had been a nasty tang about his scheme of boarding her out somewhere in the country—. It reminded him amongst other things of a case he knew of: a son of one of the parsons in Uncle Abraham's neighborhood had got engaged to a servant girl, and he sent her home to his parents so that she might acquire a certain polish, as they said. Aunt Tinni in particular was loud in her praises of the splendid way they treated her. He remembered the whole family coming on a visit to Pastor Dverberg's and the elaborate kindness the poor girl had to endure from everybody. But it seemed she soon had enough of it, broke with her parson's son and cleared out. But if there had been something distasteful in the idea of keeping Lucy in the country—it was ten times more distasteful to take a room for her in town. In a boarding house everyone would very soon guess that she was his mistress—for that matter they would guess it even if she had never been so—and he knew the kind of men who are never lacking in such places, the kind that assume that if a girl has *one* lover, she is accessible to all without respect of persons, and then they run after her like dogs after a bitch. But he wasn't going to have any of that. A room—that meant that they must find a certain type of landlady who would make a show of being discreet—that wasn't very amusing either.

In order to bolster up his own self-respect in this growing sense of moral confusion, Paul insisted on Lucy's coming out to Linlökka one Sunday at the end of January. He had just got her installed in quite a nice sunny room in one of the little streets behind Holbergs Plass—with a widow who looked as if she would make no fuss so long as they preserved a certain decorum.

She came out by the eleven-thirty, so there was a pretty long day to put in. Paul was rather nervous as he went down to the station—he had to warn her that as a matter of fact he hadn't said in so many words that they were engaged; that was not their way here. Halstein Garnaas had been coming to the house for eight or nine months before his mother adopted him into the family. All he had said to his mother was that there was a girl he had seen a good deal of lately; he would like his mother to make her acquaintance. To which she had replied, yes, of course, her children's friends were always welcome.—

It went off quite well; Lucy didn't exactly put her foot in it, and it appeared that Julie Selmer's frank and hospitable reception gradually made her feel more or less at her ease. Once or twice—when Julie had said something considerate or cheerfully familiar: "sit down here, Fröken Arnesen, and make yourself comfortable," or "you'll see, when you come here in the spring"—Lucy looked at his mother with that strangely shy and meek expression, so that Paul felt his tenderness for her hurting him almost like a wound in the breast. That was how she ought to have been, timid and hesitating, like young girls when they have undressed on the beach and are about to plunge into the chilly waters of the fiord—not frightened like one who is pushed off the pier into the muddy wash around the piers.

Sigmund was the only other member of the family at home. Immediately after dinner the boy sat down to the piano. Music was the only thing Sigmund cared about; he would have liked to devote himself entirely to playing, but his father thought he should at least matriculate, then he would no doubt continue his studies, if he didn't get ploughed next time.

Paul had seated himself in the darkest corner of the room. It was something of Brahms his brother was playing—Paul had not heard it before; he let his mind drift with the music, as he watched the two women under the tall standard lamp. The light fell on his mother's fine dark head; she held it slightly bent as she knitted some billowy white thing that filled her whole lap.

Lucy sat where his mother had placed her, with all the gaily colored sofa cushions stacked about her and her fair face against the warm brown background of the wallpaper. The lampshade threw a faintly green light over her face, skin and hair were merged into something of an unearthly blond softness—she looked like a dream of virginal youth and feminine sweetness, as she sat listening to the music with great wide eyes.

And again the impotent sadness which now lay in the depth of his being was let loose. All that ought to have been—different from what it was. And this was just what hurt so damnably—to see his dream come to life for a moment; if only his own heart could be assured that one day it would be like this—this would be Lucy's life, to sit in peace in pure and tasteful and—yes, musical—surroundings, with everything hostile shut out. Oh, Lucy—she had but one gift—to open her arms to a man and his future and his posterity, to enclose all this in her powerful embrace and defend it with her gentle hands which were so innocently bold to devise new caresses—

But now it was only when the lamp was extinguished and she lay in his arms that she was entirely herself—then her abandonment was like sinking into an ocean of generous tenderness. The daylight showed how her youth was scarred with experience—and there was none on whom he, her man, could avenge her.

Life—well, that meant that he existed and Lucy existed and besides them some two or three million in Norway, inhabitants, as they were called—to say nothing of the rest of the world—he had known as much as that at school. And how many had become dust among the dust, and how many more were destined to overrun the globe before it became uninhabitable, was enough to make one seasick at the thought of it. They all struggled to obtain what they desired and what they needed in order to avoid what they most dreaded. Life—it may mean organic life or a man's lifetime, the sum of the knocks he has received or of the capers he has cut between the cradle and the grave. But in popular language the word is only used as a sort of euphemism—to fight the battle of life, that means fighting with others or fighting with oneself. To take revenge on life—to make others pay for the misfortunes and accidents that have befallen oneself.

If only he had been born twenty or fifteen years earlier, then he could have put the blame on society. But he had come into the world at a sufficiently late period of the migration of classes to put this argument out of court. There might always be a use for social reformers, and the ancient sources of social misery would continue to gurgle and spout in the depths of the human jungle. He would gladly have taken a part in serving society, if only he could be lucky enough to come across somebody who had some sensible scheme to that end—who was willing to start from the assumption that human beings are what they are, instead of always operating with human beings as they will be when once they have progressed so far as, etc. For one thing, no doubt there would always be young females who argued in this fashion: if people won't believe I am what I am, then I may just as well be what they take me for. And there would always be girls who put a symbolic interpretation on the fact that a man is rather well-groomed and wears clothes that fit him, and that he has books that she doesn't understand a word of, and can control his voice even when he's fairly excited—she interprets these as signs that he is her superior. And nearly every man longs vaguely for something primitive in a woman—either he wants a woman of this sort as his main theme and something more thrilling and disingenuous as a subsidiary episode, or he takes the simple woman as a supplement to more piquant experiences. But probably one always thinks it will be so refreshing to find a woman in whom nature has not been too much adapted and moulded by culture. Then it must depend on what sort of a man he is, and to some extent on what the girl is like, whether he simply wants to drain her to the dregs and go his way, or whether he will adopt her and keep her in his own garden as a kind of fountain nymph. Most men must surely feel an occasional craving for this Antaeus-like embrace of mother earth—otherwise vulgar women would not be in such demand.

He had never believed in anything but his own powers. And that had succeeded splendidly, so long as he had not grown so fond of another person that it hurt. Naturally, he had been fond of a good many people to the extent that their sorrows and weaknesses worried him and gave him uneasiness. But not so as to tear at his soul like an inflammation, nor so as to make him howl in his torment that the enemy should come out of his ambush and meet him in fight, win or lose. It surprised himself, but so it was—it was really terrible to be so fond of another person as he was of Lucy.

"Well," he said gaily, as they walked down to the station, "you didn't find it so terrifying at our house, did you?"

"No," said Lucy. "I'm sure your mother is a real good sort." She sighed. "But oh, how clever your brother is at playing! I've never heard anybody play so tip-top!"

There was something in her tone—as though her commonplace little words were meant to convey a great experience—which moved Paul intensely.

"Yes, Sigmund's a regular musician. You have only to ask him, next time you're here, and he'll be glad to play to you all day long."

"My word—I'd never dare! Then he's going to be an artist, isn't he, your brother?"

"Yes, I suppose it will come to that."

"Don't you play, Paul? Aren't you musical?"

"I? Oh, not enough to hurt anyway."

THE trains ran so that he could go into town with her, see her home and catch the last train out again—an arrangement which had been heartily cursed many a time by the Selmer boys in former days, when they had had to escort aunts and whatnot.

Coming home he ran by the short cut through the fields to Linlökka. The snow crunched under his feet—there was no moon and the sky was full of stars, which were reflected in the ice of the pond, now dark after the late thaw. He slid along the slide which marked his mother's and Sigmund's path to and from the house. There were no lights showing, except in his mother's bedroom.

Sigmund was asleep when he came into the boys' room. Paul lighted the candle on his bedside table. He felt a momentary pang—of pity for his mother: they had once lived here in such close companionship, all five—now she had only Sigmund left, and he too would soon be grown up. He saw a streak of light in the crack of her door, and so he knocked.

Julie Selmer was sitting at her dressing table, in a black silk kimono, brushing out her thick hair, now tinged with grey. On seeing her son's face behind her own in the glass she gave him a little smile.

Her dressing table was of the old-fashioned sort with flounces of patterned chintz, the same as the curtains of her four-post bed and in the windows. The air of the room was sweet and spicy with toilet vinegar and lavender water.

"Well," said his mother, "Fröken Arnesen got safely home?"

"Oh yes. What do you think of her, mother?" asked Paul; he had seated himself on the edge of the little couch.

"Oh, I think she's awfully sweet. Quite attractive—I liked your friend very well indeed."

"So do I."

Julie smiled at him again in the mirror. She brushed and brushed at her hair, then gathered it in her hands and began to plait it.

"She has perfectly wonderful hair, Fröken Arnesen! I've hardly ever seen anything like it. Oh but, Paulinus—you must really go to bed now—good night!" She bent her head back to receive her son's good night kiss on her forehead. "Go to bed now, my boy!"

Chapter Eleven

About this time Paul moved from the Gotaases. He had felt uncomfortable since that afternoon—was bashful every time he came home late at night; and that was by no means the worst of it. The worst was that he did not know what Fru Gotaas would think if Lucy came up to his room after this. Fru Gotaas had said nothing since that evening, and he was almost positive she had not spoken of it to the rest of her family. And for that matter Lucy would not come to see him again, on any account. But the whole situation was unbearable—his imagination spun a web of shame and self-contempt about him, because he was living in a place where his sweetheart could not go in and out frankly and without embarrassment. He had stayed at Linlökka a good deal since that evening—but that was no real way out of his dilemma. So when Aaser said he had to move, Paul jumped at the chance and offered to take over his diggings at once.

It was down in Munkedamsvei, in a little grey-green timber house, a forgotten remnant of the old town. A small brick house had been built on to it and there was a bicycle repair shop on the ground floor. A foreman lived upstairs in the wooden house, and then there was Aaser's den, whether you pleased to call it two rooms or one big room with an alcove. This was let separately, so that the foreman and his family had nothing to do with it, except that the wife had done the cleaning for Aaser and was willing to do the same for Selmer.

From the windows there was a view of an open space with huge heaps of road metal and mountains of paving stones, now covered with a thin coat of sooty snow, and beyond lay the Filipstad creek with its grey water full of drifting ice floes, and the red buildings of the Aker

Engineering Works with the slender iron girders of the bridge—and the rocks of Tyveholmsberg with the bathing place out on the skerry.

It was cold, Aaser made no secret of that; unwarmed rooms below and only one inner wall; that was why they had to find other quarters when his wife came home from the clinic with a little baby.

Paul had only been up there once since Aaser and Martha were married—he could not deny that the little household made rather a cheerless impression just then. They were both science students and they came from the same parish; he was the son of the schoolmaster and she was the daughter of the district physician, so there had been a terrible to-do in both families when this wedding came off last autumn. But fortunately that sort of thing is not infectious, and Paul had always liked the place, the view of the boat harbour and then the feeling of solitude associated with a little inhabited snuggery like this in the midst of deserted surroundings. Even the noise here, of which Martha complained so much—the hammering of iron plates, the shrieking and rattling of winches on the wharf, the screeching of steam-whistles and howling of sirens out in the fiord at night—and the smoky air which drifted, so strangely alive, and shut out the red winter sun—all this had a certain charm for Paul.

So he helped Aaser with their move and brought in his own things.

There stood his trunks, and all his books were stacked up along the wall, and near the stove stood an old octagonal drawing room table and three low chairs which he had bought. The uncurtained windows gaped to the night, and outside the white arc lamps were shining on the wharf; when he went to the window he saw the sea with the reflections of lights in the black water between the ice floes, and far away the red beacons; and when he looked up he could make out a star here and there in the frost fog and darkness. Along the window ledges was ranged his new crockery, with bags and parcels of butter and bread and coffee and sugar, and on the floor was the Beatrice stove boiling water in a big saucepan.

The bedroom beyond was quite narrow and had only a square skylight which was on the slant. He had put the little paraffin lamp on a stool; it lighted up the whole of his furniture, one basket chair and the show piece, a sofa which he had picked up in an antique shop. It was an elegant piece of English Regency furniture, in dark mahogany with finely moulded supports to the back and ends, the whole framework carved with laurel leaves and scrolls; it was upholstered in old horsehair. Of course it was a good deal knocked about, but when repaired it would be a great ornament—the first he had acquired for their home. There was a drawer underneath which could be pulled out, so that a bed could be made up for two, and there was something in this idea which appealed immensely to Paul—Lucy sleeping on the fine old sofa and himself before her couch—in the drawer—as though on guard—

Otherwise there was nothing in the place at present beyond a rubber bath and a washstand and his shaving tackle on the floor in the corner, by the side of the blue and white Madonna, which Fru Gotaas had given him at parting, presumably that she might keep an eye on him.

He had forbidden Lucy to come here before tomorrow evening. By that time he would manage to make things a little more comfortable.

Paul made his bed on the sofa. He knocked a nail into the wall above it and hung an enlargement of an amateur photograph of Lucy on skis among snow-covered stunted birches—one he had taken in the Nordmark this winter. Then he wound up his watch, hung it on the same nail, threw his clothes into the basket chair and crawled in between the icy bedclothes. He stretched himself on his couch—it was about as comfortable as the seat of a third-class railway carriage.

HIS mother looked in on him next day about noon, just as he was taking in his new writing table—a huge unpolished drawing board on trestles. Paul himself thought it made a brave show under the middle window and a good way on either side—it looked so practical.

Julie was only moderately enthusiastic about Paul's latest notion: "You'll see, you'll dawdle away a lot of time in this way—and how cold you'll find it here!" She moved her chair nearer to the stove and fastened her fur collar again.

"Look here, Paul—I'm only asking a question, I don't want to be nasty or reproachful—but do you think you'll be able to take your degree next term?"

"I hope so—"

"You have your recruit's course too this summer. You know I'm not in the habit of badgering you to stick to your reading and so on. But haven't you taken it pretty casually the last half year—?"

Paul made an attempt to sit up on his work table, but the top tilted up.

"Oh well, mother—it's not so easy—you know, the new hours of lectures—"

"Don't put the blame on that," said his mother sharply.

"No, mother, I admit it's a shame—I haven't been working properly the last half year."

"Yes, I've seen that. Now of course it isn't quite the same for those of you who are not studying for one of the paying professions. But I am rather disappointed about you. Men like Sigurd Aaser and yourself. How passionately keen you were to start with, and then after a time you slack off and allow your energies to be diverted to—other things. God knows—well, you know very well I don't imagine that young men can be anything but young, or that it's a sign of corruption or of a wicked nature if you let yourselves be tempted to neglect your work for—other interests. But all the same I do think it's a little—unmanly of you, when you know you may count on broad-mindedness and understanding and tolerance, that you can't make it a point of honor—of your own free will—to set up for yourselves an object which you mean to attain, acquire for yourselves a certain equipment of knowledge, before you try conclusions with life—"

Paul stood with his back to her looking out of the window. Julie came over to him. An orange winter sun lay behind the frost fog, casting a coppery sheen over the slushy ice of the creek; the factories and quays stood out finely against the sooty grey snow and the water.

"Yes, it's beautiful here," said his mother. "There is beauty in everything if only you have got eyes to see it."

Paul made a little grimace. There was an Englishman his mother had met on a summer holiday in the west country; he had said this with reference to a locomotive, and Paul had heard her quote it before.

"But at any rate I'll make you a present of some curtains," she went on. "What color would you prefer?"

"Something like—rust red, thanks," said Paul without reflection.

"Yes, that would look nice—against these grey walls. *Must* they be like that, or is it only that they haven't been washed properly since the Aasers moved?"

"Oh yes, I had a woman here all day yesterday washing."

"Well, you see, Paulinus," Julie took up the thread again; "I believe I may say of myself that I'm not too narrow-minded or prejudiced. But I can't deny that I'm seriously shocked at an affair like this of Martha Hellman, wasn't that her name? Because I know what it cost the earlier generation, in struggles, and courage to defy ridicule, and sacrifice of personal happiness—before they made good the claim of girls to the same education as their brothers. And then she must needs go and trip up in the middle of her university studies."

Paul could not repress a little sarcastic smile.

"And then she's not a bit pretty! I remember her well, he brought her out to our house on Midsummer Eve the year before last and they danced—"

"Yes, yes. As a matter of fact she was the one he seriously cared for—all the time. Ever since they shared the same governess—"

"Well, there's no accounting for tastes. Of course, he's no beauty either. Poor little child, as far as that goes it hasn't much of an inheritance to look for—"

"Oh, it's quite pretty—looks as if it hadn't any joints, but so do all the babies I've seen."

"Have you seen it?" asked Julie laughing.

"Yes, I took Martha some flowers."

"That was really sweet of you, Paul—who would have thought you had so much *savoir vivre*—" She looked into the bedroom. "Oh but, Paul, what have you got hold of there?—that's a find, my boy! Are you going to use it as a bed?—well, I must say, I congratulate you!" She looked at the photograph hanging on the wall above: "You took that? You're a clever photographer, Paul," she nodded. "Now you can come and have dinner with me, will you?"

In the evening Lucy came. She brought him some flowers.

Paul had succeeded in getting the room comparatively warm, and he had prepared the supper table with Italian salad and tinned crab and roquefort cheese, all the things Lucy liked best. She made tea, and he had sherry and grapes to follow.

They were rather solemn—for this was like having a secret little home of their own, their first one. Paul felt strangely unstrung with emotion. They were so extraordinarily alone up here. It began to freeze on the windowpanes and the light from outside sparkled on the ice flowers. At this hour it was very still in the street, so still that the distant hum of the town became audible—they could hear the train rushing past as far off as Lassons gate.

He brought the basket chair in front of the stove, and she lay in his arms as they stared at the glow behind the mica panes.

"Do you like this place of mine?" he whispered with his face against her soft cheek.

"Yes. But, Paul," she whispered shyly; "—it isn't because you're helping me that you have to put up with such a poor place, is it?"

He gave a giddy little laugh:

"You think it looks empty?—Oh, but it'll be better in time. You know, the things I buy now will come in when we set up house, Lucy. But don't you think it's wonderful here—we can be together without a soul being any the wiser—nobody to notice what time I leave you. And tonight!" he whispered rapturously against her neck, "we'll be together all night long!"

THAT was what they had agreed. But next morning as they went into town together Paul had made up his mind to accept his mother's offer of one of the beds from home. He had not had such hard lying at the worst of the saeter quarters he had known.

THAT nobody took any notice of them—that was not quite correct. It was not long before his charwoman, Fru Fransen, began to talk about "that Fröken Arnesen, your sweetheart" in a very cordial manner, full of benevolent confidence. She constantly drew comparisons between them and the Aasers—they were to the advantage of Selmer and Fröken Arnesen, but all the same—. Naturally their affairs were being discussed in the Fransen household.

The workmen at the bicycle workshop knew of Lucy too—though she scarcely ever came till after half-past seven, and it was not so many times that she stayed all night. And in the shops of the neighborhood where they made their purchases the people knew about them; no doubt by degrees their relations became known to the whole street.

For their engagement was not particularly secret—several times he had arranged to meet his friends in town and taken Lucy with him. And once or twice it happened that someone or other called on him in the evening and found her there—Paul did his best not to let it be seen that the visit was inconvenient, and at a suitable time he said that he must see Fröken Arnesen home. They parted outside her door, he whispered "tomorrow"—it was a bore, but it couldn't be helped. For that matter, not many of his acquaintances were in the habit of coming to see him in Munkedamsvei—intimate friends he had none, and those friends he had seemed to understand that they would not be terribly missed now if they didn't come.

Once or twice she had been with him to see his father and Lillian, and their friendliness had been overwhelming; on Tua's part it was perfectly genuine. Garnaas let it be seen that he was no snob and did not intend to spy on his brother-in-law's doings—that was Paul's impression. It was only Hans who was entirely natural and undemonstratively polite to her. So it was not for pleasure that they went there. And the memory of that unlucky dance on the King's accession lingered in the minds of both. But Paul insisted that once in a while they must go there.

At Linlökka Lucy was really at home, Paul could see. She felt the cosiness of the place, and she regarded his mother's home as less "grand" than his father's—where Lillian's ideas of elegance overwhelmed and oppressed her. No doubt she had the same feeling about his mother—she made Fröken Arnesen welcome, was pleasant and did everything to make her guest comfortable, but was never fussy and never overdid her amiability or interest.

And then Lucy was evidently very fond of music. It was always she who sat in the corner by the piano when Sigmund was playing.

"Tell me what I'm to play to you, Fröken Arnesen," said the boy.

"Oh, thanks, it's all the same to me"—Lucy blushed with delight. "It's all so lovely—"

Paul sat in the corner of the sofa by his mother, smoking, reading a little, chatting with Julie. He was happy on these evenings—and underneath there quivered a vague anxiety lest something should slip out of his hands.

Lucy had embroidered a hanging for his wall, water-lilies on a kind of grey-blue woollen stuff. He thought it pathetic—since his loyalty forbade him to call it ghastly even in his most secret thoughts. He nailed it up over the Regency couch which now did duty as a sofa in the big room; his mother had sent him Tua's bed and a good deal of furniture besides—her daughter would not be living at home any more. It looked quite cosy at Munkedamsvei now.

He had also got some bookcases. One evening when Lucy was with him and he was arranging his shelves, she got hold of a volume of Asbjörnsen and Moe. Thus Paul discovered that she knew no fairy tales whatever—she only remembered one about a cock and a hen that she had had in a reader when she was a little girl at school.

Paul settled himself to read aloud to her—and now he found that she was altogether beside herself with delight, she laughed and she cried—it was really like reading fairy stories to a child. It affected him immensely—this great girl, this passionately generous lover who had found her true home in his arms, after being dragged through such horrible calamities—she flushed and sat breathless when he read about "Boots" and the king's daughters who were carried off by the trolls.†

Then he laid aside the book, came over and stood leaning over the back of her chair.

"Now let's pretend we've run away from the Giant who had no heart in his body—we'll creep in there and hide—"

And afterwards, as she was falling asleep in his arms, it seemed to Paul that in a way this was a fairy tale they were playing at, and the game was so serious that it was no use trying to get to the bottom of it.

NEARLY every time she brought him flowers; sprigs of mimosa, rather dry, so that the little yellow puff-balls went to powder, tulips and hyacinths. The smell of the hyacinths worried Paul, as these flowers were never quite fresh; they were such as she was allowed to take away on leaving the shop. But this scent of hyacinths that had begun to go off reminded Paul of the room in which his grandmother Selmer had lain after death—she had had white hyacinths lying on the pillow beside her face. He had not been afraid—had only thought she looked very strange and solemn. Still, he did not like this scent which reminded him of it. But he could not tell Lucy that.

MARCH came with its long afternoons; a band of clear green light lingered on the ridge of the hills long after the first stars had pierced the blue of the sky. One Saturday afternoon, as Paul and Lucy were walking along Bogstadvei with their skis over their shoulders, they met Aaser and Martha.

Paul stopped and asked after the little boy. And he introduced Lucy to Fru Aaser.

Whereupon Martha Aaser quite unmistakably gave Lucy the cold shoulder. It was the first time Paul had known anyone treat his fiancée with downright discourtesy.

He tried to smooth it over as they sat in the tram:

"Isn't it extraordinary that there are lots of women like that—they can't forgive anyone for being prettier than themselves? Imagine a woman like Martha—she really has plenty of brains, a great talent for mathematics—but she can't bear other women who are prettier than she is—which practically means that she can't stand other women."

† TRANSLATOR'S NOTE: See Dasent's *Popular Tales from the Norse.*

Lucy made no reply to this. And Paul guessed that she had seen very well what Fru Aaser meant by being nasty to her. In matters of that sort Lucy was by no means stupid—on the contrary, she was far too perceptive for his comfort. But that Martha Hellman of all others, Martha Aaser as she was now, should feel called upon to snub Lucy, that was too ridiculous for words.

AND then of course he knew very well what was meant by it.

It was that Lucy was not what the little, ugly, angular Martha with her gold spectacles understood by a lady. Martha's and Aaser's relations might pass as free love or a marriage of conscience or whatever fine name they might please to call it by. But one could not get away from the fact that he and Lucy belonged to different worlds. Everything about him proclaimed that his forbears for generations had been people who shaped their lives on predetermined lines, developed their entourage, chose their partners, brought up their children according to a definite plan. He had what is popularly called a well-bred face with the smooth, broad forehead and thin, straight brows, the delicately modelled cheeks and the pure lines of the narrow-lipped mouth. He carried his big, broad-shouldered body without being conscious of it; no later impressions and no slang could efface the character his voice had acquired, since he had had cultivated voices to listen to and to imitate from the time he first began to babble.

And nothing could hide the fact that Lucy came from a class in which life is more vegetative and the workings of the brain are less comprehensive. Her face was charming, fair and soft, but relaxed in all its lines; her sweet, pale pink lips had no firm outline, as though affected by her way of talking—in words and sentences which expressed what she wanted to say in such a pathetically insufficient and undecided fashion. She had now got herself a smart new black walking dress, but when she moved she appeared incurably clumsy, in spite of her lovely figure. But she seemed made for manual labour and open air—there, he felt, she would have been able to move with the grace of strength. She was getting anaemic from standing behind the counter in a little shop day after day—she was too big of build and her senses were too sound for such a life—it was already making her look a little overripe and slack. He recollected the spiteful comparison someone had applied to her that evening—a painted deal wardrobe. Paul had seen such things: in a timber-built farmhouse, where the windows were in their regular places and let in just the right amount of light, there the bright and richly painted wardrobe was the centre of an ensemble for which it had been designed. Then some "nationalist" idiot, who gushed about the artistic gifts of the people without understanding anything of the nature of popular art, came and carried it off, stuck it up in his flat in town between two tall windows with white curtains. And there it stands, a huge piece of lumber which proves the point of all townsfolk when they talk about boorish taste and ugh, these "national" horrors—

And yet they suited each other. They suited each other so that a thrill went right through him if he did but think of her in broad daylight. They suited each other as Adam and Eve had suited each other. It had been his luck, as perhaps it does not fall to one man in a thousand—that the first woman he met was she who was his mate. He simply would not imagine himself being ever untrue to her. But the little secret, that she was the only one—that he might fittingly keep to himself and take with him to the grave.

That it was so—that was the wonder. But at the same time it was also true that he was and would remain a young student of good family who had an affair with a shop-girl, daughter of a lay preacher from Jarlsberg. In the eyes of the sentimental section of the community a "gentlemanly" young scamp who took advantage of a poor girl's affection—the orthodox denouement of the story would be that he gave her a baby and deserted her. And in the view of cynical middle-class propriety it was she who was an impudent hussy, and it would only serve her right for setting her cap at the inexperienced son of her betters.

No one, no one could know how indescribably, how madly they were in love with one another—that whatever might come of it, the game they were playing was for their whole lives.

But that was just what he would have to show to the whole world—Lucy included. For he guessed that every time she abandoned herself to him, she got up as it were and dressed herself again in her fear that it could not last, wrapped herself in a sort of resignation in which she was to meet the inevitable.

So this story would not come right until he was properly married to her—he had come to realize that. And a thumping wedding he would have—rubber-tired carriages to take them to church and a first-class sleeping car for their trip abroad and all the rest of the symbolical paraphernalia which would settle it once for all that from now on they were to be treated as one in the eyes of God and man.

Chapter Twelve

They had arranged to have a little celebration on the Friday evening before Paul had to leave for his recruit's training. For on Saturday they had to go out to Linlökka.

He had persuaded Lucy to ask leave from the shop at five o'clock. It was never very difficult to get her to do this; especially now in springtime it took it out of her a good deal to stand in the shop all day. And when Paul had put things straight at home he went up Huitfeldts gate to meet Lucy.

The afternoon was as warm as summer and the sky had that deep, full blue that makes one think that now one can see what space is. Paul and Lucy paused on the bridge over the Western railway; hand in hand they just stood there and let the sun shine on them. In the warm yellow light even the dirty many-eyed backs of the tenement houses looked well, and behind rose the trees of old gardens like the edge of a forest, shimmering in the light with their mass of swollen buds.

The slopes of the railway cutting were already turning green, the ragwort, which was everywhere, even in the blackened ballast between the rails, was already old and dangled on its long stalks. A train passed under the bridge; even the black coal smoke it sent up, hiding the sun for a moment, had a festal gleam as it dissolved in the blue. And the everlasting boom and drone of the town seemed strangely muted, as though subdued by the light and the warmth.

They walked by the side of the boat harbour. There was a smell of paint and tar, where boats were being fitted out—the water glistened and the islands outside shone with vernal green. There were some people on the bathing place pier, and the garden at Filipstad was bright with red and yellow tulips, new-mown lawns and clean, brown mould.

Paul took in with all his senses every single little sweet and joyful sign of spring—the smell of the brackish water in the Frogner creek, the scent of gardens where the dead leaves had just been raked from the raw ground. The first spring flowers round the verandas of the villas had such wonderfully pure colors; the moss on the black stems of the old trees was emerald green.

He enjoyed the very fact that he was alive—felt his own healthy body as something so intensely good, every movement, every breath he drew, was good. And Lucy walked by his side, they walked in step—it was such a joy to be near her; her fair hair shimmered so finely in the sunshine, her shoulders and bosom were so beautifully rounded in the tight black jacket—and he loved her voice at every word she spoke, little commonplace phrases, which seemed but symbols of her strange, tender caresses.

And thus they would go on enjoying every second and every minute, hour after hour, of this wonderful spring evening, till night came and sleep enfolded them both, two young mortals weary with happiness.

"Isn't this good, Lucy?" He put his arm round her, as they walked from the ferry up into Bygdö. There were not many people about so early on a weekday afternoon—but the voices of children gathering anemones came from among the trees, and the sound of horses' hoofs on turf and the jingling of harness from beyond the little wood—they were ploughing up a field. There was a smell of manure and of burning weeds. The little neglected piece of ground by the hothouse looked so deserted; the red gardener's cottage always reminded Paul of foresters' houses in German colored prints—there was a kind of touching colored-print romanticism about the whole of this little Bernadotte park, with its doll's castle and the collection of old houses and the tarred stave church among big, dark firs.

"Oh, Lucy, don't you think this is good?"

"Yes. But if you have to go away—"

"Now don't go and make yourself miserable over that. We shall see each other in the summer, you know."

His conscience was a little sore because he was not by any means cut up about it. To speak more truthfully—he looked forward to his soldiering. Not that he was tired of Lucy, far from it—he was much more in love with her now than he had been in the beginning. Though that was no doubt impossible. But at any rate he felt more and more sure that it was with her he was to spend his life. She had restored to him the feeling he had not known since he was a child—before his parents separated—of unforced confidence in other people, of its not being necessarily difficult or troublesome to associate with others, of not having to be constantly on one's guard not to scratch either them or oneself. Until now it had always seemed as though the people he was most fond of were at the same time his enemies, without their wishing it or being aware of it. Now he felt that he could have friends with whom he could be a friend, and if he made enemies, they would be his enemies right out. He need no longer be on his guard except as to the future—need no longer be reminded of himself, but could put his whole heart into his work, his duties, all the joys life has to offer, together with his mate—in short, he could take an undivided interest in the life around him. It was a glorious feeling—the spiritual counterpart of what a man feels physically who has always been ailing and now feels perfectly healthy and strong. So he thought in any case—he could not know it, of course, as he had always been as strong as a horse.

But all the same he did long to get away from all this for a while. It was all right between him and Lucy—but there were all these external circumstances which made their position a little tangled at present. He really wanted to work in earnest now—could not make out how a thousand hindrances kept coming in his way. Lucy was in the shop all day, so he could not put the blame on her—but still it was so hard to settle down to work that he felt hot about the ears when he thought of the winter and how he could manage to get through next term.

Then there was his debt. Of course it was nothing desperate. He could clear up the mess all right when he had taken his degree. But it was a little uncanny, the way it was growing. Of course, the people who lend money to students whose families are reputed to be well off, don't do it from philanthropy; he had been quite clear about that before he entered into these transactions. And neither his mother nor his father must have any suspicion of this debt—whatever they might say or not say, he knew who would get the blame. It is so easy for others to know how a girl ought to conduct herself in such matters—a little more difficult for herself, with a wage of thirty crowns a month and some small casual earnings from her needlework. For seven crowns a month one can always get a furnished servant's room with a cellar full of cabbages underneath and a milk shop alongside; one is not likely to stay there if one can get away. And Lucy never suspected that he had any difficulty in finding the money he gave her. When all was said and done, he was only drawing on what would belong to both of them when they were married.

Then there was the other thing; nearly every month it was the same story—Lucy beside herself with fear that she was in trouble, as she expressed it. In spite of their blessed precautions which threatened to destroy the sweetness and freshness of their relations, so that at times he thought almost with disgust that this would have to go on for a long, long time. If only too much of the gilt had not been rubbed off before they were able at last to live like two normal, natural human beings. Hitherto it had fortunately been a false alarm every time. But it could not be denied that they had been more lucky than wise sometimes—and nothing was infallible.

And then occasionally he had this feeling of being tired—not of Lucy, but of always having to be with a woman, always thinking and talking in a woman's company, and listening to her. He longed—not so much to talk to other men, but to be among men and to be allowed to hold his tongue in the society of men. This had nothing to do with his love for Lucy—Romeo himself would have felt like that in time, if he had been married to Juliet, and Bendik, if his adventure with Arolilja had not ended so abruptly, would certainly have turned his back on the golden bridge now and then, with a blissful feeling that he was on a holiday.[†]

BUT this evening Paul only felt that there was something infinitely perfect in their love—in spite of all tiresome external things. And that was good.—

They supped at the Sea Baths, and late in the evening they strolled home by the upper end of Munkedamsvei with its big old gardens. This one warm day seemed to have brought on the trees noticeably—the budding twigs were no longer sharp against the dim light of the sky. The birds still sang, but in short and broken strains—it would soon be night. Down on the railway lines the little lanterns were burning, and out on the white fiord shone the beacon light. They walked slowly, close to each other, he with his arm around Lucy so that he felt her warm, round breast against his hand: "Lucy—isn't it lovely, that we're *alive*!"

Up in his room they stood for a while at the window, looking out over the yards, where the mountains of road metal shone as with a pale light of their own in the spring night, and the water had a strange gleam upon it.

† TRANSLATOR'S NOTE: The allusion is to an old Norwegian ballad, in which Bendik crosses a golden bridge to the bower of his beloved.

Outside little boats with lanterns hurried past breaking up the surface into dark oily ripples.

"Will you have a glass of sherry before we go to bed? If you'll clear away my herbarium—gently though—I'll get glasses—"

He kept his crockery in a cupboard in the bedroom. Paul lit a candle in there. For a moment he thought nothing of seeing his brown handbag standing by the cupboard—his washing had come—then it suddenly dawned on him. He had given his mother the doorkey when last at home, so that she might come and take in his washing, if he was not at home.

And there was the bed beautifully made, two pillows with crocheted borders and monograms—Lucy's "trousseau" that she had been making. And his nightshirt and her pale blue nightdress lay neatly and respectably side by side—

"What is it, Paul?" asked Lucy from the other room.

"Nothing—" but then she came to the door, and there he stood with his bag and a puzzled look on his face.

"God—has anybody been here—!"

"Only the washing—"

"God!" said Lucy horrified. "Do you think your mother brought it up herself?" It had happened once or twice that Fru Selmer herself had brought things for Paul while Lucy was there.

"Haven't an idea—anyhow it's nothing that you need worry about." Paul tried to seem indifferent. But Lucy sank into the desk chair.

"Oh, what do you suppose she'll think of me now!"

"Of you?—Of me, I should say. No, but, Lucy, this is nothing to make such a song about. What if it had been Lillian—or Tua—but mother! Mother's not that sort, she's so broadminded"—he thought himself the word sounded gruesome in this connection—"mother understands—" he corrected, but that didn't make it much better.

And in his heart he thought, if only it had been anybody else at all but mother. Meanwhile he tried to comfort the girl—at last he knelt before her and tried to make her take her hands from her face:

"Lucy dear—Lucy—don't be so miserable! No, I certainly shan't let you go. Why, if we're sold, we're sold—so we may just as well take the price, my girl!"

THERE was no question of getting Lucy to go out to Linlökka with him next day. And the end of it was that Paul himself telephoned that he could not come before Sunday morning; he had to go and see his father on Saturday night.

But on Sunday morning there was nothing else for it—he had to go.

"Haven't you brought Lucy with you?" asked his mother. She showed absolutely no sign, so Paul did not know what to believe—perhaps she had not brought his bag herself. He stole a glance at her from time to time. But once, as he did so, she withdrew her eyes quickly, a kind of quiver of confusion passed over her face—and Paul's heart began to beat violently again. Certainly she knew—

Tua was at home with her fiancé, and they had dinner early, as Garnaas was to preach at evening service in town. He was now ordained and had some work in Christiania—Paul was not very clear as to what it was, but Tua took part in it in some way or other. And they carried off Sigmund with them—the boy had promised to play at a party.

So Paul was left alone with his mother.

"Come along." She put on her waterproof and slipped her cigarette case into the pocket. "I want to show you the glacier crowfoot that you and Aaser brought me, it's flowering so nicely."

They strolled along the path looking at the perennials which were just coming up. Around the flagstaff mound Julie had laid out a rock garden.

"Why, they seem to take to a garden," said Paul. "Those little poppies from Dovre are spreading all over the place."

"Yes. But the silene aeculis looks rather sick—at any rate I can't get it to bloom properly. Just a flower here and there. But evidently it doesn't thrive in captivity—."

They strolled back again, by the path along the stone fence that bordered the little copse. His mother parted the long grass with her fingers to see if the orchids were coming up nicely. There was a mass of leaves of lily of the valley, a host of green lances. A rustling in the supple branches of the weeping birch over their heads told that the fine weather was over; it was bitter enough today, with wind and a cloudy sky.

Paul did his best to hold out: if his mother would not say anything, he too would try to pass it off. But there came a moment when he could keep it up no longer:

"Was it you who came up with my things on Friday?"

"Yes. By the by, remind me to give you back your key before you go this evening—"

"I say, mother. I'd just as soon you said what I suppose you're going to say. We may as well have it now." He turned red as fire and stood still, in a sort of challenge.

"What makes you think I should want to say anything?" asked Julie in her easiest tones. "My dear Paul. Do you really think there is anything for me to say—now?" She shrugged her shoulders.

"You know what I think about that sort of thing. You know I don't give a red cent for conventional middle-class morality. But there is something we call athletes' morality. And I think it's a little unmanly of you young people that you can't apply it to your intellectual training as well—

"And you're so young, my boy. Don't you know how it is with the reindeer in the rutting season—the young bucks are not allowed to have their way till they have fought for it—"

"Good Lord, mother, we're not mountain reindeer unfortunately—"

"No, no, Paul. I don't mean to preach morality either. It's too late for one thing. And as far as that goes, I've never had any great belief that it does any good. I've never tried to instill any morality into you except that you should always behave as gentlemen—be fair and straight with everybody, whether it's your tailor or your sweetheart—no sneaking out of any debts or any responsibilities.

"And now you've taken upon yourself a responsibility with regard to Lucy—"

"Yes, I have that."

"And she's a really sweet girl. I've come to like her."

They walked in silence for a while.

Till Julie stopped, gave a little sigh—and then began, rapidly and nervously, without looking at her son:

"Since we're talking of these things, Paul, there's a thing I should like to ask you: have you any debts?"

"Yes."

"How much?"

"Oh, nothing to hurt. I shall be able to clear it off myself, mother, at the right time."

"I know you've earned a little now and then. But I expect you've borrowed at extortionate rates, haven't you? For I may feel sure you wouldn't go borrowing of your friends?" she said quickly.

"Oh no, mother." He gave a little smile. "I haven't sunk that low yet."

"No, no. I beg your pardon. I didn't believe it either. But look here, Paul, hadn't you better tell me what your debts come to? Then I can raise the amount. If it's not too big, I should like to make you a present of it, by the way. I can't bear you to draw on your little fortune before you're in a position to earn something by your work. It's so—demoralizing. And you promise me you won't make any more debts?"

"No, mother. I won't. I won't promise anything that I'm not sure I can keep."

"That you're sure you can't keep."

Paul turned red as a fire: "Have it which way you like."

"Well, then you'd better take over your own money and manage it yourself, boy. As a matter of form," said Julie dryly, looking up at the boy's defiant eyes. "As a matter of form it would at any rate have been more becoming if you had declined my offer with a *No, thanks*."

"Yes, I beg your pardon, mother. I admit I ought to have said that. But it isn't such plain sailing, you see—there's so much that I can't explain to you."

"Heavens, Paul, do you think that's necessary?—I flatter myself at any rate I'm fairly open-minded; it isn't because I'm prejudiced that this affair of yours with Lucy has weighed a good deal on my mind. It's simply because I have rather a strong sense of reality."

Paul made no reply. His mother went on again:

"The situation, you see, is simply this, that in all probability it will be a year or two before you can stand on your own feet. And you have already taken it upon yourself to support another." She raised a hand to silence him: "No, boy, I'm not reproaching her with anything—not an atom. Gretchen driven out by her Christian parents before she was full-fledged, Gretchen alone in the great city, obliged to take what work she can get, and surrounded by fellows who think every female is fair game and no close time! Don't you think I see that it's nothing but the order of nature when she throws herself into your arms at the first opportunity and clings to you and accepts all she can get from a nice young student who is neither rough nor diseased, but willing to protect her and be kind to her? And I will add, from the impression I have of Lucy, I assume she is tremendously in love with you, as she appears to be the sort that needs both a man's protection and an object for worship and devotion—"

"I'm tremendously in love with Lucy too, mother." They were now walking up and down the path by the copse. Julie lighted a cigarette and offered her son the case. And Paul felt a slight relaxation of the tension and the throbbing.

"All that you've been telling me about Lucy," he remarked superciliously—"you mustn't think it's new to me. Lucy has told me everything about herself. So that's all right. Only I can't imagine where you heard it—about her being turned out of her home, etcetera. Was it from the Nicolaysens?"

"No—do they know anything about it?"

"Don't know. Nikko saw a good deal of a sort of friend of hers at one time, so I just thought—"

"No, it was Ina Bertelsen as it happens—you remember she was out here one day last winter when you were both here. And you know, Lucy is a girl one notices, with her hair and blond complexion. And Ina had seen her some years ago, when she was in service somewhere in the west end together with a couple of girls who had been patients of Ina's before that. They told her a good deal about Lucy, and Ina had a talk with her one day and warned her against the dangers of the town."

"And of course Ina was not particularly lenient in what she said of Lucy?" said Paul bitterly. "She and her sort are not generally so—in dealing with girls who recover themselves without troubling them for their assistance."

"No, Paul, Ina does a great deal of good. It wasn't very pleasant for me either, when Ina came out with her disclosures. At that time, you see, I hardly knew Lucy—though I had to pretend to Ina that I had heard all this before."

Paul threw away the butt of his cigarette: "oh, let me have another, please, mother—." They strolled down towards the rock garden again. "As I say, Lucy told me everything there was to tell, before we were engaged. And if you had heard the story from her own lips, you too would have had nothing but admiration for the bravery she has shown through it all. No use for Ina there, I can assure you—" he tried to laugh. And as his mother said nothing, he went on in a tone of rather forced gaiety: "So you mustn't be too sore about this, mother—the daughter-in-law I'm going to give you is worth more than a dozen of the girls I used to dance with at our own parties—

"Lucy is the most truthful person I have met in my whole life," he said, with all the emphasis he could summon, when his mother still said nothing. "I wish you and she could have a good talk one day."

Julie smiled sadly:

"O dear me, Paul—if she were to tell me what she has told you—do you think it would be the same story? No, you needn't fly at me—I don't at all mean to say that Lucy has told you anything but the truth. Only—no woman in the world tells another woman the same that she tells to a man—not in the same way. I shouldn't be able to do it myself. And both versions may be equally true—

"If you should happen many years hence to think of this day, Paul, you will remember perhaps that it was a spring day with sunshine and the birches were just coming into leaf, and we went and looked at the first flowers that had appeared in our garden. And I should remember that it was a grey, bitter, unpleasant afternoon with a northerly wind and that it had snowed during the forenoon. One would be just as right as the other—

"What is truth? A Roman official once asked, and he made himself famous through the centuries by that stroke of wit."

"To my mind the reason he became famous was that his saying was addressed to a man who declared that he himself was the truth."

"Are you still brooding over those influences you came under when you were living with the Gotaases?" asked Julie rather anxiously.

Paul avoided her question:

"And I'm inclined to think that's the most plausible explanation. If the truth is not a person, I'm afraid it's a fiction."

"But science, Paul—that gives us the key to truth?"

"I don't know anything about that. It teaches us a whole lot of things which are true, but that's quite another matter. And it has taught us a whole lot that people once believed to be incontrovertible truths, but have turned out to be untenable. About some of them people are now monstrously contemptuous—fancy anyone ever believing things like that. And then on the other hand there are a whole lot of errors which have served as uncommonly useful working hypotheses, and men have arrived at results which appear incontrovertible enough, for the moment at any rate, by way of the strangest fallacies."

"Yes, yes, but when all's said and done, you must believe in science?"

"Naturally I believe in positive scientific results. And there are a whole lot of scientific men that I believe in tremendously. Others that I believe in a good deal less. But you can't expect me to believe in the science of popular mythology—Science with a big S."

He laughed teasingly, as his mother shook her head:

"I'm afraid, mother, your children have been a disappointment to you."

"Yes, they have." Julie spoke with suppressed heat. "Don't you think

I have reason to feel that? Hans and Tua have gone over entirely to their father's family—and you can't expect me to be more than moderately enthusiastic about the man Tua's going to marry. And soon the time will come for me to send Sigmund out into the world. Then there comes this business of yours. As to your plans, I won't even speak of them—scientific studies, taking part in expeditions and so on—there won't be very much of that; probably you'll have to take to teaching as soon as you can get a job, and get married while you're still a boy, to a girl—I won't say anything against Lucy, she's sweet and strikes me as good-natured and tractable. But all your ideas and traditions are so fundamentally different. You'll both find this out more and more the older you grow. You'll find out what it means to be so unlike in everything that is determined by habit and bringing-up—when you have to share in all sorts of everyday concerns to which neither of you now gives a thought. Oh no, Paul—you can't ask me to be *pleased* about it!"

"I'm not asking that either, mother," said Paul quietly. "Only that you will go on being nice to Lucy."

"So you think I haven't been so hitherto? Then you must remember that it's over two months since Ina Bertelsen told me that. And then another thing, you must find time to come up to the office one day so that we can have a real talk about your money affairs. Amongst other things, I don't want it to come to your father's ears that you've got into debt. He would be very displeased. And then there's this about it, that his new wife is"—she shrugged her shoulders "—a stranger—"

Paul quivered a little. That disgusting palpitation again. Anger that his mother should think fit to remind him just now—that his father was married to a stranger. But to tell one's mother that one would take over the management of one's own money, because one was keeping a mistress, that wouldn't do, by all that's holy. And he felt a childish desire to blub and explain to mamma how innocent all his intentions were—

"I promise you, mother, I'll be ready by next term. You know, mother, I've worked hard the other years—and you know I've made good use of all my vacations. And demonstrations and laboratory work and so on I've followed pretty closely, in spite of everything. It's really only systematic reading that I'm behind in."

"Well well, don't promise more than you can keep. And then you understand, Paul—when you've got so far that you can think of marrying Lucy—it would be a good thing if you made a trip abroad, and the girl could come here meanwhile, and I would take over the part which would have belonged to her parents, if they had been normal."

"You—you are kind, mother."

"We'll go in now," said Julie, shivering. "It's horrid cold."

WHEN they came into the drawing room she put a match to the little pile of sticks and coal that lay ready in the fireplace. And with her elbow resting on the mantelpiece she stood and watched it burn.

"Ah, yes. It was a woman friend of mine who used to say there are three things for which we all ought to be thankful to the Lord. That we can't see into the future, and that we hadn't the pluck to shoot ourselves when we wanted to, and that we couldn't marry our first love."

"That's what I am doing," said Paul quietly.

"It's what I did." She threw off her waterproof with an abrupt, impatient gesture, drew a chair up to the fire and sat down. Leaning forward she looked into the flames.

"And when I think of it, Paul—it sometimes happens, as one grows older, that one lies awake more at night—I think of what I believed your father to be, and what he was in reality, and what I believed myself to be, and how different I was too—then it all seems to me pretty sad—"

She saw him to the station in the evening.

"Have you seen anything of Harald Tangen lately?" she asked, as they walked down.

"I met him once at the University library just before Easter. I believe he asked to be remembered to you, by the way. Otherwise I haven't seen anything of any of the Tangens lately."

Chapter Thirteen

Paul had a glorious time in camp. For one thing, it was a point of honor in his set that one had to look upon one's recruit's training as a grand time. The lads were bound to think it all great fun, even punishment drill, fatigue and stomach trouble. To criticize the rations would have meant losing caste. Anyhow they were unexceptionable, thought Paul.

"Oh well," said a faultfinder in his hut, a dark little fellow who was an instrument maker by trade; "it may be fun for upper-class fellows like you to do a bit of hard work for a change and eat off a tin plate."

There might be something in that, Paul was ready to admit. He was big and strong and thought it splendid to be free of brainwork for a while and to lead a regular physical life. In his spare time he practiced the concertina and became a virtuoso—had never suspected that he had such musical talent. Sigmund could take a back seat now with his piano-thumping.

Firearms had been his passion ever since he was a baby boy, and tramping in the dust had always had a special attraction for him. Of course mountain climbing was still better, but he had marched the whole length of Eggedal and Numedal along the high road and enjoyed it. And he liked the drill.

Naturally, there was a sort of shadow over it all—the shadow of last year's crisis. And on a couple of festive occasions he had to listen to speeches which gave him the same feeling of nausea as he remembered from last winter, when he went to the theatre with Lucy and saw "Christian Fredrik, King of Norway."

God stands behind us—faith, one must hope so; they say he takes care of all fools. However, this frontier guard business hadn't been all play-acting, he found that out here, from several things he heard. If only all these irresponsible blockheads could leave off talking about it as if it had been some mighty feat of arms.

Of his last conversation with his mother he would prefer to think as little as possible. She had paid him out two thousand crowns. He himself had thought that would be ample, but—. Well yes, he had given Lucy a diamond ring for her birthday. Not a bit pretty, he thought; they might have got a charming old enamel and pearl ring for the same price. But it was the very idea of a diamond ring which meant God knows what to her, poor girl. So she had to have it.

Then it had been settled between them that in her summer holiday she should come up to the little boarding house in Hurdal where they had first met. She would be given a week this year.

He did not care to tell his mother he was in want of money again so soon. But he managed without—wrote to Aaser and got him to sell some books which he could find just as well at the reading room.

In July Lucy came up to Hurdal, and Paul got leave on the Sunday she was there and went over on his bicycle.

The boarding house had treated itself to a closed veranda and the title of sanatorium. Otherwise it was unchanged; the same neutral temperature of food and drink, even the landlady's creosote-scented relative was there again this year. The other visitors were ladies, but he could not identify them with certainty. The yellow spots where the plate had worn off the spoons and forks had grown bigger. And he and Lucy loved one another—and that made the whole world different.

In the morning he rowed her out on the lake. The whole vast surface was gleaming white, and the forest on the other shore was blue in the heat haze. He had never rowed her before—and then a burning desire came upon him: he must and he would see her naked in the green woods with the sun on her bare milk-white skin—for he had never properly seen her loveliness, she was so odd in that way. Besides, it was so hot rowing in uniform; a bath would be good for its own sake.

But she turned red as fire when he proposed it:

"We haven't any bathing dresses—"

"No, what do we want with them—? You can wear some water-lilies," he nodded at the flowers in the bottom of the boat.

"Oh, you—"

But when he passed the next point that ran out into the lake, with dry bog moss showing white among the little spruces and firs which had a wan look here on the barren rock, he turned the boat into the creek beyond. It was like the very heart of sylvan solitude in there—on the steep hill behind the firs grew one above another drinking in the sunlight so that their tops were aflame; above the top of the ridge white swelling clouds shone against the blue. At the head of the creek was a level patch of green, where a brook ran out into the lake.

Paul grounded the boat there.

"Here there's no risk of anybody coming. Perhaps you'd like to undress in the boat?"

She shook her head, her face as red as a berry. And for an instant it was as though Paul had to harden his heart against something—he knew not what. But she looked so utterly miserable.

"Don't be so silly, Lucy," he begged her with a laugh. Then she obediently climbed out of the boat and disappeared among the bushes.

He was undressed in no time. Jolly to get out of one's trousers. He stretched himself and surveyed with approval his brown, well-trained body—admired the play of his muscles as he changed his position to get the full benefit of the caresses of sun and air. It was brown, peaty soil, with some tufts of sedge and here and there cushions of light green moss and of fragile, cool stellaria—he walked a few paces, it was so good to tread on with bare feet.

"Lucy," he called softly. "Come along—shall I give you a hand—"

She came out and stood, dazzlingly golden white, in front of an osier bush which reflected sunshine from all its shiny leaves. She raised one arm above her head—a twig had caught in her hair: the line from the elbow along the inside of her upper arm, the armpit and one breast which was raised by the movement, the waist and the arch of the hip, the thigh which was lost in the tissue of grass—it was so beautiful that he could have wept! But when he called her name and made as though he would spring at her, she gave vent to little pitiful screams, doubled up and waved him off with her arms—he saw the same agonized blush on her face and far over her neck—

Then he checked himself:

"No but, Lucy—" he tried to laugh. The sun kissed her all over; some belated buttercups bloomed in the grass at her feet—but the girl's incomprehensible fear projected as it were an invisible wall between them. The wild and joyous excitement dropped from him; he felt his heart contract at something strange and meaningless. Then he turned his back to her, took the few paces down to the water's edge and plunged in.

The sweet, cool voluptuousness of sinking into living water by degrees restored his composure—his late sense of fatality subsided, giving way to an impression of foolish and baseless fright. Lucy was merely irritatingly and inconsistently silly—

The water turned brown and muddy around him, and there was an old fallen tree with stumps of branches like iron spikes, and sharp stones in the soft mud of the bottom. He stopped when the water reached his middle, and looked back over his shoulder:

"Come along now—the water's not a bit cold!"

But she still stood there, hugging the osier bush. Then he started swimming.

"Go in just where you see I've gone—there's a tree under the surface to your left; look out you don't scratch yourself on it—"

Next time he turned over on his back and looked, she had got so far as squatting in a few inches of water. As soon as she saw he was looking at her she hurriedly splashed the muddy water over her shoulders and breast.

"No, come in properly," cried Paul. "Shall I come to you—I'll give you a swimming lesson—you just lie across my arms and strike out—like this—"

"No—ugh, no, Paul—"

Then he gave it up—swam out on his back and felt the sunshine as a blood red darkness through his closed eyelids. When he opened his eyes and raised his head again the bright summer world seemed pale and faded, and he just caught a glimpse of Lucy's back as she ran in among the bushes.

He dived, swam under water with his eyes open—it felt so good and strange to be down in the cold, streaming, translucent darkness that throbbed against his eardrums and poured along his limbs—he came up for breath, spouting the water from his mouth. Again and again he dived, swallowed water, flung himself about and swam in rings. Till Lucy's form in the light blue summer dress appeared at the water's edge.

"Paul," she called faintly, as though afraid someone might hear them. "Oh, do come out now, Paul. You might get cramp," she cried, louder.

He laughed. Then he swam to the shore. Lucy sat waiting up in the wood till he had his clothes on.

An hour or so later they lay in the wood, smoking cigarettes and crunching chocolate which Paul had brought for her. But it seemed that nothing could disperse the gloom that had settled upon them.

Paul could not get over the inward feeling that he had violated her in some mysterious way, been cruel or brutal, when he forced himself to make her give him that lovely, fleeting vision—

And that was so incomprehensible. For there were really a great many other things about which he was far more bashful than Lucy.

And suddenly it slipped out of his mouth:

"But, Lucy—we look much better without any clothes on—"

Again her face had that odd look, as though he had hurt or insulted her, and she blushed violently: "I don't think so—"

He looked down at his long legs in the baggy, grey-blue uniform trousers and heavy ammunition boots:

"That's how we were meant to be, my girl." He laughed quietly. "You know, if it hadn't been for the Fall, we shouldn't be bothered with clothes—"

"Do you mean to say you believe in the Fall?" asked Lucy with a touch of scorn.

Paul looked up into the blue sky. The clouds were spreading over it now, with a coppery light above, but down on the wooded ridge the bank lay blue and threatening.

"God knows. I almost begin to think there's something in it," he said pensively. "But we must think about getting back. We shall be late for dinner anyway."—He wouldn't say anything about the thunderstorm; Lucy was so afraid of thunder.

They got into the boat. Paul pushed off and sat down to his oars.

"If you had any idea how wonderfully beautiful you are—" he said softly.

"Ugh, can't you stop talking about that—" She burst out crying.

So Paul didn't say a word more, just rowed in bitter exasperation, and Lucy sat in the stern and cried. When the first flash flickered over the ridge and the summer thunder rolled far away, she gave a start and sat up gasping with pale lips and eyes darkened with fear.

The first drops of rain rustled the leaves as they walked up from the boatyard. And in the afternoon, as they sat drinking coffee on the balcony outside Lucy's room, the landscape was blotted out in the grey veil of rain. It drummed on the roof above them, the water splashed in through the rail of the veranda, all the gutters were spouting noisily. Paul and Lucy were silent most of the time—and he was not very enthusiastic at the idea of having to ride all the way back to the Guards' camp in this downpour, with the roads a mass of mud.

THIS incident of trying to get Lucy to bathe with him left its mark in Paul's mind. It was just as if their relations had undergone a permanent change.

So long as he was in camp he had not much time to think about it. Its effect was rather to make him more absorbed in what he had to do at the moment, he gave himself up to the daily life and avoided thinking—in particular he thought much less of Lucy, because he no longer had the same desire to dream about their relations, past and future.

But when he returned to Christiania in the autumn and they met as before, the feeling was always there—that he had done something fateful. Just like the boy in the fairy tale who cannot be satisfied with the good things he has—in fairyland or over the hills and far away—there is a forbidden door which he can't resist opening, or one single thing he is not to touch, and he touches it. Then he finds himself in the bog, or he hears an ugly roar in the distance, and now the troll is coming to take him—

Bosh, he tried to say to himself. He had been reading too many fairy tales last winter. They may be all right for children—they are not healthy reading for grown-up people, who are apt to find too much profundity in them. Or perhaps they are too profound to be good for grown-up people—?

At home they had been brought up not to be ashamed of their nakedness. Until they began to grow up their mother had scrubbed them when they had a bath. And afterwards they had to stand up with their backs to her and the palms of their hands against the wall, and bend slowly. And the only impression he retained, when once he had been called in to an inspection of this sort and noticed that Tua was beginning to grow little breasts—they reminded him of little pegtops—was that by way of a change he zealously took her part against his mother, who wished Tua to carry her books in a knapsack instead of a strap. That great big girl—it would have made them all laughed at by the rest of the school. After that he had always taken care to give Tua a brotherly warning, when they were to meet their mother after school, that she must change over and pass the strap under her right arm.

He knew to a nicety what his mother would say, supposing she had come to hear of this business. She would have been virtuously scandalized over what she called unhealthy ideas, and of course she would blame Lucy's bringing-up: it was the impure imagination and stuffy cowardice of those people that had crippled the girl's sense of beauty and purity. And until quite lately it would never have occurred to him to disagree with his mother.

He at any rate had found his mother's morality, which made beauty and purity one and the same thing, very helpful during his adolescence. He had been ashamed of other boys when they showed curiosity, like a rat peeping out of a hole and vanishing in a flash if discovered, or when they indulged in prurient talk as though they could not control themselves—some of them out of bravado and others in a feverish way, with cowardice showing in their eyes. And he had been ashamed of himself—a bitter, burning shame—when he yielded to something he knew was odious or allowed his thoughts to play with ugly and nasty things. He had prided himself a good deal on not being prudish—he could be frankly amused at coarse stories and jokes of a dry and salt kind—like cigar ash, which you only have to dust off when you get up. But the kind of obscenities which are sticky, like drops of punch, he was in the habit of ignoring with a proud and icy disapproval—.

It had only lately come home to him that one cannot dust off cigar ash so that it leaves no mark, unless one's clothes are clean and well pressed.

His mother's nudity morality might be good enough—for those who were shapely and handsome and strong. And the famous nostrum of frankness was not so bad—with children who have a reasonable expectation of not being kept waiting outside too many of the locked doors of life, begging and bargaining. If he had remained virtuously superior to bawdy stories and fastidiously observant with girls who showed off before him—why, it was small praise to him.

But one of the discoveries he had made in camp—not that he mightn't have discovered it before if only he hadn't had such a swelled head—was that the world will not be retransformed into the Garden of Eden simply by abolishing all morality except good taste. Tastes differ—and the taste of some was such that he would have denied their having any—and they were just as natural as any other people: their old Adam was by nature omnivorous and only asked to have its desires gratified as soon as it felt them. While it was his own nature to hang about and wait and look around till he discovered something for which he might possibly conceive a desire.

And it was not only such fellows as had to be glad to take what they could get—or who had no bashfulness because they had grown up in circumstances which did not give them the choice of being bashful or not. It was not only the little hunchbacked cobbler down by the station who watched with hungry eyes and dribbling mouth for every skirt that might come into his field of observation. He had seen plenty of big, well set-up men of good birth who honestly thought ten brawny wenches a better proposition than one fair Helen.

In his joy at their love being something so wonderful and perfect he had succeeded—not in forgetting Lucy's past altogether, but in forcing back the recollection of what he knew. Amor vincit omnia, etc. In the flush of victory he had made too bold a stroke. And now he had learnt, in a way he was never likely to forget, that it was not only their homes and upbringing that were different, but also their experiences.

What aggravated his pain and his vague uneasiness was that the image of her young and dazzlingly white form, as she stood before the glistening osier bush with the yellow flowers dotted among the grass at her feet, haunted him day and night. It ought to have belonged to a world in which innocence and beauty were the same, and where he could have dashed forward and thrown his brown, muscular arms about her soft white body, while the sun and the clouds and the lake and the woods were nothing but a garden planted for them.

Now that he recalled her gesture, as she raised her arm to free her hair from the twig, he knew what she had resembled—although it was very different, for the statue had a tunic—but in spite of that, form and gesture resembled the Wounded Amazon. Ever since he was a little boy he had thought that the most beautiful statue in existence. He dared not speak of it to her; it would be beyond her comprehension and would only upset her again.

By the way, he had thought too that the engraving of the fettered Andromeda which hung in his father's drawing room reminded him of Lucy. So evidently it was tragic images that she recalled—the fettered Andromeda and the wounded Amazon.

Chapter Fourteen

One evening at the end of September, when Paul and Lucy were sitting in the Teatercafé, Henrik Alster suddenly turned up. Paul asked him to join them. Alster was really one of those friends he cared most about, though they had never had what people call "interests in common." Since Henrik had gone home a couple of years ago to enter his uncle's business, they had heard no more of each other—neither was much of a correspondent. Now Henrik had started his own business in Trondhjem—as a builder's merchant.

When they had seen Lucy to her door, Henrik Alster went on to Paul's diggings. They sat talking till past six in the morning and made an end of a bottle of whisky—drank it neat when the soda gave out. And Paul had confided to Alster a good deal more about his relations with Lucy than he had imagined himself capable of letting out to anybody.

"Chuck it," said Henrik Alster, referring to Paul's examination. "Come up to Trondhjem with me and let's go into partnership.

"If you're certain you want to marry her, it's perfectly idiotic for you both to hang on here in town making a mess of the whole affair. When once an affair of this sort has reached the point where both you and the girl say that marriage is meant, it's ruined *qua* love affair. And if it's allowed to drag on indefinitely, it'll end badly, whether at last you get married or not."

Paul nodded thoughtfully from the depths of the armchair. Henrik's utterances struck him as very profound,.

"Yes, I've realized that myself long ago."

"And then you know, if you're going to be married, it'll be much better for you to live in some place where neither your family nor her former acquaintance can interfere with you. That will be a great relief—if you two are to be one flesh, as the Scripture says. Different as you and Fröken Arnesen are."

Again Paul nodded solemnly. The words were so true.

They began to discuss the arrangement from a purely business point of view; how much money Paul could put into the concern, what knowledge he had which would be useful, and in what way Alster should take in hand his business training. Alster wanted him to come north at once and let his examination go hang. He had known a good many business men and farmers who had university degrees and it wasn't a very favourable omen. Either they turned out miserably unpractical business men, foredoomed to trouble and bankruptcy, or else, Henrik Alster asserted, they were clever in a greasy, lousy way; at any rate they never had the cachet that a modern, gentlemanly business man ought to have. Of course, a science degree was not quite so bad as one in divinity or philology, but all the same—"No, come as you are, as the lay preacher said to the girl."

He could share Alster's quarters to begin with—a three-room flat on the outskirts of the town, which looked very comfortable—Alster had some photographs in his pocketbook.

They agreed to discuss the affair further, under dry conditions, when Alster returned from his trip to Gothenburg in five or six days. For now, though far from drunk, they were even further from being sober.

PAUL fell asleep as soon as his head was on the pillow and woke up two hours later, convinced that now he would get no more sleep before he had to get up—whisky always had that effect on him. With that the recollection of his whole talk with Henrik Alster burst in upon him.

His first feeling was that he *must* stick to what he had said—break off straight away, go to Trondhjern and become Henrik's partner. Since he had acquainted the other with all his difficulties with regard to Lucy. Otherwise it would be just as if he had confided to another fellow the details of his intimacy with his mistress, simply for the sake of having someone to confide in. And if he had done that, he simply wouldn't be able to put up with himself. On the other hand, if in one way or another it could be regarded as the preliminary to action—then it was quite another thing.

His heart shrank at the thought of giving up his studies—after the slacking of the winter before his interest in them had become quite keen again on his return to town last autumn. And now it was arranged that after taking his degree he was to assist Professor Ellingsen in working out the results of this year's expedition, and next summer he himself would be one of the party for Bear Island. After that he had a fairly safe prospect of a post of assistant lecturer in the autumn. Then they could marry—he would have to furnish out of his capital.

This was not very large. And the little fortune which each of the children possessed was in the main the result of their mother's management. When their father made the division among them he had lately had fairly heavy losses through speculation; it came to something under four thousand for each of the children. Now there were six thousand crowns belonging to Paul invested in his mother's business, and besides that, while the children were under age, she had put a part of the money which she received from their father for their support into first debentures; he had four thousand crowns in first-class securities which he could realize. Their mother had provided for them almost entirely out of her own resources up to the present time.

He had had his financial affairs very thoroughly explained to him that day last spring, when she had insisted on his receiving her account of the management of his property—and rendering her an account of his debts. He had then asked her to continue the administration of his funds, until he had taken his degree.

In the summer Tua would be married, and then she would withdraw at least a part of her money from the printing office and put it into some kind of philanthropic undertaking that she and Garnaas were interested in. Hans was to be a doctor, which was a long business, and Sigmund's musical training would be at least as expensive as a university course.

And so his own studies were thrown away, looked at from *that* point of view.

That being so, he could not go to his mother and say he wanted to take his money out of her business. Unless she herself would propose an arrangement.

At all events he would put the matter before her.

It chanced that he spoke to his father first about it. There was a note from Lillian by the morning post—would he come to supper that evening? When she herself opened the door to him she said it was his father who wanted to talk to him about a matter and had asked her to write that note. Instantly Paul felt a certain repugnance or irritation which in a way determined his mood for the whole evening.

Halstein and Tua were in the drawing room. Halstein was expounding something to Lillian; they took up the thread again when they had greeted Paul. It was religious education in schools, Tua explained, as her brother sat down by her under the tall standard lamp; she was sewing some big white thing, as she had always been doing lately.

"It is a living faith, not a doctrinal faith, that we must seek to arrive at in the Norwegian national church. The explanation of the second article is a piece of theological speculation: I believe that Jesus Christ is very God, begotten from everlasting of the Father—here Luther is still bound by his respect for the dogma transmitted from Catholicism. In reality it is by no means implied in the words of the article—it is human reasoning, based on a false syllogism: a son of God must be God's son, therefore he must be very God. It is the same as saying, a king's son must be a king. Of course not, but he must be *royal*, so that the king can appoint him vice regent. In the same way Jesus, as God's son, is divine—"

"God bless my soul," Paul interrupted in a rather irritated tone; "one would think you looked on it as a sort of official position to be God, Halstein?"

Halstein turned to his future brother-in-law:

"Of course not. All I mean is that what we must keep a firm hold of is the spirit of the Reformation, and we are not doing so by maintaining dogmas which still had a value for the people of that time as the expression of contemporary religious experience, but which can only act as a hindrance to the thought of the present day. We can only remain in the spirit of the Reformation if we have the courage to experience Christianity in our own way, by preaching to the people of our time the gospel of the greatest religious genius who has ever lived, whose sovereign thought was that God is the Father, whose King's speech was the Sermon on the Mount—"

"Really? I had an idea that neither was so frightfully original. The Aryans had their old Dyaus Pita, Jupiter, God the Father from time immemorial, and you can find the same ideas as in the Sermon on the Mount in lots of places. Unless the originality of Christianity consists in its asserting that a man who lived in Judaea at a definite historical date was God himself, who had incarnated himself in a virgin's womb and stayed on earth such and such a time in order to point out this and that to the men he had himself created—the lilies of the field, for instance, and the right and wrong in their way of thinking about him and his kingdom, and the way to treat their wives and their debtors and people who fell among thieves—then I don't know that there is anything original in Christianity. It is not that the Sermon on the Mount is so entirely without a parallel, but that Christ's death and resurrection are supposed to make it possible for us to realize the teaching of the Sermon on the Mount, instead of having a more or less Platonic fancy for similar ideals—"

"That too is not so original as you think, Paul. Divine sons supernaturally born and divine virgin mothers and savior divinities who are sacrificed are to be found in a great many ancient religions—"

"Precisely. That is to say, there are plenty of divine sons who are born supernaturally—to call their mothers virgins exactly, requires a strong dose of tolerance. But I think too that Christianity is only a dream which resembles a mass of other dreams—unless it is the realization of those dreams. If in short it is more than a tradition which you people dare not admit you have outgrown, it must be the solution of all the riddles—which men have amused or tormented themselves with trying to guess—published by the same one who set the riddles."

"For shame, how you talk," said Tua indignantly. "And you're not a scrap religious even. You won't believe in anything at all—"

"Won't—none of you can know that. Nobody has ever told me anything about religion in such a way that I could imagine there was any reality behind it."

"You ought to be ashamed of yourself! You had religion at school. And when we stayed at Fossbakke as children, you certainly had to go to church every Sunday, just the same as the rest of us—"

"Yes, but it never occurred to me to believe in what they said. I know very well that Uncle Abraham believes fully and firmly in what he himself preaches. For in order that all his ideas and opinions may be correct, it's a necessary assumption that his religion is the true one. Uncle Abraham would believe in any religion you like which provided a logical basis for the set of opinions he has got. For it would never occur to him that opinions which he has once got into his head could be anything but right."

"Well, but that applies to all religion, doesn't it?" suggested Lillian, rather doubtfully.

"I understand what Paul means," said Halstein. "He means that a personal religious conviction assumes an antecedent crisis, an awakening; and that is true of most people's religious life. Though one also meets with—I have met with—many excellent Christians who have retained the faith of their childhood without any critical awakening or violent irruption of new experiences. And this applies in particular to men of the older generation, precisely to men of Uncle Abraham's cast of mind. But Paul is right, unfortunately; they are not very well suited to be spiritual guides to the youth of our day. That is just why we lay such stress, in the religious education of children, on not clinging to dogmas which are no longer capable of embracing the religious experiences of people of the present day—no metaphysical doctrines about a god-man's double nature, but Jesus' own teaching, that which is the life and soul of him, his confident apprehension of God as the Father."

"Yes, but that's just what I want to know," said Paul obstinately; "where did he get that idea from? If he is God's son, begotten from everlasting of the Father, of the same substance as the Father—as the Catholics assert and as Uncle Abraham hasn't yet grown out of believing—then it's all plain sailing—teach me to worship him as God. But don't come here and ask me to go in for any genius-worship in place of religion. If he was a man of genius who felt just as if he might be the son of God and certain that nobody could bring any sin home to him and such a one in whom the Father must be well pleased—then I can only assure you that I don't feel the least desire to work up any analogous feelings in myself. That is, if he called himself God's son in the same way as others have called themselves son of the sea or I might call you son of the mountains. But perhaps God, if he exists at all, was just as indifferent to the fate of Jesus as the Hardanger range is to that of the ski runners who come to grief there or the sea to the sinking of a ship with all hands."

"Well, but, Paul—you must admit, the very feeling of unity with nature which makes a man call himself a son of the mountains or son of the sea—that in itself is a spiritual force of immense value—" said Halstein.

"As a kind of augmented perception of one's ego, yes. I am a tiny little dot in nature, and yet I delude myself into thinking that the whole mighty landscape feels and thinks in much the same way as I do. One man might go so far as to imagine the mountains of Norway as one great teachers' common room, to put it at the worst. Or another might call a country stern or smiling, according as it looks to him. I can acquire nature's secrets, but nature doesn't care a curse for acquiring mine—it can be sure of acquiring my corpse and incorporating it with itself by a process of corruption."

"That is an entirely different thing. It is our soul, Paul, which perceives the relation between itself and the origin of all things in such a way that the spirit within us makes bold to say, Abba, father!"

"Yes, but I want to know whether the origin of all things has ever expressed itself so clearly that we know it has acknowledged the paternity of us pitiful creatures? In other words, is it because God has revealed himself that we have learnt to say that—Abba, father—?"

"It is the Holy Ghost, Paul," said Tua impatiently. "You ought to know that much—"

"Yes, but who is the Holy Ghost?"

"God's spirit speaking in our soul."

"Yes, but who is there who can take upon himself to introduce God's spirit to us, so that we know it's he who is holding forth in our soul and not, for instance, our own desire to believe we have got the right hang of a thing?"

"I've never heard such expressions as you use—" said Tua, scandalized.

"Don't you see, that's just what I want to know—is it a revelation, or is it simply men headed by the religious genius, Jesus, who project into space their own dreams and surmises and desires? Has God himself spoken and said he is our father and we are his children, or is it only we ourselves who imagine God as a father of supernatural size—each of us according to his own ideas of fatherliness—a universal domestic tyrant who has us by the ears early and late and jumps on us the moment we go the least bit outside his table of rules—or a benevolent old gentleman who pays all our debts and is soft-hearted enough to pull us out of all the tight places we are careful to get into—a glorified noodle?"

"No, look here, Paul!" Lillian jumped up, scarlet in the face. "You're going too far! I can stand a good deal, within reasonable limits. But I draw the line at blasphemy here in my own house!"

Paul tried not to smile. It was the others who were talking blasphemy, it seemed to him—if there was a personal God, that is.

TUA and Halstein were invited out to supper. As they were leaving Tua said:

"Remember me to Lucy. How is she, by the way—has she got rid of her cough?"

"Yes, thanks, I think so." It was the first time anyone had so much as mentioned his fiancée this evening, Paul noted, not without a certain bitterness.

It was the maid's evening out, so Lillian made an excuse and disappeared into the kitchen.

"What kind of behaviour is this?" asked his father with annoyance. "You seize every opportunity of wrangling with your brother-in-law and falling foul of him."

"I don't at all see what Halstein's religious views have to do with you," said Herr Selmer contemptuously, when he received no answer. "As far as I know you're a freethinker—the same as your mother."

"Not the same as mother anyhow. Not so that I profess a positive faith in negations." The son smiled rather pertly.

"Then I think at least you might respect another man's personal convictions."

"I can do that quite well, as long as he doesn't bring them forward as religion. Good heavens, father, when one thinks of how it comes about that people acquire their convictions—there's no limit to what you can convince them of, or what they can succeed in convincing themselves of—. Think of Uncle Abraham and Aunt Tinni—every scrap of gossip that people came and served up at the parsonage, especially if it was about folks they didn't like or whose orthodoxy was in doubt—they were convinced it must be true. I've often wondered whether they were so ready to believe in gossip because they never had any knowledge of human nature, or whether they have lost their knowledge of human nature from listening to so much gossip.

"Good God, when you set men to teach us religion on the strength of their having passed an examination and been given a public appointment, and then let them preach according to their personal interpretations and experiences and convictions and private opinions about religion—you can't be surprised that the young, if they're ever so little inclined to skepticism, don't believe what these men tell them—even if their skepticism doesn't prevent their swallowing blindfold what the next man preaches, though it may be the shallowest radicalism or romantic utopianism or the most popular of popular science or anything else that mother swears by—"

"Well, you wouldn't ask Halstein or any other clergyman to preach something different from what he himself believes."

"No, of course not. But if Halstein's faith is only something that Halstein believes, then I don't see any sense in our going on paying him to tell us what he believes. It would be another thing if Halstein knew an authority in which he believed sufficiently to take his faith from it, like a banner for which he would fight and to which he would devote his life—with the prospect of a long, long life or a sudden death before him.

And if he failed, we should know there were others ready to spring forward, take the oath of fidelity and bear the banner. But not a banner that he himself has invented or sewed together—even if it bears the ordinary heraldic motives of Christianity arranged according to his own ideas of proportion—"

"Are you still brooding over those things?" asked his father sharply. "You go to the Catholic church too, I've been told?"

"I've been there once, a year and a half ago. And God knows, I've thought mighty little about that kind of thing the last year. But I can't help doing so when I meet clergymen like Uncle Abraham or Pastor Garnaas. Whether a religion that has any vitality must not possess an authority which sends out its priests—essentially different, that is, from a department—and whether the individual priests must not have a different kind of mandate for teaching beyond the fact that they have taken their degrees and consider themselves competent to guide others. A consecration, to put it plainly."

Herr Selmer shook his head:

"Such a form of Christianity is not suited to us. We are far too independent to allow ourselves to be led by a priesthood with a supernatural mandate of that sort. And too independent to accept such a mandate either, for that matter. Far too independent and individualistic to renounce, for instance, the right to an ordinary, natural family life. That a Norwegian priest should abandon his right to have a wife and children and a home, when the poorest cottager or labourer in his parish has these—"

"Well but, father!" Paul could not help laughing. "Do you call that independence?"

"Be that as it may," his father cut him short; "I won't have you speaking to Halstein in that tone. In the first place it hurts your sister—to be sure, you boys have never shown yourselves too pleasant to Sif. In the second place I think highly of Halstein—he is an extremely honorable young man, and far from wanting in talent. It would not surprise me if he made something of a name for himself one day—"

"I believe that's exactly what I have against him," said Paul thoughtfully. "I too know very well that Halstein is a fine fellow and idealistic and all that, and as honest as a man can be with his confidence in his own personal convictions, as he calls it. I don't suppose I really have anything against him except that, if he gets on well in the world, he will be so firmly convinced that it is for the good of the whole world that he does get on."

"Well, well, enough of that. It was to speak of your own affairs that I asked you to come here this evening."

Paul looked up, expectant. Involuntarily he felt his conscience traveling like a searchlight over his inward and outward life during the past year, and he was anything but easy in his mind.

"I met Professor Ellingsen at the Brydes' last Tuesday. And he evidently has a very favourable opinion of you, Paul. I was—I was very pleased, I may say, to hear what he said about you. And therefore I will tell you that next year, when you come home from Bear Island, you will have at your disposal the necessary funds for two years' foreign travel.

"Hitherto your mother has borne the greater part of the burden of your bringing-up and education. As you know, this is not because I have not contributed my share. Out of that Julie has succeeded in putting aside a good deal for the benefit of you all—and she deserves all honor for it. But I had rather you did not touch that. Now it is my turn to assist you further."

"Father." Paul had a sudden feeling almost of giddiness. He had spoken almost before he gave himself time to think. "I'm awfully grateful to you for that, father. But it just happens that I'm thinking of giving up my studies and going into a business. You see, Henrik Alster—he's in town just now, he's proposed to take me into partnership."

He looked at his father—had a kind of impression that the other turned pale, and then he felt strangely miserable himself. So he threw up his head and put on an exaggerated air of energy and decision.

"Ever since you were a little boy you have known what you wanted to be," said Erik Selmer in a low voice.

"Yes—"

"Business man—is it the prospect of a more brilliant financial position that makes it seem more attractive in your eyes than being a man of science? Or—is it this new—romance of commerce?" said his father with a touch of sarcasm. "The practical life and all that?"

"I've taken a fancy to it. I have a fancy for working with Henrik Alster for one thing. And then Lucy and I are anxious to get married as soon as possible—"

"And so you want to give up now, when you have taken your degree—after you have got on so well and have every prospect of passing with distinction, and the future you have had in mind ever since you were a boy is on the point of being realized—"

Paul dropped his eyes:

"I was thinking of going north with Henrik at once. Early next month."

After a pause his father asked quietly:

"Won't you tell me what is the cause of this extraordinary decision?

"Is it," he went on, when there was no answer, "that you feel bound to marry your fiancée as quickly as possible?"

"Yes." Paul felt how burning hot his face became. It was chiefly that his father could bring himself to hint at such a thing—somehow he had felt certain that his father would never let fall a hint, whatever he might guess. "But certainly not on account of circumstances of the sort which I suppose you are assuming. But if Lucy and I are to stay on in town in the way we have been living, we shall be spoiling something which is far too precious—wasting our youth in stupid misunderstandings," he said hotly.

His father looked at him, rather doubtfully:

"You're not twenty-four yet, Paul. So unless there is any special reason for hurrying on your wedding, I honestly think there are many reasons for postponing it a few years longer, before you undertake the part of married man and father of a family. To put it plainly, Paul, you haven't the ghost of a notion of the ideas that prevail in the class to which the girl belongs—I'm not saying that those people may not be worth just as much as ourselves; they are often worth more as men and women. But they are different; their ideas are so widely different, their estimate of values—why, even the same words have a different meaning and value—"

"You may be sure I know that," said Paul nervously. "But for that very reason—let us in God's name try to come to an understanding with one another while we're still young enough for it to be possible—"

"I don't think you have any cause to complain of the reception your fiancée has been given in your family. You doubtless understand that there are a few things which we might wish to see changed, but we have done our best to overlook them. As far as that goes I don't see that Fröken Arnesen has anything to complain about. She has been given every chance of finding her bearings in your social surroundings. Your mother, as far as I know, has shown herself at least equally accommodating in her treatment of your fiancée—"

"My goodness! Is that what your mean—that the fact of your having accepted her is supposed to have an uplifting effect on Lucy—"

"If you insist on interpreting everything in the most unnamiable fashion—"

"Oh no, father—that doesn't make it easier. That Lucy has no home and no parents, while I'm if anything too well provided—with two homes and three parents—"

Erik Selmer said nothing for a few moments.

"Very well, Paul. But if I haven't altogether misunderstood your mother, she has explained to you that it was not by my wish that you children lost the home of your childhood."

"I know that, father." Paul rose abruptly, looking at his father. But then he turned half from him, went over to the piano and stood up the photograph of old Sheriff Kraby which had fallen. Oh no—one can't talk about that kind of thing—but he was smarting from remorse; ah yes, they had all treated his father unfairly—and he dared not trust his voice—

"However," came his father's voice, dry and sharp from across the room—"I will not venture to deny that time has proved your mother to be right. It is possible that the atmosphere of *our* home might have become so depressing that perhaps you were just as well off with Julie. Otherwise you would have found out that things were out of joint—and put the blame on that if you had failed to hold your own—young people nowadays are like that, they must always find some excuse if things go wrong. And as regards my present wife—if you are not generous enough to feel gratitude for the kindness and friendship she has *never* failed to show my children by another woman—at least I insist on your being polite to your stepmother here in our home."

At this Paul was again more angry than hurt. Damn it, had he ever been anything but polite to Lillian—?

AFTER supper they again discussed Paul's latest whim, as his father called it. Nothing came of it, beyond showing Paul that his father greatly disliked the whole business—that he was going to drop his degree, that he meant to adopt a commercial career, that he would not wait a few years longer before marrying. While he sat talking with his father about all this, and Lillian now and again put in a word, Paul seized upon an idea which had just flashed on him: he would go and see Harald Tangen and ask him to be umpire.

BUT next day, as he walked up Akers gate, he heartily disliked doing so; it was only a kind of obstinacy that drove him on, as he rehearsed to himself the brief statement of his affairs which he had worked out during the night and morning and taken up again and again: I am on intimate terms with a girl who is employed in a shop here; she has no home, no family, and no friends. It has been understood all along that we are to be married as soon as I am in a position to keep her. My parents have accepted her as my fiancée, but I am not sure they haven't hoped it may be broken off before I get so far as being able to marry her. Now I have had an offer to go into partnership with a friend who has a business at Trondhjem. If I accept it I can perhaps offer my fiancée a home in the course of a year or so. But my father greatly dislikes my giving up my studies. On the other hand I know how it will turn out if we continue our present life here in town. And I have begun to think—quite apart from conventional prejudices—that there may be a good deal in the general view that loose connections of this kind are unfortunate. Therefore I should like to ask you what you would advise me to do—?

All the same he felt fearfully nervous when the gate swung to behind him and he found himself in the little garden behind the choir of the church. The long, greyish building, where he knew the Catholic priests lived, had a sort of retiring mysterious look. So he pulled himself together, went up the short flight of stone steps, and entered a rather gloomy hall, which had doors on both sides. And on the right-hand door he discovered a square of china plate with black letters: Harald Olav Tangen, priest.

The interval between his ringing and the appearance of someone from the darkness within was long enough to give him time to hope there was nobody at home. Then the door was opened; it was Harald Tangen himself, and all at once Paul thought the situation was impossible and at the same time extremely exciting. The long black garment Harald Tangen wore, buttoned down to his feet, made him look as if he belonged to an entirely different world from Paul's.

"I don't know if you can spare the time—could I talk to you a moment?"

"With pleasure." The priest showed the way through a dark passage into a fairly spacious room which smelt strongly of tobacco. On the whole it struck Paul as a homelike room—a study of the kind he was used to seeing, with bookshelves from floor to ceiling and a big writing table near one of the windows. But there was a *prie-dieu* in one corner, and crucifixes and pictures of saints all round the walls.

"Is there anything I can do for you, Herr Selmer?"

"I was wondering if you could advise me about a matter—although I'm not a Catholic and don't think of being one either—"

"I shall be glad to see what I can do."

There was something about the other man—not in the least unsympathetic, but so unlike anything Paul had seen of clerical sympathy—a kind of reserved interest which was more like the manner of a doctor. Instinctively Paul made an effort to speak in a dry and even tone:

"You see, I'm bound to come to a decision which will probably determine my whole future. The thing is that I'm on intimate terms with a girl—" and then he went through the whole story he had got up.

Harald Tangen sat listening with a calm, attentive expression in his grey eyes. Paul finished his story and began to wonder what he had left out. Then the priest asked:

"But what makes you come to me about this? You know, don't you, that I can't give another opinion than a priest of your own communion? That you are doing wrong in cohabiting with your fiancée?"

"So you think that too? But then I assume you can anyhow give me a real, pertinent reason for it?"

"Pertinent? What do you mean by that?"

"Well, for instance, my uncle, Pastor Dverberg—I believe you know him. Or my sister's fiancé, Pastor Garnaas. It would never occur to me to ask them—"

"No, of course I understand that. You don't want to have it treated from a family point of view—"

Paul shuddered. It occurred to him that Halstein and Tua had certainly exchanged opinions about him and Lucy. Or what about Uncle Abraham—. He had memories of visits to the parsonage, when he had to sleep on the sofa in the morning room—Uncle Abraham wandering backwards and forwards between the bedroom and the dining room as he undressed and discussing people and what they thought with the aunt, his braces dangling down his back.

"It wasn't that I was thinking of, as it happens. But of course there's that too. No doubt they'd think I was the black sheep of the family—though to be sure she comes from another fold. But it wasn't that in the first place. Oh no—I'm quite aware they would think our relations were sinful. Because it seems the mass of people still think it's immoral to live in that way. But what I'm wondering is, if it goes on the way it seems to be going, getting more and more difficult for young people to marry or to afford to have children before they're well on in years—so that the community gets accustomed to us young people making marriages of conscience or entering into un-Platonic engagements and is no longer scandalized about it—don't you think the clergy will follow suit and discover that we're not such arrant sinners after all? Since what we're doing is no longer in conflict with civil morality? You see, I remember, when I went to school, it was such a terrible thing to be a freethinker or the child of a freethinker—now even the parsons, the young ones at any rate, are quite ready to admit that freethinkers may be decent folk. And at that time too they thought divorce was frightfully ungodly. Uncle Abraham wouldn't hear of divorced people being married in church. But when his daughter, my cousin Laura, married again, he allowed his curate to perform the ceremony. And now he admits that it may occasionally be justified, and Halstein, my future brother-in-law, says it is justified in many cases."

"I see," said the priest. "What you want to know is, whether the Catholic Church condemns irregular connections of the kind you tell me about on an immutable principle?"

"Precisely. No more than a year ago I couldn't see any reason why Lucy and I should give up more than we jolly well had to—of course we knew it would be many years before we could have a home and a child, but what was the use of imposing unnecessary renunciations on ourselves? But now I at any rate have come to feel that perhaps there may be reasons—which exist independently of whether current morality at a given time may cry shame on corrupted youth, or whether it may treat young people in an easy-going fashion, saying they can't be expected to exercise self-denial until they're old and grey and can afford to marry—"

"I see. And you believe you've discovered that from your own experience?" Harald Tangen smiled slightly. "Well, for us it is enough that God has instituted marriage between a man and a woman. And God's ordinance cannot be annulled because men have done all in their power to make it difficult to live according to it. And all attempts to improve upon His institution we call sinful. But at the same time we believe that God's order is that which best serves human happiness, and if He forbids us to replace it by another, it is because such human substitutes only serve to make men unhappy. For that matter it makes no difference whether what you call civil morality cries down these 'private marriages' today and applauds them tomorrow. Perhaps the sinners get off more lightly in the former case—when others are so ready to harm them, perhaps they escape the discovery that they are harming one another or themselves."

"Yes, but that's precisely what I don't understand—why is it that we harm each other? For I see that we do so—although we are terribly fond of each other. Not merely in a purely physical way, for we are that too, though you probably think it wrong, but still there are so many things which make it easy for us to misunderstand one another, and extraneous things may come between us—I don't know how to express it—but deeper down than all such trumpery and trifles it seems that our natures belong together. It sounds so funny to say so, but it's as if Nature had picked us out because we supplement each other—perhaps it's a crossing she wants to bring about—"

Again Harald Tangen smiled slightly:

"Well, in that case it's comparatively easy to advise you. I think there is no doubt you ought to accept your friend's offer, go to Trondhjem and make yourself independent, so that you may marry the girl as soon as possible. When you yourself see that the future happiness of both of you depends on your regularizing your relations. You know perhaps what we Christians believe—that a catastrophe occurred in remote antiquity, the Fall of Man, and that it is our very nature that has got a kink—we call it original sin—so that it is thrown into confusion all through. What renders our natural desires and passions potentially sinful is precisely this, that they are in disorder, have been thrown higgledy-piggledy—nothing else. And that is why God took upon Himself our nature—to re-establish order in it."

"I understand. You teach that God created Adam and Eve with such a nature that they felt they belonged to each other—without complications. And the Fall is to blame if it looks as though the only natural morality for their descendants since that time has been what my mother's lady friends call double morality."

The priest laughed. "Yes, I dare say you can express it in that way too. But then perhaps you know another thing we teach is that grace does not change nature, it makes it perfect again. And that marriage itself is a means of grace—a sacrament, as we say."

"Yes, for those who are married in the Catholic Church?"

"Oh no; for all, Christian and heathen, who come together in order to live in a real marriage—that is, not merely in one which they themselves may consider agreeable or endurable or harmonious. The Church's doctrine is precisely that it is not the priest who imparts the sacrament of marriage; that is done by bride and bridegroom in accepting a common responsibility towards all that they understand by eternal and divine. Thus in marriage even the heathens have something which leads their nature back to the nobility with which man was created by God. Do you remember the saga of Gisle Surssön?—if you remember the description of Gisle and his wife, Aud was her name, then you'll see what I mean.† Well, for us Christians you will understand that marriage is also included under the general rebirth of the personality which is given us in Our Lord Christ."

Paul nodded: "But then why are these outward ceremonies required—a wedding in church or a visit to the civil authorities?"

"They would not be required, of course, if the result of original sin had not been such that we human beings cannot trust our own nature and the world has become a confusion in which people rush hither and thither in a kind of panic in order to secure for themselves all the things they are afraid of missing—instead of first seeking the kingdom of God and His righteousness. If people were only a little braver in that way, a great deal of external parade might be simplified immediately. You don't know, Selmer, what a help it may be to yourself one day, to have been married in the presence of representatives of all whom it may concern—besides a great many whom at any rate it does not particularly concern at that moment. Nobody can tell in advance whether a day may not come when everything within you tempts you to prove false—nay, even if you pray God to help you, you will not think He does so unless He helps you in the way you yourself desire. Then it is at any rate a help to feel yourself bound by your own word and honor. We humans are no better than that. And your sweetheart—you know as well as I do that the girl might just as easily have fallen into an—un-Platonic engagement, as you call it—with some fellow who got tired of her in the course of three weeks or three years and had no hesitation in telling her so and sending her away."

Suddenly Paul felt his nerves give way:

"She—she has been through a good deal, poor girl—" He turned his face away, pulled out his handkerchief, fussed about to keep from crying. He was immensely grateful to Harald Tangen for not touching him with any word or act of consolation. So the attack passed off pretty quickly; he blew his nose and asked:

"But if *that* is the Catholic Church's view of marriage, I don't understand—that is, I believe I do understand perhaps—what is the meaning of the celibacy of the clergy and monasticism and all that?"

† Translator's Note: This was translated by Sir George Dasent, *The Saga of Gisli the Outlaw* (London, 1928).

"Well, that would take rather long to explain." The priest smiled. "But for one thing, the Church is a church militant—she must incessantly win back souls within her own gates and go out to win souls outside—and each new human being that is born must be saved separately. Now when you yourself are married you will discover how much it takes of a man's time and attention and force to be all you ought to be to your own wife and child. And you know, we priests are not tempted to expect God to make it easy for those He loves—not here on earth. We read of the martyrs in our breviary every other day almost. Why, didn't you have old Throndsen to teach you religion at school?—he was a good and pious man, poor soul, but he would try to make us believe that virtue was rewarded in kind here on earth, and that God constantly gave the wicked fairly exemplary punishment on this side of the grave. I was near turning atheist for a while, because Pastor Throndsen tried to make out that God was to such an extent harmless that even a child could see it was nonsense—

"I am reminded of a case which comes within my own knowledge. A man who was about the same age as yourself, when his wife became insane after her first childbirth. She has now been ten years in an asylum—perhaps she will get well, perhaps not. And now he's in love with another woman. I at any rate cannot understand how a priest can bring himself to answer such a man with the words of Jesus about divorce and remarriage—and then perhaps go home, sit down at the tea table opposite his wife, take a look at the baby in its cradle. It seems to me that would stifle him—if he was a man at all.

"But we are forced to do that every day—preach patience, renunciation, resistance. And it will never be otherwise, however much they may turn social relations topsy-turvy—never so long as human nature remains the same—

"Well, you mustn't believe we don't think that some people are designed to live happily together, husband, wife and child. And it is obviously your call—to take Fröken Evensen to your wife, as a good gift from God, sent to you with plainly marked name and address. Even if profane fingers have touched it before it reached you."

Paul got up:

"Well, I owe you many thanks, Father Tangen. It was good of you to talk to me like this. So you think I ought to break off at once, go to Trondhjem and work like a horse so that Lucy can follow me as soon as possible. However much my parents may dislike my not taking my degree?"

The priest had also risen; they were standing by the door:

"Oh?—Do your parents dislike it so much?"

"Yes—you see, I was supposed to be going up for it this term."

"But if it's only a question of a couple of months—can't you join your friend's firm on the first of January? I should have thought that would suit very well?"

"If I pass well"—Paul turned very red—"and it may be I should pass very well; it depends on the papers of course, whether I get the things I am best up in—then you can guess it will be difficult for me to break off—decline my father's offer of a stay abroad to continue my studies—"

"What about your mother—what does she say to it? For she was your guardian while you were growing up, I've heard?"

"I haven't spoken to mother yet."

"If your mother asks you to go through with your examination, it seems to me you ought to defer to her wishes. But let it be clearly understood beforehand, that afterwards your first thought must be of what you owe to your fiancée and to yourself. And make up your mind not to abuse your sweetheart's devotion to you so long as you two are still obliged to stay in the same town."

Paul smiled in spite of himself. At which a fleeting smile passed over the other's face, but his eyes remained very serious as he said:

"Remember that the passions of the emotional nature are in themselves neither morally good nor evil—they only become so through their relation to reason and will. And now you of your own accord have become aware of this—perhaps more than Fröken Evensen."

"Arnesen," corrected Paul.

"Arnesen, I beg pardon. So now the responsibility rests on you."

"That is so." Paul was looking at the enlarged photograph which hung on the wall just over the priest's head. It was taken on a moor surrounded by forests; Captain Tangen with two of his sons, Harald and, no doubt, Wilhelm, sitting by an elk they had shot—Harald with his gun in his hand and an elkhound on his knee looked very young and smart.

"I suppose you don't often have any shooting now?"

"Never." Harald Tangen laughed gaily.

"I should think that must be hard. Four years ago father and some friends of his had a bear hunt up in Valdres, and I was to have been one. The day before I fell and broke my right arm. I thought I should have died of vexation as I lay in plaster of Paris—"

"Yes, that would be enough to try the virtue of a saint. No, but I have scarcely time to miss it even."

"Well, goodbye and thanks. Do you know what, Father Tangen—I could almost wish I was a Catholic." Now he had said it—he felt as if he had exposed his broadside so that Harald Tangen could give him a salvo. He waited, with no feeling of ill will, for the other to go ahead with his proselytizing.

Father Tangen looked at him with the faintest of smiles. Then he said very guardedly:

"You know I can lend you some books, if you care to have them. Are you at all familiar with the New Testament?"

"Oh no, not particularly. Then it's true that Catholics are not forbidden to read the Bible?"

"Catholics are under an obligation to use authorized translations. There is a Norwegian one, but it's in rather an awkward size. But you read English, don't you?" He took a little black book from the shelf. "You're welcome to keep that. Then you can write to me if you'd like me to send you books. But the main thing is that you yourself pray earnestly for faith—otherwise nothing will come of it. I don't know whether you have any regular habits of that sort?"

Paul shook his head: "I have never been used to pray."

"But at any rate you must have been in the habit of saying your evening prayer—when you were a child?"

Paul gave a little laugh:

"Mother taught me to say, when I got into bed at night:

Fight and, if it must be, die
For all that you hold dear;
Then you'll not find life so hard,
And death you need not fear.

I repeated that to Wilfrid and Josef one day we were walking home together—the Gotaas's boys, you know. And Wilfrid said: 'Ay, that's a nice prayer. But who were you praying to?'"

"Well, but surely you know the Lord's Prayer at least?" asked the priest, laughing.

"I hope so, anyhow. I used to hear it at prayers all the years I went to school—every blessed morning."

"Well, that's something to begin with. But look here, Selmer, what is there really to stop your marrying at once? It need not make any outward change in your relations; your wife could stay on at the shop for the present. And then there would no longer be anything ambiguous in your helping her with a monthly allowance."

Paul turned red. He thought of his father's hint:

"No, that wouldn't work very well." He himself didn't like the idea either—of having a wife serving in a flower shop in Christiania when he started as Henrik's partner. "Amongst other things it would put her in an unpleasant position with my family—

"Do you know, by the way, last year when we believed there might be war—I had an idea of asking you if you would marry us before I went to the front."

"That I certainly could not have done." Now he laughed right out and gaily. "Since neither of you belongs to the Church.—Nor is it quite so easily managed among us."

"I always thought you priests could do pretty well as you chose in such things," said Paul.

"O Dio mio!—Well, as I said, if you will write, I shall be glad to do all I can for you. And you know, you have my best wishes."

OUTSIDE it was already dark in the little garden round the church, but the street was lighted by the shop windows—and the sky above was high and dark blue. Paul went up to the little side door in the tower and entered.

The body of the church was filled with shadows, and now again it seemed vast and lofty, but homelike all the same—all the mass of things they had on the altars and round about showed but vaguely and gave the impression that the church was a place where people lived day by day. A faint light from a gas lamp outside fell through the painted windows and made the deep red, blue and green glass glow with full and beautiful tints. And high up in the darkness of the choir hung a little red lamp with a flickering flame within it.

There was no one in the church. Paul walked softly up the centre of the nave and entered a pew. With some hesitation he put down his hat, pulled up his trousers and knelt down. He hid his face in his hands—gloves were in the way, so he pulled them off, put them in his hat and bowed his head again in his hands.

How does one address God? I've never tried to talk to him before. Our Father which art in heaven—so one says *thou* to God. He gave a little embarrassed laugh behind his hands. It was so odd too, his kneeling here in Saint Olav's church to pray to God.

He tried to think why it was exactly that he had landed here, peeped up and fixed his eyes on the little flickering red flame in the darkness. And all at once it dawned on him, so that he felt shaken all over—if what that little red lamp hung there to proclaim was true—why then, why then!

If *that* was the truth about Jesus—of whom he had heard so much talk, humanly discursive, humanly cocksure talk, that he was utterly sick of the very name—if that was the truth, that here He was actually present in a mysterious way, confined in something material, a sacrament—and somewhere in the lower depths of his being Paul had a sudden knowledge of what a sacrament was, though he understood nothing of it. If it was true that He was here, present in this way and at the same time on thousands and thousands of other altars—then He must also be present in another way everywhere and at all times, an eye that embraced the beginning of the spheres in space and the interior of the atoms and the secret thoughts of men in one single glance without distinction between past and present, great and small—everything was merely His thought and everything contemporary and everything equally clear and dear.

He felt the skin of his face grow cold and stiff, while his heart was like a burning heat in his breast. If this was the truth, then the whole of life was inconceivably more wonderful and dangerous and rich, so unspeakably more serious and valuable than he had ever dreamt. He had a glimpse of paths which led out into a darkness beyond his imagining, and forward into a light that he scarcely dared to divine.

It is simply too good to be true.

He crouched still lower with his face buried in his hands.

It was as though he saw—concentrated in one point—that this was not impossible of belief. Truth might be just as fantastic as this. But he felt himself shrink up with dread at the thought that this truth was to enter into his life, as though facing a terrible effort. I am the Truth, Jesus had said. It had never occurred to him before to consider at all closely what those words really implied. Though he had had a vague presentiment that the Truth was something he did not know, and that all he knew was a kind of unreality. Although no doubt it was reality in a way; all that was lacking was the explanation of what this reality might be good for. Just as an unlighted lamp is real, but a savage who has never seen it burning cannot guess what its use may be.

—So I suppose I've got to try and find out how one sets about praying—

He looked up towards the choir—again he felt a kind of shiver: is He there really, shut up in a little box in the dark? Voluntarily—He at whose will worlds come into being and are dissolved—? Waiting, waiting, for the half-dozen people who come here every morning, for the congregation that fills the church on Sundays, for the solitary creature who turns in from the street to speak with the One and Only—

God's patience—the thought struck Paul as the central point of all this—that what we call patience is but a little image of something inconceivable—God's patience—

"Jesus, Jesus, be patient with me too—"

He would have to attempt the Lord's Prayer anyhow—try if he knew it.

Paul straightened himself on his knees. Before he was conscious of it he had made the sign of the cross, as he had seen the Gotaases do at table.

"Our Father, which art in heaven, hallowed be thy Name. Thy kingdom come. Thy will be done on earth, as it is in heaven"—when he had finished he had not thought of a single one of the words he uttered, merely felt happy to find he still knew it all by heart.

But then—? To pray *for* something seemed so cheap. The very moment he had begun to think of it as a possibility that men might achieve contact with God, he could not very well come forward with requests.

He remained kneeling against the back of the bench in front, with his arms crossed on his breast, feeling nothing but the darkness and the stillness and the little red light high up which seemed saturated with something real and good.

Somebody was coming—he caught a glimpse of a lady with two children, boy and girl. They went a little higher up the nave and knelt down, all three in a row. But presently the electric light burst out up in the choir and somewhere down by the door, and Harald Tangen entered by a side door near the altar—he wore a short white surplice with lace on it over his long black cassock. He knelt for a few moments before the high altar, then put on his head that odd black affair that Paul had already noticed as part of the Catholic priests' equipment. The priest came down the centre of the nave and entered something which Paul guessed to be a confessional. The little boy came out of the pew, bobbed to the altar and disappeared behind the curtain of the confessional.

Paul thought perhaps he had better go now, but he hadn't the energy. The boy's catalogue of sins seemed pretty short; he came back, and his sister tripped across. After a while it was the mother's turn.

Then three nuns appeared in the lighted choir. They carried vases in their hands, and they curtsied and turned about and went backwards and forwards up there. Paul observed their movements with attention, trying to make out what the ceremony might be intended to express: probably it was in some way symbolical of confession. Till one of the nuns suddenly produced a big feather brush and started dusting the paper flowers in a vase. Oh, that was it; they were charwomen. He felt kind of foolish. Presently he went out.

PAUL walked downtown and along the quays under Akershus. The water was black, with long shimmering streaks of light—up on the fortress rock the gleam of the arc lamps fell upon yellowed foliage below the grey stone walls of the old bastions. And it was wonderfully mild and fine this evening.

He had arranged to meet the Aasers in the Students' Union—a Swedish explorer was giving a lecture. Sigurd and Martha had been at home with his people this summer, and they had left their child there on returning to town in the autumn. And now Martha was reading again for all she was worth. Paul did not find the lecture fearfully interesting; he went home about twelve, with the idea of reading a couple of hours.

But on opening his door the first he saw was Lucy—she was sitting in front of the stove, had made a fire and opened the lower door. The light fell on her bare feet in the red slippers trimmed with swan's down. She was sunk in the biggest basket chair, in her thin, pale blue nightdress with a yellow wrap bordered with swan's down round her—she called it a négligée. She had taken down her fair hair and combed it out.

She turned her face towards him—had evidently been half asleep. In the light from the stove he could faintly see her little smile, apologetic and beseeching:

"I met Hans this afternoon; he said you were going to the Union, so you wouldn't be going out to Linlökka tonight. So I came up here. You—you aren't angry with me for coming—?'

"No!—are you crazy?" Paul went up behind her chair, took her face in both hands, turned it back and kissed her on the eyes. "How can you think of such a thing—?"

So much for that resolution—but after all it sometimes takes two to resolve on a thing.

Chapter Fifteen

He went out to Linlökka next day by an afternoon train. His mother was standing at the garden gate in her long white shawl. "I saw you coming—" she put her arm through his and smiled up at him—"that's nice. Will you have something to eat?" She was alone today, she explained, as they went up to the house arm in arm. Sigmund had gone into town yesterday, and he and Hans were going up to Fossbakke for the night; Tua and Halstein were there. "So it's only you and I, Paulinus."

No, thanks, he and Lucy had dined at Fröken Johnsen's, but then Jonsa was to help Lucy cut out some clothes, "so I was not wanted, you can guess."

Later in the afternoon Paul was sitting at the piano—he had been looking through the music and picked out various things he used to play, trying them over here and there. Julie was on her knees by the bookcase in the corner, arranging some sets of magazines she was going to take in to be bound.

"You know, Paul—I shall have to buy a grand—for Sigmund. Of course he could go and practice at Erik and Lillian's. But the end of that would be that he too—and I should like to keep *one* of you with me a little while longer." She remained on her knees, with her hands hanging down, without looking at him. "But what I was going to say—if you care to have it, I'll be glad to give you my piano. It's quite a good instrument—and as you only play to amuse yourself. If you think it'll be a pleasure to you, you can have it in Munkedamsvei."

"Thanks, mother—you can guess I'll be awfully glad to have it. But it's hardly worthwhile sending it to Munkedamsvei. For I don't believe I shall be living there much longer."

"Good gracious—are you thinking of moving again? What does that mean?"

"It means"—Paul swung round on the piano stool—"that in all likelihood I shall be moving to Trondhjem no later than this autumn."

"What are you doing?"

"Henrik has proposed to take me into his firm. He has a business which is doing uncommonly well—builders' merchant. And I'm all for accepting his offer."

"I never heard anything like it. Well, you youngsters take some things into your heads. And what about your work, Paul?"

"Well, it's going to be selling slates and stoves and wallpapers and odds and ends of that sort. If you insist, of course I shall go up for my degree, but after that it's—Trondhjem and business for me!"

"I believe you've gone a little crazy, boy!"

"Not a bit, mother. I'm thinking of making a future for myself, for me and Lucy. Can't you guess that, with your cleverness—this way of going on is simply ridiculous, she and I living like this in Christiania—when we get as far as being able to marry, we shan't have anything but warmed up hash to live on."

Julie had risen to her feet and came over to him:

"Well, Paul—this seems to me sheer giddy madness!"

"No! In the first place you must see that there's a good deal to be said for Lucy and I starting a new page together—somewhere away from Christiania."

"Yes, but perhaps you can get a post, at the Bergen Museum, for instance, or at the College in Trondhjem—"

"Yes, perhaps, perhaps—nobody knows what or when it will be. As you yourself pointed out to me, mother—I've made myself responsible for Lucy. And I can tell you it's no light matter to have the responsibility for her, without being able to marry her. These long engagements are the very devil—"

"Ugh, Paul—I'm not saying anything but that Lucy is a really sweet girl—"

"Look here, mother," Paul interrupted. "Can't I be spared hearing that over again—from you at least? You've said it before, and father says it, and Lillian and Tua, and Halstein would say it if anybody gave him a chance, and the devil and his grandmother and all his great-aunts say it too presumably. Lucy is a really sweet girl, I like Lucy so much—but—. *I love*

Lucy, God damn it, and curse me if I can stand it any longer hearing you all bleat: Lucy *is* such a sweet girl, we like Lucy so much—*but*!"

"Well, but, my dear boy—that's just it: Lucy is a sweet girl, but there are buts—lots of them! There really isn't one of us who doesn't want you to marry Lucy. But that for her sake you should come to a decision which will be of vital importance to your whole future—upon my word, that's quite another thing!"

"No, look here, mother—that's *too* good!"

"Yes, you're laughing! Laugh away! You're mortally fond of Lucy now and Lucy of you. It would never occur to me to indulge in moral reflections about your seducing Lucy or Lucy seducing you—I assume that really neither of you knows which took the initiative—you're young and healthy and good-looking, and it's impossible nowadays for anyone to hang around and shepherd you, see when and where you meet—and night and wine and love-making are dangerous toys to meddle with, as Wessel remarked long ago. Why on earth shouldn't you marry the girl, since that's what you've been talking of all the time. It would be treating Lucy too abominably to disappoint her expectations in that way. But it's when you two have to be together every day, Paul, when there's no longer the slightest excitement or risk about it, on the contrary, you'll be forced to hang together even when you're not in the mood and have no humour for anything but being in a bad humour—then it is that the difficulties begin: the very thing that shows up different levels of culture most of all is the way in which one bears one's bad humour. One forgets impressions of this sort in the early days, each time one's humour swings back to fine weather, that's true; but our tempers all swing up and down—and at each period of depression the thought sinks deeper into one that life with the other jars more and more, as soon as a cloud hides the sun. That is how most marriages come to grief. I'm really not saying this to cool down your sanguine expectations as a prospective husband, Paul. If it turns out well with you and Lucy, you will have great cause to congratulate yourselves, and so shall I, I assure you. But if after all you don't get on, then you may be sure it's no marriage—"

Paul burst out laughing. Julie stopped short, staring at him. Next moment she gave him a sound box on the ear—

Her son caught his breath an instant—then he laughed louder than before. Julie had turned crimson in the face:

"You understand very well what I meant, so you needn't laugh at me in that impudent way. Stop it now, before you get hysterics, I can't stand hysterical menfolk—I don't mind begging your pardon for forgetting myself, but you know what I mean. In our day an imprudent marriage doesn't mean penal servitude for life—though you're so young and so stupid that maybe you think it ought to. And that is why I think you must consider long and carefully before you give up all your plans for a career which you yourself looked upon as capable of giving a meaning and purpose to your life—apart from the question whether your marriage with the first girl you have fallen in love with may turn out a success or a fiasco."

"Listen to me, mother." Paul was now calm again. "All that you've just been saying—you can't suppose it's anything new to me. I wasn't born yesterday either. But it shall turn out well with me and Lucy. It's not only that if I failed to fulfill all that I myself have taught her to expect of me—the consequences for Lucy would probably be even worse than you are capable of imagining. But there is also the future, after we are married—if I didn't manage to treat her decently in our married life. You don't suppose *I* believe it's going to be kisses and petting and smiles and sunshine all the time, do you? Oh no, mother—but I know that I can depend upon Lucy in such a way that we can stick together just when things get difficult. She is exactly the tough and patient sort that can bear the pressure of reverses without having the buoyancy squeezed out of her—when she and I are together, be it noted—but none of you can know how sweet and cheerful she is, when we are alone.—Left to herself, betrayed once more by a man in whom she trusted—well, you can try to imagine how you'd like it, if you had her going about Christiania as my divorced wife.

"Besides, mother—I don't mean to disparage her the least little bit, when I say I have the most unbounded trust in Lucy, so long as I have her and she has me. But if I left her to herself again, I don't care to think of the eventualities that might ensue—"

Julie Selmer had stood quite still, looking at her son as he spoke. Now she turned her head away—sighing. Then she said in quite another tone:

"Fancy if I had guessed it, Paul—that you had thoughts of being a business man! Then I would have proposed your coming into my business—after your previous examination, for instance. But it never occurred to me—that any of you would think of anything but an academic career."

Paul refrained from answering. But the prospect of a business training under the firm hand of his mother did not appear at all alluring.

"You see, mother," he said, very simply and deliberately; "for the same reasons, which I see you are also aware of, I think it would be just as well for us if Lucy and I together were forced to shake down in surroundings which were equally new to both of us. In a strange town. Where the people I shall have to do with, most of them anyhow, will be our own contemporaries."

Again Julie sighed. The maid came to the door at that moment: supper was ready.

"Have you talked to your father?" asked Julie as they went in. "What does he say to this?"

"Oh, you can imagine he was a good deal less than enthusiastic. No, he didn't like it. And Lillian didn't either," Paul added, innocently.

When during the meal his mother asked for further particulars—what were the proposed terms of partnership between him and Henrik—Paul guessed that in principle she had already given in. No doubt her real resistance had been abandoned in that freakish box on the ears.

A LITTLE later in the evening she was actually taken up with his new plan—life and soul. There was something in her boy's burning his boats in this fashion which appealed to her at heart, Paul could see that.

She discussed the financial side of the question—explained to him with a little smile various things which her son was not very clear about; once, when he showed himself quick to catch her meaning, she praised him, nodding and raising her liqueur glass.

The money of his which was invested in her business could be paid out in the course of six months—some of it before, of course, if necessary. But she proposed that they should go together and see his uncle Paul: "I know he's left you a good deal more than the other children—for the sake of your name." For some arrangement ought to be made which would enable Paul to put at any rate not less than a third of the capital into the firm.

"By the way, I'll do it this evening—write to the mercantile enquiry agencies I generally employ—"

"Mercantile enquiry agencies?"

Julie laughed softly:

"Well—? You look at me exactly as if I'd said something improper! Oh, my child, you have a lot of things to learn." She had risen; stroked his hair as she passed: "I believe I like you rather, Paulinus!"

BUT still, as he walked up from the Eastern Station that night and dropped his mother's two letters into a post box on the way, he could not free himself from a feeling that mercantile enquiry agencies must have something scandalous about them.

HOWEVER, the information Julie Selmer received about Henrik Alster and his business was unusually favourable—she explained it to her son, who as yet was quite incapable of judging the value of an agency report. He was at his mother's office every day at this time, and when Henrik returned from Sweden they held all their conferences there. Henrik Alster was obviously very pleased that Fru Selmer took a hand in them—he had come to have a great respect for her business capability.

She had also succeeded in interesting old Paul Selmer, the architect, in his nephew's plans, partly by playing off Lillian in some wily fashion—her eldest brother-in-law persisted obstinately in regarding Erik Selmer's second marriage as a kind of faux pas. And Lucy's blond and somewhat massive beauty had entirely captivated him, when by a happy inspiration Paul dragged her one day to call on his uncle.

Paul himself almost felt giddy at the rapidity with which his sudden idea was being realized.

There was something funny in it—his mother taking up the affair so warmly; and he guessed that to her it meant a sort of triumph over his father and Lillian. After her having tried all these years to soften his bitterness towards those two, and finally going out of her way to reconcile him to them; having succeeded in that, she had now turned jealous. But no doubt the reason was that his brother and sister had in a way taken up their abode under his father's roof.

THE business was as good as settled before Paul mentioned a word of it to Lucy. Then he rang her up at the shop one day and arranged to dine together in town.

She sat and listened to him, speechless, with wide eyes that darkened strangely, as Paul put the matter before her with glowing eagerness.

"Well, my girl—what do you say—aren't you glad?"

"Glad," she repeated tonelessly. "Well, but—that means you're going away?"

"M-yes—that's not to be denied. But let's hope it won't be so long before I can come and fetch you."

Lucy crumbled her bread on the cloth. Her head was sunk between her shoulders.

"Now you're to be a brave girl, Lucy—at any rate you must save your tears for an affecting farewell at the station! Why, my dear—we've had a perfectly wonderful time for nearly a year—more than a year, we've been engaged fifteen months now—but you know what I mean. It's uneconomical in the long run to live as we're doing—

"Oh, I'm not talking about money," he said with a laugh on noticing her expression. "What I mean is that we can never afford to be the least bit thrifty with ourselves—or extravagant, if you like. Do you know what I long for sometimes? To put it plainly—I long for you and me to be able to go into our own bedroom and undress without any fuss, yawning one against the other as wide as this"—he showed her with his thumb and forefinger—"and give each other a very sleepy, respectable good night kiss—slee-eep well—eh?"

"Ugh—why must you say such—nasty things—"

"No but, Lucy—is that nasty? That I think it would be fun to see you in the morning curling up again under the bedclothes, while I have to go to the office—and to think, as I go off cold and peevish, that there's somebody who can take it easy and sleep on and have her breakfast in bed!"

Lucy looked up with a little shy, poverty-stricken smile.

"*Skaal*, Lucy!" He squeezed her hand under the table. "And then you need no longer be afraid of that, you know! And I'll try not to curse too much when the baby takes it into its head to howl all night long. Heavens, Lucy, don't look so tragic!"

"It isn't worthwhile your coming in this evening," he said as they left the restaurant; "I don't know what time we shall have finished at mother's—and very likely Henrik will come back with me afterwards, so—I say, mother's going to give us her piano—"

"No, then I won't come tonight," said Lucy, hanging her head.

NOT to a soul had he said anything about his visit to Harald Tangen and all that. But the memory of it was like an undercurrent in his mind, as with eager happiness he saw his affairs taking shape and moving towards a final decision.

So the last Sunday he was in town he went off to hear High Mass in Saint Olav's church.

There was still a fine mist left of the frost fog, but it was vanishing before the morning sun as Paul came into Akers gate. The sky was mild, pale blue above roof and church tower, which flung out the clang of bells.

There were still a few brown leaves on the trees, and outside the Cathedral School some children were searching for chestnuts among the fallen leaves. The paving stones rang hard and frostily under folks' feet in the Sunday stillness of the street.

The few people who were out looked as if they were all going to church. And Paul himself felt a little creeping at the stomach—it was the first time in his life he had been out as a churchgoer entirely of his own free will. The bells of Trinity Church were ringing, from the tower of Saint Olav's came a clanging peal. Seen thus from below the church looked really well on the grey stone base of its terrace, with the broad flight of steps and the reddish brown west tower, whose slender spire pointed up into the blue air. Today the main door under the tower was wide open.

A flock of black and white nuns came round the corner and went in as Paul ascended the steps. He wondered if he would meet anyone he knew at church—didn't know whether he wished to or not.

Today the church was fairly full—people were kneeling or sitting on the benches. Again the aspect of the interior was entirely changed, and a mass of candles were burning on the altar up in the choir. Paul found a place about halfway up and sat holding his hat on his knee, till he discovered that the other men had placed theirs on the floor by the kneeling rail; so he did the same. Again the stillness affected him as something good—nobody here talked or whispered as they waited for the priest to appear. An elderly man who was kneeling at his side prayed so that his lips moved.

Then the organ pealed—and some little choristers and a priest in a green vestment appeared by the altar. The priest came down through the church sprinkling water with a gadget of some sort, while the choristers held up the skirts of his vestment. The congregation sang—this was dead contrary to what he had always been told. The man who knelt at his side pushed towards him one of those little black books that the Catholics seemed so well provided with—pointing to the place. So that was what they were singing—

Asperges me, Domine, hyssopo, et mundabor. Lavabis me, et super nivem dealbabor. The Norwegian text was in the next column: Sprinkle me, O Lord, with hyssop (i.e., with the blood of Christ)—ah, that was what it meant—and I shall be clean. Wash me, and I shall be whiter than snow. Have mercy on me, O God, according to thy great mercy. Glory be to the Father, and to the Son, and to the Holy Ghost. As it was in the beginning, is now and ever shall be. Amen.

Paul tried to recall how the opening prayer went that they used in the Protestant churches—for this evidently corresponded to it. It was something about "I have come into thy holy house to hear, open thou my heart—" Perhaps it was the form and voice of Megaard, the parish clerk, that had always made him imagine God in the likeness of a schoolmaster, every time that prayer was said in Fossbakke church. And here the words too seemed more like a direct address from the creature to his Creator. And that symbol of the sprinkling was really very eloquent.

He had hoped it would be Harald Tangen who officiated, but it was another—a much older man.

Paul tried to remember what he had read in Tilmann Pesch about the Mass, and to follow; but it was not easy. Only when they sang the Gloria was he able to catch on—the text of the Gloria was in the book his neighbor had handed him.

Now it was the priest who stood before the altar and sang—and his obliging neighbor placed another book before him, pointed, and withdrew again into his own devotions. They had come to the texts for the day, Paul could see, and he read them in the book—they were in Latin and French. Involuntarily Paul translated to himself as he read:

Epître de l'Apôtre S. Paul aux Ephésiens, 4:1-16: "My brethren, I who am in fetters for the Lord's sake, beseech you to live in a manner worthy of the vocation wherewith ye are called, in all lowliness, meekness and long-suffering, forbearing one another with *charité*"—that's midway between love and compassion, no, both at the same time—"with charité, endeavouring to keep the unity of one and the same spirit in the bond of peace. There is one body, and one spirit, even as also ye are called to one and the same hope. There is one Lord, one faith and one baptism, one God and Father of all men, who is above all, who penetrates all and resides in us all. Blessed be he throughout all ages. Amen."

Graduel. Ps. 33:12. "Blessed is the nation whose God is the Lord! Blessed is the nation that has chosen him for its inheritance! By the word of the Lord were the heavens made, and the host of heaven by the breath of his mouth. Alleluiah, Alleluiah. Lord, hear my prayer, let my cry come before you"—so in French one says *vous* to God—

Evangile selon S. Matthieu. 22:34: "At this time the Pharisees came to Jesus, and one of them, who was a doctor of the law, asked him, to tempt him: Master, which is the greatest commandment in the law? Jesus said to him: Thou shalt love the Lord thy God with all thy heart, and with all thy soul, and with all thy mind. This is the first and greatest commandment. The second is like to it: Thou shalt love thy neighbor as thyself. On these two commandments hang all the law and the prophets. The Pharisees who were assembled"—no, that's not it—"While the Pharisees were assembled, Jesus put this question to them: What think ye of Christ? Whose son is he? They answered him: Of David. But then how is it, he said to them, that David, inspired from on high, calls him Lord, saying: The Lord said unto my Lord, sit thou on my right hand, till I make thine enemies thy footstool? If then David calls him Lord, how is he his son? No one could answer him a word, and from that day forth no one ventured to question him again."

The little effort of being obliged to translate the texts to himself made them affect him as something new and fresh—he had certainly had all this at school some time, but it seemed as if he had never before grasped the meaning of it. And then the fact that the sentences were printed connectedly, without the confusing division into verses with numbers in front of them. The Epistle became a fragment of an actual letter—a thing that was written straight off, incisive, burning with zeal. He had never thought of that before—had only regarded Paul's epistles as a kind of cairn of texts, from which parsons and missionaries could pick out a stone and hurl it at one another and at their hearers. St. Paul—he couldn't help smiling; why, of course, he had never thought of it, but that was the man he was named after—Paulus the Lutherans called him, and they had their own way of representing him as a terrible old bore.

He would certainly start reading some of his famous namesake's literary remains—in the English translation that Harald Tangen had given him. Perhaps they would have a totally different effect when their meaning was allowed to emerge without that disguise of Germanized old Danish which was known as Bible language. That the Reformation gave us the Bible in our mother tongue, that is after all one of those historical legends that contain a remarkably small kernel of historical truth. Of course, the Bible was never wholly incomprehensible in this country. But may not the wonderful, clear and luminous Church Latin have been just as intelligible to the people of those days as the odd twists and turns of Renaissance Danish?

Marvelously well chosen and put together these texts were. Here were no reservations or strange capers around the question—who was Jesus? Well, he had known as much as that before—the Catholic Church had always had its answer, clear and decided.

Paul had made up his mind to listen attentively to the sermon. But it was not so easy as he thought. The priest had a strong foreign accent, and his sermon was pretty ordinary, Paul thought—not so wishy-washy, to be sure, as Uncle Abraham's generally were; there was more stuff in it and fewer words that were simply padding, and the delivery was dry, like a lecture, without that wearisome sing-song. But it was hard work taking it in all the same, and every moment his thoughts were wandering. Thank God it was fairly short anyhow.

Then somebody intoned: *Credo in unum Deum*—and the whole congregation stood up, organ and choir came in so powerfully that it sent a shiver down his back: sentence by sentence choir and congregation sang the mighty confession of faith antiphonally—it was like mighty blows of a hammer driving in what they believed. Till suddenly the whole congregation sank on its knees and a voice came from the organ loft, still and clear, infinitely distinct:

Et incarnatus est de Spiritu sancto ex Maria Virgine, et homo factus est—

The congregation stood up again. And Paul, who had been sitting while the others knelt, thought he could not get on his feet now—just as if he had sat down as a demonstration against the doctrine of the incarnation. So he remained seated and felt pretty uncomfortable for a while.

Now came the most essential part of the Mass. He tried to follow, but could not remember what the priest was saying or what his movements signified, though he had read about it once.

But in the stillness which suddenly filled the church, when organ and choir fell silent—and the little handbells tinkled and he saw the little white host raised high in the priest's hands—then quite quietly he too let himself slip forward on his knees and hid his face in his hands. *If* it was this that was the reality, and everything else in the world merely derived its reality from this reality—then of course one's whole life, if it had severed its connection with this, was nothing but a sort of wading through rushes in a mist, and all the values one pursued were actually but dirt, like the food in the pixies' cups.

As he rose to go out he caught sight of the Gotaases a few rows in front—they were still on their knees, perhaps had some private prayers to say. It looked as if that was the custom here—people seemed to conclude the service each for himself.

Outside on the steps he was met by the autumn day, radiant with sunshine and blue sky. Two girls were going down in front of him—he recognized Randi Alme's jolly little profile and fiery hair and Monika Gotaas with her black plait which couldn't be kept in order, because her hair was as tightly curly. Paul ran down and spoke to them.

"Oh, good day," said Randi, without much surprise. "It's an age since I've seen you. Though I caught a glimpse of you in the Union a fortnight ago—"

The pavement was black and slippery, but there was a delightful spring-like feeling of moisture in the air, now that the sun had dissolved the night frost. They questioned each other about their summer holidays.

"Why, you might just as well have made a trip into the forest to see us," said Randi, when Paul told her he had been in camp. "It's not so far, if you bicycle from the Guards' camp to the Romsaas farms and take the old packhorse road west across the ridge. It would have raised our prestige, Monika's and mine, you see, with the girls in the other saeters, if we'd had a visit from a military man—"

"Yes, if I'd only known you were there. It would have been fun to see the Alme saeters again. Were you two acting dairy maids last summer then?"

"Well, we had an old girl with us who'd been summer dairywoman at home for many years. But I thought it was good fun to try the saeter life once more. And Monika got over her terror of cows enough for me to teach her to milk."

"Oh, you—" laughed Monika. "Oh, they were so horrid—as soon as I'd milked a few drops the cow always put her foot in my pail—if she didn't kick it over—"

They were passing a confectioner's down the street, and Paul proposed that they should go in and have a cup of tea.

The waitress came with the tray, and Paul helped to move the girls' belongings—handbags, missals and gloves—over to a chair.

"By the by, who was that priest who officiated today?" he asked casually; "I really came to hear Father Tangen preach. I know him personally, so I was interested in hearing him for once."

"I believe his name is Father van Richthofen—he's here on a visit; he comes from one of the towns on the coast. Father Tangen is traveling with the bishop, I think."

"Isn't he a very able priest—Harald Tangen?"

"Oh yes—he's a good preacher. And his penitents are very fond of him. I don't know him very well—my confessor is old Father Kindrich; it was he who received me."

"At any rate one thing was brought home to me today," Paul went on; "why you Catholics worship the Virgin Mary. Because if one believes that God came down on earth when Jesus was born, it must be frightfully difficult to worship him and try to ignore his mother. Isn't that so?" he asked, as Randi made no reply beyond a faint smile.

"Yes, of course. That is, we only speak of worship in the case of the uncreated. I don't know whether you appreciate the difference—though you obviously possess a certain natural perceptivity—"

"Thanks. It looks as if I shall have to be satisfied with that," said Paul, a little huffed. "I must say, I haven't seen any signs of the Catholic zeal for making converts. I've really got to know a whole lot of Catholics, and up to now there isn't one of you that has moved a finger to convert me!"

Randi looked at him attentively a moment:

"Perhaps that's just why. Because you know so many—and for the most part such charming and excellent representatives of papistry as Gotaas and Fru Gotaas and Father Tangen—to say nothing of us two. So that we're afraid you might take it into your head to go over to the Catholics. You see, if you go over to Catholicism, and are afterwards disappointed, you may be sure that the fault is yours—God disappoints no one. On the other hand, if you go over to the Catholics"—she laughed—"it's possible you may be badly disappointed, and that need not be *entirely* your own fault."

"I see."

He asked after Eberhard and Margrete-Marie Gotaas. They were to be married in the spring, Monika told him; she herself was attending the Commercial College, and she was to have Margrete-Marie's post when her sister was married.

The girls were going to take a walk round by Akershus, so they went together part of the way—Paul was going out to his mother's by the midday train.

"My fiancée is out there—Fröken Arnesen; do you remember we all made a trip to the Nordmark together in the spring of last year?"

"Congratulations," said Randi and Monika. "Somebody told me, by the way," Randi remarked—"the other day. Who was it now?—You must remember me to her, please—"

He had worked hard till he got Lucy to go out alone to Linlökka on the Saturday—partly so as to be free to pay his projected visit to the Catholic church. Partly because Lucy's persistent air of despairing resignation was beginning to irritate him. The silent, passionate misery of her caresses made his heart shrink up—but at the same time he could not deny that it made him pretty angry.

But there came a night which was to be their last—for the present.

Paul was shaken through and through, as though the very ground beneath them had suddenly opened in a fissure and divided them—and she stood on her side of the abyss, calling to him in mortal terror. Though the fissure only existed in her imagination, it was utterly impossible for him to talk her out of it; she worked herself up till she quite lost her reason over misfortunes which only threatened in her own fancy.

"You *mustn't* go away from me—I can't bear it. You don't know what will happen to me if you go away from me. But I know—I can't bear to be left alone once more. Though I didn't care for the others—nothing at all to what I care for you—but all the same it was far worse than you'd believe, for you've never tried it. But if you go away from me I'll make an end of myself—"

She sat up in bed between him and the wall—in the light of the candle by the bedside her face was so stained with tears that it looked scarcely human, with wet hairs sticking to the red, swollen skin, and indeed she was all a tousled mass, for she had writhed and twisted her head round and round against his chest.

Paul raised himself on his elbow, and then she flung herself upon him, bit him in the throat and the breast, tried to goad him to her with caresses which seemed to him the devices of a madwoman—and all the while she sobbed, with a sound in her throat like the wailing of a tortured animal: "Oh, don't go away from me, Paul, Paul, Paul—don't go away."

"Come, let's get up and sit in front of the fire for a bit"—but he had to pull her out by force almost. He managed to wrap his plaid around her and pack her into the big basket chair; then he made up the fire—for now she was trembling with cold, or with the after-effect of her desperate attack, so that it was painful to see her. There was a little sherry left in the bottle—Paul filled her glass and noticed that his own hands were shaking.

"There—drink that up."

She blinked up at him with tiny, swollen eyes. He was standing in his white nightshirt, reaching to his feet—Lucy had always been so impressed by his long nightshirts.

"Oh, Paul, there's no need at all for you to think of marrying me," she said in a husky voice. "You know well enough I never meant to ask that of you."

"I don't believe you have any suspicion"—Paul seated himself in the other chair, "that that is the worst and most insulting thing you could say to me. Do you think I have lied to you all the time and never meant a word of all I said to you?"

"Oh yes, I know well enough you meant it, worse luck. But I never believed it would come to that—it's only something you took into your head because you've had so little experience. It's not a thing that you can decide, Paul—"

"Then I'd damned well like to know who can decide it," said Paul furiously. "Well, of course, if you're going to carry on like this—it may be necessary to send you to a home for nervous cases—but that would only be a postponement—"

Now she was crying again, wailing softly. Paul got up and put his arm round her neck:

"Poor little Lucy—you must have had a wretched time all this year—and I knew nothing about it. If you've been expecting all the time that something mystical or other would happen—that I in my inexperience couldn't do anything to avoid—" he tried to turn her face up so that he could kiss her.

After a little resistance she gave in, and then she sat staring at the red glow behind the pane of mica:

"Oh no, I wasn't so awfully unhappy. I thought to myself, I was happy as long as it lasted—"

Paul squeezed himself into the chair at her side and got her on his knees. With his arms around her he tried to talk sensibly—picturing to her how different it would all be when they had their own home.

Lucy listened, if anything rather sulky now. Once she interrupted him angrily: "I don't care a scrap about having a child. I don't like kids—"

"Fie, that was not a nice thing to say. But you can't know anything about it, just because you didn't like looking after Fru Holst's youngsters."

Then she cried again—worked herself up till it grew worse and worse. Paul showed temper in the hope of stopping her:

"Hush now—you'll wake up the Fransens with this noise—if you don't look out they'll think I'm murdering you and send for the police—"

At long last she was so exhausted that he ventured to take her into the bedroom, and soon after she fell asleep with her head on his shoulder.

By then she had shed at least half a pint of salt water over his nightshirt, thought Paul.

Carefully he raised his head, took a last glance round the little room, half-empty and untidy in the flickering light of the candle—then he blew out the flame.

To tell the truth this was something he had not expected—he had firmly believed that they had the same ideas when they talked of a future together. But, poor girl, perhaps she couldn't help it—it was this foolish distrust of life and of everyone she met, which he had been up against so often. But now it was as if he had struck his foot against a sharp stone in the dark. Poor thing—"I know what it's like to be left"; it didn't make it any pleasanter for him when she called up such memories.

Nevertheless he was sure—in spite of what all the old aunts in the world might say about love being no foundation to build upon and common interests being necessary—that was just a lot of aunties' talk. The day they two could go into their own house and shut the door against all interlopers, then he was sure it made no difference that they hadn't what aunties call common interests. A solidarity towards life itself they had, the rhythm of their senses was as the pulsebeat of the unity they made up—he didn't know, but they two together were something far more real and mightier and so strangely familiar and warm—and all such theorizing about love and man and woman was like nothing but the wind about the corner of their home.

He was just dropping off; felt in the darkness that Lucy was still sobbing in her sleep like a child that has cried itself tired. Dimly he pictured to himself a veranda door with white curtains swelling inward in the breeze, and outside was sunshine and the green shade of creepers, and Lucy in a white dress bending over a child's perambulator.

The picture changed—he was in a hall, and the door stood open to the driving snow; beyond he had a glimpse of a dark spruce hedge. He had his gun and rucksack, and a bright little dog was getting wild with expectation—while he talked to Lucy, who was behind a half-open door scolding the children: mustn't stand there in the draught. The outward frame of the picture reminded him of his home in Linlökka, but the feeling was a calm, rather overweening joy, "my house is my castle."

If only Lucy were solemnly established in a home, so that she knew that here she had a right to be, and it was his duty—not merely a feeling which he acknowledged—to defend her right and sustain the whole thing.

Marriage—that it was really the most romantic of all forms of love affair, that had never struck him before—a sort of pioneer life—on an island—of which they had taken possession—

By this time he had calmed down sufficiently to fall asleep.

His mother came to see him off at the station the evening he left, together with Lucy and both his brothers. He had said goodbye to Tua and Halstein at his father's; they had gone to stay with Garnaas's parents the same day.

Julie was sparkling with excitement; Hans and Sigmund were cheery and mildly interested, and Lucy was silent, wide-eyed, pale and tragic. When the train swung round the curve and Paul pocketed his handkerchief, turned into the compartment and began to arrange his new baggage—Lucy's farewell glance continued to haunt him.

It reminded him of the look in the eyes of a little white cow that had sunk in a bog—they had come upon it one day when they were on a walking tour. Nikko and he, while they were schoolboys. They couldn't manage to get it out alone, so they ran to the nearest saeter for help. Then the poor beast had looked at them like that, as it lay there, lowing piteously and making fresh efforts, though it was almost done.

Well, in a way Lucy was maybe what one understands by a cow—but she was his, and he loved her more than any crofter body loves her "ainly coo." So it was his business to get her out of the quagmire she had fallen into. It was no use being offended if she didn't see why he must run away from her for the time being.

He sat down, took out his pipe, unfolded an evening paper—then he wiped the dew from the window and sat watching the lights of the train flashing past the dark wall of the cutting outside. At last he decided to turn to the papers in earnest.

Chapter Sixteen

Paul reached Trondhjem in brilliant morning sunhine over a land that was pale with rime, but with mountains around and a fiord outside so icily cold and blue that he could not help thinking of old Simon Olaus's words about byrnies blue and steel-bright shields. And the joyful feeling that he was free and his own master sank so deep into his being that he thought it would be months before he had exhausted it. And there came Henrik running along the platform: "'Morning, morning."

They drove up through the town—what a grand smell it had of sea and salt fish; yes, now he knew that smell again, he had been here for a few days one summer when he was a schoolboy. But the town was even more beautiful than he remembered it. Kjöbmands gate with the warehouses along the river and the big trees, the picturesque old town bridge, the Bakland with the charming lines of its streets which continually brought out the little, delicately colored wooden houses in a new and pretty and amusing aspect. Good heavens, a painter who came to this town would surely run amuck—he would find subjects everywhere.

The carriage stopped outside a yellow two-storied house of the old-fashioned Trondhjem type, attractive in every way, small as it was. It stood back from the line of the street, with a scrap of garden in front and a tall poplar by the corner of the house. Behind one of the small-paned windows of the upper story a round and ruddy woman's face looked down at them.

"Here we are," said Alster.

The woman opened the door. She had merry blue eyes behind her steel spectacles, a long apron covered her whole rounded facade.

"You're very welcome. And I hope you'll find it comfortable here."

Her name was Karen and she was the housekeeper.

"Well, now you can choose which you like of the bedrooms, if you prefer the one in front—"

"No, are you crazy; I'm not going to turn you out of yours—"

The rooms were small and low-ceilinged. Paul went to the window of his room: the river ran just below the little frostbitten back garden. The broad, grey-green stream was shot with blue as it reflected the sky, and on the other bank, above long, low sheds and bare trees the Cathedral rose with its solid masses of light stone and its huge spire pressed down upon a tower that was too small. The view was so fine that it was like nothing on earth—

He was starving too, and the scent of coffee and fried bacon and eggs filled the whole house while he was changing his clothes.

After breakfast they went down to the office, and Paul was introduced to the whole staff, from the lady clerk, Fröken Raaen, to the errand boy Nils. Engineer Mortensen was their authorized superintendent of installations and had his own business, but they worked hand in hand, as he said, and shared one of the showrooms on the ground floor. Then he had to be shown over the whole place. Paul thought he had already been here an age, as he undressed that night.

It was all tremendous fun and did not wear off. Every morning Paul felt the same boyish delight as he rounded the corner of Nordre Gate and saw the low, pearl-grey wooden house with their big black glass sign between the two stories, the showrooms below and the office windows on the first floor with Alster & Selmer painted on them.

There was such a heap of things he had to learn, so he was kept busy all day; often Alster and he stayed on at the office till late in the evening. It was like a game or a sport to him. But at the bottom of his heart he did not seem able to realize that now he was a business man in earnest—or rather, it was earnest enough, but terrible fun at the same time.

His work took up much more of his time now—the whole day, really. But formerly, when he was working at the University, the subjects he studied were like worlds that existed for themselves—science had its own independent life, whether he took part in it or not. Not that he hadn't felt joy, excitement, affection, interest for the world which he had thought would be his, ever since he was a boy. But these subjects rested as it were on a foundation of seriousness. He himself and his life and his work were small and fugitive compared with the permanent realms of science.

But the business existed simply through their work, Henrik's and his; it was they two who *were* it. They were so absolutely the protagonists in the little world they were building up about them that in these first months Paul felt rather as if he were playing a part; he was taken up with all these new things in much the same way as when he had taken part in a students' performance a few years before. He was fascinated even by his new winter overcoat and his astrakhan cap and his ebony stick with silver crutch, because they made him think of a theatrical costume; when he put on this uniform, and when on arriving at the office he stood listening to a message Fröken Raaen had to give him, while he took off his gloves and hung up his coat, it was in a way like a scene in a play. The letter paper with the name of the firm and the catalogues with their half-tone blocks inspired him with something of the same expectant enjoyment that he had felt in handling an opera glass. They had a kind of symbolical value besides the practical.

To a certain extent Paul himself was aware that something of the sort was at the bottom of his youthful and sportive spirit. He understood now why his father's family had always looked down with a grain—or perhaps rather more than a grain—of contempt on business people in general. Practically all the men of his father's family had done service and had felt themselves to be servants—felt it the more keenly in proportion to their position in the country; as officials, as men of science, their souls had been filled with an idea in comparison with which they counted themselves small: country, nation, State, Church, science. They might become pedants, parochial souls, but however dried up they might be, an idea ran in their veins together with the thin and scanty blood; this was so even when the idea had slipped out of their tired and dusty consciousness and sunk to the bottom as a tradition in the darkness of instinctive life.

A business man was more or less centered in himself and had to find the object of his work in something which belonged to him: his business, his home, his children's future, some artistic or social cause which he wished to promote, or something of the sort. If *that* was his only object in life, to keep himself and his family alive and to live as well and comfortably as his means would permit, why then he might easily turn into a frightful type of the kind that intellectually speaking always remains seated on his own backside, with no wider outlook than he can obtain from that viewpoint, and never has a thought that prompts a man to get up and walk. In that case the old public servants' contempt for shopkeepers was justified—the latter might grow unbearably fat about the heart and hollow and empty of all ideas but those which came of their own accord as they sat in a doze, after applying all the sharpness and enterprise they possessed to the effort of keeping life in the corpse.

For a business man therefore it was far more important to be a personality in himself. If he would serve his country, he must himself have initiative enough for it, he must find his own ideals, if one was to use so odious a word, he must square his accounts direct with God.

So there it was again—God. Paul thought it was getting exciting almost—as if God were reaching out a hand, trying to catch him. If he said anything of the sort to his mother for instance, she would of course start preaching that such ideas were shockingly arrogant. And she would tell him all the things he knew much better than she—about how far it was to Sirius and how small and old the earth was and how short the history of the human race—only she would believe it was all "scientifically proved," as they said in the primary school, when he knew it as more or less plausible hypotheses. That was of course a kind of anthropomorphism, an errand-boy mentality which estimated the value of things according as their dimensions were capable of being expressed in a multiplicity of figures, God was conceived as a sort of director general of the united solar systems; he could not possibly have a personal knowledge of all the functionaries in one of the least important establishments of the universe. Funny though, that for nearly two thousand years men had confessed: I believe in God the Father almighty, creator of heaven and earth. And then, when it dawned on them that the creature was considerably greater than they had originally believed, they cried off—there would have to be a limit to almightiness too!

If one once assumed that everything in existence is included in an almighty personality, then of course it was only rational to conclude that every single cell of a plant and every single sphere of the solar systems was present with equal intensity in his consciousness, and to believe, as the orthodox Christians believed, that he knew all about every single soul. And also that he let them know when he had something to say to them.

But in that case not even he, Paul Selmer, could escape his creator. Unless he wilfully refused to understand his overtures. But he had actually not the slightest repugnance to believing—though it was funny to think that perhaps a day would come when he would say of himself: "I am a believing Christian."

If he was to be that, then no doubt he would be. For the present he hadn't so much time to think about such things. Now and again he knelt at the window and said an Our Father and a Hail Mary before getting into bed—but he couldn't deny that it was more or less on the chance—if there might be any to listen.

HE had no time to write many letters home. They took a good deal of printing, account books and the like, from his mother—though they had to be careful to give some orders to local firms as well—and when ordering Paul sent her a little typewritten letter; then his conscience was at rest again for a while. And one Sunday he sat down and did a little watercolor, the view from his window—he didn't draw badly; this he sent home to his mother and felt quite proud of having shown so much filial attention.

To his father he sent a few words now and again, and picture postcards to his brothers and sister; nor did they ever send him anything else—except Tua, of course; she was great at letter-writing.

Then there was Lucy. He generally wrote part of a letter to her every day, kept it in the drawer of his desk and posted the whole week's chronicle on Fridays. He told her a little of everything that happened to him, especially such things as he thought might make her laugh. He abstained advisedly from refreshing her memories of their intimate life together. For one thing, letters may go astray—what if Lucy's landlady, for instance, might take to poking her nose among her things while she was out. Another thing was that Paul felt extremely bashful at the thought of writing down in black and white, as he sat alone in his office after closing time, such things as one says quite naturally when one holds a sweet, warm mistress in one's arms. Besides, he considered that perhaps it was just as well not to dwell on memories which might stir up too violent longings. He had been a good deal scared by that last night they were together. Lucy's passion was so entangled in odd and morbidly sad imaginings of which he had really seen nothing before their parting. One thing and the other resulted in his allowing very little play to erotics in his epistles to her—as a matter of fact he often confined his endearments to "dear Lucy" and "your devoted Paul."

HENRIK and he dined in a little private hotel in Olav Tryggvasons gate, where they usually sat with Jens Mortensen and a young lawyer's clerk, Arnt Hauan; Paul knew him slightly from his student days. None of them knew many people in the town, and as they got on well together it came about that they spent a good deal of time in each other's company. They played bridge one evening a week, and took walks on Saturdays and

Sundays, to a place up in Selbu, where Henrik had been shooting the year before, and sometimes over to Hauan's home, a farm in Buvik.

Mortensen was engaged to a girl named Else Sakshaug. Now and again she dined with them, and one Sunday she and a girl friend went with them to Selbu. Paul thought her charming, red hair and freckles, with a lively little face—she reminded him a good deal of Randi Alme. He regarded her from the point of view of possible company for Lucy in the future.

Else Sakshaug was employed in an office in the town and lived with her mother, whom she helped with her earnings. Fru Sakshaug was the widow of a clergyman who had been master in a girls' school and had died while Else was quite small.

A few days before Christmas Else came, bashfully enough, to ask Alster and Selmer from her mother—if they had no better engagement, would they care to spend Christmas Eve with them?

It turned out quite pleasantly. There was a little Christmas tree on a table, and Else read the Christmas gospel and played Christmas hymns, and afterwards they had boiled rice and roast pork and fruit and nuts and punch. Fru Sakshaug herself was obviously very pleased to be able to do something for these lonely young men who otherwise would have had to spend Christmas Eve alone in their diggings in the strange town, and Paul and Henrik were pleased with themselves for behaving in so exemplary a way and expressed their gratitude to the old lady as nicely as they could. The little rooms smelt of hyacinths and Christmas food and spruce branches and tobacco smoke, and for the last hour Paul sat perfectly silent, rather sleepy, in the corner of a sofa, while Else played and Mortensen sang; he had a very good baritone. Paul thought of Christmas Eve at home; Lucy was not going there, she was spending the evening with Fröken Johnsen as she had done for some years. Thank goodness he had remembered to enclose something for Jonsa, a silver spoon in cathedral style, in his parcel for Lucy.

But on Christmas Day she was to go out to Linlökka, and the following day they were all dining at his father's. For a moment it surprised him that he felt no longing to be there—on the contrary, he felt relieved to be out of the whole business. He was so deadly sick of swinging backwards and forwards between two homes; though he had no right at all to say that he and his brothers had been badly treated through his parents having arranged two separate establishments.

What charmed him here this evening was watching Else. She was so sweet to her mother—Fru Sakshaug looked as if she might be a regular tartar, to use Hauan's expression—and to her fiancé. Mortensen was indeed a lucky dog.

Mortensen went home with them, and Karen had laid out a supper for them. And they had a whisky and soda and played a rubber of dummy whist and performed on Paul's piano. How it had ever got up the narrow stairs and through the door was a miracle no one could understand. Their voices grew pretty loud—Mortensen had a rousing laugh—but the old folks who lived on the ground floor were so deaf and slept so soundly that it was known to be impossible to disturb their night's rest.

About five in the morning all three, glass in hand, walked into the little room where Karen sat in bed asleep, propped up by a mountain of pillows. They turned on the light, woke her, and Henrik made a long speech, enlarging on all her virtues; he devoted at least five minutes to thanking her for the care she took of their foot gear: she sent them to the shoemaker's as soon as a heel showed the slightest tendency to wear down; she dried them, polished them, greased them, put them on trees, and so on. Karen sat and laughed with her glass in her hand; at last she managed to persuade them to withdraw so that she could get up. She got coffee for them, made up a bed on the sofa for Mortensen to save his walking out to Ila where he lived—then she went off to early service at the Cathedral.

For Christmas Day and "second Christmas Day" they were asked out to Hauan's. It was a fine ski run out there in the afternoon, and there was a dance in the evening. There were a lot of old clothes in the house, and someone suggested that they should dress up. Paul chose a uniform of the 1820's and they corked a moustache on him. Else Sakshaug was rigged out with a jointed parasol; draped in a pair of curtains and with a Roman silk scarf tightly bound under her bust she made a charming Empire lady. For Henrik Alster they could find nothing but a dress belonging to Fru Hauan's younger days, but it suited him splendidly: with a comforter stuffed in under the jersey body and a couple of sofa cushions under the skirt behind he looked as if he had stepped out of a Krohg picture of Albertine and so tempted a druggist in spencer and Christmas mask and a youth who had disguised himself in something indefinitely southern or piratical, with jackknives, hunting knives and paper knives stuck into a red scarf round his waist, that their advances showed a passion that was positively unseemly.

Mortensen enjoyed the fun so that he insisted on their dressing up again next morning, to let him take snapshots of them outside in the snow.

The photographs were funny. And Paul enclosed them in a letter he sent Lucy at the new year, in which he broke it to her that she must not expect long letters from him for a little while to come; they had to take stock and make up their accounts and as a beginner he wanted to be well posted.

The business had made a good start—there was a good deal of building going on in the town just at that time. Henrik Alster was a born business man, descended from several generations of business men, and Paul Selmer was picking it up well. And their appearance was in their favour—healthy, well-educated, good-looking young men, with a quiet, engaging manner, an innate talent for listening with patient interest to people's arguments without putting in a word until the other had said all he had to say.

The days began to lengthen. And Paul had grown accustomed to the new life; outside the business he and Alster were now more independent in their movements. One evening when Henrik had gone to the theatre Paul took out the little English New Testament that Harald Tangen had given him and began to read St. Luke's gospel. It was Randi who had said once that St, Luke's story of the life of Jesus was addressed above all to a public of normal people who had little or no previous knowledge of the Christian faith—and among these he might count himself.

After reading the first nine chapters he was convinced that at any rate it was a perfectly wonderful story, and the impression he had retained from school and from Sundays in church and perhaps also from Thorvaldsen's Christ, of something at the same time self-sufficient and mawkish, but above all boring—was entirely absent, if one took the gospel itself and read it without prejudice. Jesus appeared to him in the first place unaccountable, a law to himself, as though he drew on reserves beyond the limits of ordinary men. But still it seemed that Jesus must awaken a feeling that this world of his might well be beyond a man's everyday horizon—though it was not wholly new for all that; it was as though Jesus came from a world where all men had once been and had forgotten all about it—he had full knowledge of all that others have heard of and divined and forgotten before they really understood what it meant.

He went to bed before Henrik came home; for he wanted to think over what he had read and not be obliged to talk. In bed he finished reading the gospel. It was wonderful—right up to the centurion's words: Certainly this was a righteous man. And then the scene with the two on the road to Emmaus—their simple-hearted invitation: Stay with us, for it is toward evening and the day will soon be done—and then all at once they see who it is they have asked in.

But if now—his heart beat fast at the thought—if that is just what repeats itself all the time? We ask an unknown to come in, to stay with us—and it is He—

Well, then one is nicely caught. Paul laughed into the pillow, for his eyes were full of tears. Daughters of Jerusalem, weep not for me, but for yourselves and for your children. Father, forgive them; for they know not what they do.

It made one giddy to think what a difference it must make in everything. Is it true that there is something within one which is afraid of God? Not of his wrath, because there's that about the forgiveness of sins and so on—but simply, one is afraid because it means something utterly unfathomable—that God reveals himself and allows one to worship everything—well, everything that is meant by God.

On the Sunday he went to the Catholic church. It was small and rather poor-looking, and the sermon, he thought, did not say much to one who was not sure whether he believed—though on the assumption that it was all true, it was doubtless quite good. But again he followed the Mass, kneeling in the same breathless excitement—what if it were true. With St. Luke's gospel fresh in his memory he thought: why not? Is it not after all the fittest continuation of that story that it should be continued eternally, taking one human being after another and turning all his habits of thought upside down—and at the same time it is only as though one woke up and began to find one's bearings again in space.

With "being waked" he had always associated the idea of the kind of "awakening" one gets in the headmaster's study. There you find out that pranks which you've indulged in quite innocently in the belief that you were a devil of a lad, are grave crimes—then maybe your nerves break down, you howl and beg pardon, whether your repentance may signify an acknowledgement or not. And he had always felt a kind of schoolboy contempt for those who allowed themselves to be intimidated by the head. But what if it meant purely and simply that one woke up—with that complex feeling of bewilderment, relief and finally calm. And the confession of sins was like the sense of shame one may feel on remembering certain dreams—a sense of humiliation that one's soul should be capable of such aberrations when it escapes the control of the will.

"*Are* you a Catholic?" asked Alster; they were sitting over their coffee and Paul mentioned where he had been that morning. They had not yet switched on the light; the sky was so fine and bright and spring-like behind the black trellis of the poplar's branches.

"I? No—not yet anyhow."

"No, no; I was only thinking, because of that madonna figure you have in your room."

"Oh, that—it's one that was given me by an old Catholic lady."

"For that matter I have a good deal of sympathy for Catholicism," said Alster. "But it won't do for me to think of it now—I'm engaged to a lady who is just getting a divorce from her husband. So I shall have to stick to the State Church."

Paul's first feeling was a kind of shame. True, neither of them had ever referred to his confidences that night in Munkedamsvei. But he saw now that he had yielded to a desire to open his heart—though Henrik's nature was such that it had not caused him any pain to speak of afterwards. But now he was to learn that Henrik had an affair of his own—and the man hadn't uttered a syllable about it. In the whole house there wasn't a woman's portrait belonging to Henrik, except the photographs of his nearest relations. Paul of course had Lucy in all shapes and sizes, both in his bedroom and on the piano here in the sitting room.

"I haven't mentioned it before," said Henrik; "because nothing was settled—the fellow, the husband, kicked up a fuss. She was living here last winter, giving singing lessons; he stayed in Berlin. But now it's all in order. Fru Eck is her name—that's her maiden name. Berit Eck-Hermann—you may have seen it in the papers; she has given concerts in Christiania."

"Congratulations." She must be a good deal older than Henrik—it was at least five years since he had heard her one evening in the Union, and then she was not so very young. Henrik Alster would be twenty-five at midsummer.

That evening Alster took some photographs out of his pocketbook and handed them to Paul:

"There, that's Berit."

Yes, there she was. She was dark, hair á la Cléo with a fillet, quite handsome, but large, hard features; she didn't strike Paul as excessively sympathetic. But no doubt the portraits were taken for exhibition purposes;

that was why they were so artificial.

"A very characteristic face," said Paul diplomatically. "She's very talented, isn't she?"

"Yes. And a wonderful voice. The husband's a cur—ought to be shot and the one who shoots him should get a bonus. Here you can see her little girl—she's three years old now—'

One afternoon in April Paul had business in Ranheim; his customer drove him to Lade; from there he had to go inland.

Paul walked down to the old church and went into the churchyard a moment. It was blowing enough to make the great trees sway and moan with their bare branches. There was a wild sky, full of clouds and sharp piercing rays of sunlight, which were now golden as evening drew on. Out on the fiord the water was alive and gleaming under the clustered rays that shot down upon it—the sun drawing water they used to call it when he was a child. A broad streak of sunshine came sweeping over the fields by the shore, lighting up the moist brown ploughed land and making the withered pasture shine. The little wooden houses down in the bay gleamed for an instant red and yellow as poppies. But the mountains on the other side of the fiord were cold and blue in the shadow, still streaked with snow.

He walked down towards the water and found a sort of road leading under the Lade crag. It was rather intricate, he came upon fences and had to try in other directions, up and down the little mountain. And once he came out on a kind of ledge where he had never been before—though he had walked here fairly often.

Just below him were two little houses looking out across the fiord. One of them was uninhabited, and the doors must have stood open, for one could see the sunset right through it—the light of the glowing, stormy sky and the reflection from the vast open fiord seemed to fill the whole house with gold.

Paul crept through a barbed wire fence, found a sort of path leading down between bare alders and bramble bushes, till he came to the door of the house.

The place was fairly ruinous, had never been much of a house either, a little weatherboard matchbox. The wooden doorsteps were half rotten and broken, bits of them lay about on the ground. The house had been painted pale green, but had turned grey with wind and weather and the paint was peeling off everywhere. The outhouse stood a comparatively long way off and a little watercourse made almost a bog between it and the house. He went round to the front and into the primitive veranda. In front of the house was a slope of thin turf and grey, withered hare's foot—where it ended it looked as if the ground fell abruptly to the fiord. The rush of the waves and the roar of the surf under the rocks filled the whole windy and luminous space—with the cry of gulls and the sight of three of the great birds flying past beyond the bushes and catching the sunshine on their white, heeling wings—

A woman with a key hanging on her forefinger appeared round the corner of the house:

"Maybe you'd like to look at the house, would you?"

Paul said thanks. The rooms were small, there was a stifling smell of newly painted floors. The place looked scarcely habitable. But he noted with thanks the name and address of the man in town who had the selling or letting of it—it wasn't anyone with whom they had had dealings.

PAUL walked on, thinking of Solstua—so they called the house under the Lade crag; but that didn't matter, the name was appropriate for once. Of course it was no use thinking about it; for one thing he had no money to buy a house with yet. And it would swallow up a fortune to get it put in a habitable state, make a proper approach and so on. Altogether the place had nothing to recommend it but its position—there could scarcely be a finer in Norway.

But as he walked he played with the thought of what he would do with it, if Solstua were his. Knock the two rooms above into one, so that the evening sun might stream right through always. The whole house would want new weatherboarding—red with white window frames. A steatite stove in the veranda room. The stream would have to be piped, and the little hollow in the rock in front of the house might perhaps be made into a pond. Over by the outhouse there was room for a kitchen garden. But round the house itself he would have nothing but mountain plants: purple gentian which grew in such masses hereabout, blue sowthistle along the edge of the thicket, Dovre poppies in the cracks between the stones, primula scotica, dryas—they had got this to thrive so well on the rocky knoll at Linlökka that last summer the whole of one side was white with bloom.

He described the place in letters to Lucy—what their home was to be like. It need not be Solstua exactly, but that had given him the idea of their house, as he wanted it.

And after he and Henrik had spent the winter mildly chaffing

Mortensen, who was entirely given up to the work of furnishing his house—he had had a dining room suite made of unpainted deal and was engaged in decorating it himself with pokerwork in dragon style—Paul himself began to develop a ravenous appetite for furniture, though in a different taste. He had come across at an auction a couch and three chairs, country work in rococo style, black lacquer with gilt mussel shells. He wanted to collect a whole set of the same—and then it was his dream to get hold of a tea table with a china top. He had the old bookcase which stood in the boys' room at home, and the sofa from Munkedamsvei was stored in the loft at his father's. Quite by chance he got hold of a mahogany corner cupboard with curved doors, very handsome Trondhjem work, and two old watercolors in flat mahogany frames, the falls of Lerfoss and Stiklestad in 1810. He wrote to his mother in detail about his purchases and asked her to keep her eyes open for anything that might suit him. Julie was at once keenly interested—it gave an immense impulse to their correspondence.

At the same time of course he kept Lucy posted about his purchases, though it was no use entering into details with her. But he sketched for her a mahogany work table in the Northern Museum of Arts and Crafts and promised to give her one like it for her birthday.

The poplars that lined the streets were out and filled the town with their fresh and bitter balsam scent, especially when the sun shone after rain. Trondhjem was beautiful beyond description. There were poplars in the street outside the office too; the scent of them poured in as he and Henrik sat at work with open windows. And their own old poplar, the huge tree outside the house in the Bakland, was just like a dear old friend, and the tiny garden in front was quite touching with its pale, half-wild pansies round the beds which Fru Aune had planted with geraniums, and the miniature lawns had the slender, shiny grass that grew in their gardens here in the north.

At the end of June Paul went south to Christiania for his sister's wedding.

Julie Selmer met him at the station, beaming with joy:

"O Paulinus! Such fun to see you! Why, I believe you've grown, boy—" she laughed with delight.

Paul laughed too—while looking about him with a trace of annoyance. But perhaps it was because she thought his mother would want him to herself a little while—for his mother could not come this evening.

She drove with him to the hotel. And Paul really thought it fun to unpack his things in this hotel room, to tell the maid about his dress clothes, to order coffee for them—while his mother sat in one of the fabulous hotel armchairs, looking with admiration at the son who now at last had entirely escaped from her leading strings.

"You'll stay and breakfast with me, won't you?" he asked from the bathroom. "I must say though"—he came back into the room, sat down and took his coffee-cup—"I think Lucy might have arranged to come and meet me too. She can't have had to go to the shop this morning—do you know anything about it?"

"Well, Paul," said Julie rather nervously; "I may as well tell you at once—Lucy's not coming to the wedding—"

"What—not coming—! But what on earth does it mean—she's not ill, is she?"

"She's not invited—

"No, no, Paul, wait and let me finish what I have to say. It's really *not* so unreasonable, I've had quite a lot of talk with Lillian about it. She hasn't put in an appearance there since Christmas. Tua has asked her several times—to working parties and at other times too—she's been to see her at the shop, and Lucy has always accepted and then stayed away without sending any message. And Lillian herself has written and invited her four times altogether—the girl hasn't answered a word, hasn't so much as rung up—"

Paul sat listening with a gloomy countenance. It could not be denied that this was not unlike Lucy—

"And I'm not going either," said his mother. "Though both your father and Lillian proposed it. But after mature consideration I thought it better not—

"—You're not publicly engaged either, you know," Julie Selmer concluded.

"No engagement ring?" said her son spitefully. "No, as far as that goes."

"Well, I'm annoyed about it too—now of course you won't enjoy yourself a bit. I have been terribly annoyed about Lucy's—what is one to call it? But really I couldn't bring myself to talk to the girl about her strange behaviour when she has been out to see me."

"How has she been when she was with you?" asked Paul quietly.

Julie shrugged her shoulders:

"One would never accuse her of being a chatterbox, you know. Poor girl, I don't suppose she felt very comfortable—but that wasn't entirely our fault, Paul. Oh, it's so difficult," she said impatiently; "for her too, of course. But I can tell you it isn't easy for me either with a perfect stranger whom it's impossible to get a word out of except yes, thanks, and no, thanks.

"Sigmund has taken her to concerts a few times, when he had tickets given him. She's very fond of music—"

"Yes, she wrote me that."

Julie glanced rapidly at her son once or twice. She was furious with the stupid girl—now of course she had spoilt the wedding altogether for Paul. Who probably hadn't been looking forward to it with any wild enthusiasm beforehand.

Paul rang up Lucy at the shop, when he came back to his room after breakfast. But he didn't get much more than good day and how are you and looking forward to seeing you again. They arranged to meet and dine together next day.

He didn't feel equal to talking about the wedding or risking any explanations on the telephone. The whole business was far too annoying.

Then he gave orders to be called at three o'clock, undressed and went to bed, firmly determined that he would sleep. It was not much use. He had smoked the best part of a packet of cigarettes and read half a Phillips Oppenheim before he fell asleep.

The wedding was at their father's. And Paul willingly admitted that in themselves the arrangements were marvellously successful, considering the space available. Lillian had done all that was humanly possible for his sister and kept herself in the background as tactfully as she could.

Tua had never looked so well in her life—there is something in a white wedding dress with wreath and veil—and many of the bridesmaids were pretty, and friends of the young couple had decorated the church and sang in the organ loft, and Uncle Abraham looked distinguished in canonicals and his address was probably the best he had delivered in his life—he was himself so moved.

Nevertheless Paul felt that never in his life had he been at all in touch with this kind of service, nor was he ever likely to be. It was fine and impressive, the singing and the organ, the lights, the mass of flowers, the bride in a cloud of white, the bright and sumptuous dresses of the ladies, the men in ceremonial clothes with orders and stars brightening the black and white of their evening dress. But it all seemed to be done in order to work up an emotion.

He longed for the poor Catholic churches—with paper flowers on the altar and plaster dolls in niches, and the few people in their workaday clothes who collected there on weekday mornings and shivered as they prayed. He wondered whether it was because he knew what the Catholics believed—of the extreme, he had almost said grotesque, abandonment of God's love in that little cage over the altar—but it seemed to him that the difference must make itself felt directly even by people who had never heard of the eucharist. The Protestant churches, whether they were ugly and devoid of feeling, or grand and inspiring—were meeting places and could be nothing else. People came there to accomplish some kind of worship of God in his invisible and spiritual presence; but one could do that just as well out in the woods or at home in one's room—better perhaps, since it is written that God is a spirit and is not to be worshipped in Jerusalem or what's the name of the other place—but in spirit and in truth. But all attempts to make these meeting places for the worship of the omnipresent God more or less instinct with feeling had such an oddly inadequate and prosaic effect—if one believed him to be at the same time present everywhere outside, and it must be admitted that he had himself decorated the outside world with considerably more taste than these good people could show—

But if one believed that he continued to meet men also in a sort of material substance, in bread, of which he had said, this *is* my body—do this in remembrance of me—then it was natural that men should make huts to receive him. They were not decorated in order to arouse feeling and devotion—it was devotion and feeling, of gratitude and joy, that impelled men to decorate his dwelling place as well as human poverty was able; the painted plaster figures of his mother and his faithful companions, the paper lilies and the brass candlesticks in the poor churches which he had here today, and in the lovely choir of Trondhjem Cathedral—they had the same meaning as the worn and ragged cloaks which the dwellers in the outskirts of Jerusalem threw down before the rider on the ass's colt on Palm Sunday, while they broke off the first green branches they could find and cried Hosanna—our King is coming—

OLD Garnaas, Halstein's father, was a tall, fair, handsome man, just what is always described in the local press as a chieftain type. He had been a member of the Storting for many years, you could see that at the first glance, even if you happened not to know it. Every time he was about to say something it looked as if he suppressed an unctuous, self-sufficient smile, enjoying his own words in advance—so that one involuntarily expected him to say something which would suit the character of a parish clerk in a play which satirized such officials. One almost felt cheated when nothing of the kind came—everything he said was excellent, natural and sensible. He spoke dialect, but freely and without affectation, and he had a warm, sonorous voice. The speech he made at dinner was really fine—beyond question the best of all the speeches that were made.

Fru Garnaas was a rather charming little woman, with a skin like ivory, mild blue eyes and an anxious voice; she was said to rule her blond chieftain of a husband with whips and scorpions.

Paul could see that his father was greatly moved at giving Tua away; she had always been his own child, as it were. And he was evidently not a little proud of his three big, well set-up sons, who looked their best in evening dress.

Lillian was a fantastic figure in a cream-colored gown, cut low in front and at the back, with miles of train, and what was it she had at the side of her golden coiffure—a tuft of ostrich feathers sticking straight up and some flashing stones! But a grand dinner she had given them—and Tua's trousseau was in good style, he understood. Paul raised his glass: "Lillian—may I have the pleasure?"

He had taken his cousin Ruth in. He had not seen her for ages—charming she had grown, a good deal like his mother, with chestnut hair and warm brown eyes. And evidently you could take it quietly with Ruth—she didn't want to be cackling all the time either. "*Skaal*, Ruth, jolly to see you again. Yes, it's a great bore that Uncle Halvdan couldn't come to town."

Hans had been given Molla Nicolaysen. And it was clear that he was hopelessly gone on that miracle of beauty and charm. Seriously, Paul had rarely seen anyone so pretty as Mollik. And she seemed intelligent too. But Hans—that young ass—Paul felt seriously and fraternally perturbed: he wasn't going to get himself engaged, when they were only children, both of them—?

There were telegrams for the bridal couple—a terrific number. Halstein's best man, a strapping young clergyman whose name Paul hadn't caught, had the task of reading them all out. There was one from Halstein's elder brother, the infantry captain—it referred to Halstein's coming sphere of activity being situated in the neighborhood of the frontier:

A happy omen for domestic peace, you'll own:

I bid you welcome to the Neutral Zone.

Paul turned crimson: something, whether shame or sorrow, gripped his heart in a downright physical way. The Garnaas side of the company laughed enthusiastically, the Selmers blushed more or less deeply and stared stiffly at the melting ice on their plates. Uncle Abraham looked round as if searching for a tip as to how he was to take it.

Directly afterwards they rose from the table. There were coffee, liqueurs, cognac, cigars and cigarettes in the drawing room, the study and the veranda. The wedding presents were on view in the boudoir. "And this we had from Lucy," said Tua, showing a long table-centre in drawn thread work. "Oh, how charming," said all the ladies. Well, it was a good thing Lucy had thought of that, anyhow. Soon after Sigmund sat down to the piano.

The newly married couple were to leave by a train from the Eastern Station at a quarter past twelve. And their nearest relations saw them off. At twenty minutes past twelve Paul was standing outside the station—the summer night was pale and mild, the town so still that every sound came through with a strange echo, and from the Palace garden was wafted the first hint of the scent of lime blossom.

Paul had a wild idea. And instantly he started off to realize it. He took the high road under Ekeberg along the shore of the white fiord.

When he had gone a little way beyond Ljan he stopped and took off his light overcoat. It dawned on him that he must have taken a tiny drop too much at the wedding party to make him think of such a thing—a nocturnal walk of about twenty miles along the high road, in evening dress, with new patent leather shoes on his feet. Nor had he the slightest idea whether he had said goodbye to any of the other guests.

But as for turning and walking back to town—hanged if he would. He took his coat over his arm, dried his forehead with a strongly scented handkerchief—heaven knew how it had found its way into his pocket—and walked on along the strip of grass bordering the ditch. At regular intervals there were irritating heaps of road metal which he had to go round—it was a scandal they hadn't been spread long ago.

The spruce forest on both sides of the road began to take on colour in the dawn. The fresh shoots had grown long and pale green and among them grew cow grass forming great carpets with its brownish leaves and little pale yellow flowers. The sky above the treetops was turning blue and a few shreds of cloud drifted high up, shining in pink or gold.

Just outside Tyrigraven a man suddenly rose out of the ditch; he asked for some pence for coffee.

Paul raked out all the small change he had lying loose in his pocket, silver and copper: "Here you are—good morning."

"You couldn't tell me what's o'clock—?"

Paul looked at his watch. As the man shot forward to grab it, Paul sent him a well-aimed uppercut which landed him on the bare rock with such a whack that Paul could feel it all up his own spine.

"Quarter past three. It won't be so long before you can slip into the inn here and get something. And you may thank your stars I saved you any trouble with the police—I won't say anything of your conscience—"

"Are you awake?" asked the man, squinting up suspiciously.

"Yes, did you think I was walking in my sleep?—'morning."

He tramped on, quietly whistling. Good Lord, what a fine morning it was—the birds were singing like mad, a cuckoo called far away in the woods, grass and flowers were pearly with dew. If only his patent leathers would hold out a little longer; it wouldn't be so pleasant to walk in his socks.

It was bright morning and the sun had been up some hours when he swung in through the garden gate at Linlökka. His footsteps crunched on the gravel in the morning stillness—and there was his mother, up among the leaves of the veranda, draped in her white shawl.

"Paul!" She jumped down and ran towards him, threw her arms about his neck and gave herself up to weeping, with her face against his shirt-front. "O Paul, Paul, Paul!" He saw, as he bent down and kissed her, that his mother had been crying a good deal.

"There now, mother, don't cry like that—" side by side they went up to the house. The cushions on the divan in the corner of the veranda were all crushed: "You don't mean to say, mother, that you haven't been to bed tonight—?"

Julie laughed and cried at the same time:

"I knew it would be no good—so I camped out here. You know, it's not that I'm not used to your all being away from me at once, but this is something different. But how in the world did you get here—walked from town, do you say—? My dear boy, whatever put it into your head to do that?"

"Oh, I must have been a little more squiffy than I thought—" Paul sat down on the divan and took off his shoes and silk socks; they were in rags, stiff and grey with road dust. "I say, mother, I hope you haven't given away that old grey suit of mine that I left hanging here? Otherwise I don't know how I'm to get back to town. You don't mind my turning up at home like this?" he asked, smiling up at his mother.

"Mind—" She kissed him again. "But you'll want some breakfast, won't you?"

When she came back with the tray Paul's coat and waistcoat were hanging over chairs, collar and tie were on the floor, and her boy lay on the divan sleeping like a stone.

His mother stood for a moment looking at him. His white shirt showed how broad he was across the chest, his fine black trousers how spare and narrow were his hips. What a notion to come out to her like this. Julie stood for a while, lost in happy contemplation. His short, light brown hair was bright and curly, and his skin was so clean and healthy and sunburnt—God, what a dear boy he was. His eyelashes still curled up a little at the ends—just as they had done when she could wrap the whole man in a piece of white flannel and carry him away in her arms.

She fetched a pair of blankets and laid them over him. Then she took the coffee tray out to the kitchen, wrapped a coverlet around her and tucked herself up on the drawing room sofa.

About twelve o'clock they met for lunch in the dining room. Paul had changed into the old suit and found a pair of Sigmund's shoes that he could wear; he told his mother about the wedding and could not help laughing at the formal way in which he was addressed by Alvilde, the maid who had been with them nearly ten years.

Julie had quite got over her emotions of the early morning and questioned him eagerly about everything, even wanting to know what the various ladies had had on. But Paul could not give any detailed description—except of Lillian, of course, and Molla Nicolaysen in sea-green with glittering sequins all over her—oh, she was worth looking at! Ruth—oh yes, Ruth looked very nice—in some yellow stuff. "But now I must fly—I don't look too comical, do I? For I shan't have time to go up and change—I told Lucy quarter past two and I can't keep her waiting, you know—"

His mother nodded. And she felt an overwhelming return of her impatience and antipathy towards this stranger, this somewhat impossible girl to meet whom her son had to gallop away.

PAUL had to wait over a quarter of an hour for Lucy in the restaurant, and when at last she came along between the tables it was as though all his displeasure with her clumsy rudeness towards his family revived in him. She had on a kind of walking dress of thick, sky blue washing material, and it was fearfully crumpled. She also wore white canvas shoes which were so tight that the flesh bulged out over their edges. In reality she had fine, shapely feet, but they were big, and these white shoes made them enormous.

He went to meet her, and they greeted each other almost as if they had met the day before. And they fell to talking in a strained way about indifferent things, for Paul did not feel inclined to take her to task just now about her behaviour to his father and stepmother. Nor did he know exactly what he could say about it—

"I was in church yesterday," Lucy herself began at last. "I was sitting in one of the back pews. But you didn't see me."

Paul said nothing.

"Tua looked so charming. Was that your uncle, the clergyman that married them?"

"Yes."

"Who was the girl you came down the church with? You drove away in the same carriage too. In yellow crepe de Chine?"

"Oh, that was my cousin, Ruth Wangen. Mother's niece."

"She's awfully pretty—" said Lucy with a sigh.

"Yes, she's grown into a really pretty girl. There's a talk of her coming to live at Linlökka in the autumn—so you'll have a chance of meeting her there. She paints—is clever, they say—"

AFTER dinner they went up to Lucy's. And at last, when they reached her room, Paul could take her in his arms. He kissed her hard and hotly, even harder, fiercely almost, because he was conscious that they were separated by an infinity of tiresome misunderstandings, and that they must love one another across a stream of trifles, of which he could not make up his mind whether they were pure bagatelles or really foreboded something serious and sorrowful.

Chapter Seventeen

On the third day Paul went back to Trondhjem. He was glad enough to come home to the business—the impression left by his trip to Christiania was rather gloomy than otherwise.

He had tried as gently and cautiously as he could to talk to Lucy about that matter of the invitations from Lillian which she had never answered. But of course it was entirely useless.

"Pooh, I know well enough they don't care anything about me. It was only for your sake they asked me—"

That irritated him fearfully—a genuine lower-class argument: not to be able to see what forms and politeness were worth in themselves, for making life a little easier and more pleasant. Always wanting to search the hearts and reins of those with whom one came in contact, from a kind of insufferably sentimental and undignified arrogance—is it for my sake they are polite to me, because they really appreciate me, care for me?—It was this in reality which gave some people their lower-class stamp—that they took themselves far too seriously and at the same time were too careless about themselves: they were always swayed by what they thought other people thought about them; they could never in all friendliness refuse to care a damn what opinion strangers might have of them, and for the rest be polite and pleasant to all indifferent persons one came across. Well, naturally he understood that it is not so easy for weak and lonely individuals with no resources to speak of in themselves or their surroundings, to preserve such an unworried attitude towards all those they are not specially interested in; so it was useless to discuss the matter any further with Lucy. But it had put a sort of damper on the joy of meeting again—for her too, without doubt.

It had also been a real disappointment that he did not meet Harald Tangen when he was in Christiania. He had rung up the priest and arranged to come and see him and borrow some books. But when Paul appeared, he was received by another priest, an elderly foreigner, who handed him a parcel of books and a note from Father Tangen—he regretted that he had been called out of town by telegram to the deathbed of a Catholic.

He had firmly made up his mind to have it out with Harald Tangen about what was to him the main question—whether one could believe in a personal God who took an interest, separate and intense, in each individual human soul. For an almighty God there was of course nothing to prevent this, even if in the course of time it meant a good many souls to look after and even if they should continue to multiply rather seriously in the future. If he could once believe that, he could believe in the whole doctrine of the Church. And then there would be nothing for him to do but to become a Catholic as quickly as possible—and to strive to be a good Catholic.

These books that he had brought away were of no earthly use to him. Every one of them consisted of a defense of Catholicism against orthodox Protestantism; that didn't interest him a scrap. It had never occurred to him to believe in Christianity so long as he was only acquainted with the Protestant clergy's version of it—the later, more liberal versions appealed to him a great deal less than Uncle Abraham's. He had gradually arrived at the opinion that the various editions of Protestantism he had come across, and his mother's freethinking, were all much of a muchness. God Almighty was to arrange his revelations so as to suit the national character of the Norwegians, or a vivacious and gifted lady's ideas of what the world and mankind ought to be. Even from his schoolbooks on church history and history generally he had acquired a deep distrust of the authors' reliability whenever it was a question of the Church or the Reformation or anything connected therewith. And now, when he had himself read through the New Testament and parts of it several times, it seemed to him that the Protestant explanations—for instance, the attempts to get round Jesus' insistence on good works or his prohibition of divorce, or estimation of virginity, or Saint Peter's primacy—were perfectly ridiculous antics.

If one were willing to admit that the Bible is an inspired book, then it was no use picking out of it what agreed more or less with one's own taste or opinions of probability, and baking one's own religious cake of that. The word was: Take and eat!

Still, he made a loyal attempt to struggle through a couple of these apologetics that Harald Tangen had lent him. He was badly bored until he had worked some way into Father Stub's "Guide from Prejudice to Religious Truth." Then he suddenly discovered what the old exiled Norwegian quite involuntarily disclosed—the sweet wholesomeness of his own soul. An intensely beautiful and noble humanity made itself felt through the odd old-fashioned language; so he came to read Father Stub's book through as a human document that gave him joy.

JULY went by, and Paul and Henrik discussed the question of summer holidays. Henrik wanted to take his when the shooting opened. And Paul decided to save up his holiday till after the new year—then he would go to Christiania and be married to Lucy. The wedding was to be at his mother's, and then he thought of combining the wedding trip with a business journey to Germany.

He had definitely given up Solstua, after going out there with Henrik one day—Henrik roared with laughter when he saw the frightful cabin Paul had fallen in love with. To make it fit for human habitation would cost double as much as building a comfortable, modern little cottage. Well, Paul knew that already, but it sounds so odd when one hears another say it. So now he was looking out for a house, but as yet he had not found one he liked—and he would rather try to get a flat in one of the old wooden houses—good-sized rooms, not too high, with a view of the fiord or the river. "Well, you know what you want, don't you?" said Alster chaffing him, and helped his friend with all his might to look for a flat which answered more or less to the schedule.

But if the business went on prospering as hitherto, he would in time have a house of his own somewhere on the fiord, Paul was sure of that.

Then there came a glorious day in August, two days before Alster was to leave for the shooting. The two partners had gone down to the office together; Alster fussed about, opening windows, unlocking drawers and banging them in again, getting out his papers. Paul had stopped short at his desk, putting down his straw hat and gloves, for he had seen a letter from Lucy lying on the top of the pile.

He slit it open. Inside was an envelope, inscribed:

"Please don't read this letter till you have left the office. L."

Then Paul tore it open and read:

Dear Paul.

I hardly know how I'm going to begin this letter. Ive been thinking for many weeks that Id rite to you but Ive dreaded it so terribly. Im afraid youll be very angry about it and sorry too when youve read it, but Ive seen for a long time that were not sewted for each other and therefore I dont believe it would turn out happily for us if we got married and therefore Im going away now from Kristinia because it must be all over between us I cant explain it any more but I believe after a time youll he grateful to me for breaking it off between us. Im so fritefully sorry as Im riting this because youre the only one Ive loved properly and that you will be as long as I live but Ive come to see now that we dont sewt to be married and therefore I do this out of love for you Paul whether you believe it or not its *true*.

I send you back all the things Ive had from you and all the letters youve sent me and I ask you to send me my letters and the bits of work Ive worked for you, if you dont care to keep them for then youre welcome but I think when you get this letter youll be so angry with me that you wont want to keep anything to remind you of me and then you can send me everything back to Jonsa's but not the photographs you took of me up in Mungedamsvei. Those you must please destroy, I beg you so earnestly to do that or else I shall be even more unhappy than I am. Well I expect youll think youve got in with a very common person after all youve done for me but Im doing this chiefly for your own good.

Goodbye dear Paul and dont be too mad with me

Your sorrowful Lucy.

Paul read the letter through once more. He had violent palpitations; the paper rustled a little from the trembling of his hand. Then he laid it down and lit a cigarette.

"Henrik. Would you be frightfully annoyed if I asked you to put off leaving for a day or two? One day would do, I dare say. I want to take the train to Christiania tonight. I can be back the day after tomorrow or the next day at latest—"

"There's nothing wrong, is there? Naturally I can wait—"-

"Yes, it looks as if there's something very wrong. It's from Lucy—"

"She isn't ill, is she?"

"Mad, I should say. Writes some bosh about breaking it off—for my own good, she says. Devil take me if I understand a word of it—"

"Why, of course you must go. And stay there as long as you think necessary—"

Paul tried to concentrate on the day's work and leave off thinking about Lucy's letter meanwhile. It was so senseless, a lot of nonsense that the silly girl had taken into her head—if only he could get hold of her and have a talk he would soon cure her of these fancies.

The moment he read the first few lines he had thought—there, now of course she's going to announce that she's to have a child. But that couldn't possibly be it. Break off the engagement and disappear—that was what it looked like from the letter—because for instance she imagined he would feel it so embarrassing if they had to get married in a hurry—no, that wouldn't be like Lucy. If that was the matter, she would have been more likely to write and tell him they must get married at once. For surely she couldn't be so mad as to do anything to herself—? Paul's heart quailed at the thought. Oh no, Lucy would never do that—take her own life when she was engaged to a man she knew was fond of her and the wedding was fixed for a few months ahead—no, no—

But he'd be damned if he could make out a word of it.

He must give up thinking of it now—he'd hear all about it when he got to Christiania in the morning.

Could anybody have been nasty to her, could she have misunderstood anything his mother had said or done—had she for instance met Lillian in the street and had Lillian said something—?

Anonymous letters—could that be it? He hadn't been incautious and frequented any Trondhjem ladies in such a way as to be talked about? Not that he knew of, anyway. Or was it simply that feeling of dissatisfaction that had come between them last time he was south—had she been brooding on this till his poor child's head had been quite confused—?

He picked up the letter and read it again—poor Lucy, at any rate she must have suffered terribly before she could write all that nonsense—

"I can't make out a scrap of it!" he said to Alster.

"No, but you'll be able to get hold of it tomorrow. What do you think—you might just as well take your bicycle and go up and see that fellow at Selsbak, he insists on talking to one of us. And if you're going to sit here, you'll think of nothing but her letter the whole day. And you may as well look in at home and tell Karen you're leaving—then she'll pack your things instead of mine—"

Paul nodded: "Yes—thanks."

He scarcely closed an eye in the train that night. And as soon as he had got a room at the hotel and had a wash, he rang up the flower shop. An unknown southern girl's voice answered him:

"Fröken Arnesen—no, she's not here, she finished a week ago. No, I don't know anything about where she's gone—"

Then he dashed off to her lodging in Linstows gate. It was Fru Skaaning herself who opened the door, in morning dishabille, looking immensely surprised to see Selmer standing there:

"But dear me—are you in town! Please walk in—I haven't had time to do the rooms yet, I hope you'll excuse—"

"Is Lucy in?"

"No, Fröken Arnesen, she's left—left the day before yesterday, for Bergen, I believe. As far as I know, she must have gone away with that Lövstö—"

Lövstö—Lövstö—Paul seemed to have heard the name. A fellow who had come up and spoken to Lucy once, last autumn if he wasn't mistaken, when he and she were having a meal at the Frogner saeter. There had been a party sitting at a table not far away, and one of the men had come across and spoken to her. He would have judged the fellow to belong to the Carling period—wonder if Lucy hadn't said his name was Lövstö. But he wouldn't know him again if he ran across him.

"Lövstö?" he asked Fru Skaaning. He was positive Lucy had never mentioned the name before or since.

"Yes, Fröken Arnesen has seen a good deal of him lately—he used to come here and take her out and that. And just these last weeks, since it's been off between Fröken Arnesen and you, he's been here pretty often—I've really had the impression that she's given him hopes—"

"But our engagement hasn't been broken off at all—what on earth put that into your head, Fru Skaaning, that it was all off between Fröken Arnesen and me?"

"But bless me! I was so sure you'd broken it off last time you were in town. Yes, I really did think that—!"

The ready blush that made Paul so furious spread over his face. Well, she must have strange ideas about the technique of breaking off engagements—

"Well, fancy that. I thought I understood from Fröken Arnesen that you two had broken it off—"

No, she didn't know Fröken Arnesen's address—he'd be most likely to get it from that friend of hers, Fröken Johnsen.

PAUL was on the stairs when Fru Skaaning came out and called to him, running down:

"Aren't these yours, Selmer? I thought of giving them back to you last time you were in town, but I always forgot—"

To his dying day Paul remembered it—the semicircular staircase where he stood against a window with red and blue glass; through one of the panes with frosted stars he had a view, without taking it in, of some backyards with stairs and fire escapes.

He took the rolled up gloves and opened them out—they were pale grey with black seams, stained violet from a copying pencil: "Yes, they're mine—thanks—" Lucy could never cure herself of putting her pencil in her mouth.

HE took a cab to Jonsa's. Jonsa was away on a holiday.

PAUL paid his bill at the hotel and walked down Karl Johan with his suitcase in his hand. There was a train to the north about three—then he would have several hours loafing about Hamar, but rather that—at any rate it was a strange place. He couldn't bear to stay in town.

In the station square Hans suddenly crossed over towards him:

"Hullo! Are *you* in town—?"

"Yes, as you see. I had to make a flying visit."

The brothers went into the station together. The hall was a mass of sportsmen and dogs—on the platform outside there was a barking and growling and whimpering of dogs in boxes. O hell, the trains would all be packed today. They nodded to acquaintances as they passed, on this side and that, but spoke to no one.

"I say, Hans"—the brothers were walking up and down the platform. "I'd just as soon you didn't say anything to mother or anybody about my being in town. As I hadn't time to run home—

"It's about Lucy, you understand. Yes—she's broken it off."

Hans looked at him—turned red and slowly redder.

"O-oh—" was all he said, very quietly.

At that moment Paul had to jump into the train. He stood at a window in the corridor—Hans waited below. The last thing Paul saw was his brother's face with that odd awkward look.

He found a place for his suitcase and hung up his raincoat in the corner by the door—the carriage was full of men. Then he went out into the corridor and stood by a half-open window.

Hans—could he know anything—the boy turned so red and strange. No, damn it all—he knew absolutely nothing. Simply hadn't an idea what it all meant. She had met Sigmund, once at least since the wedding—those two had made friends, no doubt. It was perfectly idiotic, by the way, that he hadn't been out to Linlökka—to hear if they knew anything. God almighty, what an ass he seemed to have been—he'd simply lost his head entirely and run away from town like a miserable coward. But Lucy, Lucy, Lucy—what does it all mean? I'm completely in the dark—

Lucy—could he have been utterly mistaken about her—was she just an ordinary wanton?—no, I can't believe it, not even now. But then I can't make anything of it. Lucy, what does it mean?—and then this Lövstö, what sort of a fellow is he, what has *he* got to do with it—?

No, curse it all—it won't do to think like this—

Tobacco smoke filled the whole corridor—all the compartments were packed with fellows laughing and talking about dogs and shooting. After all, that's just as well—I'd like to see myself sitting down somewhere and starting to howl. Oh, but Lucy—what have you done, Lucy—my Lucy?

He felt the little soft ball in his coat pocket—the gloves.

—Bygdönes baths and the pale-green spiraea hedge against the water outside, white in the sunshine. They two were sitting at a little yellow iron table which rocked as Lucy put her elbows on it, studying the bill of fare and sucking at his copying pencil—

The thin spruce forest above Lilleström was slipping past the window. Paul took the rolled gloves out of his pocket, hurled them through the window into the woods.

No, by gad, he wasn't the one to cry when it wasn't any use—by gad, no, he didn't cry. But God help me if I understand a thing about it.

Book II

Chapter One

Three years later Paul Selmer was married to a girl whose name was Björg Berge. When he looked back it was something of a riddle to himself how it had come about.

They had had a couple of good years in the business, so when Henrik Alster married Fru Eck he bought a really nice villa on the Island. Paul kept on their bachelor quarters in the Bakland and the excellent Karen. Julie Selmer came to stay with him in the summer, the same year Alster was married. And they made excursions to the Lerfoss falls and to Jonswater and out to Östraat, and Henrik and his wife gave a charming party for Fru Selmer.

"Can you understand—" said Julie, as she and her son walked homewards. The town lay in morning stillness; it was the hour between night and dawn—roofs and treetops still stood out sharp and black against the white sky, but on the heights around the town the colors were beginning to awaken, the farms showed bright against green meadows and thick groves. It had rained during the evening and the last grey shreds of cloud drifted below the clear vault of heaven; the air was heavy with the scent of wet mould and leaves and the salt fishy smell from the quays. The river ran broad and smooth under the bridge, and Julie stopped, drinking in the morning air: "God bless my soul, how lovely it is here, Paul! I am glad I have seen Trondhjem!—No, can anyone understand what possessed Henrik—marrying that ridiculous creature!"

Henrik couldn't have a very easy time, thought Paul. Berit was absolutely set on playing a part. She exerted herself in vain to get the entree into the old Trondhjem families. Henrik's and his circle, during the years they had lived here, had consisted almost exclusively of newcomers, stray, unattached people like themselves—well, Henrik did have some relations in the town, but they were quite ordinary people, very pleasant and easy to get on with, but not the sort his wife cared to visit: tradesmen class, no, she couldn't bear that; the old upper-middle class, that was another thing, they had style, she said—And now a good many of their friends were married; Mortensen and his Else already had two little boys, twins; but obviously Fru Berit and Else Mortensen could not bear each other. It was a kind of catchword in their circle that all the men were in love with Else, in all innocence—she was as it were the quintessence of refined and gentle womanliness. But the fact that all her husband's friends paid court to this other young wife was quite enough to make Berit Alster dislike her.

Berit took care never to let anyone forget for a moment that she was a well-known artist. It was this no doubt that had impressed Henrik's imagination—and then of course she was handsome in a way, an illusive way. And she had certainly had a bad time with her first husband. Altogether she must have appealed precisely to the romantic and chivalrous and rather sentimental side of Henrik's nature.

In his student days he had affected a daredevil air; and indeed he had lived pretty fast. Now he did his best to appear the sober, clear-headed, straightforward business man—and a clever business man he was too. He looked the part; Henrik Alster was tall and had a good figure—had had one; now he was beginning to put on flesh. And then he had a little round head with red cheeks, sandy hair cropped short like a hairbrush, and yellow kaiser moustaches. He was passionately fond of all that was beautiful, of outdoor life and sport, loved books and pictures and had a natural instinct for what was genuine and fine in art—there were charming things among the paintings he had bought in the course of years. But he came of a class in which the very word art was regarded with suspicion and despised; and then he was curiously uncertain of his own judgment, always ready to admit, if he could not see the good points of what was praised by others, that it must be he who failed to understand. Music he knew least about—and with the secret respect he felt for all who were concerned with art, it had probably been an easy matter for Berit Eck to impress him.

And now his wife thought him vulgar and dry because he was beginning to react mildly against her everlasting claim to be treated as the great operatic star. Of course she was to be pitied, in a way. She had had a glorious voice and a good deal of technique—and she had been checked in the middle of her career by that lamentable marriage with a fellow who was evidently a typical show specimen of sadism. For a year she had fought to keep life in a little boy who was born without vitality; then the child died and she was separated from her husband, was lucky enough to get an engagement at a German court opera, made a success and came into some money from a godfather. She met her husband to have the divorce finally arranged, and the result of their meeting was Lillemor. And at the clinic, where she went to have the baby, she caught cold, and it ended in a protracted throat trouble. Since then her voice had never been quite what it was before.

Her appearance was also a trifle passée—she was tall, rather massive and at the same time bony, with prominent collar-bones and hollows in her neck. The big face was narrow, with a large nose and mouth, a coarse complexion—but the eyes were wonderful, a golden brown. She had raven-black hair, smooth as horsehair, and she wore it parted and combed over the ears, with a fillet—in the evening a gold band with a scarab in front, and princess frocks in hard colors, green or red.

If she had not been rather stupid, poor thing, she would have laid herself out to be on good terms with Henrik. She had been the great love of his life, and he was certainly ready to go on loving his wife and to spoil her, if she did not take pains to make him sick of her. But she seemed to imagine she could keep Henrik in play by exacting a slightly erotically colored admiration from all the men who came near her.

And it pretty soon came to this, that Berit had hardly any women about her. The married ladies whom she would have been glad to know, did not care for her, and she did not care for those who were willing to be friendly with her. So she had to fall back on her husband's old friends.

"I should feel it as an insult," she had declared on one occasion, "if I found that a man could be in my company without bearing in mind that I was a woman—and desirable." What directly provoked this remark was something Else Mortensen had said—something prudish, it must be allowed, as Else collapsed like a paper bag on receiving this answer. But Berit Alster was an exacting lady in this way, and it was not pure fun being a friend of the family.

Naturally she meant nothing at all by her manner towards him—not for a moment did Paul Selmer imagine that Fru Berit cared specially for him. For that matter, she was certainly very fond of Henrik, in her own way; it would be strange if she were not; they were still on their honeymoon, so to speak. All it could mean was, that was her idea of how one ought to treat a lovely lady and a gifted artist. So she adopted a tone towards her husband's partner which obliged him to affect a certain air of flirtation—unless he wanted to be very impolite.

But he was not so green as to be unaware that there was some danger involved in being on this footing with the young and somewhat provocative wife of one's best friend. At all events for a man who hates having scenes with people who after all do not matter so much to him, and who shrinks from showing himself morally scandalized without any real necessity. Meanwhile this flirting tone that had grown up between him and Henrik's wife struck him as rather disgusting.

Moreover he could not imagine any house which he would care to visit four or five times a week—for dinner, for supper, for Berit's constant little parties. And one can have enough of "Ich grolle nicht—" and "Du bist Orplid mein Land—" even if she sang them finely, and especially of being told every time that she was going to sing for *him*, his favourite songs. All the friends of the house had been allotted their favourite songs.

Then there was the child. Henrik's step-daughter—a sweet little thing, to be sure, with black curls, big eyes, thin and nervous, neglected and spoilt and as fond of being petted as a kitten. She had unaccountably bestowed her affection on "Uncle Paul." Children had had a way of bothering him ever since as a big blushing schoolboy he had been put out of countenance by his fellow travelers little ones calling the attention of the whole railway carriage by addressing him as papa, papa—at the worst the little wretches stretched out and grabbed the schoolbook he was pretending to read, while insufferable females looked on with a smile. Now it was Lillemor who climbed up into Paul's lap and put her arms round his neck and teased her papa by drawing comparisons between him and Uncle Paul, not very flattering to the former. The annoying thing was that Henrik disliked it, Paul could see, though he laughed and tried to put a good face on it. Henrik was very fond of the little girl.

WINTER went by and spring. Henrik and Berit celebrated their wedding day by giving a little evening party "only for intimates."

Paul was hanging his coat up in the hall, when Berit called to him over the banisters:

"Lillemor asks if Uncle Paul will come up and say goodnight to her."

Paul obeyed the order. The moment he came into the nursery he had an impression that the furniture had been changed. Berit was standing in front of a dressing table between the windows; she was dressed in some orange-colored thing, cut extremely low.

"No, no, Lillemor—keep your chocolaty fingers to yourself—" The child sat up in her little bed; her mouth was brown and her fingers were sticky, and she was engaged in undressing a doll.

"Are those *real* pearls you've got in your shirt, Uncle Paul?"

"You'll think we have a strange way of celebrating our wedding day," said Fru Berit from in front of the glass—"that I've moved in here—"

"Mamma won't sleep with papa," exclaimed Lillemor; "for she thinks he looks so ugly when he's asleep, with his moustache tied up"—she demonstrated with a ribbon she had taken off her doll, stretching it tightly over her lip and round her face.

Paul made an attempt to escape. But Berit turned towards him laughing, as she gave her arms a final touch of the powder puff: "Well, what do you say? We can be just as good friends, can't we?—without Henrik's initiating me into all the secrets of his toilet. Ugh!" She stamped on the floor. "I much prefer a man to be clean-shaved—like you. Tell me, what am I to do to make Henrik cut off his moustache—?"

"Couldn't you take revenge?" suggested Paul. "My sister has all kinds of contrivances which I should think might do—curling papers, and long woolly sausages which she pads out her hair with—"

"Ugh, no—that kind of hairdressing doesn't suit my style. No, if I'm to think of revenge, it'll have to take another form—"

"Now you must let me go, Lillemor—good night to you—"

"Here come the other men," said Lillemor, listening attentively to the buzz of voices from the hall. "Now I can hear them singing the opening hymn."

Paul laughed, and her mother explained: "That's a thing she's heard her daddy say—"

He thought himself it looked idiotic to come hurrying down from the upper rooms—together with the mistress of the house. Tasteless, that was what it was. It was certainly not good taste to try to establish him in this role of tame cat. Sometimes of course he imagined a scene in which he spoke a few words of plain common sense to Fru Berit—you ought to be more appreciative of the excellent husband you have got and take up your singing again in earnest, instead of talking everlastingly about your old laurels from Germany and Christiania. But he knew very well he would never say anything of the sort to her.

Devil take the whole business. That time, a couple of years ago, when he used to read the Bible early and late, he had thought that those words about "whoso looketh on a woman," etcetera, were, to put it mildly, somewhat exaggerated. Now he began to see that there was a good deal in them.

He definitely did not like Henrik's wife. Nevertheless he had been driven, more against his will than otherwise, into relations with her which might become risky. Berit of course didn't mean any harm by it, as he always repeated to himself—and he was anything but keen on meeting her, never had been that. But he couldn't get out of it—and after a while she got on his nerves. Tactless she was too. But it wasn't always so easy to pull her up—without being impolite. And he could not help reflecting that pure chance—external circumstances, time and place and so on—may easily drive people into going farther than they intended. Well, that would be a lovely mess—hell! Or else he'd be forced to do the Joseph trick. After which his relations with Henrik's family would be about as pleasant as what we hear of those between the famous interpreter of dreams and the Potiphar ménage.

Chapter Two

For the ptarmigan shooting Selmer and Hauan and an engineer named Kristvik had taken the same saeter as they had had the year before. And it was arranged that Hans Selmer should come up and stay with them part of the time.

So a week after he had taken up his quarters in the Aune saeter, Paul went down to meet his brother. The sky was entirely covered with high, blue-grey clouds that day. It was very still among the mountains. Once, when a bull took to bellowing far away, it was as though the whole wide horizon resounded.

The saeter path led across some mossy wastes, and then the highest mountain farm lay close under the hill. A piercing yellow sunlight broke through under the clouds at that moment, and at one end of the long brown house the sun shone right through a room which stood out against the sky and had windows on both sides.

Paul halted—he seemed on the point of remembering, he knew not what; but this view from the hill above Rise was so fine that it filled him with the same joy every time he came. Now the sun shone upon the old log houses and the grass on the roofs shone as it waved, long and silky, with tufts of bright-colored flowers among it. Below the farm a grey-green field of oats lay in the sunshine, and the bushes along the fence threw long shadows over the corn. But the dark wooded valley with the bright ribbon of the river far below lay in shadow, and on the other side the bare rock rose brown with streaks and patches of snow on every blue knoll.

He was filled with the thoughtless well-being that comes of following a path where one knows every stone almost and every bush. When he walked here in the dark he could hear where he was by the stream that the path followed for the last few miles—it gushed swiftly over stones or gurgled in peaty soil, close by or farther away.

It gathered speed and foamed as it plunged beneath the road, and bubbled in the pool below, as if it could not swallow so much water. Then the stream appeared again and ran down through a paddock where the boys of the farm had made little mills which Paul had been to look at with them.

The gleam of sunshine seemed to shrink up; the last glimmer of it fell on the back door at Rise with the big stone step in front. A woman in white came out, carrying a little child, and as she crossed the grass of the yard Paul saw that she had thick golden plaits wound round her head in a wreath. A perambulator stood there, and before the mother put the child into it, she swung it high into the air and made it laugh; then she pressed the little one to her and kissed it passionately.

At that moment Paul reached the gate and held it open for her. She gave a little curtsy in reply to his bow, and he had the impression of something bright and soft, dazzlingly snow-white and rose-pink. A mere child she seemed to be.

He was given coffee in the big kitchen, at a window that looked on to the valley, and when he saw the cart coming along the road he went down to meet his brother. Paul had gone a little beyond the place where the stream ran under the farm road, when it happened: below him the girl in white was coming up the road with her perambulator, and farther down the cart swung round a projecting rock. Hans was walking by its side; he waved on seeing his brother. At that moment the horse shied at something or other—the cart ran against a roadside stone and the baggage was pitched out in all directions—and then the horse bolted. Hans had snatched at the reins and was dragged along, trying to get a better hold; and Paul dashed down to the perambulator and the white girl, pushed them away into the ditch on the upper side of the road—looked up again to see if he could stop the runaway horse and cart which came on at a furious pace. Then he saw them disappear with his brother over the opposite edge of the road, where there was a big drop. Paul slid down, carrying a shower of gravel and stones with him. Hans lay still in the grass, and across the fields came Anton Rise and his man to catch the horse which was still thundering along with the wreck of the cart, and along the road the driver was running up with the man he had stopped to talk to.

When Paul turned his brother over he saw that underneath the blood Hans was white in the face and was not breathing. He was badly grazed on one side of the face, but Paul could not find any sign of a fracture as he felt with his fingers under the hair—and now the lad was breathing faintly, as it were superficially. Rise and the farm hand came up, and they cautiously went over the unconscious man, but it was impossible to find out at once how badly he was damaged. They made a litter of stakes and coats and carried Hans up to Rise. Behind it walked the driver crying—he was only a boy of eleven or twelve.

Now it was the young woman in white who opened the gate for them. "O dear, I hope it isn't serious—is he dead!" she ended in a kind of stifled shriek.

"No, no," Paul hastened to reply. "My brother has got concussion of the brain, but I hope it won't be serious—"

Her face was white as chalk and she hurried through the gate after them with her perambulator, glancing back in terror at the man who was leading in the horse—it was an ugly sight, with blood on its quarters, wild-eyed and still inclined to shy.

ANTON RISE helped Paul to put his brother to bed in a room off the passage. As they were taking the boot off his left foot they found that the fibula was broken just above the ankle. Hans opened his eyes an instant, but was gone again directly. As soon as they had put him to bed there was a knock at the door, and before anyone had time to say come in, a big blonde lady appeared:

"My name is Fru Anderson, Mrs. John Anderson—I thought perhaps I might be of some use—I've been through a course of first aid—"

"Many thanks, but I don't think there's any more to be done until the doctor comes—"

But Mrs. Anderson threw back the bedclothes to look at the temporary bandages that Paul and Anton Rise had put on. Paul stood there, annoyed and embarrassed, not knowing how to get rid of her, when she turned round to him, seized his hand and squeezed it:

"But how am I to thank you for your plucky conduct—you have saved the lives of my niece and my baby—but you can understand a mother's heart—"

At that moment Elen Rise came in—the doctor would like to speak to Herr Selmer himself. The telephone was in a little room off the kitchen, and as Paul was explaining his brother's condition to the doctor, as far as he could make it out, and receiving instructions about what to do in the meantime, he heard a girl's voice, loud and impulsive, in the kitchen:

"My! Elen, did you ever see anyone so brave? Fancy, the moment he came this afternoon I thought he was the most thrilling man I'd ever seen—and such a sweet doggie he has!"

Paul could not help smiling, in spite of his low spirits.

THE doctor could not arrive for four or five hours. Paul sat at the open window; now and again he went over to his brother, who lay motionless, stretched out straight; his pale profile showed up sharply against the blue paint of the timber wall. But the pulse was a little stronger now. Just then Hans began to vomit. Paul held him, to prevent its choking him. Then he put him straight again. But when the vomiting was over his skin felt a little warmer and he muttered a few words, with eyes half open.

But it was not cheerful. All at once Paul remembered that the last time he saw his brother was that day at the Eastern Station. He himself had not been south since then. No, this was a real bad job—and poor Hans, there'd be no shooting for him this year—and he himself would hardly get back to the saeter this time either.

The window looked out over the valley, and now the wooded hills were black and the river gleamed faintly in the darkness. Just outside was the old farmhouse garden with gnarled apple trees and currant bushes looking like woolly lumps of darkness scattered over the grass; and just under the window was a rosebush which had not yet lost all its flowers, high as the farm stood.

Paul went over and laid his hand on Hans's forehead—the other moved and muttered again—now his skin was growing hot. Paul raised his brother and pushed another pillow under his head. After a while perhaps he could take away some of the hot water bottles.

The hours went by. The change had come rather rapidly; Hans was now feverish and restless, he greedily drank water with unsweetened fruit juice in it. It was quite dark outside and Paul had lighted a little lamp which he placed on the chest of drawers. He was getting fearfully sleepy—they had turned out early at the saeter, with the idea of going early to bed. He moved from the bed to the window and then back again to the corner by the chest of drawers. The rocking chair was not a good thing to sit in when one had to keep awake, and the bound volumes of a children's paper which he found in the hanging shelf were no great help. Between whiles he wondered how he ought to convey the news to his mother—better wait and see how it turned out—unless what the doctor said made it advisable to telegraph.

He was thankful for the interruption when Mrs. Anderson came to the door and asked how Hans was going on: "and then Elen told me to ask if you would have a cup of coffee—you must be tired—"

Coffee was quite a good idea. So he accepted with thanks.

Soon after there was another knock at the door, a very soft one. It was the child in the white dress with the golden plaits. She had the coffee tray in her hands: "May I put it down here? "—She put it on the table and poured out the coffee: "How is your brother now?" She spoke in a whisper and opened her eyes wide whenever she said anything.

"Oh, thanks, he's as well as can be expected. But my dear young lady, are you still up—I hope we're not keeping the whole house awake—?"

"No, Anton and the children have gone to bed, but Elen and Aunt Selma are sitting up in the kitchen. And I don't think I can go to bed before the doctor's been—"

"Oh, but you mustn't think of staying up. There can't be anything to say; my brother has a concussion and it'll take its usual course—"

The girl stood with bowed head and eyes on the floor:

"You have saved my life—" she snatched at his hand and curtsied; "thank you—"

"Oh, not at all—for that matter it was my brother who—well, he didn't manage to stop the horse, worse luck—"

She shook her head, raised her eyes to Paul—and at that moment he saw that her lower eyelids were too thick and covered rather too much of the eyes; this spoilt her face, which would otherwise have been really charming.

"Yes, it was you who saved me and baby Sydney. Auntie says so too." She was going to the door, turned round to him again: "But gee! I've quite forgotten to introduce myself—my name's Fröken Berge, Björg Berge—" and away she went.

A little later, as he put his head out of the window and listened, he heard the rumble of wheels far below. And directly after there was a movement in the kitchen end of the house—they had heard it too. It was the doctor, thank God!

Hans Selmer would have to lie where he was for at least a week—he was pretty seedy; the concussion had been rather serious. Then, if all went well, he might be fit to be taken to Trondhjem when Paul's holiday was over, and sent to the hospital for his broken leg.

"You can be pretty sure I won't hear of your hanging about," said Hans; "it's bad enough that I have to lie here—off with you to the saeter, my lad! I'm not going to spoil your holiday too!"

But Paul wouldn't hear of that. He went up one afternoon to fetch some of his things, and when he came back next evening he found his brother rather poorly, with headache and sickness and a temperature.

"Oh, it's all this chattering," said Hans. "That Norwegian-American woman has been sitting in here, and then there was a teacher fellow they call Jevne—"

"There, you see! I'll have to stay and look after you—"

He went out and shot a fox one morning, and then he tried his luck at fishing in some little tarns not far away. But he dared not leave his brother alone for long. Mrs. Anderson was extremely willing to sit with him, but she talked so much that Hans broke into a sweat at the bare mention of her name.

Hans had to be helped with one thing and another, and now and again he was rather bad, so Paul lay awake a good part of the night, kept a lamp burning and read *The Newcomes*—he always took Thackeray on a holiday, in the handy little volumes on India paper. When he had finished that, there was nothing else in the house that he could read. And at times it was rather slow sitting with his brother—you can't talk very much with a man who's had concussion of the brain.

Paul asked Mrs. Anderson if she could lend him a book, and she gave him two sixpenny editions of Elinor Glyn—totally unreadable. After that she brought him two numbers of a magazine called *The Catholic World*. Paul could not have been more astonished if she had offered him books in Sanskrit. On seeing his surprise she laughed rather nervously:

"Yes, we're Catholics, you see, Mr. Anderson and I—his mother is Irish. But they don't know that here, so I'll ask you not to say anything about it in the house—you know, people of that sort are so terribly prejudiced—"

Paul was slightly vexed, as he didn't like Mrs. Anderson much. Though no doubt she meant well—insisted on helping him and his brother all she could. Her mother had come from Rise; she was related to Anton Rise, but very distantly, and they were here as "paying guests," as she took care to explain. The little Fröken Berge who was with her was the daughter of a cousin of Mrs. Anderson's; she came from Christiania.

THE girl was not nearly so charming as his first impression of her. She had looked so attractive as she stood there with the baby in the evening light, young and dressed in white. It somehow made a difference that the child was not hers—though she was sweet for all that, when she was looking after the little ones, little Etta and the fat baby and Elen's smallest boy—a sort of big-sister motherliness. But her feet looked so huge and swollen in white canvas shoes—a thing that Paul had always thought specially unsightly. And the curls, which in the early hours framed in her soft oval face under the wreath of plaits, had a tendency to come out in the course of the day and hang down straight—exactly like Tua's straggling locks in old days.

But of course Björg Berge was pretty—she had a radiant color, golden hair, a clear complexion, fresh lips and good teeth. Her figure was rather amply developed for her age, for he would not put her at more than sixteen or seventeen—her face was quite childish, and her talk gave a very undeveloped impression.

SHE was picking currants for Elen Rise one or two afternoons, as he sat at the open window, so they fell to talking. She came up, stood with her arms on the windowsill and asked Hans how he was—expressed her admiration for his bravery in seizing the runaway horse. She would have it that she and the baby had been in danger of their lives that evening—well, of course, it might have turned out very badly. Then every morning, when Paul came in to breakfast, Fröken Berge sat there waiting to ask after the medico, as she called Hans. And it usually happened that she stayed and entertained him as he ate. And he thought it amusing enough to listen to her—Björg chatted about Karl Johan and music and the theatres and the Nordmark and the Union: she had had a brother who had been a member of the Students' Union, and evidently Björg was immensely proud of that; in her eyes it was a very great thing to have had a "university education." And Eivind had been so terrifically clever, she assured him with the utmost gravity; in fact she seemed to think it was that that killed him, for he had died of brain fever a year before. It was with an eye to Eivind's future career that he and she had taken the name of the farm their father came from, Berge; her parents were called Jacobsen, and her father kept a draper's shop in Storgate—and Björg admired her whole family in a way that was really touching. Altogether she was such a pronounced lower middle-class Christiania girl that Paul grew quite warm about the heart and rather sentimental from old memories of his student days. To be sure she was a sweet little thing, and he went walks with her along the road a few times and they went together to the local shop and he bought a mug that was painted with roses and had "For a Good Girl" in gilt letters, because she had admired it with such comical seriousness: "Gee, isn't that real peasant style, eh?" And when she found it in her place at the breakfast table next morning she turned red: "Ish, you think I'm silly, don't you—I'm sure you only did that to make fun of me! But I can assure you, I'm not half so childish as you seem to think—"

THE doctor had been up, and he thought Hans Selmer was well enough to be driven the long distance to Storen station, as Paul had to go back to his business. Two days before the Selmers were to leave, Arnt Hauan and Leif Kristvik came down to hear how things were; by that time Hans was feeling so fit that he insisted on having a whisky and soda with the others and a game of poker by his bedside.

Paul went part of the way with his friends when they walked back next day after dinner. He was on his way down again; dusk was already coming on, when he reached a big pond that lay below a marshy tract some three miles above the farm. His little setter swam hither and thither so that he saw nothing but its white back and tail among the rushes. Suddenly the dog darted off barking and wagging its tail towards a figure crouching by the side of the path.

Paul recognized the blue pattern of Björg Berge's neckerchief. When he came nearer he saw that she had taken off one of her shoes and stockings.

"Hullo, Björg—you don't mean to say you've hurt yourself? That would be too bad—if anything happened to *you*—"

Björg Berge shook her head:

"I've only scratched myself—I stumbled, and then I scratched myself on a beastly juniper stump that was hidden in the heather—"

It was a nasty gash—the round girlish calf was all bedaubed with blood, which had trickled down to the foot, and that was brown with bog water. She had been out gathering cloudberries—a tin pail half full stood by her side. Paul fetched water in the lid of the pail and bathed the wound, which was full of shreds of wool; by chance he had an unused pocket handkerchief on him, so he made a compress with that and bound her neckerchief outside.

But when she tried to put on her stocking it was in such rags that it could not hold the bandage in place; it was soaking wet and muddy too.

"Wait a moment, we'll see—" In spite of her protests Paul proceeded to take off one of his knitted stockings and to draw it cautiously over Fröken Berge's foot.

"How's that—it doesn't hurt too much, does it, when you tread on the foot? No, let me take the pail—won't you take hold of my arm?"

And they both laughed; he looked so comic with one bare leg and one stocking.

The evening was very mild, and in the cloudy sky yellow streaks, the color of brass and amber, shone in the north-west above the mountains on the farther side of the valley. The sky was palely reflected in the bogholes over the moor; the water of the mountain stream turned black under the edge of the peat, but where it ran rapidly among stones it had a yellow gleam from the afterglow. The purling of the brook and the murmur of water farther off and the soft sighing of the evening breeze were blended in a mild and melancholy autumnal note. The two young people hardly spoke. Paul only whispered, when the path ran downhill or was stony—"take my arm now," and Björg took his arm without saying anything.

"Does it hurt?" he whispered now and again. "It isn't hurting you too much, is it?"

"Oh no—it doesn't hurt too badly—"

There was only a pale light under the clouds on the horizon when they reached the bluff above the farm. The valley was in darkness, with faint glimpses of the river far below, and little red eyes gleaming from farms and crofts on the black wooded slopes. Directly under them the kitchen windows of Rise shone warm and homelike, and from the byre came a stream of lantern light—the dairy maid appeared at the open door and emptied a pail into the big milk can.

"Thank God," said Paul with feeling, "that we've got so far. Poor little Björg, I'm afraid it's been hurting you awfully—"

"Oh no," said Björg.

"What a brave little girl you are!" He gave her arm a little squeeze against his side. Then he bent down and kissed her on the lips—a gentle, tender kiss upon the childish mouth, chilled by the wind, and felt it close, innocent and coy, beneath his lips.

"Poor little Björg—I think you're a really brave girl, I do indeed!"

As they entered the passage he asked:

"Have you any iodine—or your aunt—well then, I'll fetch it—you must get your aunt to paint it with iodine and put on a gauze bandage—"

Björg drew her arm out of his and stole quietly through the dining room door.

A FEW minutes later Paul came into the dining room with the bottle of iodine and some packets of gauze bandage. Only one of the hanging lamps was lighted; it shone upon two places laid at one end of the long dining table which always had a cloth on it. Paul went towards Mrs. Anderson's door—then he discovered that Björg was sitting in the little basket chair by the middle window. She was half in darkness, but he saw that she had not yet taken off her coat.

"Oh, are you there—is Mrs. Anderson in her room?" "Aunt was going with Elen to the teacher's this evening—" Björg's voice was low and indistinct; she kept her head turned away from him.

"Do you think you can manage it yourself—here's the bottle and here are the bandages—but, my dear, you don't mean to say you're crying—? Does it hurt so much, Björg?" "It isn't that—"

"But what is it then—is there anything I can do for you?" She turned her head towards him—it was resting; thrown a little back, against the round cushion of faded canvas embroidery. Her hair was falling down, shimmering like darkened gold in the faint lamplight, and in the full, oval face the eyes were like great dark wells brimming over—the tears flowed fast down the red cheeks and twinkled as they dripped upon the soft white throat.

"No man has ever kissed me before," she said, trembling with solemnity.

Paul did not quite know what answer he ought to make to this. She looked perfectly charming anyhow, as she sat there, warm, dissolved and bathed in tears—literally—childlike and virginal—

"But, bless my soul—did you think it hurt—?" he said lightly.

She tossed violently in her chair, and then she broke into loud sobs. Paul felt like a ruffian.

"But Björg, dear little Björg—have I hurt you—I didn't mean to do that, you may be sure—" She only wept. "But, Björg—do you really think it was so terrible—?"

"I have always thought," Björg sobbed, "that I would be able to say to my fiancé, if I had one some day, 'you are the first man who has kissed me.' That has been my dream ever since I was a little girl—"

That was awkward—but at the same time it was awfully touching. Paul said despondently:

"Don't be so cut up about it, Björg—I didn't mean anything. Don't be angry with me"—he tried to take her hand—"I really didn't mean anything at all except that I thought you'd been a very brave little girl. I kissed you just as one would kiss a child—"

"That's exactly it!" she cried hotly. "If you had cared for me, why—. But I'm *not* a child, I take leave to tell you that I'm eighteen already! But you've treated me all the time just as if I was a child—.'"

"Well, but I really beg your pardon, Fröken Björg. It never struck me—. You must know that I think you're frightfully sweet—but somehow I couldn't behave differently to you—it would have been like kidnapping—"

"Do you care for me at all, Selmer—?" she looked up at him anxiously.

"Of course I care for you. You must see that."

"Properly?" Her eyes were black with seriousness—she looked enchanting, though her face was a little too red and swollen from crying.

"Properly," replied Paul, and then he smiled down at her, for she was staring at him in such intense expectation. "Properly." With that he bent down and kissed her. She threw her arms round his neck and pressed her warm, wet, soft cheek against his.

"Yes, but are you fond of me?" she whispered between her kisses.

"Fond of you—you can be sure I'm fond of you—"

"For I've been fond of you the whole time—ever since you saved my life on the road—"

He helped her to dress the wound on her calf, and they and the whole room smelt of iodine. Then Björg fetched the tea pot which had been standing on the kitchen range all this time and poured out his tea—it had the flat taste of the country shop and at the same time was bitter as ink from standing. And every moment it became clearer to Paul that he had certainly got himself into a kind of engagement—and he felt a trifle overwhelmed. So as not to show it, he proposed to Björg, when they had finished supper, that they should take a little walk. And with their arms tightly clasped about each other they strolled down the road—but it was pitch-dark out of doors and the road was stony and uneven, so that it was not inviting in itself to take a walk this evening. They kissed each other a lot, for Paul was still too staggered by the turn things had taken to be able to say much, and Björg was in a state of quiet rapture. Then it began to drizzle and very soon it was raining properly.

Before they parted in the passage it was settled that Paul was to write as soon as he got to Trondhjem, and when she and her aunt came there in a week's time, she was to ring him up. For Paul said she must not think of getting up next morning to say goodbye to him—they were leaving so early.

Hans was asleep when Paul came into the room; he undressed, feeling rather uneasy in his mind. This couldn't possibly be serious. He lay awake a good while wondering what it really was he had done.

She *was* up next morning as they were leaving, and Paul took a warm and affectionate farewell of Björg Berge in the little passage leading to the back garden.

HANS Selmer was taken to St. Elisabeth's hospital. Paul went to visit him every day, and his Trondhjem friends were very kind and sympathetic towards his brother. Else Mortensen and Berit Alster vied with one another in sending him delicate little dishes, homemade sweets and cakes. If one of them was not there, the other was, but usually the latter when Paul went to see his brother.

So when Björg rang him up one day, Paul was in the mood to greet her with some enthusiasm—she would be at any rate a change. She and her aunt were living in a boarding house at the bottom of Søndre gate.

That week there happened to be brilliant autumn weather. And Paul Selmer was always on the go with Mrs. Anderson and Björg, but more often with Björg alone, for Mrs. Anderson had been let into the secret. He and Björg went to Graakallen one afternoon in sparkling weather, and they were at the Lerfoss falls one dark, steamy, wet evening, when it was so mild that the moist air was almost muggy: they walked on the road between the two falls and the scrub that grew in the folds of the clay slopes was reeking with moisture and the river ran smooth and full with threatening eddies in its dark water which reflected the lights of the power station. The light gleamed in puddles on the road and the air was full of the roar of the waterfall and the trickling murmurs of little brooks—it was as though they were at the bottom of a strange, wet, cosy world; they kissed and kissed each other in the dark, and Paul abandoned himself entirely to his feelings. Heavens, of course he was glad that fate had thrown him and this sweet little girl into each other's arms. He was fond of her, that he was.

They supped at the restaurant by the falls, and there wasn't a soul there that evening besides themselves.

One day they took the train to Melhus; Mrs. Anderson and the two children came with them. Paul had ordered a carriage and took the ladies for a drive along the Aanöia. It was the same radiant weather with sunshine and brilliant blue autumn sky above dark forests; the big farms shone gaily with their red, yellow or white buildings against the autumn tints of the Woods and the green meadows and light fields of stubble. It was impossible to be anything but happy, even about an unintentional engagement, when the world was so fine and the girl so sweet.

The afternoon before the aunt and she were to leave for Christiania, Björg came to see Paul in his rooms. Karen had laid an elegant coffee table for two and decorated it with autumn flowers. Afterwards they sat together in the armchair by the window and watched it grow dark; the streetlamp outside shone on the leaves of the old poplar, and they made plans. Paul said yes to everything Björg said—they would have a little house of their own with a garden, and they would make a wedding trip to Paris, and Björg had always longed so much to see Nordland, ever since she read *In Fairyland*. Paul agreed to everything.

She had to do her hair again, before they went to meet the aunt at the Britannia. Björg gave him a little bashful smile, as she slipped through the door into his bedroom. And Paul sat down to the piano and played the wedding march from *The Wedding at Ulfåsa* to celebrate the first occasion when her hairpins lay on his dressing table, which by the way was an old chest of drawers. Björg called out asking if it was an heirloom, and who was the charming lady he had a portrait of on the bookshelf: "Gee, how beautiful she must have been—why, you're like her! I say, do you think your mother will like me—?"

"I'm sure she will."

"Oh no, don't muss me about any more," Björg begged him, as she came and stood by him at the piano. Then she had to rummage through his music—she played herself and sang a little too, had a sweet little voice. They frittered away the time at the piano till they discovered they'd have to fly as if the devil was after them—it was Paul who had invited the ladies to dine at the hotel this evening, and it would never do if Aunt Selma arrived first.

Next day he appeared at the station, loaded with books and flowers and cakes for the children and sweets for the ladies, and so they left.

Chapter Three

Paul heard from Björg several times a week—long letters, in which she assured him of her love and confided to him her thoughts, "but perhaps you think I'm an odd one to go pondering about all this, but you must please not to laugh at your little girl for that," and she told him about everything they did at home and the sewing circle and her friends. Paul had also had a letter from Fru Jacobsen—Björg had never had any secrets from her mother, so he had to say she might tell her mother about their engagement. The letter from Björg's mother occupied three and a half pages of scented mauve note paper and was rather high-flown, Paul thought—he scratched his head and composed a nice polite answer.

So now he was once more writing love letters every week, and he scarcely reflected that this time it came far more easily to him—he filled two quarto sheets of the firm's letter paper in a jiffy; pet names and tender expressions flowed from his pen like nothing at all.

Hardly had she left when the whole business appeared to Paul as something absolutely unreal. Even this lively correspondence—well, it was as though there were no reality behind it. He remembered how when he was a small boy at school he had once let one of the mistresses coax him into starting a correspondence with a Swedish boy of the same age who lived at Uppsala. To begin with he and Nils Gösta wrote very zealously to each other—describing their doings in the holidays and the possessions they most valued; it was much the same as writing a Norwegian exercise on a subject chosen by oneself. When they had no more things of this sort to tell each other, the correspondence came to a standstill of its own accord. Almost unconsciously Paul expected that the same thing would happen to his and Björg Berge's letters.

Now and again he saw quite clearly and soberly—it was by no means so sure that this would happen. For without being too conceited he could say to himself—it was natural enough that Björg Berge should wish to marry him. He had a good business, came of a good family, was good-looking—and he had kissed and petted the little inexperienced thing and promised her a house of her own and a trip to Paris. But time would show what was to come of it. In any case he had been a good deal in love with Björg when they were together—worse things might happen to him than being married to her.

He wondered whether Henrik had guessed anything—for he had been running round with Björg and the aunt every single day, the week they were in town, and now these long, narrow, colored envelopes with round, girlish handwriting showered down upon his table at the office. Hans presumably had thought his attentions were only a return for the sympathy they had shown while he lay disabled up at Rise. Anyhow, whatever Hans thought or did not think about it, he would never say a word until Paul himself broached the subject.

When his brother came out of hospital he stayed a fortnight with Paul, while getting accustomed to using his leg. It was a pleasant time; they sat each in his chair reading, and occasionally one or two of Paul's acquaintances came up in the evening and they played cards, Karen made special efforts at every meal, so that the student might look really well when his mother saw him again.

Paul had succeeded in avoiding Berit Alster pretty well for a time; but after Hans had left he had her on the telephone again constantly. Just at this time however her manner was rather more subdued towards other men and more wifely towards Henrik, and one day Alster hinted to his partner that a happy event was impending at the villa on the Island. That was fine—then perhaps Berit would settle down a little.

One evening in November she rang him up again:

"I say—couldn't you come round?—Henrik had to go to the Moens', but I wasn't fit to go with him—Lillemor has been so poorly, I'm afraid she's going to have bronchitis—ugh, I'm so worn out with sleepless nights and so nervous and depressed—I can't bear being left alone—can't you come and be kind to me a little—?"

"All right."—Damn the woman. It wasn't weather you'd turn a dog out in, biting wind and driving snow that came at you almost horizontally.

"Well, well, Gulla, will you come too? We'll have to go, my doggie, when the lady calls us."

He was shown into Berit's drawing room, where he was always afraid of knocking something over—it was made almost impassable with standard lamps and easels and little tables with photographs of artists, especially of Berit, in costume and in mufti, and then she always kept a subdued red light. This evening, though, it was good to come under a roof; his face was burning from the weather.

Fru Alster was sitting on the low couch before the fire, reposing on the great polar bear's skin, and she had Lillemor with her. The child was in her nightgown, wrapped in a plaid. Then came first of all the usual scene—he had to carry the youngster up to the bedroom, and Lillemor insisted that Uncle Paul should sit down by her bed and tell her a story. It was a kind of serial novel that he had started one evening when he couldn't think of anything else—about Gulla, his dog, and two little girls named Guro and Ambjörg. He had taken the names from Tua's two children, whom by the way he had never seen, but Lillemor knew them from the photographs in his rooms—in Paul's narrative they were already big girls who went on mountain expeditions and had a lot of strange adventures. Fortunately it didn't amuse Berit a bit to listen to this, so she went down again at once, with an injunction to Lillemor not to worry Uncle Paul too long—"do you hear, Paul, it's so late—it must be a tiny little story tonight—"

When he came down Berit was already at the table in the dining room—she was reading the paper while waiting.

"It's a bore that Lillemor has got such a cold—"

"Ugh, yes, I hope it's nothing—will you have your tea at once?"

She had her hair hanging in plaits over her bosom and a silver ribbon fastened on her forehead. The violet dressing gown with silver flowers was no doubt meant for a sort of morning gown—it looked fairly theatrical.

She put her arm through his as they went back to the drawing room:

"Oh, I do think Henrik might have stayed at home when I wasn't fit to go—can you guess why he must needs be running to these relations of his early and late—?"

"But it's the seventieth birthday today—there's a portrait and all in the papers—"

"And tomorrow he wants to go off with Hauan—in this awful weather! and stay there over Sunday. Are you going too?"

"I had thought of it—"

"Paul—no, sit here. Paul—you are my friend, aren't you?"

"Of course."

"Tell me—do you think I have an easy time—?" she seized his hand among the white fur, and leaned back against the silk cushions. "Do you think I have such an easy time always? When one has been accustomed as I have to live in the centre of everything in the great cities of Europe—not that I would claim that it's always the best or the most valuable life in itself, but it was my life, my own life—and then to be transplanted to a little provincial town right up under the North Pole almost. And then Henrik lets me sit alone here with my little sick child evening after evening—tell me, Paul, do you think I have an easy time—?"

He had heard this a hundred times at least. He pressed her hand in sympathy and hurriedly got up to attend to the fire.

"I can't see that it can be difficult to be married to Henrik—"

"No, I know you think he's faultless. He's your friend—and I know he's great in that way. A man's man. It's not that I'm not intensely fond of Henrik, you understand—but perhaps you don't see that one can admire a man and love him—intensely—and still there is something one misses—sympathy or an understanding of one's little childish weaknesses—" now the tears were beginning to drip—

Bah, what bad taste. And in present circumstances too—

"Paul," said Berit in a low voice. "You're so good at telling stories to little children—haven't you any for big children? You never tell me anything. Come, a fairy tale—?"

"No-o—I don't think I could make up anything that would amuse you—"

"You never tell me anything about yourself—"

"About myself? Devil a fairy tale there, Berit. You'll be bored stiff and stark if I begin telling you about myself."

"I believe you're wrong there. But you're always so close about your own concerns. I believe you like to make yourself sort of—mysterious—"

"Oh, you're talking nonsense."

"For instance," said Berit. "You see, I know a little about you. This was before I knew you. There was a girl—just a little, a little—don't you know?—but you were terribly fond of her, weren't you?"

"Oh! That was in my salad days." Confound it all—but of course, when one's friends got married one must expect them to tell their wives all sorts of things—

"Have you quite lost sight of her—?"

"She's married to a salesman at Bergen," said Paul, curtly.

"And you never hear from her?"

"No, of course not. By the way"—he sat upright—"I may just as well tell you, if you haven't heard it already—I am engaged."

"What do you say—?" asked Berit after a pause. "Is this quite lately?"

"In the mountains this autumn. I'll show you—" he took out his pocketbook. The snapshots he had taken of Björg had not turned out so well, but he had the portrait she had sent him. He took it out and handed it to Berit.

She leaned right back under the lampshade, inspecting it thoroughly.

It would bear that. Björg looked bewitching in it. Her round, childlike face had such a touching expression of serious wonder, and a little clever retouching of the eyelashes made her eyes look like dark, radiant stars. From the parting on her forehead her fair, wavy hair hung down like the ears of a setter, her heavy plait fell over her shoulder on to the young bosom; the pure and delicate lines of the throat were surrounded by something soft and white, a kind of lace shawl.

"Well!" said Berit, rather sharply, "she's just perfectly enchanting! No, Paul, anything quite so sweet—but my dear man, you can't think of marrying her for years! Don't you know that there's a law about the responsible age—?"

"That was taken three years ago," said Paul rather shortly, putting away the photograph. "When she was confirmed. Well, we're thinking of getting married in the spring."

"You don't mean to tell me this is the same as the little lady you were showing off here a couple of months ago?" Berit laughed aloud. "Well, then she has undoubtedly changed a great deal. Fancy, I didn't recognize her—oh, but she was quite sweet—dainty and pretty—"

PAUL sat down and wrote to Björg as soon as he got home. He was rather excited, and the letter turned out a real love letter. Why should they wait, he wrote—life was short, and youth didn't last so long that two who were fond of each other could afford to throw away any of their time. He would come to Christiania at Christmas—and he asked Björg to marry him in March, for instance, or at any rate as soon as she could get ready.

Then he ran down and dropped the letter into the nearest post box straight away.

And when he had gone to bed he suddenly found himself wide awake—it was as though he had been flung to a distance and saw everything from a different point of view all at once. The plain fact of the matter was that he had been a great rascal—he had won the love of this charming little child, the first love of a good, innocent girl—he had kissed and pawed a pure, inexperienced little child like Björg, got engaged to her—and the Lord knew what he had meant by it all! He supposed he had been hoping, perhaps without being altogether conscious of it, that it would blow over, that the connection would gradually become weaker, until this engagement died a natural death. But then I've been behaving like a scoundrel, he thought, burning with consternation—I've played with the warm and loyal heart of a little girl. And never thought a scrap about it. No, by God, sweet little Björg, my dear little friend—oh, but she should never know this. I was in love with her, I shall be in love with her again as soon as we meet—I am fond of you, Björg, I shall be so fond, so fond of you, my dear young sweetheart—have I really had the heart to deceive you a single moment?—no, Björg, I'll never do that as long as I live.

And he actually went to Christiania three days before Christmas, and when he came into the office again on the second day of the new year he wore a plain gold ring on the ring finger of his right hand and received the congratulations of the staff, and for the next few days he was congratulated by everyone he knew, and the cards came showering in, replying to the notice he had sent out.

Paul assured himself that the fire of love burnt brightly on the hearth within him. And his feelings swayed hither and thither like the smoke in a chimney on a day when the wind blows from every quarter.

She was so sweet, so touching in many ways. But he had had few chances of seeing her alone. It began with his dining with his future parents-in-law—the next day, Christmas Eve, he was at his mother's and she at home. But on Christmas Day he was back again at the Jacobsens', and next day Björg came out with him to Linlökka, and after that they went to his father's, and on the fourth day of Christmas his mother and Hans and he went to the Jacobsens'—and on New Year's Eve Björg and her parents were invited to the traditional party given by his father and Lillian—and they had been to Uncle Paul's and to Mrs. Anderson at the Hospice, where she was staying.

But, thank God, they were going to live at Trondhjem.

So this sort of thing wouldn't last.

And no doubt the Jacobsens were excellent people; they had received him very pleasantly. That they thought their daughter had made a good match was very natural from their point of view. Also that they were proud of Björg—she was so sweet with her simple-minded admiration of her parents—and with the education they had given her, high school, music, commercial college, arts and crafts and two or three things besides, it was reasonable that they should consider Björg accomplished enough to be able to grace any position in society, as her mother expressed it.

The Jacobsens lived on the first floor in one of the little old houses in Storgate; the draper's shop was on the ground floor. And there was something about the house and the view from the upstairs windows which put Paul into a Christmas mood—bitter driving snow round the gas lamps, little drifts of fresh snow in all the corners and windowsills and finely powdered snow on the heaps of broken ice that bordered the pavement. Greenish yellow and orange light streamed from the shop windows, struggling with the frost on the panes. And crowds of people in the street, people carrying Christmas trees and dragging bobsleighs with sheaves of corn on them, the trolley cars clanging and thundering past, striking sparks from the overhead wires. Storgate, that was one of the few streets in Christiania that put you in mind of a big town. They had always gone there for their Christmas shopping with their mother, when they were children.

"This site is worth some money," said his father-in-law to be. Herr Jacobsen was a little, thin, broad-shouldered man with a low forehead, a square and bony face, deep-set, sparkling blue eyes and reddish yellow hair that was cut straight across the forehead and plastered down with some stuff. Not many words had Paul heard him say—whether because he was bashful or because his wife had deprived him of the power of speech.

Paul had a spontaneous liking for the man. He reminded him of the shoemaker who had done their repairs when they were living in Keysers gate—a taciturn little man with whom Paul had liked to sit, saying nothing or recounting his adventures, in a narrow little shop with one window, where there was an interesting smell of leather and cobbler's wax and stale coffee. His father-in-law's name was Ole Jacobsen and he came from a farm in Dovre, Paul found out.

It took him rather longer to make up his mind about his mother-in-law. She must have been good-looking at one time, but now she was fairly massive, to put it nicely—especially when in evening dress she looked as if she would burst all dams. Her face was red—as though her high neckband caused her continual discomfort; and her florid complexion made her grey-green eyes look strangely bright. Her light brown hair was curled and crimped and piled up in a great pyramid. Altogether she looked rather—well, kind of overwhelming, but maybe that was partly due to her manner: she talked a great deal and in a fairly loud voice, was obviously accustomed to admiration from her husband and children—from Björg anyhow; to her every word that proceeded from her mother's mouth was infallible wisdom. With the son it had probably been different, there it must have been the mother who was the admirer and who insisted on all his demands being fulfilled. But now he was dead, poor fellow, so there was no more to be said about that.

Fru Jacobsen had spent some years in America—it was there that she and Jacobsen had been married. And no doubt it was in the land of liberty that she had acquired her colossal assurance: she kept telling her son-in-law that they reckoned themselves as good as anyone for all they had begun in such a small way, and she was almost pathetically snobbish, and she complained bitterly of how everything was on such a small scale in Norway and behind the times compared with what she remembered "over there."—

But it wasn't his parents-in-law he was going to marry. And since Björg and he were not to live in Christiania, it would be sheer cussedness on his part if he couldn't be good friends with her family the few times they were likely to meet.

HIS own mother had been rather silent at first, when he told her of his engagement—but then she cordially wished him joy and kissed him, and of course she was sweet and friendly with Björg when he brought her out to Linlökka. But she had given no sign of what she thought in her own mind—beyond some almost impersonal remarks as to how pretty Björg was and so on. For that matter he had scarcely had a moment alone with his mother or his people except on Christmas Eve. Nor indeed had Paul sought an opportunity of being alone with his mother. He had a feeling that it would be awkward for both of them if they were to discuss anything connected with his last engagement.

Nor had they much to say at his father's, but he had never expected they would have. His father had aged a good deal, Paul thought. But Lillian was the same as ever.

In March Paul went back to Christiania to be married. The wedding was to take place in Our Savior's church, and afterwards there was to be a dinner at a small hotel in Stortings gate—Paul had never heard of it; it was after his time.

On this occasion it was arranged that both his father and mother should come to the wedding and Lillian stay at home. Paul did not like this arrangement—of course he had always known that his parents saw each other fairly often, but he had never been with both of them at the same time since his childhood, before their divorce. But his mother-in-law declared she really couldn't see anything strange in it—such things were quite usual nowadays. Perhaps she ought to put them next to each other—?

Hans was the only brother who could come to the wedding. Tua was unfit to travel at the moment, Halstein was at a congress in Germany, Sigmund was giving recitals in Dresden. But old Uncle Paul came and two Dverberg cousins—Evald, the barrister, whom Paul couldn't stand, and Emil whom he had scarcely seen since he was a boy. Arnt Hauan had come south to be his best man.

But it was no worse for him than for other fellows who had to go through it—on the contrary; they were to get away the same evening. There were some newly-wedded couples who had to put in the time at home and receive visits.

They drank him out of the ranks of bachelors, very handsomely and correctly, at Emil Dverberg's; there were only seven of them, for he did not know so many men in town now. Paul returned to his hotel at half-past two, as sober as was decently permissible for a man in his situation.

The little red lamp on the bedside table showed him a packet and an envelope. The writing was Lillian's. Paul stood in his ulster and read the letter:

> Dear Paul,
>
> As I take up the pen to wish you joy on this auspicious day, my heart is so full. My thoughts go back to the old days at Röllstulen, when you were the charming little boy with the brown curls and the big, frank grey eyes and the sweet, manly, chivalrous nature—Aunt Kraby's faithful little cavalier. Dear Paul, you must forgive me if I strike this note this evening, but I desire so earnestly that, if you can, you will forget all that has

happened since and that in my wildest dreams I should never have imagined at that time, and will allow me this evening to express every good wish for your future happiness, not as your father's wife, for that has given occasion for misunderstandings and difficulties as the result of which I must be content tomorrow with being present in the spirit at your wedding rejoicings, but that you will try for once to think of me as an old aunt who sits at home poor and lonely, but with her heart full of the warmest desire for God's richest blessings upon you and the young woman whose fortunes from now on are to be bound up with yours.

Dear Paul, all of you, Erik's children, have always been unspeakably dear to me. As you will remember, I too have experienced a mother's joy and sorrow, and you must believe me when I say that the empty place which my little Margit's death left in my heart is occupied in a great measure by you, her brothers and sister. But especially by you, my dear Paul, and Sif—Hans and Sigmund were so small in the old Röllstulen days.

It is therefore quite impossible for me to find words to tell you how happy I am that you are now to unite your future to the charming, warmhearted, pure little person who tomorrow before the altar will give you her hand for life, if God will. For I think your little Björg one of the most enchanting and unaffected creatures I have seen for many years. God bless you two dear people. Indeed I am so glad that you have won the heart of so lovable and innocent a young woman. Now I feel convinced that a bright and happy future lies before you, my dear boy—I must be allowed to call you that for this once. Not if you had been my own son could I have felt it more when a few years ago it looked as if you were about to throw yourself away. But God be praised that tomorrow you will appear before the altar with one who I am sure is worthy of your affection!!

The silver is from your father and me for both of you. But in the accompanying case you will find a gift: the diamond brooch which your father presented to me on my fiftieth birthday. It is at the same time the most valued and the most valuable jewel I possess, and therefore I entreat you to give it to

> *your young wife*, when you two young people arrive at the hotel where you are to spend your first days together. Convey to her at the same time my warmest wishes for a long, bright and blessed life for both of you.
>
> Your devoted old friend
>
> Louise (Lillian) Kraby Selmer.

There. She meant it well. Poor woman, in a way it was really quite thrilling—when he remembered how proud she had been of that jewel.

NEXT day then Paul Selmer and Björg Barge were married. And then came the dinner and the speeches, and they changed their clothes and drove to the station. And suddenly bride and bridegroom found themselves alone in a stuffy second-class carriage; the little lamp in the roof shone sleepily upon the red plush seats, the curtains were drawn on the side of the corridor—the train gave a jerk, and they were off.

Björg, in a new grey walking dress and a marten coat, looked up at her husband, pale and round-eyed. Paul felt inclined to laugh—poor little puss, she looked as if she expected her new-fledged husband to pounce upon her like a tiger upon its prey.

"There, kid—now you must lie down and try to get a little sleep before we have to turn out—we don't get to Haugerud till past three—give me your hat, I'll put it up in the net—

He settled the cushion under her head, covered her with the plaid, and then took his place in the corner of the opposite seat.

The lamp in the roof jingled, the door of the carriage rattled and the woodwork creaked. Outside the night swept past, white fields with a gleam of silver and long shadows over the snow; the moon was just up. It was blowing a good deal tonight.

Björg stole a glance at him now and again—seemed still a little afraid of an ardently amorous attack—and perhaps a little disappointed that her husband just sat there looking out of the window. But after a while she fell asleep. Poor kid, it must have been a strenuous day for her too.

Somehow he could not get it into his head that it was real. In church, during the ceremony—he had stood up and he had made his responses and he had knelt down. He had listened to speeches at the dinner and he had made a speech himself, and all the time he had had a feeling exactly as if he had been acting a part in a play. His mother and his father had carried on an animated conversation sitting under a talipot palm, his father-in-law had wandered about in a swallow-tailed coat, and the whole thing had been like a comedy. Björg had been like a vision in her wedding dress—white silk, wreath and long frothy veil. Hauan had taken some flashlight photographs. The champagne was vile.—

Paul got half up and felt in the pocket of his ulster which was hanging by the window, searching for his cigarettes. What was this he had hold of?—ah, Lillian's letter with the little packet. Now she might very suitably receive the present tomorrow morning at the breakfast table—a morning gift!

At half-past three in the morning he stood in an icy hotel room—the fire that crackled and blazed in the stove had not yet made itself felt—outside it was dazzling moonlight. And Björg was rummaging in an open trunk which stood on trestles at the foot of two iron beds with innumerable brass knobs.

And all at once Paul had an irrepressible feeling that now this adventure had been carried too far, he had got himself into a frightfully illegitimate position—and he must really be a very immoral young man to have enticed this good little girl into an hotel, with the object of passing the night with her in a double room—

"Paul," whispered Björg bashfully—"couldn't you go out for a little, while I go to bed—?"

Paul took her in his arms and succeeded in putting an entirely appropriate degree of passion into his voice, as he whispered—"But you'll be quick, won't you—"

Then he walked up and down an infinite length of coconut matting in a corridor with a blind, smooth, ochre-yellow wall on one side and a row of grained and numbered doors on the other. At the end of the corridor the moon shone in through a colossally high naked window—outside was the forest, black as coal around the lake, where the frozen snow gleamed like silver. From the edge of every drift the dry snow was blown like fine, light smoke into the bright, greenish blue air, which was lashed by the pliant boughs of the weeping birches. The building creaked and groaned under the howling blasts of the wind upon its walls.

Paul wandered between the window looking out on the wild moonlight night and the farthest door at the corner of the landing. Outside it stood a pair of gaping men's boots, down at heel. Otherwise the whole row of narrow yellow doors with black numbers seemed to exhale a confession of the emptiness and biting cold within. Then a door halfway down was opened a little way—a pair of new brown ladies' boots was placed outside. Paul went to the door and knocked.

"May I come in—?"

"Wait just a moment—"

Paul continued his march between the window and the mournful men's boots. At last the door of number nineteen was opened again—a hand and part of a white arm beckoned in the streak of light. And Paul betook himself to the bridal chamber.

THREE days later they went on to Finse and stayed there a week. There they got on together far more comfortably than he had expected—Björg was as clever and plucky on skis as any little Christiania girl could be, and they had very good weather. They came home giddy with sunshine on snow and fresh air and exercise and holiday humour, and as they dressed for dinner up in their room they caressed in a kind of free and easy comradeship.

FROM Finse they went to Bergen, where Paul had a lot of business to see to, and then they were to take the boat to Trondhjem. On waking the first morning at the new hotel Paul was aware that he had been dreaming—he was still wrapped in a mood of infinite, sensuous sweetness. He was holding Björg's hand upon his breast, he discovered—had been holding it there while he slept—and he released it as he felt himself shrink with cold and disappointment, with himself and everything. The warm and painful voluptuousness that had belonged to the dream had nothing to do with Björg—could never in this world have anything to do with her. But the only part of his dream he remembered was that he had been standing outside a shop window full of blue hortensia, masses of flower pots with blue hortensia arranged so that they sloped inwards, and among them were some bunches of golden doronicum. The rest, the erotic part, was only the reflection of—

Cautiously he took Björg's hand again, drew her whole cool underarm against his breast. She stirred slightly and muttered in her sleep. There was however nothing remarkable in his having dreamt of the window of a flower shop; they had passed more than one as they drove to the hotel the evening before, and he had thought he would go out today and buy some flowers for Björg. There was a limit to everything, and it was absurd that he should lie here feeling upset because he believed he might have been unfaithful to his wife in a dream—of which all he remembered was that he had been standing outside a flower shop and looking in at the window. It wasn't even that window—it was a much bigger one.

Björg wanted to stay in bed and have breakfast sent up, and Paul took his hat and ran down to buy papers. It was full spring here by the sea—dry pavements, green lawns and big buds on the trees in the little park—warm, and spring-like morning sunshine over the town. Paul strolled along the first street round the corner till he found a flower shop, bought tulips and narcissus and birch leaves, a whole armful.

The porter had letters for them when he came back—three for Björg. It was the first time Paul had seen the strange name on an envelope: Fru Björg Selmer. He could not help seeing before him another name which he had scrawled on blotting paper and inside the covers of notebooks—Fru Lucy Selmer. Well, well, perhaps one does that kind of thing the first time and never again.

Björg had fallen asleep. A chambermaid brought him empty vases with a discreet smile—Paul arranged the flowers by the bedside and on the dressing table and about the room, before he woke his little wife. And he sat on the edge of her bed while she ate, took a drink of coffee from her cup, and she had a pull or two at his cigarette.

"But look here, you little sluggard—you must hurry up and get dressed; meanwhile I'll go down and get a bite of food, and then we'll take a carriage to Fantoft—in weather like this we can't go trailing round to Haakon's halls and churches and that kind of thing—"

Neither of them had been in Bergen before, and the town looked simply *too* beautiful and interesting on a sparkling clear day like this, with real mountains around, down whose sides little streams and watercourses were glistening, and at the bottom of the basin the swarm of old reddish brown roofs and big budding trees was bathed in sunlight. They drove along the Kalfar—all the villa gardens that lay terraced on the steep hillside were covered with ivy and evergreen bushes, in a luxuriance which he had never believed possible in Norway. And among the dark evergreens new pale green leaves and grass and bright tulips were sprouting.

Along the path under the big old trees two women were pushing perambulators. As they drove past Paul saw that one of them was Lucy—

He put his arm round Björg, pressed her to him impulsively, as they sat back in the carriage:

"We're quite happy, aren't we?"—Lucy hadn't seen him. And again he squeezed his wife round the waist: "Don't you think so, darling—we're quite happy, aren't we—?"

Chapter Four

They were to live in his bachelor rooms till they found a house to suit them. But Björg found it very slow, when Paul was at the office all day and Karen insisted on doing everything about the house. So Björg contrived to get rid of Karen.

In June Björg moved to a farm above Melhus where they took summer boarders; Else Mortensen had praised the place highly. Paul came out once or twice a week. It was quiet at home in his rooms; the atmosphere was close with a peaceful smell of dust and loneliness, for the woman who looked after the place for him always shut all the windows before she left—Trondhjem wasn't Paradise, no, she said, there were thieves even here, and the old people downstairs had gone away to visit their married daughter.

Paul was comfortable in the empty, summer-like rooms. Soon he would be leaving here for good. This flat was very small, all the same, for two people. Naturally it felt a little strange, to have to be constantly with another person, a mere girl, whom after all he had known very slightly before he married her. She was so sweet, but perhaps very undeveloped if the truth were known; she never felt any need for silence or solitude—seemed a little depressed if he didn't talk to her; or rather, if she didn't talk, while he answered what was necessary and appeared to be deeply interested in what she told him about her home and her friends and her little adventures in town.

But he was in love with her in a way, and she was in love with him in her way. The boarders at the farm had the impression that the Selmers were greatly taken up with each other: Paul took not the slightest trouble to make acquaintances here, nor was Björg particularly desirous that he should do so; she had indeed made friends with several of the women and could tell him a great deal about them when he came out to see her; but she assured him that the others understood so well they wanted to be together, the short time he was able to stay there.

In the autumn they were to move into their own villa—a pretty little newly built house that stood on rising ground beyond Ila. They stayed at an hotel while their furniture was being moved from the Bakland to the villa. Paul somehow could not bring himself to feel that this was serious; that this was to be his home and here he was to live—though it amused him in a way to do his share of getting the house ready and buying things for it: Björg's ideas of what was pretty and cosy and necessary and practical were so different from his own that it was almost like helping a dear little girl to furnish a playroom.

In the little bedroom upstairs the huge polished mahogany furniture was crowded together so that there was hardly room to move about—it seemed perfectly fantastic that to all appearance he was going to undress and sleep and get up and dress himself again in this room—perhaps as long as he lived. The pieces of furniture were not so ugly in themselves—with the notable exception of the monstrous edifice that Björg proudly called her dressing table—but they took up such a fearful lot of room. And the big, highly polished wooden beds with yellow down quilts and lace bed-spreads had an air of hotel. He felt a kind of premonition of heart-sinking when he reflected that now he was *always* to have another person in the room with him.

The ground floor rooms were gradually filled with things Björg had brought with her. Paul looked at them with a sort of ethnographic interest. For the dining room he had the old corner cabinet and the chest of drawers for table linen, and he had since picked up a very good English sideboard. Björg covered everything she possibly could with big embroidered cloths, on which she set out a vast number of odd articles—of nickel and copper and delft with blue patterns and plated mounts. They looked like the electric hot plates and coffee machines and egg boilers which they had in their showrooms and which he had thought it quite natural that other people should buy. For that matter they had some similar electric appliances themselves, which they were soon tired of seeing on the breakfast table. Then there were all the wedding presents in silver and, electroplate, which Björg insisted on displaying.

On the wall by the door to the kitchen Björg had hung a couple of trays in a style which made you think of embroidered braces. To Paul's eyes the arrangement had an almost thrilling effect, something like the Lappish medicine drums Ingstad had shown him once at the museum.

So they took possession and gave a housewarming party—it was like a game, living here as man and wife, and in this spirit of play they continued in good humour and grew still more in love with each other.

THERE was something touching in Björg's having been so young and inexperienced—and being now so immeasurably experienced and married. Her mother's ideas of a nice refined girl evidently took it for granted that she ought to ignore everything human that was situated lower than the tonsils—at most she might properly be interested in those regions of her body which are involved in an attack of heartburn. The result was, of course, that Björg had the funniest notions of everything that concerned the relations of the sexes—they appeared to be inspired by the situation of her home in the neighborhood of the market hall and to be common to her whole circle of girl friends. Now she was positively collecting experiences—she showed no little curiosity. Very amorous she was too, but at the same time afraid of everything she called "passion." Paul handled her monstrous cautiously and with a little secret smile, as though she had been a doll—she was both sweet and comic with all the things she "wanted to know," since now it was no longer "unbecoming" for her to be informed. Before very long, no doubt, she would be as cocksure in her pronouncements about husbands and marriage as a tourist lady who has spent a winter in a Rome boarding house and knows all about the Italians.

ONE evening in March—when they had been married a year—she came into Paul's den; that was her name for the third room on the ground floor, which Paul had been allowed to arrange more or less according to his own ideas. Properly speaking she ought to have gone to a ladies' party that evening—and Paul would not have been sorry to be left alone for once—but the dressmaker had let her down, "and I've worn that green dress so often that I thought I'd rather stop at home with you." And Paul kissed her and laughed and said it was sweet of her.

He lay on the sofa trying to read, and Björg sat at his writing table with her work. All at once she asked breathlessly:

"Paul—may I ask you one question—but you must promise you won't be angry—!"

"No, no, ask away—"

"Have you had a child—? I mean, before you were married, of course—"

"I?" He burst out laughing: "No, worse luck."

Björg looked rather offended and seemed to be considering; .

"Magda told me that *every* gentleman has at least one illegitimate child before he is married—"

"Magda—what Magda is that?"

"My dear—Magda Prysing of course—she was one of my bridesmaids, you know—it was she who wore red and black roses on her shoulder—"

"Ah yes. And how has she found that out?" he smiled rather quizzically; "has she any experience or did she get it from the Statistical Department?"

"Oh, you—you're always trying to tease me. No, but Magda's father is rather given that way, you see—so she knew a whole lot about that kind of thing—"

"M-yes. Then fate has dealt unkindly with me and my friends, for it's been very stingy about presenting us with offspring," he said as before.

Björg turned red:

"You know very well, Paul, it isn't that I don't want to have a child—but you remember what you promised mamma—"

"Oh yes." He would have promised Fru Jacobsen anything on earth to get away from the confidential *téte-a-téte* with his mother-in-law. And there might be something in it, that Björg ought perhaps to be allowed to grow up herself first. But he hated to hear it talked of. But Björg had every intention of continuing the conversation:

"But I think I might fairly be let off a little longer—only a year, then perhaps I shall want it myself. You may be sure, I shall be frightfully glad to have a dear little baby. But all the same I should like to be allowed to enjoy my youth and my freedom a little while longer first."

Heaven knew, by the way, how this little person got through her time—giving orders to the maid, doing embroidery, giving ladies' tea parties and going out to tea. Paul imagined she must be miserably bored.

"But I wouldn't like us to wait such an awful long time—for I'm sure you have a terribly strong paternal instinct—"

"Bosh," said Paul, getting angry. There had been such an abundance of superficial psychological twaddle about maternal feeling and paternal instinct and percentages of masculine and feminine in all intellectual circles throughout his early years that he hadn't much patience when people began to talk about sexual problems in words of several syllables. His experience taught him that people who preached about maternal feelings and paternal instincts generally behaved to their own offspring in such a way that the Council for the Protection of Children had to intervene—

"Yes, for you are awfully fond of children, Paul, I've noticed that long ago."

"I can't bear brats—as a rule. If they're sweet and nice, then of course I like them—"

"Heavens, the way you go on with Eirik and Svein when we're at the Mortensens'!—I won't say anything of Berit's children—"

"Well, those—they're Henrik's, you see—and Lillemor is a sweet little girl, and Tassen's my godson, so it's natural I should take an interest in him—"

"Paul—what do you *really* think of Berit?"

"Really?—I think she's pleasant, of course—it's always very pleasant at their house. She's never been anything but kind with you, has she?"

"Ugh, she always seems so superior. Just as if I was nothing but a little infant. I must say, I wouldn't trust Berit any farther than I could see her. She's had some experience of one sort and another, I should say. I'm not talking about her divorce, you understand—we're not so old-fashioned as all that at home; mamma always says it's the only sensible thing to do, when people can't get on. You don't get married to be worse off than you would be alone—"

Paul turned half round to his wife and put his pipe down on the little copper table—Mrs. Anderson's wedding present.

"I'll tell you what, Björg," he said reflectively. "I really think your mother is uncommonly liberal, when it's a question of how people are to manage *after* they have passed through the turnstile—"

"How do you mean—?"

"After they are married, of course."

"Well, I declare! I assure you we're not so—absurd. Even if mamma is downright strict and serious about morality and that."

Paul laughed, and Björg said in an offended tone:

"But I expect you think it's better when people are a little bit—you know—before they get married, eh?"

"Exactly."

"Oh yes, I know that—you were pretty bad in your bachelor days—led a tolerably fast life!—you needn't deny it—!"

"My dear child, have I denied anything?"

"No, but you never say anything. Properly speaking you ought to have told me all that—I ought to have known it before I became your wife!"

"Do you think I would tell such horrid things to my young and innocent wife?—oh no, child, it wouldn't do to confess such wickedness to you—"

"Ugh, now I believe you're making fun of me. But seriously, Paul, *you* can't possibly think divorce is wrong—seeing that both your parents are divorced—"

Paul made no reply.

"And you're terribly fond of both your father and mother. And your stepmother is simply one of the sweetest and kindest persons there is—"

"That doesn't make it necessary for me to approve of everything they do or think."

"I don't understand that. If you are fond of your parents, I don't see how you can admit, for instance, that anything they've done is wrong—"

"Can't you understand—that one may be fond of a person even if one thinks something he's done is absolutely reprehensible? Suppose someone you were fond of committed a crime—of course it would have to be something that one could understand a person doing, not anything downright infamous or shabby—couldn't you imagine that you would go on being fond of the person—and at the same time would never call his crime anything but a crime?"

Björg looked at him, rather terrified, and shook her head.

"Suppose it were myself for instance—?"

"But you won't do anything wrong!" She threw down her embroidery, jumped up and came over to him. And she flung herself upon him and kissed him:

"You won't do anything wrong, Paul, I'm sure you won't—"

Paul gently freed himself from her embrace and stood up:

"Come, put on your things, Björg, we'll go for a sharp little walk—"

But Björg thought it was too cold. So Paul whistled to his dog and went out for a solitary walk by the side of the water, which lay black with gently swaying streaks of light, under the frost-bound, white and black mountains.

THAT summer Björg was to stay with her mother at a saeter in the neighborhood of Lillehammer. Paul took her as far as Tonset and then returned home, not very depressed at the prospect of being a grass-widower for two months. He enjoyed the quiet of the villa, worked in the little garden or made trips to the mountains for plants—there was some rough ground where he could carry out his plans for a rock garden to his heart's content. Henrik and Hauan came out, and they had their quiet drinks on the veranda and their evenings at cards, and Hauan had bought himself a motorboat. Every now and then, right out in the fiord or close under the rocks for choice, the *Blue Bird* would suddenly break down, and they gathered much experience about the whims of motorboats in those short weeks.

Then a telegram from Björg disturbed the idyll: "Must speak to you at once, coming home Friday." She had only been away half the time they had arranged.

"I have some strange news for you," she said as soon as he entered the railway carriage and began handing out hat boxes and bunches of birch leaves.

"Paul dear," she crept close to him the moment they were seated in the cab. "What do you think—I'm going to have a baby"—she caught at her breath, and then the tears began to flow: "Ugh, it's only that I'm so horribly nervous—I don't know whether I'm more sorry or glad about it—"

"Make up your mind for the latter then," whispered Paul, putting his arm round her—"my little girlie—"

There was no doubt about it. She had been to the doctor at Lillehammer. The middle of March, he said.

"I haven't told mamma yet," said Björg, as they stood in the hall at home. Paul quickly drew her to him. "I thought I had to come home to you at once," she whispered in his arms, and he held her more closely.

"But gee, how frightened I am, Paul—oo, I believe I'll dread it so I'll go crazy!"

THERE followed some months when the little villa they lived in closed about their life together and became a home. True, Björg preached a good deal about her condition and the impending event—indeed she preached about it incessantly, and the house was full of little books with such titles as *Mother and Child and What Every Married Woman Ought to Know and Practical Clothing for Infants with Paper Patterns,* and the sewing machine hummed at all hours of the day and night, and there were half-made garments in all the rooms. A strange skeleton-like basket on four wickerwork legs with a long giraffe's neck wandered about the house; sometimes it was upstairs and sometimes down, and sometimes it stood on the landing looking out of the passage window. Björg was continually devising fresh plans for its decoration.

But now, as Paul listened to his wife's ceaseless chatter, he felt a new and patient tenderness towards her. It was naturally somewhat strange and solemn that he should be to blame for a new little human being who was soon to start on the racecourse of this world. Of course he would be extremely fond of the youngster, when once they had it—and it would be affectation to pretend he didn't know that it might have made its appearance in far less favourable circumstances; he would certainly give his child the best chance he could. And then it was rather touching about Björg that she was so young and so childlike—though in sober truth a mother of one-and-twenty was not so egregiously young either.

Björg and her mother exchanged letters several times a week. And at the beginning of December Paul had a letter from his mother-in-law, who had discovered that it would be too great a strain for Björg to make all the Christmas preparations herself—it was couched in such terms that he had scarcely any choice but to accept with thanks Fru Jacobsen's offer to come up and stay with them for a while.

His mother-in-law came, and then it was fixed that Jacobsen too should come and keep Christmas in the young people's home.

It was Paul's idea that on the evening of Christmas Day he and his father-in-law should go up to the Aune saeter and stay there a few days. And hardly were the two men seated in the train when a kind of wordless understanding established itself between them, and during the sledge drive at night from Stören up to Rise they came to feel like bosom friends—almost without exchanging a word. Next morning they started off across the mountain, absolutely silent and in radiant humour.

They had the glorious feeling that they need not talk in each other's company. Though actually old Jacobsen became quite chatty as they sat by the fire in the evening. In town Paul had had an idea that his father-in-law felt constrained or ill at ease in his company. No sooner had they got away from their womenfolk than everything that might divide them ceased to exist—difference in education and external conventions. They had a good dose of brandy with their coffee, smoked and made up the fire, and meanwhile Jacobsen described the hut he had by Harestu water—not on the lake itself but a little way off, by some small tarns—yes, Paul knew well where it was, and they agreed that Paul must go up there with his father-in-law next time he came to Christiania. Then Jacobsen told him a little about his time in America—and about the farm in Dovre from which he came; it was a cousin of his who had it now, but he generally paid it a visit every other year or so. Well, it wasn't any very big farm; Andora thought it altogether too primitive, but Björg had been there with him many times when she was a child—and such grand mountain pasture, my boy!

Then they both hit upon the idea of making a trip over to the Berge saeter—south to Hövringen perhaps, through Rondane and Foldal. They had food, they had tobacco, and enough brandy if they were strictly economical—and anyhow it was Paul's turn for a holiday between Christmas and New Year.

They started off next morning, came home at midday New Year's Eve, and were met at the garden gate by Fru Jacobsen, who exploded at them. Paul's telegram from Hjerkin had only arrived the day before, and poor Björg had been almost out of her wits with anxiety—it might have had the most terrible consequences. "Well, of course it was not to be expected that Paul should know anything about such things"—the whole shower of abuse was addressed to the unfortunate Jacobsen, but Paul felt that he too got his share of the wigging—there stood he and his father-in-law side by side with skis and guns and full equipment, facing the angry lady like two naughty little boys. They were only two days later than arranged, and their telegram had been received here the day before, but of course there was nothing for it but to hold their tongues.

And he willingly admitted how wrong and inconsiderate his conduct had been, as he sat on the edge of Björg's bed: she was so exhausted with crying and anxiety that she was not fit to get up before evening.

Then she came out with some nonsense that mother of hers had put into her head, to the effect that her old father and he had naturally met some pretty young ladies at one of the boarding houses, and that was what had delayed them.

"That would only be natural—you may be sure I know as much as that—if you thought it fun to flirt with other ladies now that I'm looking so awful and can't be a bit amusing—" "Bless my heart—would you think that natural—?"

He would have to see about getting that harridan out of the house as soon as possible, thought Paul. Yes, they'd be in a nice mess if it came to what his own dear mother prophesied—that morality must always conform to what ordinary decent people feel to be natural. If mother could only guess how many mean ideas he had come across among people who were quite decent in their way—as to what is natural.

He himself saw the comic side of the situation, when on the evening of New Year's Day he accompanied his father-in-law to the station—he felt so deserted and unprotected when the old man had left. But when his mother-in-law began to talk of how dreadfully Björg needed her now and so on—Paul felt he simply couldn't forsake his newfound friend, Jacobsen; he must invite the lady to stay a little longer. He himself was young, a mere recruit in this campaign, and of course he was really independent of the woman—the old sufferer must be sorely in need of a little respite. And besides, Björg was delighted to have her mamma with her now.

He tried to force himself to pooh-pooh the tales of mothers-in-law. Fru Jacobsen was vulgar, but she was fond of her child. And she must have been a good mother, since Björg idolized her so. But good Lord—

What Björg needed most was amusement and cheering up—Fru Jacobsen had read this in an American lady doctor's work on maternity hygiene, and surely there was nothing improper in a young wife being about to have a baby. So Paul had to trail round everywhere with his two ladies. What annoyed him particularly was that it was so unfortunate for Björg's social prestige that this mother of hers should be exhibited freely everywhere. He had never believed himself inclined to be snobbish, but when his mother-in-law advanced in full panoply of bursting silk and flung herself upon any who had not fled in time from her deluge of talk—well, it made him shudder.

Berit Alster, for instance, had always been very pleasant to his young wife—though she did like to play the superior and take Björg under her wing. Several times he had had to make it plain to Fru Berit that he hadn't married Björg because she was so "touchingly naïve and young," and he never expected that Björg would "find it rather difficult to feel at home in surroundings which were so entirely different from those she had been accustomed to"—so Berit's assistance was by no means necessary, thank you. It could not be denied that Fru Jacobsen's loquacity lent support to Berit's attitude.

It was more surprising that Björg and Else Mortensen did not get on at all well together. This was probably due in the first place to a piece of stupidity on Björg's part: she had entirely misunderstood the Mortensens' predilection for everything simple and unostentatious—they lived as it suited themselves and gave a cordial welcome to those of their friends who liked things the way they did them. To outward appearance their home was already somewhat knocked about; the earls Eirik and Svein were terrible young brigands, and Sirianna was inconceivably enterprising for a child of less than three. But Björg's interpretation of this was that they were not so "genteel" as the rest of their acquaintance, and she had said so to Berit, and Paul had been sickeningly ashamed and vexed at the time over this solecism of hers. Now Paul discovered that his dear friend Else was just a trifle vindictive and could easily be spiteful in her sweet little way—blandly and amiably she trapped his mother-in-law into giving herself away most blatantly on more than one occasion.

Now and again he was seized with an inordinate longing to run away from the whole affair, if only for a few days. To escape the sight of womenfolk and the sound of womenfolk's chatter about insults and parties and the hygiene of childbirth and pork and beans and his expected heir's sex and wardrobe and bringing-up and his friends' characters and doings.

So when at last the evening arrived when he helped a mortally afraid little wife from the cab into the waiting room or whatever they called it, where he handed her over into the custody of the clinic—it was beyond his power, among all the thoughts and feelings by which he ought legitimately to have been filled, to prevent a bright hope dancing incessantly before his eyes: now his mother-in-law could not drag out her stay at Trondhjem much longer. When Björg was up again, she would have to beat a retreat.

Next morning came a message on the telephone: he had a daughter; both doing very well.

THE faint smell of disinfectants which lingered in the open staircases and the bright, airy corridors, the hovering nurses in blue and white and the patients wandering about in dressing gowns—the bright emptiness of the room itself and the bare white bed in which Björg lay—all had that atmosphere of clinic and of isolation from the fullness of everyday life, in which the mind keeps itself warm through its conscious and unconscious workings. Here time was as it were sterilized of all petty joys and vexations and drolleries and graces. The vertiginously marvelous and unutterably commonplace fact that now Björg and he were mother and father—this conveyed no impression of reality to him. For the present the young mother and child were not much more than a numbered case, and in the atmosphere of the clinic all jubilant feeling was cooled down or side-tracked in the discussion of the physiological aspects of the matter.

The voice of the blood kept mum and the paternal instinct stirred so feebly that Paul was quite shocked at his own want of feeling, as he stood looking at the little reddish brown mite that appeared to be his daughter. Are they really as tiny as that when they come into the world—and as ugly—? Aloud he replied to Björg's enraptured whisper: "Yes, I should think she *was* sweet—"

On some days it was irritatingly inconvenient to have to run from his office in the busy hours to pay his daily visit to the clinic—and he was irritated with himself for not being able to muster more becoming fatherly and connubial feelings. And when he reached Björg her mother was always there, and as a rule there were other visitors, and for decency's sake he had to say thank you and taste cream buns and the contents of paper bags—and everything he put into his mouth was almost impossible to swallow in this atmosphere, where the scent of hyacinths and tulips on the white lacquered chests of drawers was blended with traces of *lysol*. And then all the idiotic questions from one female after another—whether he was "proud" to be a father—"ah, there we have the proud father"—phew!

At last, one afternoon when he came up to Björg's room, there was no one else there. She was giving the child the breast.

It was a week old now and had improved to such an extent that even the father was glad to agree that it was a pretty little baby.

Paul drew a chair up to his wife's bed and took her hand—it was so soft and white now. A crack of the window was open and long, bright drops of rain swept past on the south wind which stirred some twigs in a treetop outside, and the light was warm and yellow with the approaching sunset.

"Paul dear—have you thought of what her name is to be?"

Of course they had discussed it in advance—in a vague way, hundreds of names. As it turned out a little girl, he had assumed as a matter of course that they would call her Julie—Andora was pretty well out of the question. But he had a feeling that he would do best to keep quiet—it would come better from Björg.

"I've thought of such a darling name—oh, I'd be so frightfully glad to have her called that—it just suits our lovely little sunbeam, I think—"

"Well—let's hear it—"

"Sunlife," said Björg solemnly.

"Are you utterly crazy?—you can't give a live youngster a name like that!"

"Did anyone ever hear the way you talk to me!—I'm really not at all crazy. I think it's a duck of a name, I do. It's American; it's the name of the heroine of a perfectly charming novel mamma read when she was there—"

Paul listened absently while Björg gave a sort of resume of the novel.

"Yes, but we can't make the poor kid suffer for that, can we?"—He raised the most obvious objections, that they would call her Sunlight Soap at school and so on. Björg began to howl, so that he had great trouble to quiet her without promising to let her call the baby by this inhuman name. And Fru Jacobsen informed him at the supper table at home that Björg was not at all well—it did her no good to cry so much—and of course it would affect her milk—

"Well, it makes no difference—I won't agree to let my child be ill-treated like that. Julie is to be her name, and that's all about it."

BJÖRG came home with her baby—and at last, a fortnight later, somebody or other in Christiania was at the point of death, and Fru Jacobsen came to the conclusion that she must hurry away and take charge of that affair.

Paul sat at home one afternoon, a few days later, glancing at the evening paper, smoking and enjoying the peace of the house which at last had become his own again. He would soon have to go up and change—he had invited some business friends to dinner at the Britannia—but it was so good to be alone in the house. Björg had gone into town and the maid was in the basement.

From the room above came that odd little sound—an infant screaming and screaming, in pettish insistence. Paul got up, stretched and yawned—he would have to go up and see what was the matter with the kid—awful the way it howled—

The little creature was purple in the face, and Paul was met by a peculiarly soft and moist warmth, as he leaned over her nest beneath the long tulle curtain. He picked up the little packet of white flannel—it was soaking wet, so he took her little down quilt and wrapped it round her. She stopped crying suddenly on being lifted up, and Paul was ridiculously proud at his success. He carried the baby to the window, stood there holding her sideways and shaking her, much as one shakes a medicine bottle; she liked that, evidently—so he shook a little harder: ah, there, you see, it was fun when daddy came and took you up. Just as if there was anything awkward in handling a little thing like this.

Suddenly he realized—it was the first time he held her in his arms, except by orders and in the presence of others. The first time he was alone with his daughter.

He stuck his forefinger into her incredibly small hands and stroked his own cheek and mouth with them: papa, papa—as the womenfolk had done at the clinic. He forgot to shake her—touched the soft, moist downy hair on her crown with his face.

"Maybe you like your daddy a little bit all the same, eh?—There, shall we look out of window now, you and I?"

The mountains on the other side of the fiord were grey-blue and still streaked with snow—the light was cold and pale. Great long-drawn dark clouds floated in the sky, like a shoal of giant whales; the biggest whale was dark grey, but with a silver rim under its belly, and from behind it rays of light poured down, making a broad glittering patch of dead-white sunshine on the waters of the fiord.

Paul held the little girl so that she too might see the gleam of sunlight over the sea—he gazed down into the tiny pink face; her dark eyes had the strangest unfathomable expression. At that moment a reflection as it were of the gleam of sunlight passed over his child's features—she smiled. It came and vanished so quickly that he hardly knew what he had seen—but then she smiled again.

He felt something happen within him, as though the lowest layers in the depths of his being moved and changed their places. It was a trust beyond all understanding—that the little newborn human being he held in his hands had smiled, and it was to set out and begin its life. But God, God, God, what a trust it was—that men continue to smile, every fresh little one that comes into the world—what a trust that Power shows us which places a little one like this in a man's hands.

He gazed intently—would she do it again? And there came up in him something like a feeling of shame—O God, life is serious after all—and he had not taken it seriously all these years, and he had imagined he was grown up. In all these years he had not cared more than so much about anything—chiefly about himself, but not so that he thought it mattered greatly what became of him. But it was a lie to say it was all one which way things might go. And this little destiny he was holding in his hands, it had smiled at him, in perfect trust.

Some strange spasms came over the child's face again—then she gave a little cry. Quickly her father began to shake her—and then she was quiet.

Paul walked with her up and down the little strip of clear floor between the beds and the wardrobe.

Then there was someone on the stairs—Björg flung the door open.

"But good gracious me—what are you doing with the child, Paul?—I've never seen anything like it—well, I must say we shall have some fine ways of bringing-up here—" she threw her outdoor things on to her bed and slipped on her apron: "Come here, let me take her—so now, Miss Selmer, you've learnt how to get round your father, have you?—I can see it won't take him long to spoil his little girl—"

Paul stood with his back to her, smiling slightly, as he began to undress.

"Is it your platinum studs you're looking for?—I expect they're in the wardrobe, in that pink flannel blouse of mine—I couldn't find my cuff links that day Fru Kristvik and Fröken Jensen came—"

Paul got them out—stopped to look at Björg and the child. It lay in its mother's lap—Lord, how sweet she was with her little pink body, naked from the waist down—it was like the hindquarters of a frog when for a moment she stretched out her little legs stiffly and rubbed one foot over the heel of the other. Björg put on her the shining white linen garment that smelt of washing and the heat of the fire—turned her smartly over on her back and wound it round her legs.

A moment later Björg set up a loud twittering cry like a bird, making Paul turn from the glass and go over to her:

"Be quick and you'll see—she smiled! Ugh, you're not half quick enough—but I assure you—fancy, Baby smiled at me!

"—Oh Paul, do you know, I think it's quite solemn, I do—that I've seen my little child smile at me—her first smile!"

"Yes—" was all he said.

She sat with the child at her breast, when he came back, ready to go.

"Paul," whispered Björg, as he bent over them both: "you like her too, don't you?" she laughed quietly.

"Oh yes—she's not so bad—"

"Can't you say you're terribly fond of her—?"

"I certainly can. I'm terribly fond of her."

"And of me too?"

"Of you too, yes."

"Say I may call her Sunlife then?"

"Oh, call her Lilleborg if you like," he said with a laugh. "—No, but now I haven't time to play about with you any longer—"

But afterwards Björg asserted that he had given her his word—the child was to be called Sunlife. And the end was that Paul gave in. His own grandmothers had been called Sif and Minona—those names had probably sounded rather affected when they first came into use. Besides, they could just call her Sunnie for everyday—the other would have to be something like the secret names of mythology. He had known a lot of girls who were never known by anything but pet names—hadn't an idea for instance what Molla Nicolaysen had been christened. And then it covered something that he himself had felt—but for which it was nevertheless impossible to find an expression that was not inadequate and commonplace. Sunlife—at all events it was not quite so bad as Liv—for instance.

CHAPTER FIVE

In the spring of 1914 Paul arranged things so that he could redeem his promise to Björg and give her a trip to Paris. He had not been abroad before either—this at once created a fellow-feeling between him and his wife. They were together in a place where everything was equally new to both.

They were lucky with the weather too. There was a radiant silvery shimmer in the morning air as they left the hotel and walked along the boulevard to their cafe—so they called it after they had taken their coffee there two mornings. Great bluish clouds drenched in light sailed in the misty air over the roofs, which were the first things Paul fell in love with in Paris—the broken line of black roofs with comb-like groups of chimneys against the sky; then came a party wall like a precipice, sheer down to the ravine of the street, and under its lee lay funny old houses, the remnant of an earlier city, withdrawn from the pavement, with the furniture and other wares of an old curiosity shop exposed in the open air. This little shop lay like a backwater away from the stream of traffic.

No matter whether everybody shouted in chorus that Paris was wonderful—it was true all the same. Paul sat in quiet happiness, blinking at the sunshine, smoking and listening with half an ear to Björg's bright chatter. Across the square St. Germain des Prés raised its fine, solemn tower which ended so abruptly in the funny hat—the traffic of the boulevard flowed past, a continual stream under the trees—their leaves were already a little brown and sickly from the town air, though it was only the end of May. Pedestrians, bicyclists, cabs, automobiles, omnibuses and goods wagons with huge piebald horses from Northern France—a glitter, a clatter, a jingle and a shouting; it was just as good as looking at running water. And the tall houses were so fine; long facades of a soft, sooty grey color, with tall windows and greenish latticed shutters and railed balconies all along. Till the perspective of the street met far away in the heat-haze.

And as he sat thus in pure enjoyment he thought Björg's unceasing stream of talk was like a little melody—it chimed in so well with his own feeling of joy and new experience. For Björg too discovered something every moment: "Fancy, they go about the street in curl papers—and morning wrappers. Ugh no, I don't think I should like French gentlemen—they look to me like dolls. Oh, look at her sitting there—at the end table—do you think she's pretty? Ugh no, I think they're horrid when they're so frightfully made up and painted—I'm sure that's her lover, the one she's with, don't you think so?"—Paul smiled indulgently at his young wife; her complexion was red and white like apple blossom, her hair had a perfectly golden sheen under the big pastel blue hat she had bought the first day they were in Paris, and she had got herself a new dress of light, sea-blue silk. A trifle podgy she had grown after the baby business—now and then Paul couldn't help thinking of his mother-in-law, whether in her young days she might not have been something of the same sort—plump, rosy-cheeked, yellow-haired. But in any case Björg was perfectly charming now, reminding you of a full-blown rose of the small innocent kind that you see on old bushes in country gardens.

"Oh Paul, oh look—only five sous for those wonderful roses"—a row of hand barrows had halted just at the edge of the pavement under the chestnut trees. It was a glorious sight, there was a barrow that was one mass of dark red roses and the scent reached them where they sat.

"Would you like some—I'll run and buy you some—"

Soon after there was a barrow of downy orange-colored apricots piled high, with green leaves among them for decoration. But the apricots in the bag they got were pretty hard and unripe. Björg crunched them as she chattered on:

"Fancy their letting such big children go about with bare legs—no, I don't like *that*. Give me Norwegian children—ugh, I think the French children look so precocious. Yes, I dare say they're charming in a way, but they're so thin and pale. Ugh, I don't believe southerners have any idea of how to look after little children properly—what do you think? Oh Paul, I'm always thinking of Sunlife—do you believe she misses her mammy a tiny bit?"

"No, you may be quite sure she doesn't," replied Paul heartlessly.

"But gee, how I long to come home and dress her up in all the ravishing things I've bought for my baby. I say, what kind of a fish do you think he's got in that barrow?—ugh, it looks so nasty—"

They were big, gristly-finned fish, pink in the semi-transparent flesh, a dull pearly white underneath. The man was cutting them up with a big knife and selling them by the piece.

"That?—it's ray, we ate it the other day with black butter; don't you remember we thought it was so good—?"

"Gee, was it *that*—fancy, if I'd known it looked like that I don't believe I could have touched it."

THEY strolled along the Rue Bonaparte, stopping to look at the windows. Before they had come as far as the Seine they had already two or three parcels to carry.

The bouquinistes standing by their boxes along the quay interested Björg, funnily enough. What she wanted to get hold of was old fashion plates—she would have them framed and hang them up at home on the stairs; wouldn't that be cute? Paul was happy; she might rummage as long as she liked.

It was this marvellous sky, a paler blue than at home, full of light blue and dove grey and bright silvery clouds—the sky of the flat country which had captivated him already as they went up the river to Antwerp. The grey waters of the Seine, tinged with yellow, streaming past the light stone quays, the subdued green of the plane trees against the grey of the houses, and the air which combined all the cool, delicate tints so finely. And then down on the island the church with its two towers and the depth of its porches and the rosewindow sunk into the rich, living filigree of the facade. The grey stone was streaked with black below and had a peculiar chalky whiteness on the surface of all the sculpture, so that it seemed to shine with its own light against the sky behind, which was now beginning to be thick and grey with heat-haze.

They were to go into Notre Dame, and afterwards they would look for the shop close by, where Ruth had bought all the amusing flowered earthenware that she had in her studio. In particular there were some long-necked cats in green faience that Björg was madly in love with.

Paul waited with the patience of an angel while Björg turned over the boxes *of soldes et occasions* outside the shops. He would not have cared how long he stood there—the sights, the sounds, the smells of the ever-living movement of the boulevard with the tall grey houses, closed and retiring, the treetops roofing over the throng, the bright colors of the placards, the silky grey sheen of the asphalt and the way it deadened the sound of horses and carriages—it was so good, so good, simply to stand still in the middle of it. And he answered with inexhaustible amiability "yes, I think you should" every time Björg held up a new find she had made in the heaps of colored scraps and asked him if he thought she should take it.

They had déjeuner at a restaurant on the pavement, where a hedge of ivy in boxes barely separated them from the street. But after that they had to take the metro home to get rid of all their parcels—the hotel room was overflowing with bags and parcels and gaily colored cardboard boxes. After all they were mostly trifles, all the things she thought "so cheap," and there was a good deal of rubbish among her purchases, and Paul did nothing to check her.

It was impossible to be in this town, in the bright early summer, with a young, charming and delighted woman, without behaving as if one were wildly in love with her. Paul did not cudgel his brains to find out just how much he was in love with his wife—he loved her as if she were a mistress whose conquest he had just made, and she yielded to his tempestuous caresses with a sweet and comical audacity: "Dear me, yes, here—while we're in Paris we may surely let ourselves go a bit—"

And every single evening and night they were out amusing themselves.

Sigmund was in Paris; he had gone there immediately after his debut in Christiania a year and a half ago. The concert had been a great success, his mother wrote at the time, and she sent Paul some of the notices—they were extremely appreciative. All the same Paul had had a feeling which he could not explain. It was so ludicrous to think that in future a few strips of paper like these were to play a fairly important part in his brother's life. Sigmund had been such a straight and spirited boy when he was small, never any nonsense about him—little by little it was as though music took the place of everything the lad had been interested in before. And now all the music his brother had in him was to be in some way or other valued or encouraged or repressed by these little paragraphs in the papers. Well, it would have to be the boy's own lookout.

He had great talent, as far as Paul was any judge. He lived in one room with an alcove in the Rue Monsieur; in a kind of outbuilding looking on to a little old garden with a single great elm tree standing in a green lawn and ivy growing up the wall of the house. He gave a party for them there the first evening they were in Paris. The guests were mostly artists, Scandinavians. Björg's eyes were round and wide—she knew all these people's names from the papers, many of them anyhow, and some of them had written books which she had read.—"I say, you know, I liked her—I think she's charming company," said Björg the morning after as she sat brushing out her hair. She was referring to an actress whose private life was supposed to be somewhat wild. "Ugh no, Paul, do stop that—I can't get dressed if you carry on so—" she pushed his head away, as he bent down to kiss her bare shoulder. They were to meet Ruth and lunch with her, and then Ruth was to go with Björg to the Lafayette and help her to choose a frock that would do for dancing.

RUTH had grown very good-looking and dressed extremely well—had quite a distinguished air. She knew Paris inside out, and on one or two mornings when Björg wanted to stay in bed till lunch time, Paul went out with Ruth. The Ile St. Louis, Belleville, the Place des Vosges, the old quarters north of the Panthéon—Paul would have liked to loaf about there all day long. But Björg was not so much interested in the streets where there were no shops.

Paul and Björg usually met Sigmund somewhere for dinner, and afterwards they adjourned to some place where they met Scandinavians. Ruth was often there and some of her circle. And then on to Montmartre—they had been to the Bal Bullier and the Noctambules and a lot of the places that one is supposed to go to. Paul didn't exactly find these haunts so thrilling—but Björg enjoyed herself in a wild and panic-stricken way; no doubt she looked forward above all to relating her experiences in Christiania and Trondhjem. And Ruth's and Sigmund's friends were quite pleasant to racket about with one evening, two evenings—when it came to the third Paul found it getting very dull. To be sure, he could stick it for the week or two they were to be here—but if he were obliged to associate with these people for a year or so and hear them saying much the same things about much the same people and topics evening after evening, he would probably break out pretty soon.—They had an expression in English: "bored to tears."

But the streets at night, as they moved on from one place to another—he really thought that in this town every moment one was not out of doors was thrown away. And the annoying part of this nocturnal revelling was that they got out far too late in the morning—the mornings in Paris were the best of all.

THEY had been to the Halles one night and had got to bed at five—and Paul had risked what was the nearest approach you could get to a whisky and soda. So he woke up about seven and knew it would be no use trying to go to sleep again.

He got up and dressed—glanced at Björg; she slept like a stone. Poor little thing—she had been taken ill when they came home last night, or this morning—and when she woke she would feel repentant and ashamed—to say nothing of a headache—that is, if she remembered anything at all about her little escapade.

He would loaf about the streets a couple of hours—and then he would go and buy that necklace they had seen in a second-hand dealer's shop in the Rue de Vaugirard. He had half promised her this—she must have some proper souvenir of their "wedding trip." True, she had now discovered that she would rather have a little silver handbag—they were very tasteless, thought Paul. But the necklace was a real find—goldsmith's work of the 1840s, bold and handsome, with large, very dark amethysts, mounted in coral red and dark blue enamel and set with little pearls and turquoises. It might positively be an heirloom in the family—Sunlife might have it one day. Sunnie—how was she getting on? Splendidly, of course; she had been altogether wild with delight on being allowed to stand on a chair at the window and look down into Storgate with all the cars and taxis. She would be properly spoilt at the Jacobsens'.

From St. Sulpice he walked along a narrow street with high garden walls overhung with ivy. The elms inside caught the sunlight so finely on their dark, rough leaves. It was grand to slip out again while the morning was still fresh.

The shop in the Rue de Vaugirard was not yet open. Paul turned back to a little café he had seen at a street corner.

It had that dead, stuffy air of spirits and stale beer. A sofa covered with peeling American cloth along one wall, little chipped marble tables before it. A stout, untidy woman was serving something in glasses to a couple of workmen over the zinc counter. A dirty boy in a green apron stopped sweeping up the sawdust on the floor and brought him a glass of coffee. *Croissants*—one moment—

Paul lit a cigarette while waiting for the rolls. He looked out of the window—she was chic and no mistake, that young lady crossing the street there—in beige from top to toe, tailormade—red hair. Odd, that's the type the Scandinavians here never notice—they haven't any eyes for a Parisienne unless she's painted like a poster. Wonder what a lady like that is doing out of doors at this time of the morning though—perhaps she's going to church—

The lady in beige entered the cafe, nodded familiarly to madame and the garçon, seated herself on the sofa at the end table, put down her missal, drew off her gloves, raised her veil. Why, of all the—! Paul looked at the lady—the lady glanced at him—they rose simultaneously:

"Why, what are *you* doing here—?"

"That's great—may I move up to your table, Randi?"

"I'll move down to yours—that's where I always sit—"

"—You've lived here three years, you say. Fancy my not meeting you before—we've been here three weeks already; I'm here with my wife. But perhaps you don't mix much with Norwegians?"

"Not so much latterly. No, I came here to work at research—records and so on. And after a while that led to my seeing more of French people. Who are working more or less on the same kind of stuff, you understand—"

"Yes, I know, you're preparing for your doctor's degree—Ingstad it must have been who told me. But he thought it was something to do with Norwegian ecclesiastical history. It's mediaeval of course—?"

"No, it was the eighteenth century. And not specially ecclesiastical. No, it was really the ideology of the eighteenth century—particularly Rousseau. You know, his fantastical notions about the superiority of primitive man—how amongst other things they have transformed the rational mediaeval view of the sovereignty of the people and the rights of the people. As you find it expressed, in one way in our ancient laws, and in another way in St. Thomas Aquinas. Till modern democracy has become a superstition pure and simple—the mystagogue Sars's version of our history, for instance. But of course, you know, I came to deal with the influence of all this on popular religion too—the compulsory union between old Lutheranism and so-called free-thought and so on. Since Norway has a State Church, so that its religious doctrine is always obliged to accommodate itself to the current ideas of its citizens—"

"It sounds interesting. Are you going to stay here long?"

"I presume so."

Her father had died three years ago and the farm was sold. But she had made a couple of summer trips to Norway—had spent some time in Christiania last autumn, staying with Fru Gotaas: "you know she was left a widow the year before last?"

"No? But tell me about the Gotaases—" He had heard nothing of them since Margrete-Marie's and Eberhard's wedding.

"Yes, you may be sure they appreciated your sending a present." Eberhard had his own business now—a glass shop in the eastern quarter; it was doing well, thank God. They had four children already; Josef was in the business too. Wilfrid was an electrician and lived at home with his mother; Monika was a Carmelite nun in England.

"Monika!—Great heavens! Has Monika gone into a nunnery—she was such a regular Christiania flapper—cheeky and full of go—"

Randi smiled faintly and shook her head:

"Monika has known what was to be her future ever since she was a little girl."

"She was always so full of fun—laughed at the slightest thing," said Paul, wondering.

"Well, well—don't you think that'll help her in the convent too? I'm sure most of the nuns I know have very good spirits. Otherwise it might be rather difficult."

"My word—Monika!—I suppose I'll hear next that you're going into a nunnery yourself—" said Paul.

Randi slowly turned red. But then she laughed aloud:

"I may just as well admit it after all—that's precisely what I'm going to do."

"No, stop it now, Randi. You're only chaffing, aren't you?"

"No, it's true."

"But in heaven's name—what on earth's the good of your turning nun? And what about your work? You can't very well take your doctor's degree if you go into a nunnery? Our royal and ancient University would collapse with dismay if it saw a candidate for the doctorate present herself in nun's veil and rosary!"

"No."—Randi chuckled at the idea. "That won't be in my time anyway. All the same—there are not so few sisters who have a doctor's degree, in America anyhow. But there won't be any use for that kind of thing in Norway—girls' schools and colleges conducted by nuns—for many a year to come. And if they put me to be class-mistress or school sister in one of the small towns it won't be a doctor's degree I shall need."

"No but, Randi—you can't possibly be quite right in the head. Seriously, you know *I* have always had great sympathy with Catholicism. And as far as that goes I can well understand that young girls may feel a call to take the veil. But not such as you—you have long years of study behind you and a task in front of you at which you've been working a long time. You must surely be able to accomplish much more for the Church in other ways, my girl.—Why, even I know that there are whole periods of our history that have never been dealt with in a really scholarly fashion, because the folks who have handled the documents had no idea of what was in them, because they knew nothing of the Catholic tradition, either in our history or in that of Europe—and what's worse, they imagined they did know something, though all they knew was the usual Protestant legends about Catholicism—and so they arrive at the most nonsensical results.—Good heavens, Randi—just think of all the material that's waiting to be taken up by a historian or philologist who can see what there is in the documents—"

Randi nodded.

"All that I have said to myself a thousand times. Oh yes—I have tried to persuade Our Lord—and myself too—assured God that I could serve Him better, if I were allowed to do what I myself wished instead of what He asked of me. But it was no use my offering Our Savior this thing or the other in place of what He desired. Unless I were willing—well, to give up my close and intimate daily life with Him. Of course, one can withdraw oneself from Him—content oneself with practicing just that minimum of religion which the Church demands of her idlest and most stubborn children, before she is obliged to cast them adrift. Do you think I haven't tried that too?—I excused myself with having so much work to do—I could not collect my thoughts for prayer and meditation, I was not not in a state to go to Mass and communion every morning.—But then I couldn't get my work to go properly—there was no savor or substance in the day without—bah, it was like living on nothing but canned food—"

"But don't you even *wish* to go into a nunnery?" asked Paul seriously. "Then how can you think any good will come of it? For you can't hold that you ought to take the veil simply because you don't *wish* it?—At any rate that's not the impression I have of Catholicism—that it is intolerant of the joy of life and demands that everyone shall do only what he least wants to do?"

Randi Alme shook her head, slightly nettled.

"No, certainly not.—Ugh, it's so difficult to explain to you, as you're not a Catholic.—No, if that were it, that I had a distaste for convent life, then it would be plain sailing—I might be tolerably sure that I had no business there at all. But it's not that. No, it's the *price* that I don't like paying. And the joy of life, as you say—I know very well the Church always says, Rejoice in the Lord! But I'm not speaking of the joy that comes of clinging to this and that, scraping together and piling up human values, for that won't stand either washing or sunshine. Not even joy in one's work, if one does it for one's own sake or for the work's sake—unless one works in the first place for God's sake.

"But what I shrink from is having to renounce my own will and my plans and habits. The mere fact that one can't dress as one chooses"—she shivered a little as she laughed—"I have always been so terribly fond of pretty clothes!"

"Yes, but there's no sin in that, is there?"

"At any rate I have never had to commit any sin to get myself pretty clothes."

Paul gave a low whistle.

"I begin to get a glimmer of light.—Is this what you mean—that in order to own the good things of this world honestly and rightfully one must begin by giving them away of one's own free will? It's no use preaching to those who have little or nothing that they must be content with that. Apart from the fact that it sounds so damned mean coming from those who themselves have more than a little or nothing."

"You know," said Randi quietly, "*my* work—God knows, *it* was not boring. Sometimes, when I got my fingers into some good stuff, it was like an electric shock, it positively tingled through all my nerves. A lovely feeling that, I assure you. So if I were to say I had nothing to live for, as long as I had my work, you know I should deserve to be whipped. But if I took to preaching that to such girls as have been given liberty to live by and for their work—which leaves them exactly as free as Fenja and Menja at King Frode's mill—or to such elderly modern nuns as have never pretended they had any call for a nun's life and nevertheless pass their lives in the seclusion of a cash-desk—why, then I should simply deserve to be burnt as a heretic. Yes, you smile—you know, don't you? that it wasn't the Church that burnt heretics; they were handed over to society, which burnt them as traitors. And that is what all heretics have been—traitors to mankind, for they have always tried to give universal validity to their own subjective experiences and opinions."

"I believe *that* is true, Randi—truth with some exaggeration."

"Of course—all human truth has some exaggeration."

"Well, you know, in a purely theoretical way I too have a strong sympathy for monasticism and all that kind of thing. I reacted strongly against it in my young days—for instance, I was ordered to go and hear some lectures for young men given by Pastor Dverberg, brother of the one who is married to my aunt. He himself was using up his third wife; his second died in January and, would you believe it? before the year was out he had found a substitute; the children wouldn't have to go without a mamma at their Christmas tree that year either, only it was a brand new one. When I said something about it to Uncle Abraham, he answered with fearsome dignity that Johannes was a strong man with a powerful nature—"

Randi was gazing before her—her face was stiff with seriousness:

"*That* is in reality the only happiness they have to hope for—all those whose work is dry as ashes—and who have no home in which they can feel themselves rooted. One may tell them they must find something or other to interest them—it's much the same as asking them to sit down and make shadow pictures on the wall with their fingers. A love affair—that's the only way in which they can have a sense of signifying something to somebody in this world. You see, one must remember that 'old maid' has been used as a term of contempt, at any rate wherever the tradition is Lutheran. And that not only in the kind of would-be profound psychological books which solemnly and laboriously discourse about unapplied eros and unsatisfied maternal feeling and all that. But the so-called innocent and nice little-girls' books too—they always assume that an old maid must be comical and odd—generally sour and bad-tempered and wicked as well.

"There was a time when I saw a good deal of the Norwegians here in Paris. That was one of the excuses I tried—for it happened occasionally that I was able to be of use to some of them. But what earthly use can it be for sour old women of all sexes and ages to fret over young Norwegian girls in foreign countries, or in Christiania if it comes to that. They will fall in love, and they will have someone fall in love with them. If I would say to them, God is the only one who really loves you, He is the unchanging and perfect, who became man and died in order to give you a share in his perfection and immutability—He is the only one who loves you without fail—He is the only one whom you can never love too much, without your own love being exhausted and without the one you love becoming surfeited with you. Sometimes it may have been a good thing that I said it—I don't know. Though they ought to have heard it at home—that they should love Him who loved us first. Only they can't get beyond wanting something in addition—or something else in the first place. Is God only to be all in all to those who in one way or another are condemned to be wallflowers in this world?

"O God—there was a little girl here once. She wanted to be an operatic singer. Slightly deformed—she had evidently suffered frightfully from rickets as a child—and then she had a face like a camel and her arms were much too long. There was no beauty in her voice either, but it was extremely powerful. And this unfortunate child, you see, was in despair lest life should pass her by, as she said—and somebody had put it into her head that she must have an affair before she could really become an artist. She was ready to go to any depth of humiliation and—and—depravity—in order to find one. You understand, ugly as sin and a nymphomaniac—that was the impression she gave in any case. Enough to make one weep. Then there are all those who are born with some kind of repression—so that their very inclinations run in an opposite direction to the ordinary—unnatural, as it is called, though often enough it is *their* nature—"

"Randi," said Paul quietly after a pause; "can it help *them* that you sacrifice your life and your whole work? Isn't this—a kind of desperation?"

Randi shook her head.

"No. You see, Paul, one thing is that I'm a country girl; it's not in our nature to make sacrifices merely to have the sensation of being self-sacrificing. Any more than it's in our nature to fuss about merely to have something to do. On the contrary, we are glad enough when we can take it easy for a day. And I should be glad enough if I could escape doing anything but what I myself feel inclined to do. But it's like the work at home on a big farm—what must be done, must be done, and if it means sticking to it early and late, it's best to go straight at it and think as little as possible about oneself and as much as possible about the work. It's exactly the same with the sacrifice—one sees that it has to be made, and so—

"Since I know it is of use. To make a stand against this—phobia, this dread of not grabbing enough for oneself out of life, which goads people nowadays. So I must say yes, when my God asks me, will you let me be your all in all—not merely your love, but your employer too, the one who feeds and clothes you, not merely as he feeds and clothes us all, but exactly as the head of a household feeds and clothes his family. I know it is not solely for my own sake that I have received the call, but that He chooses individual persons for the sake of his whole economy.—

"So at least I must go to Chambery and test my call there. And really, I'm glad of it now—at most times. It was only today, amongst other things because it was the last time I could go to Mass at the Carmes—I have been there almost always, as long as I have been in Paris. For this afternoon I am to move over to some friends on the other side of the Seine, and start from there the day after tomorrow."

Paul was silent for a moment.

"And you feel you can depend on what you tell me—that you have heard the call and that. Are you certain it's not your own subconsciousness—?"

"Oh!" She laughed. "Do you think I haven't kept an eye on that good old subconsciousness—?"

"I dare say you know William James—*Variations of Religious Experience* or whatever the book's called—"

"Ask me if I know Mother Goose—"

"Perhaps you're not particularly impressed by it then?"

"Well—for its day I suppose it was quite an imposing work. But it always made me think of something like an agricultural handbook written by a man who held an important position in a zoological museum and was in correspondence with experts at laboratories and experimental stations. But who had never milked a cow or helped her to calve, or had to drive the milk to the dairy before schooltime or helped to dig potatoes in pouring rain—or tried to get within range of the crow—I won't say anything about seeing a bull turn mad and go for one's father in the narrow byre, when there was nobody else there but oneself, a little girl of nine. It was the same spring mother died that happened to me—

"Religious experience—" Randi got up, drew down her veil and put on her gloves. "I should like to show you something—very few Scandinavians go and look at it when they're here. As a rule they haven't even heard of it. Would you care?"

"Yes, thanks.

"I'm ashamed to say," said Paul as they went out, "we've been to the Invalides and twice to the Louvre—but apart from that we haven't been to see any of the sights yet. We've been so busy seeing the town itself—"

Randi crossed the street and opened a gate. She led the way through a kind of portico which opened on to a paved yard; there was a building with a dome—Paul had walked past it many times without noticing it.

At the end of the passage they came into a church—it was not very big and was fairly dark, the air felt used up and had a scent of wax candles and stale incense. Otherwise there was nothing strange about it—it was a fairly ordinary baroque church.

Before the high altar Randi knelt for a moment and bent her head, and Paul performed a kind of salute—as one bows to an acquaintance of the lady one is walking with.

"Properly speaking the crypt is not open at this hour," Randi explained; she spoke a few words to an old man in an apron who was sweeping the floor. He opened a door near the altar and went before them.

"You know about the Septernber massacres—. It was here in the Carmes that they kept the priests prisoners; well, there were some in St. Firmin and some in l'Abbaye—that was close to St. Germain des Prés. But most of them were here. Presently you'll be shown the passage down which they were ordered to go, to where the commissaire sat at a table and they were asked whether they would take the oath which they could not take without being unfaithful—and outside where they were massacred. There were a hundred and ten men here in the Carmes. A few who were young and active had escaped over the wall into the Rue d'Assas—but then they heard the shots and the shrieks in the garden—and one of them said: 'They are shooting our brothers—come, we must go back to them—'"

What struck Paul as most affecting in the little, low crypt chapel where they were standing, was the almost commonplace tastelessness of the whole arrangement. There were niches in the walls, with great panes of glass in front of them—and the way all the bones and skulls, some of them broken and bearing marks of weapons, were laid out in rows on a bed of faded velvet, reminded one of a jeweller's window of the commoner sort. The whole arrangement seemed to betray such a hardened intimacy—familiarity, one might say—with martyrdom and manly courage and faithfulness unto death. Not all the beauty in the world, nor any attempt to make a dignified or impressive picture out of this memorial chapel, could have had so pathetic an effect as just this—that its setting was quite homely and unadorned. An altar stood by one wall—it had a rather poor appearance, and the linen cloth that covered it could not be called clean.

Randi had taken a rosary out of her handbag—held it for a moment against the glass before one of these collections of skulls:

"Will you be so kind as to take this with you—when I am a nun I shall not be allowed to have so fine a rosary. So I want to ask you to take it with you and send it to Margrete-Marie Eberhard's youngest girl. You see, I'm beginning already to develop nunlike ideas," she gave a little laugh. "Nuns never send things by post if they can find anyone to trouble with a commission—"

"I think you ought rather to give it to me, Randi." Paul was laughing too.

She looked at him a moment:

"All right. By all means; there you are!"

"No, but really—" he felt how heavy it was and took a good look at it. "Of course I won't take it—I had no idea it was such a handsome thing." The Ave Maria beads were garnets, the biggest and darkest Paul had ever seen, cut in facets, but old and worn, which gave them a wonderful deep crimson lustre. The paternosters and the crucifix were in a kind of silver work.

"No, look here—you asked for it, and now you've got it. So you must certainly keep it. I had it of a friend, a German—he gave it me, by the way, because he was going into a monastery—he's now a Franciscan monk, and he had inherited it from an aunt who also went into a convent. But there can't be any danger with you, as you have wife and child—"

They were standing in the little garden where the murders had taken place.

"Children always liked you, Randi," said Paul. "Do you remember, when we used to sit reading on the bench in the Studenterlund, some youngsters would always come up to you to ask the time—"

"Perhaps that was a presage of my call. There must always be somebody to answer the questions of other people's children. Those who have children of their own have a legitimate right to say keep quiet, get out with you, don't worry me—now and then."

THEY had come out into the Rue de Vaugirard again.

"I had some shopping to do in this street as a matter of fact—but if you'll allow me, perhaps I may walk with you part of the way first?" He told her what he had come for.

"But I'll tell you what, Paul—I'll go there with you if you like. I know exactly what necklace it is—but you mustn't give more than three hundred francs for it. If you like I'll talk to madame. Because!—excuse me—but perhaps your French is not so very fluent—?"

"No, isn't it annoying?" said Paul, a little piqued. "I read French without any difficulty, but when I try to speak it they don't understand me here."

They entered the shop—Randi smiled and laughed and bargained with the woman, and the woman beamed and smiled and shook her head and insisted on Randi trying on the necklace. She appealed to Paul—obviously took them to be husband and wife. Randi looked as if she were greatly captivated by her own reflection with the necklace on. It ended in his getting it for two hundred and eighty francs.

They walked back in the direction of the Luxembourg. Paul nodded as they passed the Carmes: "I'm glad you showed me that, Randi. For of course we've heard of the September massacres. But it was never pointed out to us that the revolution was a fight against all acknowledged authority—on the part of those who sought to make themselves authorities. And naturally their wildest hatred was directed against those who acknowledged a divine authority."

Randi nodded:

"No, we are told about corruption within the Church and the scandal it aroused. But we never hear that this scandal was nothing compared with the *hatred* of the Church's sanctity—and there was much sanctity at that time too. For of course all those who say, *Our* kingdom come, are likely to hate those who have the world's power and honor in their hands. But that's nothing compared with their hatred of those who pray, *Thy* kingdom come. And it isn't even any use being scandalized by the fact that those circles at home who believe themselves to be defending the remnants of Christianity in Norway are far more interested in a priest who breaks his vows than in two hundred who assert them in the face of a firing party. The fact is simply this, that they believe in every story of traitors, because that is a thing they can understand. And the other thing doesn't interest them, because they can no longer understand it."

"No. I remember how I felt as a boy. I reacted against all that naïve freethinking in mother's circle, and therefore I was quite ready to sympathize with religion. But I couldn't manage it. For instance, I came across a book—I've forgotten what the fellow's name was who wrote it, but it was about Kloster-Lasse. It didn't occur to me at that time that perhaps the Norwegian Jesuit's strength might lie in his possessing the truth—I regarded him as a kind of Don Quixote. But his biographer was a pure Sancho Panza riding his donkey at the heels of Pater Laurentius. That preface of his—I expect you know it better than I do—the profound patriotism that it expresses—his biographer can't see anything but calculation in it. I believe that book more than anything else gave me a distaste for Protestantism—with its lack of sympathy with everything that is venturesome and chivalrous and high-spirited—it seems to me there's something castrated about it, in spite of all parsonage idylls—"

"Of course—as it goes on cutting away more and more dogmas, it becomes more and more emasculated. Because dogmas in the body social are like the ductless glands in the human body—it is they which secrete the substance that determine the body's harmony and healthy growth. Without them the power of acting and contending goes to the winds. Take something away, and metabolism is disturbed. Take away some more, and the body becomes swollen with pale, dead fat—private opinions and personal convictions—till one is reminded of Constantine the Second's court eunuchs, who may be able to quarrel and intrigue, but are no use for fighting—at any rate for fighting to the death against heathendom.

"But have you thought," she said after a while, "of what it means that the whole of human combativeness, which the Church in days gone by directed into the supernatural sphere—as your godfather Saint Paul says—we wrestle not only against flesh and blood, but against the spiritual powers of darkness—that this warfare has become disorganized in a great part of Europe even in Christian circles? The faith is represented as something relatively mild and soothing, and the fight as merely a series of small skirmishes which could never interfere with any person's worldly activities. And human beings are combative—we can't live without fighting. If we don't fight with the Devil and the world and our own flesh, we fight with each other for worldly success. Till it comes to this, that in addition to fighting with their neighbors for places in the sun, men will one fine day demand of the rulers of States that they secure them, as nations, places in the sun and victory in the struggle for the world's markets. And then perhaps we shall have a war such as the world has never seen—"

"You believe that too?" asked Paul seriously. "I've had that impression since I've been here—that these people believe in a great European war, in the course of the next few years perhaps. We went to a cinema here one evening, my wife and I—saw a film about the Franco-German war. But it happened that the hero was an Englishman, a war correspondent, and he and his Alsatian girl roused terrific enthusiasm. Finally there was a scene which was nothing but tricolors, and the band played the Marseillaise, and the public cheered like mad. And of course, if it comes to a rupture between Germany and England, France will have to be in it from the start. And we ourselves—the Germans know our waters much better than we do, right up to the innermost arms of the fiords. And God knows if we have coal supplies for our fleet to guard our neutrality for as much as three or four months. For we don't generally keep any considerable reserve of stores in our country."

"But tell me, Paul, you business men—you must at any rate have got some inkling of the feeling of anxiety abroad? Haven't there been signs, in the money market for instance, which might give you something to think about?"

"Yes—. There has been one thing and another. But since 1911, when we got off with a fright—most people at home have comforted themselves with the assurance that it will always turn out the same way. There may be threats of war, but it will always be averted. When it comes to the point no one will take the responsibility for a breach of the peace. Of course, I don't suppose anyone pays attention to what our professional politicians say. And our brand new Foreign Office—well, it's new, isn't it? Otherwise that business of the North Sea treaty would be none too pleasant.—Altogether, I'm afraid there's no reason to place any exaggerated amount of confidence in our leading men at home. To a certain extent it must be the same in every democratic country, that the politicians shrink from uttering truths that they know the people won't like to hear."

"Well, well," said Randi with a sigh. "*Qui vivra, verra*—at any rate I'm horribly afraid of it. Well, Paul, thanks for your company—this is where I live—"

They had stopped outside a house in a narrow street close to St. Sulpice. On a sign which stuck out like a crooked arm was painted *Hôtel Bourdalue.* Two priests who came out of the door bowed to Randi as they passed. She turned round to look at them and laughed:

"This is a very Catholic hotel, I must tell you. One day last winter we were given some oysters which didn't look to me quite irreproachable—one can get one's meals here. And the gargon's reply was: 'It doesn't matter, mademoiselle—if we all get our death of them, there are so many priests in the house that we can all be given extreme unction at the same time'—"

They stood for a moment looking at each other.

"And so they're going to cut off your pretty hair, Randi!"

"Ugh, yes; don't talk of it. That's the worst part." She smiled nervously.

"Well—what's the proper thing to say on these occasions—is it usual to congratulate?"

"Yes, you may safely do that. It was jolly meeting you—tiresome that I couldn't meet your wife. Well, goodbye, and all the best!"

"Thanks—the same to you—"

Paul stood there a moment, watching the slender beige figure disappear into the darkness of the doorway.

He had a feeling of coming back to everyday life—and a very humdrum everyday, rather flat and insipid, as he ran upstairs in their hotel and knocked at the door of the room.

Björg, in her pink kimono—she persisted in calling it kin-nomo—was trying on some new shoes. She was rather pale about the gills and looked a trifle dashed as she turned to her husband:

"Why, where have you been all this time, Paul—I was beginning to get quite unhappy, not knowing where you'd gone—"

"Went for a morning walk. Tired, Puss?" He took her head in his hands from behind and kissed her on the forehead. Then he slipped the case out of his pocket, and when she sat up to get her breath after putting on the shoes, he clipped the necklace on her.

Björg put her hand to her throat—cried aloud with joy, ran to the glass, back to her husband and threw her arms about his neck, then ran to the glass again:

"Paul—you're an angel, you are indeed!—"

The jewel looked ravishing on her throat—and it was a very pretty throat, round and white, and her skin shone like silk. She was sweet—jumping with joy like a little girl—

"Oh, Paul—you are so sweet, I could eat you up—oh, but let's see, what's that—something for Baby, isn't it?—oh, how charming, let me see it—"

It was the rosary; he had pulled it out of his pocket with the case, and he had left it lying on the table. Hurriedly he put it back into his pocket.

"No—it's something for myself—"

"Ugh no, Paul, don't tease me—let me see—but, goodness, isn't it a rosary—like what the Catholics use?"

"Yes."

Björg's face grew serious, her eyes were round with alarm:

"Gracious, Paul, what do you want with it—? It's not true, is it?—you're not a Catholic? Else said so once—but I said I was sure you weren't—"

"No, I'm not. But if I were, do you think that would be so awful?"

"Oh, gee, that would be terrible!"

"Why?—Your aunt Mrs. Anderson is a Catholic, you know—"

"Ye-es—she is. But that was only because the Irish mother-in-law made such a row when he wanted to marry one who wasn't. But surely you can understand that she must be a different kind of Catholic—she can't be like these southerners. Why, she's Norwegian and all—she's an enlightened person who's been to a Norwegian school, thoroughly refined and that—"

Paul laughed.

"But what if I turned Catholic—do you think that would be such a disaster, Björg?"

"Oh, *gee*, it would be terrible! Ugh no—just think of all the horrid places we've been to here. And you should just hear what Fru Ahmann told me about the place where she's living—her landlady's a Catholic—"

Paul smiled at the recollection of his Christiania landladies.

"Well, well. But remember, if I turned Catholic, I could never get a divorce from you, for example."

"Oh but—I'm sure you'd never have the heart to do that anyhow—just think of our little Baby, Paul!"

"No, no, Puss, I'm not thinking of it either."

"Besides"—Björg looked at him attentively. "Then I suppose I couldn't get a divorce from *you*, could I?"

Paul shook his head with a very serious air.

"So you know *that*. Have *you* any plans of that sort, little one?"

"Fie, how horrid you are!" She was in his arms again.

"There, my dear. Now see about getting dressed—it's getting on for twelve. And Ruth said one o'clock, you know, at Charenton. It's a good way out."

"But Paul—supposing we can't find the place where we're to meet the others?"

"M-well—we shall have to eat, shan't we? So we'll have to find some other place and lunch alone, you and I. Terrible of course—but we needn't imagine the worst—"

PAUL had one or two business items to attend to while in Paris. So he told Björg he had to go up to the factory where they made bathroom fittings and proposed that she should stay in bed till midday, then he would come back to the hotel and fetch her.

He had found out that a train left the Gare de Lyon at 11:15, connecting with a train for Chambéry. That must be the one Randi would go by. At all events he would go to the station and see.

He had been hanging about for ten minutes or so in the huge and dirty station—the noise was deafening and the taste of coal smoke such that one had to have something to wash it down. So he found a bar and had a bock, bought some papers and went out on to the platform to read them. At that moment she came past.

She was walking between two stout old nuns in stiff black skirts and waving black veils. And she herself looked so small and light and slender in her beige costume. A French lady in black, a priest who was obviously her son, a pale, dark girl, very chic, and a young man were also of the party.

And the whole Protestant tradition, which Paul had done nothing but laugh at all his life, rose within him. All the popular serial literature about convent prisons and crafty priests—Uncle Abraham's whole fantastic world. And all the primitive distrust of foreign races—they are not like us, so they must be rascally.

The charming, fair Norwegian girl who was being dragged away to God knows what terrible fate by her two big black wardresses. The swarthy foreign devils who followed at their heels cackling aloud their unholy joy. The tall young priest who looked suspiciously intelligent, with dark, deep-set eyes, was the secret instigator of the crime—

"Bosh," he said to himself, and followed them along the platform.

Randi was standing on the platform of the carriage beside one of the nuns—a smiling, brown-eyed old lady with an imposing grey moustache. Randi looked more embarrassed than anything else on catching sight of Paul.

"I thought I must come and say goodbye to you—I hope you don't mind?"

"No—it was kind of you—thanks for coming—"

Introductions followed, of which Paul only gathered that the old nun with the moustache was called Mère Angélique—and a sort of attempt at general conversation, in which Paul's French failed him badly. So he made haste to say goodbye and disappear.

The last he saw, when he turned round some distance up the platform, was Randi's bright figure in the arms of the two French ladies—they were kissing her no end—

Bosh, he said to himself again. On the basis of her belief and her way of thinking, what she is doing is consistent. She is just as intelligent as any other girl I have met, and knows more than most. It is simply a boundless naïveté for people who don't know a tenth part of what she knows, and not even that properly, to imagine she must have been taken in and talked over. Besides—let me see; yes, she is thirty—she's no little girl either. Idiotic that one can't prevent reminiscences cropping up—Chiniquy and all that reading matter that Uncle Abraham sent me when I was last on dangerous ground—though I never thought it had any interest beyond characterizing Uncle Abraham—

Randi—when he came to think of it, there were a thousand things he would have liked to ask her. Though—wouldn't she get sick of him? It dawned on him all at once that when they met he had done nothing but pump her about her faith—since he had heard she had turned Catholic. Properly speaking it wasn't even polite—for there were masses of other things he might have talked to her about, her work, how she spent her time in the ordinary way, what her amusements were. In their schooldays she had been wildly fond of dancing, he remembered—and interested in all sorts of things, really. Even politics seemed to occupy her; and not merely as they did his mother, for instance—who picked out isolated facts and current political phrases and wove them into her own fantastical web; Randi was obviously at least as much interested in actual happenings as in what she thought ought to happen. But he had never done anything but try and coax out of her information about her religion.

He had been boundlessly taken up with it at one time—remembered the feeling of something brisk and alive, warming and sparkling in the depths of his being, a merry little fire lighted in his spirit. Every new thing he read and learnt about the faith was like an armful of fresh wood thrown upon the fire. The whole of life was brightened and warmed by it—supposing it is true: then life is not merely something one may as well attend to, since one finds oneself in it—it is a marvel. The happy seriousness that had filled his days at that time, the glad conviction that henceforward no days would any more be indifferent—was not that the result of his perceiving the Faith as a possibility, at least as much as of his love of a woman—?

And was *that* his greatest loss—that he had trodden out the little bright and living fire within him, turned away from God, offended because he did not get what he wanted—?

Of course, it was his relations with Lucy which at last had caused his suppressed presentiment of the divine to overcome obstructions. Previously he had never permitted himself to think about God—because all the religion that had come in his way had appeared to him a medley of obscure ideas and worn-out phrases, on the spiritual side, and a comical self-confidence on the human. But he had been so fond of Lucy that he could no longer silence his own questions: Whom have we to thank for life, for love?—why do we ourselves destroy so much of the riches that are placed in our hands?—who can help me to bring order into the turmoil that is our life?—who can arm me to stand fast and defend what is good in our happiness?

Paul had reached the Louvre—now it was time he took a taxi to that earthenware factory.—Hang! It could wait till tomorrow. He continued to wander at random through the town.

Faith, that was a gift of grace. He must pray to be given it, Harald Tangen had said. And he had done so—almost indifferently, God knows, without any special humility or fear and trembling. Nevertheless he had been given it—he knew that now. He had not had any real doubts or difficulties—he had been perfectly sure then that it was only a question of time when he would become a Catholic. There had been nothing between him and the Faith but his own blind and ignorant levity: he had not seen that there was any hurry, had not seen how serious it was. He had not had sense enough to fear God.

He remembered the last Sunday he was in Christiania, when he rushed up Akers gate to go to Saint Olav's church. Had he not felt like the prodigal son returning home—a self-important little prodigal son trotting homeward nose in air, sure of being received with roast veal and new shoes and finger rings? And no doubt he had thought he deserved it—!

Then, as God had not at once let him have things as he wanted them, he had gone his way again—and felt himself wronged.

Of course, the way in which Lucy had chosen to break it off had been fairly brutal—and he himself had been green enough.

This last had been the worst. That day, as he hung about the streets of Hamar waiting for the train to Trondhjem, he had been struck by an idea—and sitting in a little temperance café he had composed an advertisement for two Bergen papers, asking her to give her address, "must have this misunderstanding cleared up" and so on. He posted the letters from Hamar and asked to have copies of the papers sent him. They came, and in one of them he found besides his advertisement the notice of a marriage between Fröken Lucy Snippen—that was the name of her father's farm, he knew—and Herman Lövstö.

Fru Lucy Lövstö. By degrees he had persuaded himself to believe that the whole story had been so colossal a naïveté on his part that it made one feel small and foolish to look back on it. It was perfectly simple—he had been very young and very inexperienced, and the whole atmosphere in which he had grown up had given him a certain fastidiousness and a distaste for ordinary vulgar affairs with women. And then, as the first girl he happened to come across had a certain talent as a mistress—he had glorified the whole affair with mighty emotions and solemn intentions. Somewhat pathetic to look back upon—but pretty foolish, as he was thinking.

And if it should ever occur to Fate to arrange another meeting between him and Fru Lucy Lövstö—then he would presumably be utterly unable to understand how he could ever have been so green as to be romantic over such a fairly ordinary young female. Probably he had tormented and frightened the poor creature all the time by his determination to tow her into harbour—in his own class of life. No doubt she had been fond of him—but never particularly keen on being married to him. And when in a purely physical sense he had left her, no doubt her lack of imagination and her slow nature had caused her to allow herself to relapse into the conditions in which he had found her. It was to be hoped she had now found her right level and settled down as Herr Lövstö's mate.

But he had dismissed his longing for a religion as a component part of that overstrained and childish love story.

And afterwards. He seemed to have taken life more or less as a kind of entertainment—by no means a bad one, and anyhow, there it was. Even if one didn't think it was so superlatively well arranged, it was not good form to show one was bored. Try to be pleasant and companionable with those who are naïve enough to think it's fun being here. The business was what he had taken most seriously. Whether it had been worth giving up his studies, when the reasons for doing so had disappeared—well, it was no use going back to that now. The main thing was to feel oneself competent for the work one had in hand and to see it go forward. Then one thing might be as good as the other.

He had allowed himself to be caught in a marriage—but he had done it with his eyes open. As one lets oneself be caught by a dear little girl, when one is playing kiss in the ring with the children—on the grass outside a summer boarding house when on a walking tour. Why not—? Although, if she had been there with her mother instead of with that aunt—but he would have to take the consequences of having got engaged to a girl of whom he knew so little. Besides, there had been a certain cynicism involved on his part, when he let Björg attain her little object: it suited him to marry, he valued order and cleanliness in his private life. But little Björg knew nothing of that—and she was no doubt very happy with him. They were well off financially, he was always in good humour at home, and he remembered to bring back with him fruit and sweets and new books that people were talking about—proofs enough for Björg that he loved her and was what she understood by a chivalrous husband. Not to mention that she was a sweet little person and he was really fond of her.

The child—yes, at times she made him long for—what could he call it?—for getting into closer and more intimate touch with life itself. When Sunnie was playing on his lap he knew that it was he who had frittered away something precious when he imagined that being grown-up was equivalent to letting all one's feelings drop to a mean temperature. It was incredible how fond one grew of a little creature like this—how intensely interesting it was to follow a little child's development and growth. Since the new year they had moved her little cot over to the side of his bed, as Björg was so sleepy in the morning and Sunnie always woke at an unearthly hour. But she was sweet—rosy-pink with sleep, with all her fine golden baby hair in curls; bright as a lark she sat up in her cot crooning and babbling the little words she had learnt to say. He lay dozing and passed her one by one the things she liked best to play with—a shoe horn, empty cigarette boxes, the sheath of an old knife—as she got tired of what she had in her hands and threw it on the floor. He would often have liked to take her up into his bed—but then she always forced her way on to her mother and woke her. At times there was a deep silence in the little cot; and when he looked he found she had fallen asleep sitting up, with her nose buried in the quilt.

At times the little girl would keep on for hours, babbling and busy with her games—she was absorbed in her own joy with such holy zeal that it seemed as though her play was really more serious than all the pursuits of grown-up people and her delight belonged more essentially to life than all the world's sorrows. Was it a kind of reflection of a reality which men had obscured and distorted by their own stupid and criminal devices? And it is only in the play of very small children in the early hours of the morning that one sees as it were a mirage of the distant city—life in its archetype.

In the spring, while he was working in the garden, she would get in his way everywhere. All at once he would find her tramping up the loose mould in a bed he had just made—before he knew what she was doing she would sit down and howl after sousing herself with the garden hose.

"Sunnie, what do you think mamma will say to us when she sees the state you're in?"

"Pig-gy," said Sunnie, with a terribly serious face.

"That's it. Piggy. You're a piggy-wiggy, that's what you are." That made her laugh. Then he carried her up to the house. Oh, you little child of mine, I love you, he said fervently, within himself—he did not even whisper it to her.

The mere thought that such a little human bud might die appeared to him an insufferable brutality; it could not be allowed. And yet—. She had been very little in his thoughts these last weeks in Paris. He had scarcely looked at the little photograph of her that he kept inside his watchcase. If—. Did one even forget one's own little child—in time?

Paul had reached a little square, where he had not been before. Around it were ordinary-looking houses with shops on the ground floor—some of the windows displayed images of saints in colored plaster, crucifixes in all sizes and materials, books of devotion, rosaries, cheap decorations for altars. On the far side of the square stood a church—it looked quite commonplace, not to be found in any guidebook.

Paul stood still a moment—then he crossed the square rapidly and entered the church.

The interior was dark and warm, and within the darkness twinkled hundreds of little living candle flames. They were crowded together like constellations, but were not powerful enough to light up the great gloomy vault so that one could see anything clearly—they only gave the air a golden glow and made it quiver and beam and filled the church with warmth and the scent of molten wax. When his eyes had grown accustomed to the strange lighting he discovered that the hushed church was full of people—they hung kneeling over every chair.

A great side chapel on the right seemed one mass of light and flowers and glittering jewels. And above all the flickering flames of wax tapers, thin and thick, a tall white statue of Mary reared itself, a crowned queenly figure with a crowned royal child standing on something at the height of the mother's hip—with an almost violent turn of the waist she presented her Son to the world.

This chapel was even more crowded with silent worshippers. Paul tiptoed his way to a vacant stool. Beside him knelt a grey-haired officer who was saying his rosary with his eyes unswervingly fixed on the queen-like figure of Mary.

The candles were burning on great holders in the form of pyramids with iron spikes. People came forward continually with fresh candles which they lighted and fixed on the spikes.

My God—I do not even know myself what I have done, against Thee, or against myself, or against all those with whom I have dealings—when I chose to withdraw into myself instead of opening the door to Thee—

"Behold, I stand at the door and knock. If any man hear my voice and open the door to me"—he remembered that from the Revelation. Any man—! Yes, he himself had been one of those who were unwilling to open the door. At that time he had imagined it was God alone he sought—he would not pray for this thing or the other. He had assumed he would receive it in any case; his life would arrange itself in any case, as he wished it to be. When his own childish little plans came to grief, and God did not intervene and put everything right for him—then he had slammed his door. But at any rate he knew now—there was not a thing between heaven and earth which did not seem to him utterly flat and tasteless, since he had heard God himself offer to come in and sup with him.

Even his love of his little girl was felt only against a background of sadness. It was so charming to see how completely she could become absorbed in every little thing or happening that made her glad—now. The worst thought was not that he would be unable to protect her from sorrows and disappointments as she grew older. It was worse to think that when the time arrived at which she lost the capacity for perfect joy in the delights of this world—he would see no means of helping her.

"By thy holy childhood—deliver us, O Lord" he remembered having heard in one of the litanies. He had not understood till now how much it meant—more than just the Christmas idyll of the newborn babe in the manger and the young mother bending over it, while angels and shepherds met and rejoiced together. It meant much, much more—

Maria Mater gratiae. We have been told that she is only one among all the divine mothers with a child in their arms whom the world has worshipped. Perhaps that is what we have to atone for, that we have not seen the difference between them and the Mother of Mercy. Isis who conceives by a corpse, Leto who urges her children to destroy the sons and daughters of Niobe, Tanit, Astarte, Cybele, the whole host of savage and bloody mystery-divinities who impel men to beget new generations—and the new generation lives a few short decades, fights, is cruel from fear, cruel from inclination, cruel from desire, until the Great Mother reaps it like corn and puts it back into the earth. Human mercy—it is true that it exists as a feeling, an impulse; but the whole of history teaches us it is an impulse which always yields to fear in us, to distrust of other men, and afterwards comes cruelty for the pleasure of it. But what must we pay for our error, if we imagine that these goddesses of the heathen nations resembled God's Mother—if we fancy we can recognize her features in nature—a human being, but full of grace; a woman, but with the Word which was made Flesh in her arms—?

Hail, Mary, full of grace, the Lord is with thee, blessed art thou among women and blessed the fruit of thy womb, Jesus—Paul continued to repeat the Angel's Greeting under his breath.—By thy holy childhood, deliver us, Lord.—Help me to overcome my fear of Thee—for it is fear of Thee which has held me back. Teach me to believe in Thee, not in order to gain this or that, but to learn to know Thee. By Thy holy childhood—one cannot be afraid to open the door to a child, one must rather be afraid of injuring it. And let me not find peace until I have become reconciled with that peace which Thou callest thine, of which Thou hast said that the world can neither give it nor take it away—

As he got up to go he discovered where the people got their candles—a woman sat in a corner selling them. He had a sudden idea—he too would light a candle before this image of Mary with the Child.

He went across and bought one of the biggest. He was not very clear as to the meaning of this symbol of lighting a candle, but when he came back to the chapel and planted his among the others he meant it vaguely as a manifestation of his prayer—let me not be allowed to extinguish the spark that has again begun to glow within me.

At the end of June Paul and Björg went to Chartres and stayed there a few days. It was Ruth who had advised them to make the trip.

On the way back they had stopped a few hours at Rambouillet to see the palace and the park. On returning to the station Paul went off to buy some papers. The paper seller was surrounded by a group of men who had got off the Paris train for the same purpose—evidently there was some rather sensational news. And Paul overheard one man say to another: "*C'est la guerre*—" pointing to a heading in the paper he had just bought.

Paul turned to his own copy, below the big headline which the Frenchman had shown his friend. The Austrian heir apparent and his consort shot at Sarajevo—now where's that?—the assassin a Serbian student. Telegram from Vienna.

But then they had to hurry back to their compartments. The train started. Paul tried to catch some of his fellow travelers' conversation. Those shots in the turbulent corner of Europe had evidently stirred them greatly.

Björg asked what it was, and Paul had to translate the news to her.

"Pooh!" said Björg; "they have such heaps of archdukes down there that it can't matter so very much. And we're always hearing of these attacks on princes and such like—"

She had all her mother's hostile contempt for titled persons at a distance and the same touching interest in them when they approached her field of observation closely enough for her to go out and see them drive past or hear stories of their sayings and doings at third or fourth hand.

Chapter Six

They came back to Christiania on the first of July. The town was agog with the Centenary Exhibition. Alster & Selmer had a stall there. The year before—not without considerable hesitation—they had become interested in a small steatite concern in the Gudbrandsdal, and now they exhibited a collection of really handsome stoves and fireplaces, door-fittings and other small articles, lamps, urns and the like, made of soapstone. Quite a number of orders had come in, so Paul began to think that perhaps in time the business might not merely justify itself but actually become an enterprise with a future.

The evening before Paul was to return to Trondhjem a kind of family gathering had been arranged at the restaurant in the exhibition. The concourse had a rather casual character, Paul thought, as he arrived with his father: Lillian was already there with Tua and Halstein, Hans and their cousin Evald Dverberg with his wife and their half-grown daughter; Laura had come with her new husband, a German engineer named Auwein. They were still a newly married couple and showed it rather too plainly. Laura Dverberg had been divorced from her first husband; the second had shot himself, an affair which had given rise to a good deal of talk. So perhaps it was natural enough that she should be delighted at the prospect of accompanying her Fritzchen to Mannheim that winter.

Paul was not too pleased that Björg was again to stay in the south and spend six weeks with her mother in the country. He would miss the little one—Sunnie had known him again and received him graciously; she dived into his waistcoat pocket and pulled out the tick-tick the moment she was in his lap. But now it was settled.

Fru Jacobsen came heaving along among the tables, red and exhausted, with Björg in her wake—and Paul felt a fresh whiff of annoyance. It was incomprehensible—but as soon as she came within the vicinity of her mother, the likeness between them was most strikingly intensified. To think that the child could have no more independence.

His mother-in-law was profuse in her apologies for being so late, showering greetings and protests around her, while the younger men of the party, helped by a waiter, struggled to make room at the joined tables for the new arrivals.

"But—you're not poorly, I hope, Herr Selmer?—fancy, I thought you were looking so tired!—don't you think so, Paul—good evening, Paul, I was forgetting—don't you think your father looks poorly—?"

"Father and I have been going round the exhibition all the afternoon—it's pretty fatiguing"—he stooped down and picked up all the catalogues she had dropped in taking her seat.

He could not hear her saying that—especially as he had noticed it himself the last few days; his father gave him the impression of being downright ill. During the previous winter he had been in hospital—for digestive trouble, it was said. He would find an opportunity of speaking to Hans this evening; his brother and he were staying at the same hotel. Hans Selmer was now assistant physician at a municipal hospital in one of the small coast towns.

He found it impossible to get rid of his ill humour. He was sitting next to the big window, and outside the flowers in boxes still shone with strange, pale tints in the reflection of the sunset. The sky was lemon-yellow along the horizon, and on the pond the reflection of its light, bluish green was blended with that of the illuminations. That was effective—and this temporary restaurant building had quite a festive air: all the little tables with colored lampshades and uniform bouquets and food and glasses. The place was filled with the buzz of voices and the clatter of plates, the band was playing a potpourri of Norwegian folk tunes—and from the amusement park came the noise of a different music, while ever and again they heard the thunder and shrieks of the mountain railway.

The melancholy which had been the basis of his feeling for his father ever since he had been really grown up—it was not that alone which welled up in him now at the thought that perhaps his father was a doomed man. It was a kind of indeterminate apprehension of more than that. He had been really impressed by this exhibition—nevertheless his satisfaction at the evidences he had seen of Norwegian ability had only increased this sinister feeling of uneasiness. He heard fragments of the conversation between Halstein Garnaas and Evald—Evald was chairman of various Christian organizations—they were talking about an educational scheme that was planned for the winter, lectures for young men and young women; evidently there was no doubt in their souls that lectures were a great help—"contribution" they called it!—against social evils and the difficulties of youth.

Björg sat between his father and Auwein; she looked uncommonly well this evening in her sea-blue Paris dress. All at once it struck him—that he had taken his marriage to her so lightly was another matter—but that two grown-up people who had been married three years and had a child should never be on any other footing than that of chaff and triviality—why, that must mean that he had neglected something. He longed for seriousness—not any such nonsense as forcing themselves to discuss serious subjects together, exchange ideas, as people called it. It was another kind of seriousness he hungered for, a really earnest seriousness that was deep enough and broad enough to get along with just such light and playful words as this cheap love of theirs had used.

Oh, it must have been something like this that he had missed behind it all—behind the pride and satisfaction in Norway at this moment. It is said in season and out of season that we are such serious folk—and by that is meant sourness, sermonizing and the solemnity which takes itself solemnly.—God knows if that isn't the reason for there being so much sourness and so little gaiety in this country—because we don't know much of any seriousness but the cheap and short-sighted kind.

"But I say—there's Uncle Halvdan," said Tua joyfully—she half rose and made eager signs to a man some tables away. "Paul, you must go and get hold of him—as you've just been seeing Ruth; I'm sure Uncle Halvdan would like to hear news of her—"

Reluctantly Paul rose and went off—met Dr. Wangen halfway.

He was a fairly tall man—and now he was pretty broad too, growing rather corpulent; but somehow the added flesh had been distributed across his frame, leaving his legs still slight; it didn't look so well. He had a handsome face, with an aquiline nose and a high color; red cheeks, red lips, dark hair and a dark pointed beard—now by the way it was pepper-and-salt. His eyes were dark blue and very bright—he had a way, when looking at a lady, of trying to stare her out of countenance; Paul had always thought it detestable, though perhaps it meant nothing more than that it had been a kind of trick or password in his day and his circle. He practiced it on Björg when Paul introduced her—Dr. Wangen had not met Paul's wife before.

The doctor greeted the whole company in a loud voice, took his seat next to Paul and asked him what he thought of Ruth's pictures—then he started giving a little explanatory lecture on his daughter's art, without waiting for the other's reply. He was evidently immensely proud of having a daughter who was an artist—he had always been bitten that way. Paul thought Ruth painted quite well, her pictures were pleasing and sympathetic, but somewhat impersonal. He was wondering whether he should carry his neighborly charity so far as to ask Uncle Halvdan to look in at his hotel next morning to see the two pictures he had bought of Ruth—a couple of little street scenes from Paris.

He had never been able to stand the man. But his mother had always been very good friends with this brother-in-law—of course they had been "saved" about the same time, in the 'eighties. But what he thought rather charming and becoming in her—this radicalism which reminds one of little children cutting caraway sprouts, when they take just as much of the roots as will flavour the soup—was not to be borne in a grown-up man, who moreover had the name of being a capable country doctor, but who always preferred to talk of things he did not know very much about.

Then first Lillian and after her the whole company began waving rapturously again. Paul gave a start—why, great heavens! if it wasn't his mother advancing towards them with both Tua's little girls. And it seemed to have been arranged beforehand, though he had heard nothing of it.

She looked splendid—her hair had turned much greyer in the last few years, and she was dressed all in white, a kind of heavy crochet lace, which made Lillian shout with delight:

"Oh but, Julie! What a wonderful frock you've got—I believe it's real Irish lace—no, come and sit here on the sofa, little girls—oh, poor things, how tired they must be—!"

"Yes, they're walking in their sleep." Tua's two eldest were quite pretty little girls—in Halling dress with embroidered caps—they were like their father, pale, with curly yellow hair. They began to whimper at once, from over-tiredness.

"Oh yes, we've been on the mountain railway," laughed Julie; "I too! No, thanks, Erik—we've done nothing but eat—yes, a glass of champagne you *may* give me. Five!" she said laughing to her brother-in-law; "fancy,

Halvdan, I have *five* grandchildren now—Paul has a little girl—great fun, oh yes! but going round an exhibition and acting the grandmother—it's *wearing*!" Paul however by no means had the impression that his mother was a particularly enthusiastic grandmother; he had felt a little hurt at the moderate feeling she showed for Sunnie when they were out at Linlökka the other day. "Oh no, Tua dear, they've been very good and sweet the whole time—but now they're quite done up, poor little things. No, Erik, just leave her alone, it'll pass off—hush now, Ambjör, grandpapa's not angry at all—he only wants to comfort you—"

PAUL drove his wife and mother-in-law out to Storgate and went up to look at Sunnie asleep. Fru Jacobsen proposed a cup of coffee.

Scarcely was she out of the door when Paul went up to his wife. He seized both her hands and pressed them hard:

"Björg dear—do come home with me tomorrow!"

Björg opened eyes and mouth in surprise:

"Are you crazy! It wouldn't do—what do you think mamma would say?"

"Do come, Björg!"

"Besides—you can understand I daren't risk that long railway journey for Baby in this heat—when her stomach's been so upset last night and today—"

"Bah—that's only because she's been stuffed with sweets morning, noon and night. As far as that goes, it would do the child good to come home—"

"No, look here! You may be sure mamma knows best—"

Paul stopped her mouth with a kiss:

"Oh, Björg—I shall long for you so much"—and he was quite surprised at the sound of his own voice, there was such a querulous note in it.

Björg stirred slightly in his arms. Then she looked up at him with a little smile, coquettish and sly:

"Oh, is that it?—poor boy. No, I'll tell you what, Paul—I don't believe it'll do you a bit of harm for once. I believe it'll be *good* for you, I do, if you're obliged to have a little holiday now—"

Then he released her.

"But you know," whispered Björg, "I could easily come home with you to the hotel and stay there the night. Mamma wouldn't think there was anything odd in that, I'm sure—as you're leaving tomorrow—"

"No, my dear, you know very well I wouldn't ask you. As Sunnie's not quite the thing—"

ON reaching the hotel he went up and knocked at Hans's door. But evidently his brother was not in. The time was not much more than one anyhow—.

He took out a book, one of those he had bought in Paris, and lay down on the sofa. When he awoke it was full daylight. The hotel room with the electric light still burning had a peculiarly loathsome look—and the cheerless mood of the evening before was wide awake within him. Paul hurriedly switched off the light and got into bed.

He awoke so late in the morning that he wondered if he could still catch Hans. They had met every morning in a little breakfast room apart.

The door of the room was half open when he came down—and through the opening Paul saw a couple by one of the tall windows—Hans and a girl. His brother was standing in a strangely bent attitude, with his head thrust forward under her breast, while his arms were clasped about her hips—she was bending over backwards so far that it make him think of proving a steel blade. And she was dressed in something bright and steely blue.

Paul made haste to disappear. But that one glimpse he had had of the couple had given him the impression of something so manifestly and triumphantly sensual—and shown him that she was dazzlingly pretty, a finely shaped little head with close-lying black hair and a white cameo-like profile—and it had hung over backwards, with closed eyes and a kind of impetuous smile, while her slender figure quivered in long, voluptuous waves under the man's embrace.

Who the deuce could she be—? Paul went back to his room and fetched his hat and stick; dropped the stick outside the door of the breakfast room as he was hanging up his things.

The young lady was sitting at a little table drinking coffee; Hans Selmer stood facing her. Hans nodded on seeing his brother, came to meet Paul, and the lady took up a paper. The brothers sat down at their usual table in another part of the room.

They chatted—but Paul's attention was inclined to wander to Hans's friend. She was even prettier that he had thought at the first glimpse: her head was so charmingly poised on her neck and the black hair clung so smoothly, showing its fine shape, but lower down it was arranged in plaits in the style of the Empress Elisabeth; the features were quite regular and the complexion white and compact like a flower. She looked positively mysterious—not in any ironical sense—could she be Norwegian?

Hans too was obviously preoccupied—so for the present Paul had no opportunity of broaching the subject of their father's health.

"But look here, tell me—have mother and Lillian begun to meet as friends now?"

"M-yes. You know Tua was in hospital here last autumn for a pretty severe operation. And Lillian has always been a brick to Tua. So that's where they met. And when Tua went out to Linlökka to stay during convalescence, it followed that Lillian was there a good deal. And now they see one another regularly. Mother's at their house now and then—" Hans gave a little laugh—then he started up.

"Oh, Doctor Selmer—may I speak to you a moment?" The lady was ready to go, very picturesque in a long cape of the same glossy grey-blue cloth as her dress. She was just a tiny bit too stylish to be quite elegant. Hans followed her into the passage.

"Who was that?" Paul could not resist asking when his brother came back. "She's a perfectly charming young lady!"

"Fröken Hansen's her name. She comes from where I am—the family have been awfully friendly to me. Her father's a shipowner—"

"I shouldn't have taken her for a Norwegian—"

"Her mother's name was Kurud. But it's quite likely, with those old skipper families on the coast—there may be foreign blood in the family."

"But what I really wanted to speak to you about was this—I don't like the look of father. That time he spent in the clinic last winter—has he been well since?"

"No. He has not. And I haven't been able to get him to see a specialist. Old Nicolaysen is a good doctor of course—but his diagnoses are not always equally successful. But father won't hear of going to anyone else. I don't know whether he's afraid of what he might be told—or whether he doesn't care to prolong his life a few years by an operation—"

"You think it's as serious as that?"

"I'm afraid so. I'm trying to get him to come down to us—you know my chief, Bang-Arnesen, is an uncommonly clever surgeon. And now that father has so much to live for"—Hans gave a thin, sad smile—"sitting like a pasha with his wives on each side of him and a constantly growing posterity—"

"BUT write and tell me as soon as you know anything for certain about father," Paul asked him, as the brothers parted in the street.

Paul had a good deal to do in town that morning. And tried in vain to shake off his feeling of depression and anxiety. And it continued to gall him that Björg had guessed nothing of it. He didn't know how it was, but when he told her the evening before that he would long for her, he had really felt it, felt it intensely. And for the first time; for to tell the truth he had usually taken Björg's absence from home as an agreeable change—a peaceful and cosy interval in a married life which no doubt was happy enough in the ordinary way, but came to feel a little tiring now and again. And in spite of the turn it had taken yesterday evening, he did long—for something which had not come to anything.

Chapter Seven

The month of July passed very peacefully; there was enough to do at the office, and in the evenings Paul had his garden. It was now at the most interesting stage, when everything was coming up.

Henrik Alster had been infected by his interest in gardening and repeated Paul's experiments in putting in alpine plants and growing vegetables that were not to be had in the shops. Mortensen talked about starting a society for the Suppression of Gardening. He and Else lived in a modern flat in the neighborhood of the College; they would not be so hard on themselves as to turn house owners, they said.

"The risk of war—when you come to think of it, it was at least as imminent in 1911," said Henrik Alster one morning, when he and Paul were discussing the latest telegrams. "It's only that people have given it more attention since the Morocco affair—they follow things more closely now."

Paul did not answer. With rather gratuitous ostentation he took his sliding rule and began to look up some prices.

"Besides, even if it ends in another Balkan war, it's sure to be localized again. When it comes to the point Western Europe will hardly allow Russia to go any further than a diplomatic action for the sake of Serbia."

"The sake of Serbia. Good Lord, what do we really *know* about Serbia, man? What the papers told us while the war was on. And before that, whenever there was a dramatic scene in the Konak. About so essential a thing, as the country's resources, for instance, I'm sure we know very little indeed. But we know the Serbians from the *Simplicissimus* version of them. I wonder, by the way, how much influence that paper has had on our views of European affairs—among the so-called educated classes in Norway, at any rate—"

"Yes, I know you don't like it—I don't myself for that matter. It's for Berit's sake I take it—"

"I suppose we'll have to give them forty per cent," said Paul, looking up from the estimate he was making out; "since it's a kind of charitable institution—"

Next day the papers announced the Austrian ultimatum to Serbia. Paul avoided speaking to anyone about it. It was too revolting. But wasn't there behind it the history of a European State that stemmed the flood of Asiatic hordes—and it had been deserted and attacked in the rear and humiliated so many times that it would resort to anything rather than share the fate of the northern bastion, Poland—? Treat your neighbor as your neighbor has treated you—even if it's another neighbor—otherwise a third neighbor will come along and treat you the same way again. Wasn't that approximately the train of thought that underlay the policy of States—because it represented the conduct of most individuals—?

All the same one would think it must end in some solution of the conflict being found—at the last moment.

HENRIK read aloud everything that the papers quoted from the Socialist press of the world. Paul laughed at him: "All the times you've abused me for being half a Socialist—"

"Well, well, well, when you come out with such rubbish as believing there might be nations in which socialization would lead to increased production and more equable distribution—"

"For a time, I said. And in the case of particular nations."

"No, I don't believe in any of that. Not in their social systems, no. But that idea of brotherhood—the ideal of brotherhood—the brotherhood of mankind, at any rate I should like to be able to believe in that."

"*I* believe in it," said Paul rather gruffly. "I believe in brotherhood between you and me and the man the sheriff of Orkedal arrested the other day for flogging his horse with a dog's chain. And that fellow in the slum here who ruined a little girl of three—the foster child they had adopted as their own against payment once for all, as it says in the advertisements."

"What rot. Damn it, no, I don't acknowledge that kind of relationship. And you!" Alster laughed. "Who couldn't even harm a cat. How many times do you think you've let yourself be taken in, even in the few years we've been together here, by people who came and told you a yarn about their troubles and borrowed money of you?"

"Never. In money matters I believe neither in legends nor in miracles. If any of those folks chanced to pay me back, it would upset all my principles."

"Then it's for the sake of this relationship you help them?" laughed Alster.

"I suppose it is." Paul laughed too.

"Well, but then you must assume that your less fortunate brethren might perhaps be equally kind and helpful, in certain circumstances?"

"I don't assume it; I know it."

"I see. Well then, how do you explain their turning out like this, these two monsters that you assert to be relations of yours? Do you attribute it to social conditions?"

"No. Have you never heard of cruelty to animals or diabolical treatment of children among people who pay heavy taxes? On the contrary, I assume society is what it is because we all belong to the same dear family."

"You only say that to be paradoxical."

"No, I say it because it beats me that people can't see how much this talk of the brotherhood of mankind is worth. Brotherhood is a fact, and in the last resort there can't be any other reason for most wars than this fact that all men *are* brothers. You know how things generally go in a family, when they have to divide the property—

"What has caused the confusion of ideas is simply that Christianity has talked about a brotherhood of an entirely different nature—among those who have experienced a rebirth to a supernatural life. And even with them, who had gone through this supernatural process and become brothers in Christ, it constantly happened that they suddenly dropped out of that life and found themselves again as brothers in the good old style—like Cain and Abel."

"Horrid pessimistic you are. But you can't deny that there is some good in the great majority of mankind? Sympathy and so on is really something that belongs to human nature?"

"No, I don't deny that. It belongs to a tigress to have dugs—and milk. But I don't believe it would have any future if one set up a model dairy of tigresses. At any rate I wouldn't take shares in the concern that distributed the milk."

"That's a lot of damned nonsense all the same. If it were as you say, one could never feel safe in this world."

"Just at the present time I don't believe there's any reason to do so either, worse luck.—To be sure, there's something about a little child shall lead them, but—"

"You've got the Bible on the brain, that's sure. Well, it shows what comes of this freethinking. One fine day it gets you far worse than the rest of us who have kept to the faith of our childhood—more or less—"

Paul laughed:

"I can't ever remember having one—unless it was a faith in progress and evolution and more and more culture, till the measure ran over and the very soil of the countries was saturated with culture. As far as that goes it may be just as well that I never had any child's faith. At any rate I have none that the robbers can take from me."

"Hm. All the same I don't know whether I oughtn't to telephone for Berit. In case of accidents. It might be more comfortable to have her and the children at home—"

"If I were you, I would let my family stay where they are. With the German fleet outside in the North Sea there may easily be a panic in the coast towns, if war breaks out and England is in it. Though as far as I can see we may have good grounds for being alarmed on our own account too—"

"I see you really do believe there'll be war? Although our own Bourse is quite calm—"

"Oh yes. And it may well be that high finance will step in and save a war. One thief doesn't rob another. And I dare say they feel the same horror at the thought of such a catastrophe as all the rest of us—who have nothing to gain by a war, either for ourselves or for what we believe will guarantee the safety of our country in the future."

SUDDENLY the panic was there—all over the country. There was something in the manner of its coming which reminded Paul of the wave of a steamship suddenly breaking on the beach. The Christiania papers of the day before arrived—the rates of exchange were unaltered. And today this violent feeling of anxiety and suspense. The war machinery had already begun to revolve—Russia's masses were in motion—and people had a sort, of intuition: they cannot be stopped. And those who stood looking on gasped already, or held their breath, or screamed aloud in anticipation of the shock, when the monsters should come into collision and the wails of the crushed should shrill from under the wreckage.

Paul and Henrik and Mortensen discussed the situation together. Clearly it was impossible to foresee anything except that, if there was war, all building operations would probably be brought to a standstill. They had arranged with their bank for the payment of the necessary sums for wages pending further developments. Apart from that they had several acceptances which fell due about the tenth of August and one or two important sums which ought to come in before that time. But sufficient for the day—if there was war, then of course all the conditions of business life would have to accommodate themselves accordingly.

Paul could not help it—in this oppressive feeling that what was coming was perhaps worse than anyone had imagined in his wildest dreams—there was at the same time a terrible excitement: but what is it? What are we going to see?

He came home about eleven at night—stood at the foot of the veranda steps where the bushes had grown to the height of a man this year. There was a pale white light over the fiord and the glimpses of sky between the clouds showed white; he held his breath and listened: gunfire out at sea—? He had heard in town today that folks in the islands had thought they heard firing in the North Sea. Rumors no doubt—like so many more that had been flying about today.

Below him lay the town with all its lights—the view he was so fond of. A big passenger steamer with her ports all lighted up was making her way in from Munkholm.

—Have I ever really believed it possible—war in Europe? Perhaps war in our own country—we may be dragged in by circumstances beyond our control. Of course I have never believed it. Only I have never believed in a single one of the reasons everybody else brought forward when they declared it was impossible. I believed that egoism—the egoism of individuals, of parties, of States—would be a guarantee of peace. I believed it because, when I was young, I was a witness that two small States kept the peace—and we at any rate did so because we thought peace was worth a humiliation.

There must have been some real desire for peace among our rulers at that time too—there certainly was. Much, perhaps. But when we youngsters ground our teeth and didn't know where to look in our sorrow and shame—they answered us with talk of the horrors of war and the advantages of peace, the blessings of peace. By God, we had the will to give our lives for our country's honor.—

And yet we have imagined, we who ought to have known better, that peace can be based on egoism—between States which are neither small nor weak, between men who are not kept down in the shade nor live so closely packed that they cannot grow to their full natural stature in good and evil.

If there had been less talk of the blessings of peace and the advantages of peace—but more of the dangers and humiliations of peace, if anyone had been willing to preach, not that we should be afraid of war, but that we should not be afraid of men—not because of any goodness there may be in them, but simply urging us not to be afraid of men even as they are—then Peace would have had no palace at The Hague. And Peace would certainly have had fewer declared peace-lovers.

But then perhaps there would have been men who loved Peace as men have loved War. Then Peace on earth would at any rate have begun to loom as a distant possibility.

He had stayed behind alone at the office—had finished a couple of estimates and written some business letters, and as he did so he could not help thinking: God knows how things will be when they reach their destinations.—He had let the typist leave early; she had to go and fetch her old mother from the summer boarding house where she was staying. Henrik had decided to see about getting Berit and the children home; tonight he was going to motor inland for them. Mortensen had gone to meet Else and the children at the boat. People came rushing back from the country as if for their lives.

He himself had telegraphed to his wife asking her to stay where she was for the present.

The veranda doors stood wide open. Paul went through the rooms, out into the kitchen; there was nobody. He knocked at the door of the maid's room—no. In the dining room the cloth was on and a place was laid, but there was no food on the table. Dina must have thought he would have supper in town.—So he fetched a bottle of beer from the cellar and found some food in the larder. But it was a strange idea of the maid to take herself off like that and leave the house standing open.

The perfect stillness of the little villa affected him strangely—got on his nerves, to put it plainly. Though of course that was nonsense. He went and sat in his own room and read the papers over again. And he gave a start when something came bounding noisily up the veranda steps—and it was only the dog. She dashed up to him, wagging her tail and yapping. When he ordered her to lie down, she stole in to the drawing room and took the opportunity of lying on the sofa.

She must have her key with her—Dina. Paul locked the outer door and went upstairs. The coverlet had not been taken off his bed. And he thought it looked strange and uncomfortable with the two beds and the little white cot gleaming in the dusky room. Quickly he pulled the coverlet from his bed and threw it on to Björg's; then he undressed in no time.

NOBODY brought him hot water in the morning, and the dining room table was as he had left it. Evidently Dina had not come back. He telephoned home from the office, but got no answer. And when he looked in about midday the house was still empty, bedroom and bathroom had not been touched.

He thought he would have to notify the police—something might have happened to her. She was an elderly person, rather odd in her manner. He couldn't help thinking she might have been scared by the excitement around her and had gone off her head.

ON Monday morning there was a letter from Björg—she and her mother had returned to Christiania, of course. Enclosed was a list, enormously long, of things he was to buy for the house. Paul just glanced at it: 10 sacks of wheat flour, 5 sacks of rye flour, it began with. He threw the letter into the drawer of his desk, rang up and asked for an urgent connection with the stoneworks in the Gudbrandsdal.

The whole forenoon was taken up with telephoning—to business connections, to the banks, to people who could give news of the war: French cavalry had crossed the German frontier in several places; Belgium was yielding; the feeling in London; rumours of a German occupation of Christianssand; raids on the shops in Christiania; Nuremberg bombarded from the air; would the Bank of Norway follow the example of Stockholm and Copenhagen? Fröken Raaen told him that two German spies had been arrested at the Britannia. There was a telegraphic confirmation from Grossmann & Weinberg of their last order: hope to deliver without material delay and "Gott mit uns." Hm.

Paul went out; perhaps it was safest to make personal inquiries, and he thought he must find out whether the police had any news of the missing maid. After a lot of trouble he got hold of a man who knew about the affair. Oh yes, Dina Snemo had arrived at her parents' home in Verdal on Saturday; it looked as if she had been scared out of her wits by some servant girls in the neighborhood.—By the way, she had been a year in an asylum in her young days, the sheriff informed him. The police had heard nothing of spies at the Britannia.

So he went off to read the latest telegrams that were posted up in the newspaper offices.

He felt it like a wound in his mind—and thought it must leave a scar for life—this preoccupation with his own affairs. His horror at what was happening in the world outside was unbearable, but how much of this oppressive feeling was due to uncertainty on his own account? Belgium, what state was it in today? What would be happening there tomorrow, the next day—in a month, what would it be like then? What multiplication is one to use to get some kind of idea of the misery involved in a war? And like a tiny mote carried on the wind, far away on the outer fringe of a conflagration, there was Dina, their quiet elderly maid—he could not help thinking of her the whole time, how that poor creature must have suffered.

He was invited to take his meals at the Alsters' in the meantime. But he declined. He was in no mood to listen to Berit bubbling over with German enthusiasm—and Henrik had an extraordinary notion that he, Paul, not only didn't think the war was such a terrible disaster, but actually wanted to crow over him in some way, because he had turned out right. Strange, in such a sensible man as Alster usually showed himself.

Paul felt it was positively a good thing that he had an empty house to go home to.

BUT on the third morning he was roused by somebody shaking him, and it was Björg.

"But bless me—where have *you* come from?"

"From the train, I should think—oh my! I was in such a state when there was nobody to meet us—but make haste and get up now, the chauffeur won't be able to carry in all my cases by himself—and what sort of a mess is the house in, downstairs and everywhere—you haven't given Dina a holiday now, have you?"

Paul turned out of bed, full of misgivings of unpleasant explanations to come.

"Where's Sunnie—you brought the child with you, I hope—?" Then he explained about the maid's absence.

"And you've done nothing to get hold of another—?"

He had written to Dina and asked if she intended to come back or not—"I thought I couldn't do anything till I got her reply—"

"Just like a man! I believe you're crazy—do you imagine I'd have a maid in the house who's off her head! She ought to be made responsible, she ought, leaving her place at an awkward time like that and putting us to inconvenience—"

"Poor thing, it's not surprising if she lost her head, like so many others just now—"

"Oh yes! You're always ready to take the part of the maids against me—"

"Well but, Björg—you're not such a very good hand at dealing with maids either—always nagging at them—"

"Am I! Just as if you had the remotest idea of the work there is to be done in a house. Pooh! You take the part of the maids because you fancy they're ill-treated and kept under—just as if it wasn't they who keep us mistresses under. You're always far more polite to the maid than you are to your own wife. I'm sure it's a good thing I'm not given to jealousy—"

"Yes, it evidently is."

It suddenly dawned on him that here they were quarreling—about paltry trifles—they who had never quarrelled before. That was how they met again—at a time like this. So he went up and put his arm round her:

"All the same you have a right to complain of my want of politeness—I haven't even wished you welcome home. There—welcome home again, little one!"

Björg submitted to his embrace and kiss: "But now we must go down, the chauffeur's waiting—"

On the way through the drawing room he picked up Sunlife, who stood perfectly still, smart as a doll in her new hood and cape from Paris. She looked about the strange room with serious interest.

"But, my dear, have you bought a grand piano—?" Paul ventured to be jocular as he helped the chauffeur to bring in the biggest case.

"It's food, you might guess that—mamma shared with me, I can tell you she's frightfully clever at provisioning. Thank God for it—as you don't seem to have got my letter with the list of all the things I asked you to buy here—"

Paul decided to postpone his explanation till they had had some breakfast.

But when at last they sat down to the table—he had Sunlife on his lap and was feeding her with egg and anchovy—he thought he would have to confess.

"I must have overlooked what you wrote about coming home today—because I did get your list. But I didn't think I could do anything about it. It won't do for those who have the means to buy up masses of necessaries and forestall those who have only their wages to live on, and don't even know how long they can count on earning them. It's impossible to say what employment there will be this autumn—"

Björg looked at him—her eyes grew dark and wide:

"So you did get my letter—but you simply didn't take the trouble to read it properly—"

Paul humbly admitted that he must have chanced to overlook some of it.

"Well, I never—a letter from your wife—and you don't even read it! I write to my *husband* about a serious matter like this—for let me tell you, it's *frightfully* serious, nobody knows how difficult it's going to be to get things this autumn—"

"Yes, Björg, unfortunately I do know that difficult times are coming—if not exactly in the way you housewives believe, so that you have to buy up all you possibly can and stuff your houses from cellar to attic. Sixteen sacks of flour or whatever the number was you put down—you may be sure they wouldn't have let you have so much—"

"Do you suppose I meant you were just to ring up the store?—of course I meant you to try a lot of different places. Oh, one has to keep one's eyes open—"

Paul put down the child and got up:

"Well, I haven't any more time, I must go to the office. Goodbye, Björg. You must ring up and see about getting someone to help in the meantime—"

But she followed him out into the hall:

"Just as if fifteen sacks of flour was such an awful lot—in this house where we bake all our own bread—"

"Yes, but fifteen sacks of flour, think of it!—that would be enough to bake for a whole garrison for months on end—"

"The war's quite likely to last for months—"

"I can't find the money for it either, Björg," said Paul seriously. "You must be able to see, my dear, that in a situation like this Henrik and I can't draw more cash than is strictly necessary for our private housekeeping. I know that Berit has bought two sacks of flour and paid seventy-five crowns for one of them; even that Henrik thought was too bad—"

"Berit! Such a wretched housekeeper she is. And besides, it'll have to be the Govetent's business to look after those who can't look after themselves—"

"I haven't any more time, Björg—"

Sunnie had toddled out into the hall and stood regarding her parents with a doubtful little air. Her mother took her up in her arms and began to cry:

"And Knorr's oatmeal that I put on the list—you haven't bought *that* even! Don't you think it's a shame to forget her—poor little tot, having to go through such terrible times—"

"Oh, Björg, do stop talking like that," he begged her, dropping his voice. "Think of all the little tots out there where there is war—in Belgium today—"

"Yes, but *I* can't help that, can I?" said Björg, sobbing. "God knows I wished all the time there mightn't be war—But it's just like you excitable menfolk—you think of everybody but your own wives and children—"

He was revolted out of all proportion, he confessed to himself, as he walked into town. But it was so—pitiable. Father and mother and child to meet like this at a time when fathers and mothers and children over half Europe were being torn from each other in fear and suspense, when homes were being shelled and burnt down. And such a sickening, paltry quarrel—it was actually the first they had had too; he could not remember their having disagreed once even in all the time they had been married—not in earnest. Never an angry word between them. As far as that went their marriage might almost be called ideal.

CLUNY MEDIA

Designed by Fiona Cecile Clarke, the Cluny Media *logo depicts a monk at work in the scriptorium, with a cat sitting at his feet.*

The monk represents our mission to emulate the invaluable contributions of the monks of Cluny in preserving the libraries of the West, our strivings to know and love the truth.

The cat at the monk's feet is Pangur Bán, from the eponymous Irish poem of the 9th century. The anonymous poet compares his scholarly pursuit of truth with the cat's happy hunting of mice. The depiction of Pangur Bán is an homage to the work of the monks of Irish monasteries and a sign of the joy we at Cluny take in our trade.

"Messe ocus Pangur Bán,
cechtar nathar fria saindan:
bíth a menmasam fri seilgg,
mu memna céin im saincheirdd."

www.ingramcontent.com/pod-product-compliance
Lightning Source LLC
Chambersburg PA
CBHW020930310726
48980CB00007B/712/J

* 9 7 8 1 9 4 9 8 9 9 9 3 1 *